GUNFIGHT ON EUROPA STATION

BAEN BOOKS edited by DAVID BOOP

Straight Outta Tombstone
Straight Outta Deadwood
Straight Outta Dodge City

Gunfight on Europa Station

GUNFIGHT ON EUROPA STATION

Edited by
DAVID BOOP

BAEN

A Baen Books Original

Baen Publishing Enterprises
P.O. Box 1403
Riverdale, NY 10471
www.baen.com

ISBN: 978-1-9821-2572-1

Cover art by Dominic Harman

First printing, November 2021

Distributed by Simon & Schuster
1230 Avenue of the Americas
New York, NY 10020

Library of Congress Control Number: 2021042033

Pages by Joy Freeman (www.pagesbyjoy.com)
Printed in the United States of America
10 9 8 7 6 5 4 3 2 1

To the Scientists and Engineers,
Whose minds and hearts are out in space,
Despite their feet being stuck here on Earth.
While we may all be made of "star stuff,"
Your dedication to bringing us
Closer to those stars gives me hope
Each and every day.

Yee-Haw, Space Cowboys!

CONTENTS

IS SPACE ACTUALLY THE FINAL FRONTIER?

David Boop

When I was little, I begged my mom to buy me this small, portable TV for my room because, as she recalled, it reminded me of *Star Trek*. Mind you, this was before *Star Wars* ever came out, so I must have been six or seven at the time. Now, I'm sure some of you are thinking, "What parent allows the child to have their own TV at that age? Certainly, that would be a distraction from schoolwork and family time," and so forth. And you wouldn't be wrong. It was.

But that wagon train to the stars had already left.

Many of my earliest memories involved watching TV, due to my parents working and running a ministry. They were often hosting bible studies and television had become the great baby-sitter in that era. I connected quickly to shows like *Star Trek*, *The Addams Family*, *The Six-Million Dollar Man*, and Saturday afternoon pulp serials. I knew more about television than a TV Guide, and I certainly knew more about entertainment than I did my history, math, or science lessons.

Star Wars, and all the phenomenon that came with it, hit when I was nine years old. It just took me not just to the future, but to a galaxy far, far away. I studied the industry and always wanted to be a part of it. Now, I became interested in science and the stars and dreamed of traveling to them one day. None of those flights of fancy, such as space travel, or even making movies, have come to pass...yet (knock on the pseudo-wood of my desk). Instead, I wound up becoming an author and in doing so, understood for the first time that Gene Roddenberry lied to me, all those years ago.

Space was *not* the final frontier.

"What?" says the disbelieving reader. "Gene loved us and gave us a grand design for the future that involved exploring the galaxy in perfect harmony with one another."

Yes, I know no one talks like that, and even if they did, they're not wrong there, either. He did. I'd never besmirch the honored name of Roddenberry especially in print, where Paramount could see it. No, I'm only talking about the concept of there ever being a final frontier.

Merriam-Webster's second definition of the word "frontier" is the one we most think of: *a region that forms the margin of settled or developed territory*, as in the western frontier. And while there are several other definitions, the one I tend to think most relevant to science fiction is the last: *a new field for exploitative or developmental activity*.

"Why this one?" you may ask. Well, because we can look at space exploration as just settling unexplored territories but, in truth, it's so much more. Space is the realm of God or The Creators or the theoretical physicist looking for an opportunity to turn a theory into a fact. And not just one theory, but all of them.

In my novel *She Murdered Me with Science* (Wordfire Press, 2016), I use a quote from the philosopher Johann Wolfgang von Goethe, "God could cause us considerable embarrassment by revealing all the secrets of nature to us: we should not know what to do for sheer apathy and boredom." This is one of my favorite quotes about science. And whether you believe in a divine being or not, the quote hits home. There must always be new things to explore. We've seen it in recent fiction and film and television. We can't *just* have space exploration in science fiction anymore. No, we must also add in time travel, alternate worlds, microcosmic dimensions, or any one of an infinite number of concepts. And explore them, we must. For even if we do someday have the ability to travel the entire universe, what would we do then? Would we then know the mind of God? Would we have *all* the answers?

No, we would just have new questions, new realities to dream up. We can never stop exploring, never find the actual *final* frontier. Because as Goethe said, we would be bored out of our evolved-lovin' minds.

Here in these pages are eleven stories about exploring the penultimate frontier. Much like the frontiers of the past, these stories are filled with settlers overcoming adversity, rule breakers and justice seekers, the discovery of new creatures, and previously unexplored scientific anomalies. They might not contain any answers to the great unknowns waiting out there for us, but maybe they'll help us ask new questions in preparation for that day we finally leave the shackles of Earth.

I may never get to physically journey to the stars, but these authors have taken me to places I'd never read about before.

And that's exciting enough for me.

For now.

D.B.
12.19.20

GUNFIGHT ON EUROPA STATION

GREENHORN

Elizabeth Moon

I. The Dude

Josiah Horatio Titweiler arrived at Wichita Station in Open Range wearing a mask. That was the first problem. It wasn't in period; it was a modern, non-western, rebreathing mask with little doo-hickeys on the sides. He said he had allergies.

His horse was the next problem. Yes, a range-riding, rock-herding rancher had to have a horse. Bio or mechanical or whatever . . . it had to be vaguely horse-shaped, of a horselike color, and it had to have its name painted on the front. Black, with or without white trim, was good. Pink and silver was not. Tan with white trim was good. Green with blue spots was not. As for names, Silver was good. Aluminum was not. Trigger was good. Barrel was not.

Titweiler did not understand the underlying logic, and it was not something he could ask anyone at the factory building his custom horse. He decided he would go with "laughable" to undermine suspicion. After all, one of the tropes in the books and vids was the idiot who wasn't an idiot, who gained respect by proving it and then was trusted and befriended.

His horse slid out of the freighter's belly looking like any other Tesper 1700 except for being painted in a swirling pattern of turquoise and lavender. The swirling pattern also concealed the custom modifications for Titweiler's unusual anatomy and need for firepower. The cartoon horse on the nose with the name

1

Sunnydancing in curly letters around it was bright purple. Big green eyes. Sparkling silver hooves, mane, and tail.

In his carefully tailored suit, Titweiler knew he stood out among the other passengers claiming their belongings: they wore work clothes, rumpled and stained, and their horses being unloaded included only two Tespers—both older models—and a dozen mixed of Gorins, Pedins, and Dolloks in various shades of brown and rough-patched scars. All with realistic horses painted on their noses in black, some shade of brown, or tan with black trim. Names like Buckshot, Bullet, Lightning, Stormy.

Eyes stared at him, looked at each other, nodded, looked again at the shiny and obviously new Sunnydancing and back to him. Sizing him up. Sizing the horse up as she sat unscarred on the pad. The clerk at the desk called, "Titweiler! Josiah Horatio Titweiler!" He stepped forward, careful to walk neatly to the counter, and there receive the keys to Sunnydancing. "You want we should have that thing moved around to launch for you?" The woman's eyes were laughing.

"I have a certificate," he said, pulling out the case and showing it. "But perhaps it would be better—it is crowded here. I'll be staying at the Grande Lodge."

"That'll be two hundred for a tow," she said. "Seventy-five for a bounce."

"Tow, please," he said. The choice of someone who did not want his horse scratched up by the other rough mounts. The choice of someone who might have a piloting certificate but wasn't that skilled. She entered the order, and his card, with the corner of her mouth puckered tight to hide a smile.

He walked back past the others and had just reached the compartment hatch when one of them said "You call that a horse, mister?"

He turned and smiled, keeping his lips down over his store-bought teeth. "That is what the catalog called it."

Various sounds reached him he assumed were humorous at his expense. Excellent. Everything was going according to plan. From behind him he heard "—bought a horse from a catalog! Can you believe—" and then the hatch shut, and he was moving swiftly along the passage to "lodging."

The Grande Lodge had fake log walls; every fake window had videos of mountain vistas. The bar boasted both a bucking bull ride and a bucking rockethorse ride, though both were unoccupied when Titweiler entered, an hour after checking into his room. A few cowboy types slouched in booths around the sides, vacuum suits hung on foot-long pegs and jeans tucked into their boots. Plenty of time for some of the locals who'd seen Sunnydancing arrive to show up here.

"Well, if it isn't that fellow from the landing bay," one of them said loudly. "Hear about him? He bought a horse from a catalog!"

"No!"

"He did. Purty thing, too, if you like something that belongs in a little girl's bedroom." He looked at Titweiler. "Hey, why'n't you show us how you can ride on that'n over there?"

"Uh...no thanks. I just came in for a lemon soda. Say, do you know how I can find the Ranch Exchange?"

"He wants the Ranch Exchange...imagine that."

"What ya gonna do, buy a ranch, sonny?"

"Actually I...I have one." Titweiler smiled at them, and they didn't flinch, so he was doing it right.

"You? Have a ranch? Where is it?"

"Whatcha gonna do with it?"

"I'm going to herd...um...boulders." He sipped his lemon soda.

"He's going to herd boulders!" one said to another, loudly, and then, "You gonna herd boulders with that fancy-pants little pony you brought in?"

"They said it would do everything I needed," Titweiler said, spreading his hands carefully. Only five tentacles...er...fingers on each. "I won it," he said. A half truth, as it happened. "The ranch, not my, uh, horse."

"And you got a license to fly...yanno, sonny, you oughta join up with the Big C."

"Is that near the Ranch Exchange?"

Hoots and grunts, quickly suppressed. "Where's your ranch?"

"I—I am not certain until I've been to the Ranch Exchange. It was the lottery, you see. The angles were given, and the range stated to be unencumbered, but I was told I'd get the coordinates after checking in with the exchange."

Glances exchanged again among the other men. One of them stood up. "How 'bout I show you just where it is, so you don't get lost. This is your first time on a big station, isn't it? The gravity shifts can get to you, 'til you're used to them." The man—tall for a man, he could tell—looked him up and down. "How far in you come from?"

"Mars," he said. "I worked for Allied Metals, in the accounting department, and there was this lottery—"

"Sure, sure, we know about lotteries. You got any duds but that suit? Not too comfortable to ride in, is it?"

"It is not, to be honest, but I have the right . . . um . . . outfit. Jeans, boots—"

"Good vacuum suit? Gotta have a good vacuum suit."

"Oh, yes. I asked Tesper when I ordered Sunnydancing, and they directed me to a catalog that had complete outfitting for the aspiring rancher."

The others had stood up by now, and he had five new friends, or the local syndicate equivalent, who escorted him to the Ranch Exchange. They waited in the front lounge, chatting with a woman with bleached hair and a fringed skirt who had greeted them with, "Why aren't you boys out on the range?" while a more subdued clerk ushered him into the back room for New Properties. There, Titweiler handed over the packet he'd obtained from the former Titweiler, who really *had* been an accountant with Allied Metals, and in return was given a pair of saddlebags. In one were the deeds to his ranch and the code to signal the boundary beacons that he was legit. In the other were books on local regulations and communication codes he might need.

"It's a repo," the man behind the desk said. "That's mostly what lotteries offer, is repos. But the guy who had it was a claim jumper, and he didn't really herd his own; he was all the time sneakin' in on other folks and rustlin' their rocks. So he didn't have it long, and before that it was in legal limbo until they found the heirs of the guy before that, and none of them wanted it. Nor anyone else for awhile. It's farther out than most want, so aside from claim jumpers—and they mostly stay in close so they can sell and run— it scans as nicely populated with Class III to V types, and they're small enough to herd easy. You got your horse yet?"

"Yes. A Tesper 1700, new. And my certificate."

"A new horse? You are aware new horses attract thieves—?"

"Surely not here? Isn't there a marshal here?" It had been in his briefing: Wichita had a law officer, called a marshal, named Bart Manley.

"The marshal's office is back on Main. You'd better register your horse right away."

Titweiler noticed that two of his new friends found a reason not to come along to the marshal's office, but the others did, having endorsed the Ranch Exchange's warning about horse thieves. "Sunnydancing is not a common color," Titweiler said. "That would make her hard to steal, wouldn't it?"

"Nothing a kill pen couldn't get rid of in an hour or less," said the one called Slim, who was not. "You get your mount registered and chipped—official chip, o' course—and frankly you oughta add in a custom chip only you know the code for."

Titweiler nodded, though he knew Sunnydancing already had custom chips with many more functions than just proving his ownership. But time enough for that later. His game was more complex than these simple cowhands could guess. Up ahead he spotted the marshal's office with a gold-lettered sign in the window: OPEN RANGE, WICHITA TERRITORY, MARSHAL OFFICE.

Marshal Manley, slouching back in an old-fashioned banker's chair, was paunchy, age-wrinkled, and garrulous. More important, he seemed helpfully unsuspicious, handing over a tracking chip for Sunnydancing immediately. *Clearly a third-rate lawman at best*, Titweiler thought, though something about the man tickled his instincts.

Back at the Lodge, Titweiler changed into his ranch clothes: snug jeans, plaid shirt, vest, leather jacket heavily fringed, glittering stones edging the pockets and cuffs, and cowboy boots elaborately patterned with turquoise, purple, and black leather. With his vacuum suit over his arm, he checked out and went to get Sunnydancing out of the corral where all the guests' rockethorses were kept. His new friends came with him, to help carry his luggage, they said, and they headed off with it. Then he stepped into his vacuum suit, custom-made back home though designed to look the same as others, and hitched it at his waist. He wanted his fringed jacket to show as he walked down to the corral.

When he went through into the Customer Waiting Lounge, his friends all pinched their mouths against smiles and nodded. "Lookin' good. We got your luggage loaded on that mule." The mule was nothing but a trailer all sealed up, its towline coiled in front.

"Thank you," he said. "I'm all set now—"

But the corral attendant disagreed. "Bein' as you're a new customer, we want to be sure you're actually safe to ride through our nearspace on that overpowered horse you got there. We require every new customer to take a riding test on our equipment."

"But Sunnydancing is a custom—"

"I know that. But it's the rule. Now we got a nice, safe arena, guaranteed to contain any mistakes, where you can take Old Smokey and show us you know how to handle a horse. A circle or two, a figure eight, stop, back him up, walk back to the start. Simple. Otherwise, it's eight thousand to tow you out to your ranch, plus another four thousand if you're one of the outliers, which Ranch Exchange says you are."

So it was here and now, the test of riding. He glanced at the others. They'd known. Slim nodded at him. "You'll be fine, Titsy, it's just Old Smokey. Remember what they told you in your flight training."

"He can be a bit cranky; you really have to get after him to get him moving, but then he wakes up," Tiny added. Tiny, who overtopped him by a handbreadth.

"Fine, then," he said. "I want to get home as quick as I can. Let's get this over with." He pulled his vacuum suit up all the way, easing the helmet over his head, and sealed up.

Smokey certainly looked old; a dark gray covered with dents and streaks of something that might be corrosion; the control bubble with its saddle had scratches and streaks on the inside. Titweiler climbed up from the mounting block, patting the dirty skin with one glove as if this were a live horse. In the headphones he heard what might've been a suppressed chuckle.

Once in the saddle, Titweiler ran through the checklist: power, steering, controls, electrical faults, gravity stability, while in Preflight Mode. The long neck extended and retracted, the head went up and down, rotated sideways. The grippers opened and shut. Landing legs moved, joints worked as designed. The little control bubble smelled faintly of something nasty, but his own sensors detected nothing actually toxic. Titweiler slid his customized control pod out of its holster and held it in the two lateral tentacles of one hand, with the other four on the throttle. He held the other hand up, visible proof he wasn't grabbing leather. "Ready," he said, to the corral attendant, and the man grinned and switched the horse to Flight Mode.

There was a moment of stillness. Titweiler pushed the throttle forward to "walk." A grinding noise, a slight shift to the left, a jerk forward maybe a meter, and then Smokey reared up, the long neck swinging back over the cab and the rear legs shooting forward. Classic trick. Titweiler countered easily, his legs gripping the seat as Smokey turned upside down and then rotated its rear legs to push off against the arena fence. Meanwhile, Titweiler's other lateral tentacles sank into the control panel, sending codes that modified the horse's programmed bucking pattern. Smokey shuddered to a jerky halt, drifting across the arena.

Now all he had to do was analyze—

An electric shock broke his contact with the seat, and Smokey rolled sharply right. Titweiler shoved his toes out the ends of his custom boots, both leather and vacuum suit, and his sucker pads clung to the cab deck. The rockethorse bucked wildly, changing its pattern repeatedly as his lateral tentacles sent code after code deep into its system.

He took what would have been bruises for a human from the inside of the cab, but his sucker pods held, and eventually he had control of the yaw and was able to damp the acceleration in the vertical—that bouncing up and down had put his head on the canopy more than once. He had that down to short jerky movements, and the horizontal whirl down to mere twitches. Now he moved Smokey around the arena, almost level, controlling the pitch axis to a canter-like rocking movement, first in big circles, then a figure of 8, a full stop in the middle, then backing up, then going to the docking tube, lining up with the mounting block, and holding it still. He put Smokey back in Docking Mode, retracted his tentacles back into his boots and his left glove, and called in. "Well?"

"I never saw anything like it," the corral attendant said. "You got Old Smokey acting like a show pony in under a minute. How'd you do that?"

"I rode a lot of sims," he said, which was true.

"Well, mister, you can take your Sunnydancing any time you want. Come on back through when you're ready."

Titweiler checked that all his tentacles were now imitating human digits again, and the toes of his vacuum suit boots had properly resealed, then opened the canopy and climbed down to the mounting station, patting Old Smokey as if thanking him for a good time, simultaneously retrieving nanites he'd put on when he mounted. Then back through the tube, into the Customer Waiting Lounge, where several screens were replaying his ride over and over for others. His erstwhile friends insisted on buying him a drink from the Lounge bar, and he insisted on buying a round for them, and they gave him a new cowboy nickname, Buck, before he hitched the mule to Sunnydancing, mounted up, and rode off into the darkness, there being no sunset within many, many millions of kilometers.

II. Home on the Range

Sunnydancing proved as easy to handle as the manufacturer had promised, and Titweiler reviewed his mission profile, then sent an update to his supervisor. He was certain, he said, that he would soon be provided with informants, after which he expected to retrieve the fugitives he'd been sent for. Having spiked their drinks with a neurochemical binder, his new cowboy buddies Tiny and Slim would be following the chemical trail he left for them. Easy to handle, these humans.

His first boundary beacon signaled: from here, the directions to his ranch house were clear, and he told Sunnydancer to "take us home, old pal," a line from some long-gone western adventure story he'd liked. He pinged the house to start warming up while he was still fourteen human hours out. The dwelling, like most such, had few rooms or amenities but was supposed to boast a converter unit and fully stocked oxygen and water tanks, as well as heat, according to the lottery's inspection. When he came in sight of the irregular blob, he felt almost smug.

He put Sunnydancer into the small corral without difficulty, winched in the mule, and used Sunnydancer's head to push the mule through into the entrance tunnel. Then he shut Sunnydancer down, clambered out, hooked the power cable to the ranch house output line to recharge the powerbank, and prepared to enter his own domain.

The airlock codes worked; he moved his luggage from the mule's pack into the lock and cycled through. Yes, it was aired up and yes, it was above the freezing point of water, though not much. Artificial gravity gave him a definite vertical reference in the darkness. He found the control panel right beside the airlock, turned on the lights, and saw the half sphere, perhaps seventy meters across and thirty-five meters high, the floor a smooth composite over the other half of the sphere; under it would be the water storage, gas tanks, and machinery that kept the habitat livable. To his right was the end of the small building, the core of his ranch house, perhaps four meters by six. He dragged his luggage over to the door and pushed it open. In here it was warmer, and all the numbers were green on the house screen, so he opened his helmet.

This was home on the range until his mission was complete. The furniture included a simple bed against one side wall, a square table, and four chairs. He got out of his vacuum suit, put it in the recharge closet, unpacked his largest suitcase, and stripped out of his cowboy outfit, then the shaper he wore in human form, and pulled on the soft, voluminous *krrm* he'd have worn back home. As his body softened, reshaped to the krrm, reconnected to its neural net, he felt better. Relaxed. He investigated the recycling alcove, the food storage—to his surprise, half full of human food—and the water storage, full. The scans were on, automatic with his command for the power to come on and warm the place up. He could see his range, all the beacons winking the code for "owner in residence," and also the colored lines of rockethorses moving beyond his boundaries. Nothing within them. One very distant faster blink that meant something—someone—was headed his way, but a long way out.

Tiny and Slim, probably.

Then he stepped outside, into the dimmer light of the hollow sphere, and went through restorative exercises as he could not have while in human-occupied spaces. With the krrm expanded, he could reach within a few centimeters of the ceiling; shifting in another dimension he could stretch sideways to touch both sides. He stroked each tentacle with two others—outward, then inward. The krrm shifted from rock-colored camouflage to the soft shades of early excitation, a little brighter with each tentacle receiving attention. Faster... ripples of color moved across the krrm as ripples of sensation flowed through his body.

But no. Not all the way, not now. He had no time for the aftermath of conjugation, when they would lie motionless as the cells joined, divided, divided again. He went back inside, and, regretfully and with respect and affection, peeled back his krrm, explaining the reasoning. His krrm accepted it, released its connectors all the way, and he rolled it carefully into something that could pass for a folded bedcover before laying it carefully on his bed.

By the time Slim and Tiny arrived, he had eaten, slept, organized all his clothes and tools, and attached his larger portable corral to Sunnydancing's harness, with the mule hitched for easy pull-out. Then, dressed in appropriate garb, he backed Sunnydancing into the corral, along with the mule, hitched the mule to the center post, and checked his appearance one more time before riding out to show he was actively ranching. Sunnydancing rocked along at an easy pace. He tried deploying the corral as if he'd seen something to catch; it flipped open as advertised, but instead of folding neatly on the way back, it made an unsightly mess. He kept an eye on the scans, and let them know he'd spotted them by rotating Sunnydancer's spotlight, the accepted "Hiya" wave. But there were three of them, not two. Was this a raid, instead?

He hailed them. "Hey, Tiny! Slim! You brought a friend along?"

"An' our own food supply," Slim said. "Marshal wanted to make sure you were all right out here. We thought we'd stay a few days, help you with that new corral in case it got sticky. Sometimes it takes them a few catches to loosen up."

"Very kind of you," he said, thinking something else entirely. *The marshal? Why was the marshal here?* "It *is* being a bit difficult."

One of them accelerated and came nearer. "I see—what you need to do is swing your horse's neck toward that tangle and use your grabbers to get hold of a piece. Want me to show you?"

"I'll try," Titweiler said, working the controls. Sunnydancer's neck rotated leftward, and Titweiler extended the grabbers.

"Just like that," Tiny said. "Good job. If you don't have your mag screen on, do that now."

He did have his mag screen on, so he saw a closer view of the grabbers approaching a frame member of the corral and then closing around it.

"Now move your horse's neck the other way, not too fast. I'm going to grab onto a piece on this end. When it's open enough, we can refold it nice and tight. Yes, like that. Easier with a helper, the first few times, but the joints work smoother later."

He had to ask them in, of course. They'd brought a glowstone pot and some steaks, sausages, loaves of bread, as well as plenty of beer and wine, which he didn't plan to drink. They used the sanitary, commented that when he brought his herd to Wichita to sell, he'd probably want to get some furnishings to fancy his place up a bit. Even enlarge the cabin, if he'd been lucky.

"But we're fine like this," Tiny said, looming over him, a can of beer in one hand and a huge sausage wrap in the other. "I got my bedroll—we all do—you just go on inside when you feel like it. We can make an early start tomorrow, get your corral thing all ironed out and workin' easy, and help you get your first roundup started."

He admitted to being a bit tired; he'd eaten the steak grilled over the glowstones, and it didn't entirely agree with him. He'd avoided the alcohol and went into the house while they were still chatting and drinking by the glowing stones, leaning on their bedrolls.

In bed, he felt the krrm nudging against his feet, wanting to join again. He dared not change now, with humans going in and out to use the sanitary. Finally, they settled down, and he slept, only to wake when someone sat on the bed.

"We need to talk."

Titweiler opened his eyes, reminded his lower tentacles to go back to foot shape, and said "What?" before he realized the marshal had the krrm laid over his lap and was stroking it. He jerked a little; he couldn't help it.

"I know what this is," the marshal said, his big meaty hand gliding across the velvety surface. "Those boys outside don't; they thought it was some fancy quilt. But I do. Which means I know what you are, because these aren't bedclothes. You're a Gordaunt."

That isn't what we call ourselves, Titweiler thought and then remembered who did call them Gordaunts. "Skassant?" Enemies of his people for eons. He had to let his people know. Skassants weren't supposed to be in this system.

The marshal nodded. "Thought you were smart. And I'm a lawman in both jurisdictions—and that's what we need to talk about. You're the fifth Gordaunt I've spotted out here. Same gang?"

Titweiler shook his head. "No. Not a gang."

"Spy?"

"No. Not exactly. I'm with the . . . you won't know the name, but it's essentially a division of enforcement. I have ID. Let me take the krrm."

The marshal handed it over. Titweiler slid his hand under, to the control, and spoke gently; a fold opened and released an ovoid into his hand. He brought it out on his opened hand, and touched it with the tip of a finger that now looked more like a tentacle. "This opens the file," he said.

"That's your badge?"

"That's my ID, authorization for assignment, but not the assignment itself."

The ovoid glowed, split in half, and opened to form a small screen divided by a blue line. On one side, Titweiler as he looked on the human ID he'd showed at Wichita Station: slender, dark-haired, dark-eyed, sallow skin. His cover name, his height, and an entirely false story of his origin and employment on Mars. On the other, himself at home, robed in his krrm, the ovoid on his upper stalk where the krrm was, for the image, open. There was writing, but in the wrong script; Titweiler touched the device again, and the writing morphed to English.

"Special Agent," the Marshal said. "Important, then. I don't suppose you want to tell me your mission."

"Certainly," Titweiler said. "I am sent to find and, um, deal with fugitives of ours, before the humans discover them, if possible. They are evading our laws and causing trouble here; they are, I was told, stealing from other ranchers."

"The Big C gang?"

"So my supervisor told me."

"It's not them. The Big C are just vigilantes who think they don't need a marshal, that they can uphold law and order by themselves." He smiled. "I let them think they're getting away with it."

"But you don't," Titweiler said, thinking hard.

The marshal shrugged. "Thing is, frontiers attract the lawbreakers, son. Had to decide if you were one of them or one of us. So it's a good thing your krrm kept your badge for you."

And that our peoples haven't declared war again. Yet. Titweiler nodded. "Happy to be able to satisfy you," he said.

"You don't need to worry about your fugitives; they won't bother anybody again." The marshal stroked the krrm again. "So soft," he said. "Is it true this is your mate?" He grabbed a double handful of the krrm, stood, and flung it at Titweiler. "Show me. Alien sex turns me on—"

Titweiler reacted instinctively, stretching an upper tentacle under the flung krrm; the neural mesh connected, and the krrm whipped around over his head and settled on the marshal. *It's not really edible*, he thought at it, but the krrm's reaction flooded him with stimulant as the krrm made its way through the faux human façade and the Skassant reality.

Absorption...elimination...the toxics of two species lay in an untidy pile on the floor.

Well, the chemical sanitary will take care of that. He rose from the bed, no longer tired at all, and swept up the debris. One thing remained: the marshal's badge. It too could go in the sanitary, but maybe...maybe it could be useful.

Slim and Tiny, though...he peeked out the door. Snoring still. The krrm fluttered closer, its soft upper surface beginning to show colors even without the joining. Clearly it was approaching peak fertility, but he could not leave two aliens within his home when he would be immobile for hours after. He touched the krrm and forced his will onto it.

"Just this much—they're already drunk—keep them asleep until I wake." The krrm released two patches, and he put one on each sleeper. Back in the house he turned off the lights.

Too long since he had joined and propagated. In his native form, he lifted the krrm and slid it over him. Its glow brightened and began to move up and down his tentacles, teasing, demanding. He reached out, curled up, his stalk broadening and lengthening as the krrm and he danced. When all the eggs were laid, and sealed safely away, when the delights of the dance had peaked again and again, the krrm stretched them both out on the floor, and they did not move for a long time.

III. Roundup

Chill air woke him as the krrm slid away and rolled itself up. Titweiler wavered toward the bed, and pulled the shaper from under it. Getting the right tentacles into the right opening of the shaper took several tries, and once he'd returned to human shape, he discovered that the eggs he now carried made his jeans far too tight. He hadn't expected to be nursing eggs. He tried adjusting the shaper, but his own internal anatomy was unforgiving. Eggs belonged where they belonged, and he could not shift them much at all. Both his pairs of jeans were the same size, and both had fit his former shape snugly, as he'd read cowboys' jeans should. He faced the possibility that he would have to kill the two cowboys to keep his secret, but they had helped him. It was beyond discourteous. Absolutely against the protocols and his mandate. He would lose points with his service unless there was another reason to kill them. But they must not know what he really was.

He pulled the jeans off and looked at them. If he'd considered the possibility of reproduction, he'd have chosen a cowgirl disguise and worn a skirt. He looked at the jeans, now stuck partway up his thighs. If he cut open the seams of both pairs, and patched in extra material, would they fit then? It would take a lot of work, and the cowboys would certainly notice bulges in his supposed thighs. Well, could he make a skirt that would fit over his egg sacs?

First things first: he checked on the cowboys. Still sleeping peacefully, as expected. Perhaps under the krrm's influence, or not, they had rolled closer together and now were almost wrapped in each other, sharing the blankets.

Then, with the shaper's help, he got into the space suit, and went out to deal with the marshal's horse. It would be a Skassant-operating system, though it looked like a human design—a pretty yellow with cream trim and a rearing horse on its front named Justice. He had been briefed on such things. He used the marshal's keys, and then his own nanites and tentacles to reprogram it for a complicated but ultimately fatal course. He made it to the airlock again before it took off, its triple exhausts glowing blue.

The skirt, when he finished with it, covered his fake legs adequately, and had a split so he could get into the space suit and sit in the saddle easily. He pulled up a picture of a human woman and stared at it long enough to morph his skin into growing longer hair, this time curly, and produce a few additional bulges that made his shirt a bit too tight. He picked up the krrm and put it back on the bed, reminding it not to move in front of the humans, then set about making breakfast for them. Pancake mix, dried milk, dried eggs, oil, water . . . and as the first pancakes sizzled on the griddle, he went out, removed the patches, turned up the lights, and waited.

When they came in, following the smell of pancakes, butter, and reconstituted syrup, they stared at him. "What the—?"

He smiled at them. "I know you thought I was kind of...
you know..."

"But—but you rode Old Smokey!"

"What, you don't think girls can ride?"

"No, of course not, but why—"

"The lottery. It was for men only." He smiled again. "I'll
understand if you don't want to stay for the roundup, boys. But
I'd like it if you did."

In another hour, they were all mounted; he led them off with
Sunnydancing bucking a little so he could prove "she" could ride
a rockethorse, and by what counted as sundown, they had a
good forty rocks rounded up and were pushing them back to the
holding corral at the ranch. The next day, as he caught on to the
nuances of herding rocks, they brought in more than a hundred.

Back at the ranch, he was just starting supper for them, for
he understood that with a woman on the ranch, the cowboys
wouldn't cook even so much as a steak themselves, when they
drew on him.

"Was my cooking that bad?" Titweiler asked, facing the replica .45s, a stupid choice in a rock hemisphere, unless they really
used lasers. He roused the krrm across the room.

"We have to kill you," Slim said. "You know too much."

"Know what?" Titweiler said. The two men glared at him.

"You know what! We saw you looking."

"I don't," Titweiler said. "I don't understand." What he did
understand was that if they attacked him, he could kill them
legally. Why did they stand there talking?

"You're really a woman, so you know—women have intuition
about these things."

And he couldn't kill them until they made the first move,
it was in the protocols. Killing out of protocols meant stacks of
paperwork. Why wouldn't they get on with it?

"You saw us. Lying together."

He shrugged. They'd done it every night. "So? That's your
secret? What's wrong with that?"

Their voices tangled, eager to explain. "We're not supposed
to—"

"But everybody knows, really, it's that it's never supposed to
be seen, and you—"

"You could tell and we'd be kicked out—"

"Sent to that other colony—"

"They're like us only they don't like horses, they just like arty stuff."

"See, Open Range has a strict period-realism rule, and back then, the Old West on Earth, it wasn't legal."

"So to be us, we have to pretend it's bad, and you're a woman and women talk too much, that's period realism, and so since nobody else knows you're a woman we can kill you and send you and your horse off somewhere and nobody will know."

"*Women* talk too much?" Titweiler raised his brows. Behind them, the krrm had raised itself, trembling with eagerness and effort. He signaled it to wait. Perhaps there was a way to end this without killing them...thus no paperwork. How to explain?

Then he remembered a bit of dialog.

"I am no WOMAN," he declared as he shed his disguise and appeared, tentacles and all, and lifted the denim skirt to show the egg sacks lining his stalk. He signaled *immobilize*; the krrm flowed up their backs and brought them down before they could fire. Alive. But weighed down by a pulsating prickly mass with bright blue rings flashing on its upper surface.

"You're an *octopus*?" Slim said, eyes wide.

Tiny was staring at the flashing blue rings.

Even a human should know better than that. Titweiler sighed. "No, I am not an octopus. An octopus can't change into human shape. I'm an alien from another world. That's *my* secret. And if others find out, they'll want to kill me. I'll keep your secret if you'll keep mine. If you won't, my krrm will inject you with its favorite flavor additive and consume whatever parts of you aren't toxic to us."

"You'd kill us?"

"You were going to kill me." Titweiler waited a moment. Slim and Tiny looked at each other then up at him. "Now, I trust you boys will honor a handshake, won't you?" He gestured to his krrm, and it slid down enough for two human arms to come out. "The deal is, you don't kill me, I don't kill you, and we keep each other's secret forever. Are we pardners or not?" He re-formed his right-side upper tentacles into an arm and hand, four fingers and a thumb, and held it out.

"It's a deal, pardner!" Tiny said, reaching out.

"Yup, it's a deal, pardner," Slim said.

Titweiler shook both hands. "Pardners," he said, and gestured. His krrm slid away from the two. "Now, tell me what you were really up to."

"Well..." Tiny looked at Slim and Slim looked back. "We had this deal with the marshal. Drive newcomers off their ranch or kill 'em, and then him and us would divvy up the profit."

"He knew about us, but said he wouldn't tell if we'd work for him."

"Thank you for your honesty," Titweiler said. "Here's the deal. You can have my ranch. And—" He bespoke the krrm again, and the marshal's star dropped on the floor. "One of you can be marshal if you want. He doesn't need his badge anymore."

"Really? Where will you be, what's your cut?"

"I'm going home. I have a family to raise." He patted the egg sacks. "You boys be good now."

"And that," Titweiler said to his egglings as they listened in the jelly pool, "is how your krrm and *vlln* escaped from human space and brought back word of the Skassants' infiltration."

The End

THE PENULTIMATE STAND OF PINA GRACCHI

Michael F. Haspil

There would be trouble, no two ways about it. After all, one didn't hire an all-call posse if engines burned smooth. However, Danavan Wilner concerned himself with trouble of a different sort.

He sat at the edge of a grand reception area. Pina Gracchi, his partner by circumstance, fate, and eventually choice, walked back from the hygiene station and unwittingly became the target of two drunk roughs.

The holo-guide spouted a banal greeting for the hundredth time in a pleasant female voice.

"Governor Sidney Chassum and the Tanguroa Cooperative welcomes you to Churius 161. Or 'Aguilar' as we like to call it. We apologize for extended processing wait times due to an ongoing security situation."

Danavan's seat gave him a good vantage of all the roustabouts, ne'er-do-wells, desperados, and other troublemakers apt to answer the localized posse call-up. There were no volunteers among this bunch. They were all guns-for-hire including himself and Pina. It was a good thing they were all unarmed while they awaited processing.

There were mercenaries—professionals with skills in demand who provided a service for a fee—and then there were mercs—thugs and bullies who liked to hurt people and pretended it was for the money. He saw too many of the latter among this bunch for his comfort. Something about this job reeked.

Pina had insisted they take it, and he owed her.

19

Their end of the reception hall held an autobar that dispensed libations—some intoxicating, some not—chit free. Liquid courage for the two idiots following Pina.

"Though Aguilar is considered a settled colony, it is also an active water-harvesting facility. When exiting the reception zone, please watch your step and observe all signs. While gravity is stable throughout the hab zones, pockets exist where gravity boots are mandatory. Sections requiring the use of pressure suits are off-limits to visitors."

Pina had nearly returned to the table when the first stalker made his move.

The dance was on.

"Hey, what unit is on that jacket?" The tone of his voice told Danavan the answer didn't really matter.

Pina stopped and answered over her shoulder. She wore an old-style pleather flight jacket a century or so out of style. "The 58th. Why?" The brightly colored unit patch was a tad faded but still clearly visible.

"My grandda got killed by the 58th."

Pina turned to square off with the man. Two more men crossed the room to flank Pina. Four on one. Now things were getting interesting.

Pina answered, "Don't see how that's my problem."

"It's your problem because you're wearing that jacket, and it offends me."

Pina made a show of seeing the two new players and backed toward Danavan. She put her hands up in a placating gesture. "Okay. How do we make this right?"

"I think you should give me that jacket."

Pina unzipped the jacket and took it off. She wore a black tank top underneath, revealing tattoo sleeves on both her arms. She'd gotten them to help cover up the bioluminescent electoos put there by the Judiciary. Sometimes, if the light caught them just right, the original electoos shone through the coverup.

The first man snatched the jacket from her and tossed it to the ground without even looking at it. "I think you should say you're sorry."

"I'm sorry. Look, that fight was long ago, friend. It's not between us," Pina said.

Danavan placed one hand on the alcohol tumbler in front

of him, ready to send the contents flying into a face if the situation warranted.

"I say it is. Apologize again. I don't think you meant it the first time," the stalker said.

That was when the stalker's buddy saw the electoos. "Oh, hell." He pawed at his friend. "Hey, Tyler, just let it go."

"Get your damn hands off of me!" his friend shouted and pulled away. The other two men tried to sort out which side they should take.

Danavan cleared his throat theatrically and got their attention. "Gentlemen. Do *they* have a problem? Or do *we* have a problem?"

The other men decided their drinks needed a refill and headed for the autobar.

The second man pulled at Tyler. "Let's get some free drinks." He addressed Pina, "I'm sorry about this, ma'am. He's just drunk." He turned his attention back to Tyler and tried to pull him away. "She took the jacket off."

"I want my apology. She needs to say it again." Tyler tore away from his friend. "I'll beat it out of her if I have to."

Pina took an obvious defensive posture.

"Don't hurt him too bad!" the second man yelled.

Tyler threw a wild haymaker that Pina easily blocked. Then she snaked her blocking arm through the crook of his elbow as he pulled his fist back and wrenched his shoulder out of its socket. As he fell backward, off-balance, Pina moved with him and knelt, smashing his back onto her upright knee. She chopped his throat with the other hand and, as he crashed down in what looked like agony, she stood, swept the jacket off the ground, and put it back on in one smooth motion.

She joined Danavan at the table, as the second man attended to his friend. It had all happened so quickly, all but the nearest tables didn't even notice the commotion.

The holo-guide droned on. *"Please enjoy shopping, gambling, and other entertainment along Fremont Street in First Settlement. There is no water ration on Aguilar. Visit the Tangaroa Water Emporium, its baths, and artificial hot springs. The Tangaroa Cooperative would like to remind you it is only through the harvesting of Aguilar's ice layer and pockets of liquid ocean that we can settle throughout the system and conduct the terraforming operations to make this system a new home."*

Someone moved from Danavan's four o'clock. Despite himself, his hand twitched toward a sidearm that wasn't there.

Augustus Croyle sported long salt-and-pepper hair tied in a neat ponytail and had an impressive mustache and beard to match, though the latter tended more toward salt than pepper.

"Gus. Been a few orbits, huh? Thought you were playing Guerra?" Danavan asked.

"My dice turned to shit, and I had a bad hand, so I got outflanked. Figured it had to be you in that godawful red jacket and silly top hat. What'd I miss?"

"Normally, I'd let you get away with a crack like that." Danavan took false offense and took on an affectation to match. "But if you are besmirching the uniform of the most vaunted and ancient order of the Black Royal Colonial Marines, then, sir, I shall have to ask you to step outside."

"There's naught but vacuum outside."

"The offer stands. If, on the other hand, you admit it was only your lack of fashion sense and manners made you utter that statement, I'd rather you sit," Danavan said.

"I am an uncouth boor." He stayed standing for the time being. "You have to admit, though, it's a hell of a getup and more than a little dated."

Danavan sighed. "It's all part of the branding. Fella's gotta do something to stand out." Croyle prided himself on being something of a dandy, but Danavan recognized the style of Croyle's suit, which was a rare and bad sign. Croyle always wore clothes on the cutting edge. The suit looked more gray than silver in parts. His friend's finances weren't doing well.

"No doubt. Work's been dry for our sort," Croyle said.

"Time passes. Speaking of which, you got old."

"Relative. I settled for a bit."

"And?"

"Didn't work out. Now, aren't you going to introduce me?" Croyle asked.

Danavan started introductions, "Gus Croyle—"

"Augustus, please. No one calls me Gus unless we're in a fight."

"Fair enough, if we're going to be formal. Augustus Croyle meet Agrapina Gracchi," Danavan said.

Croyle laughed incredulously. "Yeah. Sure."

Pina held out her hand.

Croyle took it and grew very serious. "*You're* Pina Gracchi." He said it like he needed to reassure himself.

"Of the New Anatolia Gracchis," Pina said.

"Any relation to CEO Peter Gracchi of New Aveline Gracchi Holdings?"

"Yeah. I'm his great-aunt," Pina said.

"So, that's a real Stetson?" Croyle asked, unable to hold awe, and a little greed, out of his voice.

"Wanna touch it?" Pina said.

"That's all right." Croyle finally sat down. "I'd heard some stories a couple decades back about a Justiciar resigning over an Adjudicator getting wrongly drummed out of the Service. Then there were stories of you cracking heads beyond the Perimeter."

"That's true," Pina said.

Croyle turned to look at Danavan. "And the wronged Adjudicator?"

Danavan smiled ruefully. "*Ecce homo.*"

"Now, that *is* interesting." Croyle turned back to Pina. "Meaning no offense, just thought you might be older, is all."

Danavan laughed. "Come on, she doesn't look a day over thirty-nine. Relative. At least that's what she's told me for the last three years."

Pina scowled at Danavan. "Faster-than-light travel and relativity are truly marvels of the modern age."

The PA suddenly came on, interrupting the holo-guide's announcements. Three men and two women entered and stood on the small stage in the center of the room.

A tall man with a prodigious bushy beard broke apart from the others and stood with his arms locked behind him. He wore blue composite military-style armor and a pearlized energy pistol at his side.

"Thank you all for answering the call on such short notice," he said. "As you may have heard, the harvesters here have something of an uprising going. The situation is a bit more serious than we've let on and this insurrection has put the water supply across the system at risk. I'm afraid as long as this crisis continues, water rationing is in full effect, contrary to the holo-guide's promise."

Groans rose from the crowd.

The man nodded in acknowledgment and continued. "What few forces the governor has at his disposal are now providing security for hydroponics, the Tokamak reactor, and other essentials. So, it falls to us to undertake the solemn duty of returning law and order to this rabble and getting things running smoothly again. Your contracts have all been ratified, and you will be compensated in currency of your choosing."

Some light applause. This was all expected.

"In a minute, we will begin processing into Aguilar. As of this moment, consider yourselves all agents of NJK Security. And for those of you who don't know me, I'm Commodore Elias Grant, and I will be your commander."

As Grant said his name, Danavan glared at Pina. "At least now I know why you wanted this job."

Croyle spoke in a low tone, "What's with NJK?"

"Well," Danavan answered, "remember the story you heard about me losing my Adjudicator status, and Pina having to resign?" He turned his attention back to the people on the stage. "Though they might not know it, them there are the sons of bitches behind it."

Danavan tore his eyes away from the sky so he didn't trip. Gravity sat at around eighty-five percent of standard. Just enough to put him off his gait.

The Tangaroa Cooperative built First Settlement in a naturally occurring cavern. He'd been unprepared for the size of it. They'd polished the ceiling and ran one of the best sky simulations Danavan had ever seen. If he didn't know exactly where to look, the holo-projectors were just about invisible. The feel of dirt under his boots instead of flooring helped the illusion of being outdoors. First Settlement's shops and habs lay ahead. The main street curved to the right and made it seem the town stretched onward. This was set up like an R&R resort. A lot of illusion to keep people from going bugnuts in limited spaces.

He turned his eyes ahead and onto the flow of other mercenaries stumbling along and caught sight of Bryn Horton and Richie Carr watching from under a shop awning—two notorious NJK operatives with reputations for responding with disproportionate and excessive force. He'd seen Carr on the stage with the commodore, but hadn't guessed Horton would be here too. The only reason they weren't war criminals was that there wasn't currently a war on.

NJK as an organization had a scary reputation for strike busting and enforcing what passed for a sort of order. They didn't recruit the honorable, but their people got their job done by letter of contract, no matter who or how many died in their wake. And they'd gotten rich doing it.

Danavan got into a staring contest with Horton, and he'd be damned if he looked away before she did. The woman smirked, nodded in his direction, and muttered something to Carr, who laughed. In another time and another place, he'd burn both down without hesitation. He felt naked without his weapons and looked back to confirm his gear followed him. The carbon-fiber trunk trundled along on its tracks, staying close like a loyal pet.

Pina interrupted his thoughts. "How long you planning on staying sore?"

"A while longer. NJK? Really. After the Grigio Massacre? After Foamfall? And now we're working for them. If I'd have known, I wouldn't have come," Danavan said.

Pina grinned at him. "You hate them as much as I do. You'd have raced me to the transport."

"She's got you there," Croyle said. The scent of roasting meat permeated the air. It was divine. "Ooh. Do you smell that?"

"You know this far out, that's probably not lab-grown," Danavan said. His mouth watered despite himself. Some animal had given up its life for them to eat it. The thought made him lose his appetite a bit. But only a bit.

Croyle broke away from their group. "I'll be right back."

Almost immediately, a holo-guide appeared and herded him back into the flow of mercenaries.

"Please proceed to the accommodations on Fremont Street. Dinner will be available in the main mess between thirteen hundred and fourteen hundred. A light supper will be provided at the same location at eighteen hundred."

"Well...shoot," Croyle said. "Guess they're running a tight ship."

At the intersection, the crowd turned left. On the corner stood the governor's main office and residence. Governor Sidney Chassum stood on his balcony flanked by two NJK guards as if in review. Flouting convention, he openly smoked a cigar. From the looks of it, it was real, not a sim-vape.

"Look at this prick," Croyle said while smiling and waving enthusiastically at the governor.

"Careful now, that's our boss," Danavan said. "We're bought and paid for." He tipped his top hat courteously.

"Doesn't mean I have to like it."

"Something seem strange to you?" Pina asked.

"Lots," Danavan said. "What're you getting at?"

"Where is everybody?"

"Maybe they cleared people out just to get us settled," Croyle said. He sounded unconvinced.

"So how many folk are here?" Pina asked.

Danavan consulted an info pamphlet he'd swiped when they left the holding zone. "Says here between eight and nine thousand. Wait, that doesn't make sense..."

Pina said, "So, the governor probably has what, maybe a hundred troops and guards—max—to be augmented by militia in an emergency. Far as law goes, maybe one or two Proctors. Maybe an Invigilator and some deputies if they're particularly troubled."

"If the harvesters were gonna throw an insurrection, it'd be over before even NJK could get here," Danavan said.

"Exactly."

"Mayhap they have some canny intelligence?" Croyle suggested.

A chorus of groans and grumbling arose from ahead. A tent city had been set up on three vacant lots at the edge of the street.

"Well, that's not what they promised at all," Croyle said.

A holo-guide directed traffic ahead to the tents. *"For those of you with room and board included in your contracts, please cite your contract number for verification, and you will be directed to the appropriate accommodations. If you do not have room and board stipulated in your agreement, lodging can be rented for Co-op scrip. Co-op scrip can be acquired at a number of establishments in First Settlement at reasonable and competitive exchange rates."*

"Sixteen tons," Pina said.

"Sixteen tons of what?" Croyle asked.

"Coal," Pina said. "Back on Terra Primus, afore every corner was bought, sold, and settled, companies had workers mine coal. They built whole towns to bring work forces into forsaken spaces to feed the growing industry. Workers would arrive from everywhere seeking opportunity in exchange for hard labor. They'd come without equipment, often with nothing more than the clothes on their backs. The company would sell them the equipment they needed, and everything else. Not for money. For company scrip.

Which was only good in company stores. And the workers were paid in scrip so they couldn't leave. The only way to earn scrip was to meet your quota. Sixteen tons. Of course, the men who ran the scales worked for the company too."

"I'm not agreeing with it, but that sounds like a hell of a good scam," Croyle said.

"If you're not a miner," Danavan said.

"Or a water harvester in this case," Pina said. "If they've resurrected this scheme, that's reason enough for an uprising."

Danavan nodded. "I'm liking this job less and less."

It was their turn at the holo-guide. Danavan referenced his notes. "Wilner Five. Five. Seven. Oh. Four. Two. Eight."

The holo-guide gave him what was supposed to be a genial smile, but made him want to punch it in his rapidly souring mood. It displayed a map of where their tent was on the grid. Their luggage recognized an accompanying code and rambled off to await them at the location.

Danavan started walking in the tent's direction, then stopped to wait for Croyle. Augustus Croyle sidestepped the holo-guide and gave Danavan a sheepish grin. "Guess I have to get myself some scrip."

"You need a better agent," Pina said.

"Apparently. I shall have words upon my return to civilized climes," Croyle said.

"For the time being, shack up with us. We can sure use an extra set of eyes," Danavan said.

"Much obliged," Croyle said.

"Let's get heeled." Pina headed to the tent.

Danavan double-checked the pistol magazines on his belt, the bandolier across his chest, and made sure the mags with different warheads were where he wanted them. He maglocked his helmet on his belt.

Pina emerged from the tent in worn and weathered, but nearly identical, matte-black Judiciary-grade armor. The armor clung to her form and showed a composite material pattern. It sported reactive-camouflage—deactivated for the moment—SA sensors, standard strength and speed augment servos and, with helmets incorporated, offered class three pressure seals. Even decades out of date, it was still worth a small fortune.

She jammed her pistol into an ident-locked cross-draw holster on her left hip and slung the satchel so it maglocked in the middle of her back. The satchel contained an Armat C8 Carbine. The components folded down into a concise package Pina could deploy in seconds. Armat developed the C8 as a capable backup to battle rifles. Only it had been so effective that many users, like Pina, dispensed with their primary weapon systems entirely.

Croyle emerged in his civilian-grade armor. Though newer, it paled in comparison to Danavan's. He carried a standard-pattern Shepherd autogun. Danavan didn't recognize the make and model, so it had to be new. Aside from some engraved filigree, it looked stock. Croyle had definitely fallen on hard times; he didn't even carry a pistol for backup.

"There's an extra energy pistol in my trunk if you need it," Danavan said. He summoned his trunk, and it crawled over to him.

"I might, if things get hairy. If you don't mind, I'm feeling right peckish and thought I'd fetch some dinner. You want me to bring some back?"

Pina laughed. "You've really been out a spell, huh? You can't eat the food here."

"Why not?" Croyle said.

Danavan crouched and rooted around in the trunk. "Say you're running an uprising, and the enemy gets up some reinforcements. You're out-resourced except for sympathizers. Where would you put those people where they might be the most effective?"

"Yeah, okay. I see your point. But they can't poison us. Health and safety sensors would pick that stuff out in seconds," Croyle said.

Danavan held up two protein bricks. "Does this look like the kind of joint running H and S sensors?"

Croyle pursed his lips in resignation.

"Look," Danavan continued, "I'm not saying the food isn't safe. I'm sure it is. Why chance it? Now, I've got Spiced Pork Dish and Turkey Dinner."

Pina walked over to Danavan and snatched the pork brick. "Fair warning. The turkey dinner is the whole turkey dinner. Turkey and all the fixings in one go. This pork dish may sound generic, but I quite like it." She sat down cross-legged in front of the tent.

Croyle took the remaining brick. "Fine. So help me if you're wrong, though."

Danavan nodded, reached into the trunk, and produced the

promised energy pistol. "And here you go. Decent enough backup piece."

Pina said, "Eyes up." She tossed the protein brick onto the trunk and stood.

The four men who had approached Pina in the reception area were headed their way.

Armed this time.

Danavan and Croyle stood. They instinctively spread out to maximize the angle between them.

The leader—Tyler, if Danavan remembered—addressed Pina. "You're Pina Gracchi. A lot of folk don't like you. You're lucky the autodoc was able to fix me up easy enough. Two slipped discs and a dislocated shoulder costs. Way I see it, you owe me some chits."

Danavan looked for an out. This didn't have to turn to gunplay. He recognized the man who had tried to hold Tyler back before. "Now, friends—"

"Shut your damn mouth, it doesn't concern you," Tyler said.

"I beg to differ. It appears *we* have a problem," Danavan said.

Pina cleared her throat, and the men turned their attention to her.

Danavan drew his pistols. "Don't look at her. Look at me. I'm the one who's got the drop on you."

The men turned toward him, their faces shades paler than moments before.

"Now, I know your type. First big job. Heads full of hydrazine and oxidizer and hearts full of glory-seeking. Someone might have told you to take on someone with a big enough rep, and you might be able to trade on that for a spell. That kind of thinking gets folk killed. Besides, you've chosen the wrong mark, *and* you're being used for pawns. Though I don't know if you've sussed that out yet or not. You're lucky we're currently of a generous mood."

Danavan gestured with a pistol to the man who'd pulled Tyler back. "You seem to have some sense. What's your name?"

"Ernan," the man answered.

"Well, Ernan, I like you," Danavan changed his tone to an avuncular one. Step one to de-escalation. "Might I guess from your dress and disposition that you may be firearms enthusiasts like myself?"

Ernan nodded.

"And might I guess that you're from in-system, so you've never taken any FTL hops and are therefore uneducated in some of the more exotic and perhaps out-of-fashion weaponry?"

Danavan continued. "Well, you are in luck. For while my partner is sporting a run-of-the-mill Mosely 'Volcanic,' I myself am holding a pair of Heim Model 2242 Gyrojet pistols."

Danavan stepped backward several paces. "Do you know what a gyrojet is?"

The men shook their heads. Good. He had them focusing on information instead of the fight. He hoped he'd engaged enough of their curiosity and intellect for the severity of their situation to hit home in a moment.

"A gyrojet is a little rocket. Launches right out of the ceramic-coated barrel like a bullet from a normal pistol. Now over the last couple of decades, advances in propellant have allowed me to load less weight-wise. Lets me make that up in payload. There's a drawback to gyrojets. Want to know what that is? They need a bit of room to get up to speed. About ten meters or so. Which is right about where I'm standing now, give or take. Afore you decide to undertake in any foolishness, consider with modern propellant and the additional payload in these rounds, that armor you're sporting is like as not to be as good as your birthday suit. Same goes if Pina uses her Volcanic, as well. Nod if you understand."

He waited for the men to nod. "Okay. Ernan. Here's what we're going to do instead of doing a live-fire gyrojet demo. You're going to collect your friends' guns and get on to more profitable business. Get moving."

Ernan got to the business of filling his arms with the others' weapons, and they began to walk off.

Tyler turned to Pina as he walked by. "We'll see you around."

Pina answered with steel in her voice. "Not if I see you first. Normally, folk don't get warnings. You've had two. There won't be a third."

Tyler sneered at her but moved on. They watched the men walk toward the mess hall.

Croyle exhaled loudly. "That's the most I've probably ever heard you say."

"Well, them being dumb is no reason to kill those fellas."

A loud horn sounded followed by an announcement along the town's PA: "All agents to the ready line. All agents to the ready line. Condition One."

Danavan and Pina headed out.

"Aren't you going to bring your hotshot rifle?" Croyle called after them as he trotted to catch up.

"Didn't have time to charge it," Danavan said.

Holo-guides activated along the street and pointed to the muster location.

The mercenaries poured out along Fremont Street and back onto Main. They followed the street where it curved off to the right and stopped in front of two massive pressure doors. These guarded the primary route out of First Settlement and into the rest of the complex.

A terrified guard in a threadbare uniform ran back at the group. "They're hacking the doors. They'll have them open any time now." If his demeanor didn't give it away, the uniform did. This man wasn't an NJK agent. He belonged to the governor's forces.

The doors slid open a crack and hissed as the pressure equalized. The line of mercenaries purred and rattled with the sound of charging energy rifles and mechanical bolts slamming closed on loaded rounds.

Danavan threw on his helmet. Pina already wore hers.

The doors crept open slowly and revealed a crowd of harvesters on the other side. His armor counted roughly three hundred. About a third of them held rifles and other weapons. The rest held signs.

Pina's voice cut in on his comms. "This looks more like a picket line than an uprising. Just like NJK to say otherwise."

About a dozen harvesters broke away from the mass. Some of them held an enormous banner that read THERE IS LIFE IN THE WATER. The leader, an Asian man, yelled something, but he was too far. Danavan blinked the command for his armor to augment the sound.

"...been lied to. They don't want you to know—" A deafening horn blast interrupted the man, and Danavan's armor immediately tempered the decibels.

Someone had activated the First Settlement PA. "Drop your weapons. Place your hands over your head and lay on the ground."

Danavan scanned again. None in the small group were armed. He activated his armor's PA and shouted a warning. "Hold your fire. They aren't armed."

NJK's Bryn Horton, Richie Carr, and two others knelt and fired, starting a chain reaction as mercenaries opened up all down the line. The harvesters turned and tried to make it back to the pressure doors but were cut down.

"Damn it. Hold your fire!" Danavan yelled. The armor's PA amplified his voice, but it was useless.

Now, sporadic fire came from the harvesters at the pressure door. The mercenaries returned a murderous stream until a figure ran out in front of them.

Pina.

Oblivious of the danger to herself, she planted herself in front of the mercenaries, arms outstretched. Her voice crackled on all channels and the settlement PA. "This is Justiciar Gracchi. Cease fire under penalty of law."

The fire from the mercenaries abated. The harvesters took the opportunity to retreat behind the closing pressure doors.

The commodore broke away toward Pina as the mercenaries reloaded. Pina and he had words for a moment over a closed circuit; Danavan couldn't hear what was said. Then Pina walked back.

"We're going to have trouble." She spoke across the squad comms. "I've stalled with some bluster and threats, but he's got the governor. Legal arguments aren't going to hold."

Danavan's eye swept across the line of mercenaries. None seemed eager to do anything rash. Except . . .

Croyle saw them too. Tyler's bunch.

"Pina!" Croyle yelled.

Pina drew, spun, and dove, firing as she rolled back onto her feet. The Mosely barked four times.

Four men fell.

The NJK All-Stars—Bryn Horton, Richie Carr, Nash Lawson, and Rzia Pacheco—broke from the crowd of mercenaries.

"Gracchi. Should have known," Horton said.

"Turn over your weapons. There's going to be an investigation," Carr added.

"Like hell," Pina said. "You people started the shooting out there, and you probably set those four onto me."

"So you say," Horton said.

"So do I," Danavan said. His armored fingers caressed the Heim pistols' polished handles.

Everything grew very quiet.

Seconds passed like hours.

Croyle spoke and tried to make light of it. "Hasn't there been enough killing for one day? We don't want to exceed our quota, do we?"

A few mercenaries laughed nervously.

Commodore Grant stepped out of the crowd. "Stand down." His people backed off.

His voice crackled across the comms. "We need to talk. You've placed this entire operation in jeopardy."

Pina answered. "You've done that yourself. NJK is fantastic when it comes to shooting people in the back and cutting down civilians. Your people are reckless, and I suspect are following orders to deliberately let this get out of hand. Maybe this is just a scheme to inflate Tangaroa's stock prices. I don't know. I *will* get to the bottom of it, I promise you that. This entire operation is under my jurisdiction until my investigation is complete."

"That's up for discussion. You can't just suspend—" Grant said.

"I didn't stutter." Pina turned and walked back to the tent city.

As the sky simulated evening growing to night, the three sat close together on a small ledge partway up the cavern side wall. They had some slight concealment, no real cover, but good sight lines down onto First Settlement. Pina and Danavan had set their luggage so the overlapping sensor proximity alarms would give them a bit of warning.

Pina stared down into the tent city. "'There is Life in the Water.' What do you suppose that meant?"

"No idea," Danavan said. "You know they're going to come after us for this."

"NJK? The other mercs? Who exactly?" Croyle asked.

"All of them *and* the Judiciary," Danavan answered. "Word's bound to get back on this one. How long do you figure we have before Grant checks up on us and gets a response?"

Pina grunted. "Oh, this whole affair will be long over by then, I suspect."

"I'm a bit confused. Did I hear wrong? I thought Pina and you were done with the law. Down there, she mustered the authority to shut everything down," Croyle said.

Danavan answered. "I'll come clean. We're on our own here. Just right and wrong. And oaths some still take too seriously." He looked at Pina.

She put her hand on Danavan's shoulder and bent her head. He returned the gesture, so their foreheads touched.

"Authority don't come from a badge. Badge don't make the law," Pina said so quietly Danavan was sure Croyle hadn't heard.

But he had. "That's a hell of thing. An ex-Adjudicator and an ex-Justiciar lying about still being on the job."

Danavan looked at his friend. "This is our trouble now, Augustus."

"Glad you understand. Yours is just the kind of trouble I don't need. I want to help, but I'm too old to get mixed up in any more misadventures. I gotta get paid." Croyle stood and started walking back down.

"Hey, if you change your mind, or if you don't, you know... we could use some help. So, if you suss out anyone with sentiments like ours..." Danavan said.

"I'll send them your way."

Pina called after him, "And passage off this rock to anyone with their own transport. I can pay well. And for you. You know I'm good for it. Interest doesn't stop building up just 'cause you're in FTL."

"Then why the hell are you out here?" Croyle asked.

Pina just shrugged.

"Fine. I'll keep it in mind. Just in case you see me on the other side... well, I'll try not to hit you." Croyle continued down.

"Likewise," Danavan shouted after him.

Soon, Croyle was out of sight.

The proximity alarm on Danavan's luggage activated. At first, he thought it was Croyle coming back up. He gave Pina a sign, and they both spread out and readied their weapons.

It was a young girl, barely twelve or thirteen. "You're the law?" she asked.

Pina nodded.

"Daiyu sent me to come get you. She wants to talk to you."

"Who is Daiyu?" Danavan asked, even as he and Pina stood ready to follow the girl.

"She's in charge now."

"Lead the way."

The girl led them through narrow access tunnels built during First Settlement's construction, now only used by workers to come and go unobtrusively. The tunnels were so narrow only one person could move through at a time. The workers had carved cubbies every fifty meters or so, allowing folks to squeeze by one another whenever they encountered traffic coming the other way.

"Do people know about these tunnels?" Danavan asked.

"Everyone does," the girl answered. "Just we use them."

"How many people—" Danavan began.

The girl interrupted him, "I don't know nothing. Ask Daiyu. Your people killed my friends. They told me to get you. I'm getting. Doesn't mean we have to talk."

"Fair enough."

Finally, the seemingly interminable tunnels opened into a hab section for the harvesters. Repurposed cargo containers stacked together formed living areas. It wasn't the first time Danavan had seen such an arrangement, yet this was the most squalid. Here, the cavern tunnels still bore the marks of excavators. Tangaroa Cooperative had done little to make them more than just barely habitable.

Conversations stopped and harvesters stood and gave them hard stares as they walked between them.

Danavan expected nothing less.

They moved to a set of pressure doors labeled DISTILLERS: AUTHORIZED PERSONNEL ONLY.

A guard with an antiquated rifle punched a code into a keypad as they approached. He barred the doorway while the pressure doors opened.

"Your weapons stay here," the man said.

"Not happening," Danavan answered.

"It's not negotiable," the man said and puffed himself up to look bigger.

"We'll just go back the way we came, then," Pina said. "You want to talk to us. Not the other way around."

A voice called from inside the next room. "Liam, let them through. If you knew who they were, you'd understand they could kill everyone in here without their weapons."

Liam stood aside, but his sour expression stated that he wasn't pleased about it.

Danavan and Pina stepped into the next room and faced an Asian woman in her mid-thirties. She had a hard-lined face that made her look old, and it was clear she'd been crying.

"I'm Liang Daiyu. I know that doesn't mean much. But it was my father your people killed today, and now, somehow, I'm in charge."

"Wasn't our people," Danavan said.

"Does it matter?" Daiyu said.

"No. I suppose it doesn't," Danavan said.

"My father wanted to give you the benefit of the doubt. He believed if you knew what was at stake you'd understand. Instead, you . . . they . . . killed him for it. Well, in the aftermath, we heard about the other shooting, and that there was a Justiciar taking control. Gives us a chance."

Pina cut to business. "What's at stake other than work and living conditions? I know now this is a strike and a contract dispute, not an uprising."

Daiyu ignored her comments about the strike and moved to the distiller line. "Look, a lot of my people think we're stirring the tanks here for no reason. We have so many of our own problems, why promote new ones? But there's a small group of us who think this is wrong. How trained are you in science?"

"Normal schooling, why?" Danavan asked.

Daiyu filled a tumbler of water from the inlet pipe into one of the distiller units. "This water is coming from one of the recently discovered underground freshwater oceans Aguilar is famous for. It's supposed to be pure and sterile except for potential mineral contamination."

She moved to another piece of equipment. "This is an electron microscope. We use it to verify the number of contaminants on the output side of the distiller remains negligible. Everything was fine on input and output until we tapped a new ocean. Then this happened."

Daiyu poured the water from the tumbler into the microscope's sampler. The screen lit up. Thousands of tiny creatures scampered and crawled across the sample area.

"What the hell?" Danavan said.

"There is Life in the Water," Pina said.

"New life. Undiscovered and unknown *alien* life. This has never happened. Across more than three hundred worlds, there has never been life that didn't come from Terra," Daiyu said.

"And you're sure this isn't somehow Terran life-forms that have contaminated your equipment and therefore the water?" Danavan asked.

"Pretty sure."

"Does the governor know?" Pina asked.

"That's when the trouble started," Daiyu answered.

"This is going to affect the entire system. Tangaroa will never let this get out." Danavan shook his head and marveled at the creatures on the screen. "They're not going to stop settling and terraforming over a few microbes."

Daiyu smiled ruefully. "And if you dipped a spoon in old Terra's oceans, would you know about whales or fish or anything else in those depths? We don't even know what we're killing here."

Pina exhaled loudly, and Danavan didn't like the look on her face, even if it was the right thing to do.

"You put together evidence for me." Pina looked at Danavan. "We'll get it out."

The start of Aguilar's artificial diurnal cycle found Danavan and Pina halfway up the cavern side wall, arming for the morning's activities. Each knew what they had to do. The future held an unpleasant promise of frustration, the judicious application of violence, and loss of life. Hopefully, not their own.

Daiyu made them a data chit containing enough evidence to warrant an investigation. They just had to broadcast it. Instead of using the settlement's common transmitter, Pina figured they could make two maneuvers with one burn since the governor had a private transmitter, and he needed to be arrested anyway.

They headed down the path. Danavan hoped his helmet visor revealed nothing of the tension and consternation his face wore beneath.

Danavan's proximity alarm sounded internally. He and Pina paused.

Augustus Croyle came into view, hands raised.

"Figured you'd be coming down this way. I have bad news and funny news," Croyle said.

"Bad news first, always," Danavan said.

"You've got plenty of folks who aren't liking this job. They didn't sign up for union busting. But they won't come over. Most of the guns down there are hard up and need this score. Myself included."

Danavan nodded. "And the funny? Could use a laugh."

"You were right about the food. About half of the force has

been rendered invalid on account of something in the food. They're crapping their guts out. The commodore's fixing to have a fit. Wants workers whipped and such, but no one can find any."

"Yeah. We might have had a thing or two to do with that. Came into some critical intelligence. We've had a busy night," Danavan said. He told Croyle about the discovery of alien life on Aguilar and how the harvesters' living conditions weren't the only cause for the strike. Then he told him about the morning's plans.

"So," Danavan concluded, "if you could go spread the word down there among whoever's still going to be doing some fighting, we'd owe you."

"You really think I would let you take down the governor without help? I may be broke and a near-coward in my old age, but I'm not spent yet. You know this is beyond crazy, right?"

"Hang around Pina long enough, one ceases to notice," Danavan said.

Pina laughed. "How else is one to become a legend in her own time?"

"In her own mind, maybe," Danavan said.

A shrieking alarm pierced the otherwise quiet morning.

"That'll be the mess hall on fire. That means we have about ten minutes until the pressure doors open and set off another alarm. We'd better get a move on."

They jogged down the path and passed the tent city at a quick trot. People ran to and fro and didn't offer a second glance. Then they were in front of the governor's quarters. Two of the governor's guards blocked the ground floor entrance.

"Justiciar Gracchi here on Judiciary business. Stand aside."

"We have orders not to—"

"Adjudicator," Pina ordered, "get idents on both these men. If they don't move in the next second, take them into custody."

The guards nearly fell over themselves standing aside.

Pina barged through the double doors. Twin stairways flanked the lobby heading to the second story. She ran up the left, and Danavan bounded up the right. He snatched a glance over his shoulder. Croyle barricaded the doors they'd just come through.

He reached the top of the stairs an instant after Pina. Two armored NJK guards stood in front of the governor's desk about five meters away. Pina had their attention.

Danavan didn't give them a moment to react. With the speed

of thought, his Heims were in his hands and roaring. He peppered each guard with a half dozen gyrojet rounds.

He turned to the governor. "Hands. Now."

The man sat utterly dumbfounded, a terrified look on his face as the remains of a half-bitten muffin dropped from his mouth. "You killed them."

"Naw, they'll be fine. I was too close. I'm betting they might wish they were dead, though, when they wake up. That couldn't have felt good."

Croyle topped the stairs, his autogun at the ready. He relaxed after taking stock of the situation.

Pina crossed the room. "Sidney Chassum, I hereby serve you formally with a Writ of *Quo Warranto*. You are hereby charged with Murder by Proxy, Murder for Hire, Improper Governance, and Trafficking in Indentured Peoples. Other charges will follow. How do you plead?"

Chassum just sat there, too flummoxed to say anything. No way he was the brains. "But I didn't do anything wrong." He found a measure of his authority and stood behind the desk. "Besides, good luck proving anything."

"'Sin was in the world before the law came, but no record of sin was kept, because there was no law.' Law is here now, and we have records aplenty." Danavan said. He pulled out a vest made from composite mesh. "This is a custody garment. For your safety and ours, I'm going to put it on you. It gets tighter if you struggle. Looser if you don't. Once knew a gal who could relax enough to get out of it." That last part wasn't true, but it tricked perps into keeping calm.

Danavan forced Chassum into it and pushed him into a corner.

Pina sat behind the desk and brushed the remains of Chassum's breakfast onto the floor. "Now, let's just hope they didn't change the backdoor, or we may be humped."

Danavan held his breath and Pina's fingers flew over the interface. In a moment, the holo-screens appeared, and Pina began getting the transmitter ready.

Croyle called from a window looking out on the balcony and the street below, "We've got some trouble. They may have detected our escapades."

Commodore Grant's voice came over the PA. "Pina Gracchi, we have the building surrounded. You are grossly outnumbered and outgunned. You've overstepped your authority and are engaged in illegal activity. We will not allow you to take the governor hostage."

Danavan crossed to another window to get a view for himself. "Shit. That was faster'n I would have guessed." He looked out on the NJK All-Stars and about two dozen mercenaries. Their weapons trained on his position.

"Pina! We may have to shoot our way out." Danavan loaded fresh magazines into his pistols.

"You're joking, right?" Croyle laughed nervously. "Even at the top of our game, that's about ten for each of us."

Danavan nodded in agreement. "Good at math, are ya? This is the path to becoming legends, right?"

"Ha. I'm having second thoughts along that score. No need to be a verse in a ballad about the last stand of Pina Gracchi," Croyle said.

Pina chimed in. "The penultimate stand. You never know when it's your last stand. Besides, I can't vouch for you two, but I'm fixing to walk out of here. Chassum has to stand trial."

"Well then, get up here," Danavan said.

The PA came on again. "We're going to give you ten seconds to come out unarmed."

"Well, at least I'm going out for a good cause and in good company," Croyle said.

"Ten." Grant began his countdown.

"If it was just the NJK crew, I bet we could take them," Danavan said.

"Nine."

"So, surrender is out," Croyle said.

"Eight."

"Never was an option. Pina?" Danavan wondered what took her so long.

"Seven."

"I'm busy trying to prevent our life-abort," Pina said.

"Six."

"The hell are you doing back there?"

"Five."

Danavan watched the mercenaries lower their weapons and walk away. The commodore shouted at them to stand at their posts, but they ignored him. Only the commodore and his five NJK All-Stars stayed. Grant's face was fiery red.

"Commodore looks pissed. What did you do?"

Pina answered as she took position next to Danavan. "Well, first, I sent a command to the Exchange to dump all my Tangaroa stock. It's about to turn to shit. Then I sent out Daiyu's evidence on wide. Every receiver in-system should get a copy. Lastly, I remembered Croyle saying how hard up everyone was for chits. And I thought, what use is currency if you don't spend it? So, I offered them all contracts via PDA paying twice what NJK promised. All they had to do was leave us alone and go have a beverage of their choice. And I promised not to pay in company scrip."

Danavan's jaw hung open in surprise.

"Now, did I hear you say you think we could take just the NJK idiots? I think you're right. Shall we?"

Croyle spoke up. "Hold up a sec. I'm too old to go jumping off balconies. I'll head out the front." He went down the stairs.

Pina looked at Danavan. "On three?"

He nodded.

"One...Two..."

The End

SHOWDOWN ON BIG ROCK 27

Gini Koch writing as Anita Ensal

Patsy finished drilling her section of Big Rock 27, where they were working today. The moment she was done, their ship's robot, Zeller, tugged twice on her tether. They had communicators in their helmets, but they were old and faulty, so they used the old miners' signals whenever they could. Two tugs meant Zeller wanted her attention.

She looked up and around. Zeller pointed off into the Blackness. There were lights coming. Definitely lights, not stars. And there were many of them. The Belt was huge, there were only two groups that traveled in force, and no conglomerate mining ships worked this far away from one of the Stations.

Which meant only one thing.

She tugged on the tethers that kept her little brothers attached to her, and they all stopped working and came to her. Zeller came, too. He leaned his helmet against hers. "We need to send out the call."

"I agree," Patsy said, as they started for their ship, the *S7*. She was normally proud of how her family had maintained this ship since before she'd been born. It looked ancient and vulnerable to her right now, though, because what it wasn't was equipped to handle what was coming.

Once they were all in the ship, her parents looked confused. So did her little brothers. Patsy steeled herself, because they were all going to look terrified in a moment.

"Send the signal—we have pirates coming. A lot of them."

☆　　☆　　☆

43

Captain Eric Delgado wondered what he'd done to get this assignment and crew.

The duty could have been worse—he could be cruising around Charon Prison to ensure no one escaped. That was considered the worst duty in the system, and it was rare when any team could last there more than three months.

Cruising this part of the Belt was fine. Not as interesting as being around Ceres, Pallas, Vesta, or Europa Stations, not as dull as monitoring Earth or Mars. The Lunars were fine—the job tended to be escorting passenger ships or shuttles, which was important, though not the same as flying around the Suspended Cities of Venus, Jupiter, and Saturn. That duty was always exciting.

Of course, the Belt mattered the most. Without its miners getting the resources needed to keep the system alive, humanity would die out. Belt duty was many months of boredom flying through the Blackness interspersed with the occasional rescue of a mining ship that had been hit by a stray rock or had another malfunction. It was important work, nonetheless.

No, he had to admit it—it was his crew on this assignment that was the real problem.

There was nothing wrong with them, at least not individually. Marcus West, the most experienced officer with them, would retire at the end of this tour assignment, meaning he was focused on what he was going to do when he was done. It was interesting to West, but not to Delgado—who was decades away from retirement. And retiring wasn't what he wanted to do, anyway. What he wanted was to find a woman who wanted to do the job with him—a life mate in uniform, saving the system together.

Rory Simons came from one of the wealthier Belt families. Why he was in the Galactic Police, though, Delgado couldn't determine. Even though he was an excellent communications officer, and was extremely adept at accessing and repairing all the ship's systems, Simons wasn't excited about anything they were doing, and Delgado had to keep an eye on him to ensure Simons didn't sleep on the job. Simons did as he was told, but *only* as he was told.

Jack Price, though, was the biggest challenge. The kid was from Earth and thrilled to be a part of the GP. He considered himself a hotshot, which was the real issue, and him ending up top of his class at the Academy meant Price thought he knew everything about everything. While Simons couldn't care less about being in their ship, Price wanted to fly the *1963* at warp speed everywhere to rescue every miner in the entire Belt, preferably all at the same time.

A sound pulled Delgado out of his moody contemplations. "Distress call," he said crisply. "Marcus, let's determine who's closest." Price sighed audibly behind him. Delgado ignored it.

"Huh," West said. "I know this ship. It's the *Sure Thing, Independent Seven-Seven-Seven*. They're good folks, and they never call for no reason or for something small."

"Rory, who's where?" Delgado asked.

Simons whistled softly. "We're the only ship close. Everyone else is at least a day away, probably more."

"Then it's us," Delgado said. "Marcus, let them know we're coming."

Before West could send the message, the distress signal shut off. He and Delgado looked at each other. "False alarm?" Delgado asked, as Price heaved another sigh.

West shook his head slowly. "I've known Doug and Sally Stevens since they found their claim. They're good miners and good people, and they do nothing by accident."

"One claim?" Simons asked snidely.

"One claim," West said mildly, though Delgado could tell the older man was annoyed. "Thirty rocks, a family group, all of good size. Well, less than thirty now, since they've been working this claim for years. I checked them out when they first made their claim, helped them get it all straight."

"You had to help them?" Simons was still unimpressed.

Delgado resisted the urge to slap him.

"I did," West said, voice still mild. "They were young and were grateful for the assistance. I like this section of the Belt and, when I get the assignment here, I always check in on them. Would have suggested it once we were a little closer, as a matter of fact." He still looked worried.

"Kids on the ship?" Delgado tried to find a reason for the false alarm.

West nodded. "One girl, Patsy, three boys, Bobby, Eddie, and Joey. The boys are a bit mischievous, but there's no way even the youngest would do a fool thing like that."

Delgado had to agree. The fines for a false call to the Galactic Police were harsh. "Visitors?"

"Not likely," West replied. "They have no other family—Doug had his father and her mother with them when they came out to the Belt. Those two have since passed on, and that's the entire family."

Delgado nodded. That was common for a good chunk of the independent miners. "Then why?"

"Why what?" Price asked.

"Why did experienced miners send out a distress call, then cancel it?"

"At the Academy, they said we should always assume the worst," Price said helpfully.

Delgado stiffened, and he knew West had, too. "The worst?" West asked.

"Out here," Delgado said, "there's only one worst—Boser Geist is paying them a visit."

The system was, for all intents and purposes, lawful. Out in the Blackness, humanity had finally realized they were in this together and, as far as they'd ever found so far, they were *alone* in this together. That didn't mean there weren't criminals—that's why Charon Prison existed, after all.

There were military and police forces on the planets, the Lunars, and the Suspended Cities, but the Galactic Police were the force that kept the Blackness safe. There were a lot of them— Delgado had heard they'd had to go to five digits recently for ship designations—because the solar system was huge, and there was a lot of Blackness to fly through. There were never going to be enough GP cruisers to cover it all.

The Belt, however, was where the worst of the worst did their work—specifically Boser Geist and his pirate armada.

Boser Geist had been around for hundreds of years. He wasn't immortal—when the current Boser Geist was captured or killed, the title was passed along to whoever in the organization was ready or able to take over. Stopping the current one was always the number one thing the GP wanted its officers to do.

"That makes the most sense," West said. "It's a rich claim for an independent. There's so much Blackness in the Belt, I was hoping Boser Geist wouldn't find them, though, way out here."

"What we want and what we get are rarely the same things," Delgado mentioned.

"In training, they said the pirates take the claims for themselves," Price said.

"They really coddled you at the Academy," Delgado replied. "There are very few ways for someone to claim jump—our systems are set up specifically to avoid it. However, the ways Boser Geist and his ilk have found are both effective and horrific."

"And it's almost impossible to catch him doing it, too," West added. Then he chuckled morosely. "Of course, Eric and I have both done so."

"You've caught Boser Geist?" Simons finally sounded mildly interested.

"Killed," Delgado said. "Not caught. And I'm all for doing that again. Right now, though, we need to do two things—set a course for the Stevens' claim and find out every single thing about them: both what Marcus knows and what the records at Ceres Main tell us."

"Why?" Price asked. "Can't we just get there and blast the pirate ships to smithereens?"

Delgado wanted to ask West who he'd pissed off to get Price assigned to his ship. He bit it back—the Academy took two years of intense, constant training, but they didn't prepare you for what it was really like to patrol the Blackness, let alone the Belt. "Because it's unlikely we're going to be able to do that and not destroy the claim and the miners." He turned around and looked right into Price's eyes. "And we're here to protect and serve those miners first and foremost. If that means we have to let the pirates get away, then that's what we do. If we can destroy the pirates without harming the miners and their claim, then that's what we do."

"What other options do we have?" Simons asked.

Delgado shrugged and turned forward again. "We can run. Or we can die." The others were quiet. Delgado ensured their course was set, though he didn't engage the engines yet. "So, now's the time."

"The time for what?" Price asked.

"The time to see what kind of person you are. Are you in or are you out?"

"You'd actually give us that choice?" Simons asked.

Delgado nodded. "I would. All four of us have to be willing to do whatever we're going to have to do in order to save those people. One of us shirking, trying to fly away like a comet, not following orders, and we're dead—the miners and all of us. Two of you are young, lots to live for. West is ready to retire, different things to live for. So, make your choices."

"Kind of forcing the decision, aren't you?" Simons asked.

"Boser Geist demands the decision. If you're not in, then you get into your gear, get into the shuttle, and we call for another cruiser to pick you up. No loss of rank, no loss of status. Not everyone can do what this is going to demand."

"What are you doing, Eric?" Simons asked.

"I'm going whether the three of you go with me or not."

"I'm in," Price said. "I didn't work like I did to not actually perform my duty now that the comets are actually going to start flying."

"I'm in," West said. "I know these people. I can't leave them to be destroyed by these Charon-damned worthless fish."

Simons didn't say anything. Delgado sighed to himself and looked over. To see Simons busily working at his station. "What are you doing, Rory?"

"Pulling up all the history we have on the pirates, as well as the other information you mentioned we'd need." He looked over his shoulder and grinned. "Oh, sorry. I'm in. It just dawned on me that I was taught the pirates learn and pass the learning on, meaning they know whatever we did in the past. But the four of us might not. So . . ." He shrugged and turned back to his station.

Delgado was pleasantly surprised. "Then, we're heading out. Rory, while you're at it, send a call to whatever GP ships you can reach and let them know where we're going and what we figure we're up against. Preferably using a channel the pirates won't have jumped."

"On it," Simons said.

"Good. Now, while we fly toward imminent excitement and potential doom, Marcus, start telling us all you know about the Stevens family."

The pirates had sent two robots over to their ship. Zeller had warned them that ship's robots were loyal to their ship, and the people that belonged to it, meaning there was no hope they could appeal to any of the pirate's robotics. And reprogramming would take time they were unlikely to be given.

One of the robots stayed in the ship with their parents and

Zeller. The other escorted Patsy and her brothers into one of the pirate ships. Both were heavily armed. Patsy had never seen an armed robot before. She didn't care for it, but that didn't mean that, somewhere along the line, she wouldn't be able to use that against them.

There were ten ships surrounding their claim—the one they were taken to was sitting the closest to Big Rock 27. Patsy figured they were being herded to Boser Geist's command ship so he could have them nearby while he threatened their parents.

Once inside the pirate ship, they'd been instructed to remove their helmets. They'd obliged, though Patsy had insisted she and her brothers hold onto their helmets and, so far, no one had argued against this.

True to expectation, they were taken to the quite-roomy cockpit, to meet the person in charge of their capture.

She'd been expecting someone large; however, the man she was taken to was more on the wiry side. He wasn't impressive-looking, either. In the books she'd read and holovids she'd seen, most of the pirates were described as big and hairy, handsome and romantic, or lacking teeth and limbs. This man just looked ordinary, nothing exceptional in looks or size.

He gave them a curt nod. "Welcome to my command. Your jobs will be simple, no one will molest you, you'll sleep together, and you'll be fed what the rest of us eat. You can call me Captain."

"What's your real name?" Patsy asked.

A smile flashed across his face, like he wasn't used to doing it and didn't like the feeling. "Boser Geist."

The way he'd said it, it was clear he expected a reaction. Pity for him. "I meant your real name. I know Boser Geist is just a title."

His eyes narrowed. "My real name doesn't concern you. Learn that quickly—you're going to be with us for quite a while."

"You're going to raise us well into old age if you think our parents can work this claim out themselves," Patsy said.

He stared at her. She stared back. "They'll have assistance," he said finally.

"Besides us?"

He nodded. "We're not fools, and we're not trying to be unkind. This is just how we . . . do business."

"So I've heard tell."

Boser Geist eyed her. "You'd make a good pirate—you ask the right questions and make the right points. Consider it."

Patsy controlled her reaction. She wanted to spit at him. Instead, she nodded. "I'll do that."

"Keep them quiet," he said to the robot that had escorted them in. Said robot moved them to the back of the cockpit. No one else paid them any mind.

Boser Geist turned back to look out at her family's life's work. He began telling Patsy's parents what he expected them to do, who would be with them when they went to Vesta Station to change their claim ownership, and so on. There wasn't going to be a lot of time to get out of this, and none once her parents left the claim in the *S7*.

Patsy spent the time looking around, pretending to be awed. She looked down at her brothers. "You should try to learn the ship as soon as you can."

They all nodded and started looking around like she was. She'd told them what the pirates wanted to do to their family—the boys were ready to do whatever they had to in order to ensure they'd survive as unscathed as possible. Hopefully one of the four of them would spot a weakness that could be exploited.

Simons shared that they were close to the Stevens' claim, meaning they had to decide how to approach.

West had filled them in on all he knew about this family, but Delgado wasn't sure if it would be enough.

Simons had given them a listing of all successful attempts against the various Boser Geists that had come before. He'd also found all the unsuccessful ones. The information hadn't been heartening—the four of them were going to have to be more creative than Delgado thought they could be, and that was if he wasn't selling any of them short. He and West had each been creative enough separately. And most GP officers didn't get a chance to take on Boser Geist more than once.

"Guaranteed by now they have the kids on one of the ships," Simons said. "That's been their *modus operandi* for the past two decades at least. If there are children, the pirates take them. If there aren't children, then they take the weakest people, women, for preference. If it's a single miner and a robot, they take the miner and make them program the robot to do what the pirates want."

West nodded. "The threat is obvious for the women—gang rape. But for any males it's the threat of castration."

All four of them shuddered. "There's no way any parent is going to go against a threat like that," Delgado said. "Or anyone else, really."

"No wonder the robots do what they're told," Price said. "It's the only way they can protect the ship's owners from harm."

"Per the history, they're democratic, in a way," Simons said. "They give the miners the option to join them as pirates. Some have taken that offer. Some of the captives taken have chosen to stay with them, too."

"You eat well, if you're following Boser Geist," West said. "No laws, other than his. It's appealing to some."

"Or else those captives took the easier way out," Price said. "Probably no risk of rape or castration if you embrace the pirate lifestyle."

"Not that we have a record of," Simons said. "But they don't kill the miners after the claims are dried out. At least, not all of them."

"They kill plenty of them," West said darkly. "They just make it look like a stray rock or a snowball hit them."

"Sadly, this claim isn't near the snowline," Simons said, "so chances of comets showing up to help us save the day seem slim."

"This gets us no closer to a plan," Delgado said. "And we have to have one, or we all die, and we doom this family to a fate that, honestly, might be worse than death." He looked over at West. The older man was staring out into the Blackness, looking thoughtful. "Marcus, want to share what you're thinking?"

"We have to fool the pirates," West said, still staring off into space. "That's what I'm thinking. They have to know the distress signal was sent, right?"

"Right," Delgado agreed, "because otherwise it would still be going. It was turned off because the Stevens family was told to turn it off or die."

"So if we show up looking ready for action, they're going to blast. But . . ." West turned to him. "But what if we come in doing what I'd planned to ask you to do anyway?"

"You mean act like we're just dropping by?" Delgado shook his head. "Going to be hard to sell."

"Not necessarily," West said. "Not if we can get the Stevens family to play along."

"Can we?" Delgado shook his head. "You have to remember that this event is now the single most terrifying thing that's ever happened to them, and it's happening as we speak. Not everyone can work under pressure."

"Belt miners can," Price said. "Per everything I learned at the Academy, those who are mining here are independent thinkers, willing to do dangerous, dirty work. They have to be able to think fast when an asteroid can rip their ships apart."

"Does one of the kids want to join the GP?" Simons asked.

"Not that I know of," West replied. "Why?"

"Because, based on the tracking data, someone on that ship has been accessing all GP training manuals, system alerts, and more. You've accessed them, as well, but not as many and not nearly as often."

"It must be Patsy," West said. "I gave her an old manual years ago, when she was out of new things to read and waiting for the family to be able to afford new transmissions for her."

"So," Delgado said slowly, "she's a reader?"

"Yes," West said. "She likes some really old books, too. Before-expansion old."

Delgado was thinking. "What's her favorite book, do you know?"

"I can make a guess, but that's all it would be."

"Based on her entertainment transmissions," Simons said, "she's enamored of some ancient texts. Some match her holovid transmissions, too."

"She read the books and wanted to see if the vids were better?" Delgado asked.

"No. I think she saw the vids and wanted to see if the books were better," Simons replied. "Based on timing. And, to get ahead of your next question, Eric, based on transmissions, the books she's rented the most are *Alice's Adventures in Wonderland*, *Through the Looking-Glass*, and any vids made from those original source materials."

"Marcus, have you read any of those?" Delgado didn't hold out a lot of hope—the original texts were ancient. Everyone in the GP read—you had to have something to keep your mind occupied while you cruised the Blackness—but most read authors who'd been born in the last century.

"I have, actually," West said slowly. "I read *Alice's Adventures in Wonderland* because Patsy told me what a wonderful book it was. That's what my guess would have been for her favorite, too."

"Perfect." Delgado felt his plan solidify. "Do you know it well enough to quote it incorrectly?"

"Maybe?"

"I can send the text to your station," Simons said cheerfully. "All our stations, just in case."

Delgado considered how to phrase his next question and decided being blunt was probably best. "Rory, why are you here? I don't mean philosophically, or why you're on my ship—I mean why are you a part of the Galactic Police? And before you consider lying to me, realize I'm asking because I have some strong suspicions it will waste time the Stevens family doesn't have to confirm your story."

"Why do you think I'm here?" Simons asked carefully.

Delgado turned and looked at him. "I think you're here because it was us or Charon Prison. Your family has money, which is why you got the choice. Am I right?"

Simons nodded, but he didn't speak. He looked worried, though.

Delgado chuckled. "Relax. Right now, having the best hacker in the System on board is a bonus, not a problem. And in case it matters—which, based on what you've already done, I know it doesn't to you, but might to the people we answer to—I authorize you to hack whatever you need to in order to save these people and keep us all alive."

Simons grinned. "My dad said he was getting me assigned to the best crew possible. I see he didn't lie."

"I'll be flattered if we're all alive tomorrow."

Price was staring, openmouthed. "Wait. Are you saying Rory is The Demon?"

"I am so saying," Delgado confirmed.

Simons shrugged. "I didn't choose that handle."

"The handle you chose was rude by the standards of every civilized community we have," West said dryly. "And, in fact, was offensive to everyone in Charon Prison, too."

Simons grinned again. "I wasn't hacking the systems to make everyone like me."

"Why were you?" Delgado asked.

Simons shrugged and turned back to his station. "I was bored."

West shook his head. "Kids today."

Speaking of which, Delgado looked back at Price. "Jack, are you up to working outside our ship?"

"Sure. I'm up for whatever you need me to do, as long as it's not sitting around and doing nothing. Though, I'll do that," he added quickly, "if those are your orders."

"No. If we're sitting around doing nothing, it's to fool the pirates."

West's idea would get them close enough, and Delgado knew the refinements he'd already thought up would ensure it. They'd also hopefully alert the Stevens family that the officers were aware of what was really going on.

He had an idea of how to give the girl clues they were trying to help her and her brothers. If she was smart enough—and someone who was reading all the GP manuals for fun was probably more than smart enough—she might even be able to give them coded replies.

How to stop the pirates once they'd fooled them into relaxing, *that* was the problem.

Simons and Price were talking quietly. "What?" Delgado asked.

"We were just looking at what you and Marcus did to beat Boser Geist," Simons said. "Both were pretty impressive."

"I want to know how you got on board a pirate ship without them knowing," Price said excitedly. "When we have time."

"I'm more impressed with how Marcus got the pirates to basically kill themselves," Simons countered.

"I was lucky," Delgado said. "There was only one pirate ship. We caught Boser Geist on his way to a function on Ceres Main, if you can believe it. The rocks on these pirates are unbelievable. It was easy to fool one ship, we just pretended we were verifying entry to the event, and they had to let me in or be blasted out of the Blackness. Once in, I didn't take off my helmet and released our fast-acting paralysis gas. I still had to kill Boser Geist, because he reacted faster than the rest, and it was either him or me. The rest of that crew are in Charon Prison."

"And we didn't have them kill themselves," West said. "We stuffed their exhaust vents with toxins, so there was feedback."

Delgado jerked. "How?"

"How what?" West asked.

"How did you do that without them knowing?"

"We were transporting a new polymer from Earth to Europa

Prime, and we had its creator on board. We had four ships and while three of them kept the pirates busy, we were able to put the polymer into the torpedo bays and shoot it at the rear of their ships. We got away with it because there were only three pirate ships, and we had four GP cruisers and, like I said, we were lucky to have the polymer on board with us."

"We don't have anything like that on the ship," Price pointed out sadly.

"Sure we do," Delgado said. The other three men looked at him, clearly questioning. "We have at least a hundred patch kits and fifty patch extinguishers on board. We carry them for us and for the miners. They'll fill an exhaust hole just as well as some polymer would. We shove in an activated paralysis bomb and 'patch' the exhaust outlet. The only downside is we have no idea how many ships we'll be facing, and it's unlikely they'll fall for anything we toss at them that would allow us to leave our ship unmolested."

"Plus, it's been done," West pointed out.

"But pretending you're just doing a routine check out here hasn't," Delgado countered. "Combining what we both did could be something they aren't prepared for."

"Plus, we're only one ship," Simons agreed, "and no one other than Eric has been successful against them alone. It's a combination of plans I don't think they've seen before."

"How do we get out of the ship?" Price asked. "And back in again, because if Eric's right, it's going to take more than one trip for us to do this."

"Oh, as to that, leave it to me," Simons said. "If the pirates don't blast us immediately, I can hack their systems."

"You're sure?" Delgado asked.

Simons snorted. "Trust me."

"We will be," Delgado said. "Jack and I will be the only ones going in and out. Marcus is going to be conning the pirates, and you're going to be hacking them."

"This is going to be the greatest," Price said with much enthusiasm. Delgado didn't share it, but at least they had a plan that was, for the moment, solid.

"Okay, Marcus, here's what I want you to do..."

The pirates had latched onto the *S7*'s radio, and Patsy and her brothers were still in the cockpit, so she heard what Boser

Geist heard. Which was Officer West. She held her breath—she and her brothers had known this man all their lives, and she didn't want to see him murdered in front of them.

"Howdy there, Doug and Sally," West said cheerfully. "Just thought we'd drop by and see how you're all doing."

"Routine visit," Boser Geist said, on a separate channel that went to the rest of his ships and to the robot with her parents. "Let it play out. I only see one GP cruiser."

"It's good to see you, Marcus," her father said. Good. No one in their family ever called Officer West by his first name, no matter how often the officer asked them to.

"Looks like you've finally gotten the help you were hoping for," West said, still sounding cheerful and completely unconcerned. "These ships carrying the relatives you told me might be coming out from the Lunars to assist?"

"They are indeed," Pa said heartily. "It's taken some time, but both Sally's kin and mine are with us now." They had no other family, and Patsy knew West knew this.

Which meant West understood these were pirates. Which also meant he knew she and her brothers would be on one of the pirate ships by now. She had to figure out how to let him know which one.

"Wonderful news! We'll leave you to it then—oh. Wait a moment."

She felt all the pirates stiffen, and she knew Boser Geist might give the kill order any second.

"Yes?" Pa asked, sounding confused.

"Are you going to change the claim status? If so, do you want me to help you with that again? You two had so much trouble with it when you first staked this claim, if you're planning to share with your relations, that's going to be even more complicated."

"Oh," Pa sounded relieved. "Would you help us, Marcus? You're right about the complexity, and it would save us the trip to Ceres Main if we processed via the Galactic Police."

This was true, and Patsy felt proud of Pa, and Officer West, too—he'd never struck her as sneaky before.

Boser Geist laughed softly. "We have a helpful public servant here, boys and girls. Let him stake the claim for us—that will be a true first." He started giving orders for whose names needed to be added and what relation to the Stevens family they should say they were.

"If you don't mind waiting," Pa said, "we're figuring out the right folks to put onto the claim, and who the beneficiaries will be."

"No problem at all," West said. "It's quiet out in this part of the Belt right now, no one needs us for anything, we're happy to relax. So, while we wait, Sally, how's your little Patsy doing?"

Boser Geist snorted a laugh and turned around to look at her. "Been a while since he's dropped by?"

"What of it?" she asked defiantly.

Another one of those obviously painful smiles flashed across his face. "He still thinks you're a child, not a pretty, young woman."

She shrugged. "What does it matter?"

"She's fine," Ma said before Boser Geist could reply, her voice shaking only a tiny bit.

"I wanted to tell her I read the book she recommended. While you folks deal with the claims situation, you mind if I while away some time chatting with her about *Alice in Wonderland*?"

Geist raised his eyebrow at her. "Seriously?"

"I like to read, and it's my favorite book. Marcus likes to read, too, and he's a nice man. Also, we talk books every time he comes by. If you want him to stay unsuspicious, you're going to have to let me talk to him."

"I don't mind," Ma said. "Let me get her."

"Letting the girl talk," Boser Geist said on the pirate channel. He indicated she should come to him.

She looked down at her brothers. "Be sure you three are extra good," she said slowly and clearly, "and really well behaved while I'm talking with Marcus." She winked at them. They all grinned at her and nodded. Good. Before the pirates had arrived she'd told them if she winked, or sounded overly polite, or spoke slowly, or seemed "off" in any way that they were to do the opposite of what she was saying and to remember the games they liked to play. "Keep your helmets no matter what," she added softly. "And make me proud."

With that, she went forward.

"Feel free to sit on my lap," Boser Geist said.

"I thought you said we weren't going to be molested."

That smile flitted across his face again. It was far more frightening than anything else, because, by now, she was sure when Boser Geist smiled it wasn't because he was thinking kindly or friendly thoughts.

"If you behave yourselves. You've given that instruction to your brothers. I'm going to make sure you follow it. I've seen several of the *Alice in Wonderland* holovids, you know."

She sniffed as she sat in his lap and did her best not to shudder. The good part of this was he'd be unlikely to pay her brothers any mind while she was on his lap, and if he spun them around, she could block his view, at least momentarily. "The book is better."

"We're a little too busy to read ancient space dust like that."

Good, he hadn't read the book. She really hoped West had a plan beyond stalling, though.

"Hi, Marcus," she said. "Ma says you finally read *Alice in Wonderland*." He'd read it years ago, and she and he had both used the full title to differentiate from the holovids.

"I have. Loved it. I wanted to tell you that. Such a fun book." He didn't correct her not using the full title. Hopefully this meant they were on the same side of the moon on this.

"And so different from all the holovids, too. Most people only watch those. It's sad." She hoped this was a clue he'd get, that the pirates hadn't read the book.

"They don't know what they're missing," West said. "A raven is like a writing desk because they're both black, after all."

Patsy forced herself not to hold her breath. "Exactly. And, like the Red Queen says, there's always time to take off someone's head."

"Right!" West said, while Boser Geist just sighed in a bored way. So, Belter's Luck was with them. Thank Sol. "One of my favorite parts was when Alice had to put a fishbowl over her head so she could swim in the lake."

"Oh, I loved that whole part!" So, West wanted them to have their helmets on. They couldn't do it now, but at the first sign of something, she'd have to risk it and hope her brothers followed suit or had correctly interpreted that clue for themselves. They might be younger, but they were all smart. "Like Alice says, turn at the fourth fish from the left and go straight on until the bottom." She hoped he counted from the *S7* outward and also looked for the ship that was the lowest—Boser Geist's ship was still hovering just above Big Rock 27.

"She had to wear a helmet?" Boser Geist asked, sounding interested, versus suspicious.

"No, a real fishbowl," Patsy said. "With water and a goldfish in it. So she could swim deep into the lake with the fish. I told you, the book was much better than any of the holovids. They have to leave too much out."

The screens blinked and the sound crackled for a moment. Then everything went back to normal.

"Huh. Everyone okay out there?" Boser Geist asked. The replies were all affirmative, then the pirates had some questions regarding the claim reassignment, and he got distracted with that. Patsy and West continued to share false quotes to trade information.

There was a ruckus from behind them, and Boser Geist did indeed spin his captain's chair around. Patsy would have blocked his view, but there was nothing to see. Her brothers, and the robot guarding them, were gone.

West was doing a great job sounding like a clueless idiot. Thankfully, the Stevens family had caught on immediately. The girl was as smart as Delgado had hoped, and she and West were exchanging information well. The pirates seemed to have no suspicions raised, even when Rory's hack had caused a momentary blip. Delgado wasn't sure if Belter's Luck was going to hold, but he hoped it would.

"I've got the tanks and paralysis bombs out by the emergency hatch," Price said. "I pulled half of the patch kits out, too, just in case. You ready?"

"Yes. Rory, you're sure no one but the four of us can hear what we're saying on the channel going into our helmets?"

"Positive."

"Then we're rolling our part of the plan."

GP officers were equipped with a variety of spacesuits. The ones they were in were called wetsuits, because they were based on ancient Earth prototypes that sat tight against your body. They were heated and reinforced, and they allowed you to move more freely than standard spacesuits. The helmets used for wetsuits were also more contoured than the standard fishbowls.

Added to this, they had utility belts that allowed them to clip whatever they needed to their waists, and they wore small jetpacks on their backs. They'd still have to aim themselves carefully, and the jetpacks wouldn't last long with continual use—they were made to be utilized in short bursts—but they'd help them get to the ships quickly and, hopefully, accurately.

He and Price went to the emergency hatch, sealed this area from the rest of the ship, each clipped six bombs and two tanks to their suits' utility belts, and aimed.

Patsy had indicated she and her brothers were in the fourth ship that was also the lowest. Counting from her family's ship, that meant the ship hovering just above the big rock the family's ship was tethered to was the likely culprit. So they'd hit that one last.

Price had insisted he wanted to take the farthest ships because there were more of them, and he'd be faster, and Delgado hadn't argued, because he knew he needed to be the one to get inside Boser Geist's ship. It had the most risk and required the most finesse, as well. Price wasn't experienced enough to give him that part of the mission.

"If they spot us, we're dead, so be sure you don't get spotted," Delgado said, as they pushed off from the *1963*.

"Can't catch me," Price said. "I'm a leaf on the wind."

"You'll be a splat on the side of a ship if you go in too fast."

He had to stop paying attention to Price, because he was coming up on his first ship. Because of how the pirates recruited, their ships were all of different designs and years of manufacture. Of the ten ships they were going to have to hit, no two were alike. However, one thing was standard—exhaust went out the back somewhere.

He reached the first ship with no issues and was able to catch an outcropping so he didn't slam into it. Hand over hand, he moved to the back, searching for the exhaust port. He found it quickly, activated two of the paralysis bombs, tossed them inside, and sprayed the insta-hard foam over the exhaust port.

The next ship had two exhaust ports. He sent one bomb into the left port, sealed it up, then did the same with the right. On to the third ship, where one gigantic exhaust port waited because it was a larger ship than the first two. He tossed in the rest of the bombs and had to use both tanks of patch foam.

He cursed in his head. Three down on his side was great. However, the moment Boser Geist realized he had problems on any of his ships, the hostages were in trouble.

"I got four of them," Price said. "I'm out of gear and heading back to the ship for more."

"Same."

The return to the *1963* was relatively easy from where he was, but it would risk his being seen by the ship identified as being Boser Geist's. Delgado gnashed his teeth—Price was sailing directly in front of that ship to return to the cruiser. No reason to be careful now. Either the pirates would see them or they wouldn't.

The jetpacks ensured they both got to the hatch quickly and accurately. "That was foolhardy," Delgado said as they dropped the used tanks and re-equipped. "They could have seen you."

"They didn't."

"We don't know that."

"We do," Simons said. "There's some kind of ruckus going on in what we're now certain is the ship Boser Geist is on. Marcus thinks the boys did something while he was talking to the girl. No one's on the comm with him right now—they stopped talking mid-sentence, then he heard a lot of shouting."

"I need to get into that ship," Delgado said. "Can you handle the last two ships alone, Jack? They're the biggest in this fleet, meaning more exhaust ports, most likely."

Price snorted. "Of course." He clipped four tanks to his belt and ten bombs. It was a good thing they were weightless, or Price wouldn't have been able to move.

"Be careful," Delgado warned, as he took two tanks and six bombs.

"It's going great, we have nothing to worry about," Price said. "I'll come back you up when I'm done." With that he shoved off, once again choosing a straight line that sent him across and above Boser Geist's bow.

"Does he realize what he just said?" Simons asked, sounding worried for the first time.

"I doubt they teach about Belter's Luck at the Academy now. They never did when I was there."

The Academy didn't focus on superstition—the Belters did.

Belter's Luck was a real thing, everyone out here knew and believed in it. But the Luck was capricious. And the moment you said aloud that Belter's Luck was with you, that everything was going great and nothing bad would happen, the Luck would leave you like a snowball running away from Mercury.

However, he didn't have time to dwell on this. He had to rig, then get inside, Boser Geist's ship. "Marcus needs to get a signal to the kids—they need their helmets on as soon as possible, because I'm heading to their ship and, if they're all paralyzed, it's going to be close to impossible for me to get them all out."

"Understood. Be careful, Eric."

"As careful as I can be." Within reason, of course, because there was nothing cautious about what any of them were doing right now.

The distraction the kids had likely caused wouldn't last forever. He had to follow Price's lead and just head straight for his goal, being spotted or not. He made it to the command ship quickly, then had to determine where he could enter safely and remain undetected. Meaning he had to waste precious time crawling around the ship, only to discover his best option was the man-sized exhaust port.

"Rory, is there anything I should know about the ship I'm about to enter via the riskiest means yet?"

"Nope," Price said, as he joined him. "These kinds are only a problem if they fire up. Watch and learn." Before Delgado could grab him, Price had clambered into the exhaust port.

"Don't go in," Simons said urgently. "They've figured out no one on the other ships is responding. They'll move any minute—"

Delgado tried to grab Price, but the kid was too far into the port. Instinct and years of being in the GP made him fling himself to the side so the sudden push of ionized exhaust didn't hit him.

Price blasted out of the port, and Delgado missed him again. The kid sailed away fast and, based on how his limbs and head moved, he was unconscious.

Delgado had two choices—abandon the miners and go after Price, or try to salvage the mission.

"Let us pray that the Blackness does not take us today," he said to Price's retreating figure. "But if it does, let us shine as brightly as Sol when we die."

"In Sol's name," Simons and West said in unison.

Delgado cleared his throat. "Rory, I need a way in, and I need it now."

"Hang on, I need a minute. Go to the left side. There's an emergency hatch there I'm pretty sure I can open."

"They're getting ready to send people to the other ships," West said as Delgado worked his way around the ship. "Not sure what's going on with the Stevens kids, no one's talking to me at all. I'm still on with them, though. I've muted my side, but they haven't. We have less than five minutes before they blast us, if that."

"Got it! The door's open, Eric. All you need to do is pull the exterior handle."

Delgado would have done so. Only the hatch opened before he could get to it.

Boser Geist had dragged her along with him to search for her brothers before Patsy had been able to let West know what was going on.

Boser Geist had run all over the ship, which, because she was good with memorization, was helpful and instructive, but Geist's firm grip on her arm meant escape wasn't an option. Not that she was going anywhere without her brothers.

Who—as they followed the trail of screams, shouts, and broken ship and robotic parts, along with a lot of human blood—had done their work well. Presumably, the robot wasn't used to children, let alone those who were good at working together as a team.

They ran into another crew member. "Those three kids are riding the robotic," he said. "Don't let them see you."

"What?" Boser Geist sounded furious. "Why shouldn't I let them see me?"

"Because they're controlling it." The other pirate shook his head. "Boser, they've disabled half the crew already."

Patsy did her best not to smile. Her brothers loved playing virtual reality and holovid games. They were particularly good at first-person-shooter games. Pa and Ma were going to be amazed at how useful the "time wasting" the boys had done for years was turning out to be.

"Stop running like a coward. Find those brats and kill them," Boser Geist snarled to the other pirate. He dragged Patsy back to the cockpit and shoved her at the communications console. "Get on the radio and tell your parents to get your brothers under control, or you all die."

Patsy saw a figure flying across the Blackness, going from the Galactic Police cruiser to one of the pirate ships. Now wasn't the time to acquiesce to anything.

She turned around and shoved him back, so he'd hopefully not see what she had. "No."

"No? You realize I—"

"Always planned to kill us? Yes, I do." She shoved him, hard. Either he wasn't prepared for a woman her size to be strong, or no one else had ever fought back. As he staggered backward, Patsy put her shoulder down and rammed into him. He went down.

She didn't hesitate. She ran.

While she was running, she put her helmet back on. "Boys, if you can hear me, we need to get off this ship. Where are you? I'm being chased by Boser Geist and trying to get to the escape hatch."

"We found the self-destruct," Bobby said.

"Can we pull it?" Eddie asked.

"We'll wait for you," Joey added.

"How close to the escape hatch is it?"

"Right next to it," Bobby said. "Hurry."

She rounded a corner and saw her brothers. They were still riding the robot. "Duck!" Eddie shouted.

She did, still running for them. She didn't see the laser shots that went over her head, but she heard them hit. She didn't turn to look back until she was close enough to grab Joey and could see the escape hatch's activation light was on already. "Now!"

Bobby and Eddy pulled the self-destruct as Patsy slammed into the hatch. She grabbed Eddie and Bobby did, as well. "Shove that robot back inside!" she shouted as she turned to make sure she had all three of her brothers. As she did, she saw that Boser Geist was hit but not dead and was, therefore, still coming.

The boys did as they were told. However, when they tumbled out of the hatch, they slammed into something hard.

"Are you all the Stevens kids?" the officer who had her in his arms asked, putting his helmet next to hers.

"Yes, Boser Geist is still coming!" she shouted as the pirate leader reached the hatch doorway and started shooting at them. How he wasn't dead from the lack of oxygen she didn't know. Maybe he really *was* immortal.

The man holding her let go with one hand and threw something right at Boser Geist. It hit him and knocked him back.

"The ship is going to explode!" Patsy shouted now.

"Get a firm hold," the man said. He moved her so he had his arm around her waist with her back to him. She tucked Joey against her tightly and managed to do the same with Eddie. But Bobby's hold slipped.

"No!" she screamed, as he floated out of reach.

The man holding her cursed. Bobby was heading toward

the ship, and she saw flames ignite inside. The ship was already blowing itself up. Her brother was going to die, and she knew the man was going to have to choose to save the three of them and himself instead of Bobby.

Then a different flaming light came up out of the Blackness. It was another man, who grabbed Bobby and kept on going.

The man holding her laughed, and suddenly they were flying after the man holding her brother. They made it to the Galactic Cruiser just as Boser Geist's ship exploded.

Price had somehow returned from the dead and gotten the one kid and himself into the *1963*.

Delgado was able to shove the kids he had in just as the pirate ship exploded.

The girl pulled him inside and got the hatch closed just in time. "Shields are up on our ship and the miner's," West said. "No damage from the explosion, though the same can't be said for the rest of the ships in this fleet. Rory hacked into the Stevens' robot and was able to get it to overpower the pirates' robot. We have ten cruisers on their way. They should be here before the paralysis gas wears off in those ships that weren't structurally compromised by the explosion."

Delgado took his helmet off and hugged Price. "We thought you were dead. Impressive return."

Price grinned. "Told you I was good, Eric. Belter's Luck is always with me, even when you think it isn't."

"Thank Sol." Delgado addressed the kids. "I think you're safe to take your suits and helmets off. We'll be bringing your parents and ship's robot over here where you'll all stay until the other cruisers arrive. Good job. *Great* job, really."

The kids took their helmets off, and Delgado felt stricken. "Did we lose your sister?"

The three boys looked confused. "No?" the one Price had saved said. "Patsy's right here."

The beautiful, sexy young woman who had just shimmied out of her spacesuit and was helping the boys with theirs looked over her shoulder at him. "Why didn't you think I was their sister?"

"Marcus, Officer West...he kind of insinuated...you were a kid." Delgado felt embarrassed for no good reason. "I was really impressed with how smart and brave a kid you were."

"So I'm not impressive now because I'm twenty, not twelve?"

"No, you're definitely impressive." Delgado felt his face flush.

She noticed and laughed. "Whose plan were you following? *I* was impressed they were thinking like I was."

"Eric's—Captain Delgado here," Price said. "He's the one in charge. The rest of us just followed his orders and added in as necessary or requested." He winked at Delgado, then looked down at the boys. "Let's go see Officer West, kids. We all want to know what the four of you did inside Boser Geist's ship."

The boys looked at Patsy, who nodded. They trotted off with Price. "How long are we going to be with you, do you think, Captain Delgado?" she asked him.

"As long as I can possibly convince you to stay." He hadn't meant to say that aloud. She looked at him thoughtfully. "You'd make a great GP officer."

"Really?"

He nodded.

Patsy smiled slowly. "Tell me more . . . Eric."

The End

HYDRATION

Alan Dean Foster

Miriam Fethri was dying. She found this immensely frustrating because she was now rich. Several weeks ago she'd had a grubstake and no money. But plenty of water. Now she had hovering before her the prospect of millions of credits. But no water. She would gladly have traded all of the former for a cold glass of the latter.

She could not put the blame on her leased crawler's subsurface scanner. It had done its job by warning her of the crustcrease ahead. Traversing a geological zone that was seemingly sound, she had felt safe making tea. The thought of tea, even hot tea, caused her parched throat to clench. She fought not to cough. Because where she was now physiologically, if she coughed she might choke. Dying of thirst was something every prospector prepared for mentally.

Choking to death was not.

When the alarm in the crawler's cabin had cried out she abandoned the tea making and rushed back to the driver's seat. She was too late. Camouflaged by heavy sand, the crease had appeared with shocking suddenness. By the time she was seated and back at the controls the vehicle was already nosing downward into the abyss. Frantic jabs and finger thrusts at the control screens had sent it howling into reverse, but there was too much pulverized grit and not enough stable stone for the treads to get a grip. Slipping, slipping, toward oblivion, she had no choice but to jettison.

The crawler's treads had been unable to find rock, but there was plenty of it where the driver's seat landed.

The impact was enough to send her spilling out of her restraints. Though they had deployed automatically upon jettisoning, they were as old and indifferently maintained as the rest of the crawler. They snapped, sending her flying out of the seat but, fortunately, onto soft sand.

Dazed, she carefully checked herself before trying to stand. Legs, straightening. Arms, functional. Eyes, ears, nostrils, all present and accounted for. Brain—brain was very, very angry. Only anger, though. It was too soon yet for it to fill with fear.

Spitting out sand, she made a quick search for the crawler. Thanks to the randomness of her emergency eject, it took her a while. The sand-covered crevasse into which it had fallen was so deep she could not see the bottom. Or any sign of the vanished crawler. So, no recovery of supplies, then. Redirecting her attention, she walked back to the ejection seat. Old and dated though it was, it had saved her life.

Her spirits sank as she examined it. Like her hopes, it was crushed, having smashed itself against the flank of one of several pale, pillar-like rock outcroppings. The portable cylindrical concentrator that fit neatly into one armrest, and was capable of drawing moisture out of the air, had cracked. Another compartment held multiple packets of dehydrated food, largely useless in the absence of liquid. She could consume the powdery concentrates straight, if she could stomach eating the gourmand equivalent of flavored sawdust. As for the emergency communicator and transponder that would send out a signal indicating a problem, she couldn't even locate it in the wreckage.

Ordinarily, she would have been delighted to encounter protruding rock pillars. The buried ones she had located, before she had turned back toward town, had set her to dancing with glee. They were richly veined with chromal. Chromal was what had brought her to Nonus III. It was what brought everyone to Nonus III. There was no other reason, earthly or otherwise, to come to the undistinguished, largely featureless world of Nonus.

But chromal was enough.

Scientists still did not fully understand the complex chemical structure of the mineral or its unique internal bonds. Found in the spidery veins of local sandstone, the best of it looked like pinfire opal flecked with stainless steel. Only, the mineral's internal play of color was more spectacular than anything else known and, unlike opal, it rated a 9 on the Mohs Hardness Scale. Impossible to synthesize, the gemstone commanded absurd prices. Finding a single short vein of gem-quality chromal a few centimeters wide could make a prospector rich. Finding multiple, thicker veins would make one the envy of old man Midas.

That was what she had discovered, concealed beneath a massive dune. After using the crawler's powervac to remove the overlying sand she had carefully chipped out enough chromal on which to support herself comfortably for the rest of her life, fully intending to come back for more. Now her hard-won stash lay at the bottom of crease along with the crawler and the remainder of her dreams.

Rich one moment, poor the next, dead the following. It was not how her last-minute decision to risk everything on adventuring to distant Nonus was supposed to end.

Maybe it wouldn't, she told herself determinedly. The coordinates of the deposit were locked in her memory. She could find the location of the strike again. All she to do was come back.

If she could get out.

There being nothing useful to salvage from the crumpled ejection seat except the small packets of food concentrate, she stuffed those into her pockets and started off on what she hoped was a course that would lead her back to Haze. There were three towns on Nonus: Haze, Blech, and Sunburn. None was situated more than thirty kilometers from another. So if she missed Haze, she'd make it to one of the others. It did not matter that she was now dead broke. Prospectors took care of their own. Because the ruined, down-on-their-luck prospector you helped today might be the one to save you tomorrow when you found your own ass on the line.

Some systems had two suns. Some three. Nonus had only a single solitary star. It didn't need any help to fry a lone trekker. There were no landmarks save for the occasional rock outcropping, most of which were indistinguishable from one another. No trees, no aboveground vegetation of any sort. Other than the rocks, there was only sand.

She tried to maintain what she thought was the correct route while keeping as much as possible to the more solid ground between the dunes. Maintaining a straight course was possible in the powerful crawler. It was not possible on foot. Even a strong woman would be worn out after surmounting and descending a hundred meters or so of soft sand. She also had to keep alert for slingers, mots, and other dangerous local fauna. Envelopment by a poisonous slinger would bring a faster death than from thirst, but she did not relish the prospect.

The argument could be made that her best chance of survival was to remain with the derelict ejection seat. Except that prospectors purposely kept their course vague lest eager colleagues track them to their diggings. Better to ensure security and take one's chances with possible equipment failure.

I can do this, she told herself. She was healthy and strong. Too strong for most women, not soft enough for most men. Her independence further mitigated against any long-term relationship, though she had engaged in plenty of short-term swapping of bodily fluids. She was lean and muscular while her height gave her the advantage of a long stride. Black eyes set in a narrow, almost girlish face were framed by dark green hair cut short. While her mouth was small, full lips were fully capable of disgorging the most inventive expletives. As a soloing prospector on a backwater world, she had to be able to hold her own verbally as well as physically. She would have cursed up a storm right now save for the need to conserve as much energy as possible. Cussing out a sand dune blocking her intended path was a sign of incipient madness, not strength.

Reaching down, she adjusted the color of her singlesuit from brown to off-white. Bright red would be more likely to draw the attention of a passing craft but would soak up more heat. Black would be better still for catching the eye, be it human or electronic. It would also be suicide.

A light breeze blew granules off the top of the dunes she was walking between. The sky was a solid, almost metallic blue. It would have been a beautiful sight—from inside the air-conditioned crawler's main cabin.

Before long, the chromal was forgotten. The crawler was forgotten. All she could think about was water.

Miriam reached the point where she was not sure how many days she had been walking. Her lips were now painfully chapped, and it was increasingly difficult to keep the sand out of her eyes. An object floated in the sky ahead of her. A cloud, not a skimmer. White and pregnant with implied moisture, it taunted her. She fought not to lick her lips. Digging into a pocket she drew out a packet of powdered food. Beef stroganoff. She almost laughed. Mixed a little at a time in her mouth with her dwindling supply of saliva, the resultant paste supplied some energy. It also tasted only a little different from the sand surrounding her. She trudged on, her increasingly irregular thoughts filled with images of thundering waterfalls and deep, dark forest pools.

The wadi she had been following dead-ended against a massive slope of sand. She could not go back, could not turn around. Maybe, she thought tiredly through the shimmering heat, the ravine was intersected only by this one dune and continued on the other side. Keeping a wary eye out for slithering mots, she started to climb.

For every two steps forward, it seemed she took one back, slipping and sliding on the unstable slope. She persevered, using her long legs to advantage. Her calf muscles screamed. Eventually sand disappeared from her immediate line of vision, to be replaced by a descending curtain of cerulean sky.

Triumphant, if only momentarily, she stood staggering at the crest of the dune, staring at the eastern horizon. It was filled, overwhelmed, with more dunes, more sand, stretching as far as the eye could see in every direction. Only—off in the distance, slightly to her left. Something broke the otherwise straight line of the horizon. A thin, barely perceptible irregularity. Buildings? Rough-and-tumble Haze, or one of its equally sorry-ass sibling urbanities? She couldn't tell. She did not have scope glasses on her, and her visual perception, like the rest of her senses, was succumbing to the heat. If it was a mirage she was looking at, at least it was a goal of some sort. She took a step forward.

And went down.

On her side, rolling, rolling, picking up speed as she tumbled, too weak to put out an arm or leg to stop or even slow her descent. The sand beneath her was hot, soft, and abrasive. She did not stop rolling until she reached the base of the dune. The only thing that saved her was that the surface was covered in deep sand instead of rock or hardpack.

Breathing one heave shy of wheezing, she lay motionless on her side and took stock of what was left of herself. As with the ejection from the crawler, nothing seemed to be broken. How fortunate she was, she mused sardonically. She could still walk, still stumble toward her goal, the thin irregular line that was possibly Haze. If she could stand.

Get up. It was an internal shout, directed solely at her leg muscles. *Get. Up.*

No response. There was no movement in her legs. Her brain insisted they were functional, but somewhere along the neurological line there appeared to be some disagreement. A foot moved. That was insufficient for her purpose.

Catch your breath, she admonished herself. *Don't rush things. Just because you're dry as a desiccated goat, just because you're starting to hallucinate, just because the big crazy forking round oven up in the sky is trying to cook you, doesn't mean you have to rush it. Just relax. Maybe take a nap. That's it: a nice, long, motionless nap. Right here in the pleasantly hellish sunshine.*

She lay like that for what might have been an hour. Or four. Until something besides blowing sand aggravated her eyes. Movement. Her eyes grew a little wider while her brain determined that, irrespective of the identity of what she was seeing, naptime was over.

The creature emerged slowly from near the base of the dune down which she had taken her interminable tumble. Grains of quartz and feldspar slithered down smooth, hairless, curved flanks. Not as long as her but much stouter and heavier, the alien resembled a cross between a pile of golden potatoes and a freshly scoured pig. Its body was a mass of lumps and bulges, some twice the size of her fist. Each was a slightly different shape and tinted to match a slightly different color of sand.

Cryptic coloration. Camouflage. She wondered what for. It was too big for a mot to tackle and a slinger's net would not be strong enough to restrain so much mass. Which implied there were other things as yet undocumented on Nonus that were big enough to kill one of these creatures. The thought was unsettling.

One lump slightly more protrusive than the rest was the nearest thing the being had to a head. Two very tiny, almost vestigial, pupil-less black eyes glistened in the sun. Set well below these miniscule oculars was a larger black circle that pulsated slightly and appeared to go deep. She could not see any sign of teeth. No dentition in the indentation, she told herself wildly.

The creature advanced slowly toward her. Humping along the ground like a spasmed seal in the absence of limbs, there was no mistaking its route. The slow-motion charge, or attack, or whatever it was, provided sufficient motivation for her to get one leg up under her right hip. Shoving with all her strength she managed to get her hips and right thigh a few centimeters off the ground. When even this meager effort proved too much for her enfeebled, overheated body, she collapsed back onto the sand.

The creature was now perhaps a meter away from her face. This close she could see that its face, if that was indeed what the three black circles represented, was surrounded by dozens and dozens of slender cilia. Reaching outward from the body, they were fluttering hypnotically in her direction. Even for an alien creature, the hydra (as she had decided in her semi-delirium to call it) presented a particularly unsettling visage.

If it was going to eat her, she mused, it ought by now to be showing some teeth. Unless it was going to use its tiny toothless mouth to gum her to death.

It stopped about half a meter away from the supine, weakly breathing creature lying before it. She had the impression it was studying her. Would it wait for her to die and then somehow, via some as yet unperceived alien gustatory mechanism, begin consuming her flesh?

It walked, or rather oozed, still nearer. Insofar as she could tell, it gave off no odor. So close now that she could make out hundreds of pores pockmarking what heretofore had appeared to be smooth skin. Tiny hairs grew out of the pores.

The hairs started to extend toward her.

She couldn't move. Nothing functioned below her waist, and said non-functionality was beginning to creep down her arms, as well.

Try to look on the bright side, she told herself. *You are now potentially wealthy beyond the dreams of avarice, whoever he was, and you are also most likely the discoverer of a new charismatic alien species, which may try to kill and eat you.*

So very near it was now, the lumpy desert hydra-thing. Scarcely a couple of handsbreadths away from her face. Long filaments extending outward from dark pores, quivering in her direction like hair in the wind. Something glistened at the tip of each of them: a clear liquid.

Hydrochloric acid, perhaps? Or something similar, to dissolve her flesh into easy to consume porridge. Surely not water.

It couldn't be water. Why would a sack of alien lumpiness be offering her water?

What the hell. Even if it was some kind of acid, maybe it was diluted enough not to kill her. At least, not outright. Whatever it was, it was wet. She was out of options anyway. Making a supreme effort, she raised her right hand and brought the index finger down toward the nearest filaments. When her hand drew near, a dozen of them curved toward her trembling digit. Contact was made.

There was no burning sensation, no irritation. Only dampness, surprisingly cool. Dare she, she wondered? If not, dead she. Carefully she brought the fingertip to her lips. It was only a couple of drops, but inside her mouth it felt like a long draught of a spring freshet.

Advancing, the creature cut the distance between itself and her face in half. No sound emerged from the tiny maybe-mouth. Glistening with moisture, dozens of light gray filaments extended in her direction. Was it, could it be—offering? But why? Not that it mattered. The droplets that had all but evaporated inside her parched mouth had caused no damage. Her entire body cried out for more. She grabbed at the nearest cluster of water-laden filaments.

They withdrew, sharply. The creature started to turn away.

No. Nonono. Come back.

She did not know if she whispered it or merely thought it. She lowered her hand. It required too much of her wisp of remaining energy to hold it out any longer, much less grab at anything.

After a few panicky moments, the inhabitant of the dune turned back to her, and its filaments extended toward her mouth once again. They fluttered around her perspiration-streaked face: testing, questing, exploring. For a second time, they found what they were looking for.

She might not be certain where the hydra's mouth was, but it did not have the same problem with regard to her.

Dozens, maybe a hundred or more of the gray filaments pushed just inside her half-open mouth, past chapped, crusted lips. Then they began to exude—water. Still only droplets, but dozens at a time now. A continuous flow measurable in milliliters. Unexpectedly soon, there was enough to swallow. She felt pain in her dried-out throat, mixed with delight. Lying there, her breathing shallow, she let the alien dribble life-giving liquid into her. It was slightly alkaline, but utterly delicious.

She felt a pinch on the back of her left hand. So exhilarated was she by the slight but steady flow of water that she almost failed to notice it. Which was likely the evolutionary idea.

Tilting back her head, she saw a single filament that was different from all the others. Instead of being a light gray in color, it was nearly transparent. The tip that had eased its way into the vein on the back of her hand was probably very sharp. She could only assume such was the case because she could not see the tip. Could not see it because it had pushed its way into her vein. Fluid was flowing through the filament.

Not from the hydra to her, but from her to the hydra.

Her first instinct was to draw away. To break the connection. But her mind, recharging now toward sensibility, told her that if she did then the hydra would likely also retract every one of its life-giving water supplying filaments. Forcing herself to remain calm, she struggled to hold still and gauge the exchange. The creature's actions toward her were neither philanthropic nor symbiotic. This was something else. A little blood for a lot of water. What did the hydra get out of the exchange?

Various proteins. White blood cells. Red blood cells—containing hemoglobin. Iron. Proteins and iron.

As near as she could tell, the hydra was supplying her mouth, which for the first time in days was able to gulp, with far more water than it was extracting in blood. Which suggested that water was easier for the creature to find than certain proteins or other necessary impurities. Useful information for a prospector on Nonus to know. Not that it mattered to her. Because she was going to leave this wretched sandbox of a world. Her memory was solid. She would go back to the chromal deposit. What she had mined was now gone, returned to the planet's innards. But millions remained in the stone matrix, waiting for her to return and carefully, triumphantly, extract it. A few of the best chips, samples intended for assay, still rattled around in the depths of one tightly sealed side pocket. Not enough to purchase or lease an entire new outfit, but enough to attract all the investors she would need. She was going to make it. She was going to be rich.

And she was going to live.

She lay there on her side, trading blood for water with an

unclassified alien dune dweller that seemed perfectly content to accept her otherworldly proteins, letting it sip of her self through a flexible organic straw, and feeling better and stronger and more optimistic than at any time since her expedition had come to near disaster.

It was not sex. But it felt like it.

The End

WINNER TAKES ALL

Alex Shvartsman

From the observation deck of the Commonwealth cruiser, Elise stared at the plethora of stars. Hundreds of them filled the impressive wall-sized display, shining and twinkling at her, sprinkled across the majesty of the cosmos. They were a lie, of course. Were she to call up the actual view outside, she'd see a scattering of dim pinpricks of light. The projected image existed to impress the tourists, just another layer of technology inserted between reality and the people, to coddle Commonwealth citizens in a false sense of security and comfort against the sort of things that existed beyond their line of sight. Of course, there were no tourists on this flight, no passengers to gawk at the fake stars. The ship had been commandeered for a black ops mission. The deck was all hers, and she preferred the solitude of this space to the solitude of her cabin.

"Spectacular, isn't it?"

She turned to find a lanky man, probably in his early thirties, standing in the doorway. He was a little thinner and taller than an average human, his elongated limbs a testament to growing up on a world with lower gravity. How long had he been watching her watch the screen?

When Elise's silence grew almost uncomfortable, the man stepped forward. "Tobey Choi. It's an honor to meet you, Elise. I'm so glad you were available for my operation."

The man exuded naiveté, so much so that she held back the urge to bite his head off. Instead, she asked, "First field assignment?"

Tobey blanched. "How'd you know?"

"You're an accountant, and you're junior enough to be disposable. Seemed like a safe bet."

There was a flash of something like anger in Tobey's face, but he got it under control remarkably fast. When he spoke, his tone was even and reasoned. "First, I'm a forensic accountant smart enough to locate one of the most wanted criminals in the Commonwealth. Second, I've used those same skills to identify and request the most experienced operative based on the mission parameters. Are you telling me I made a mistake and that you can't keep me safe down there?"

"You'll be safe enough on the planet," said Elise. "But that's not what I meant. I can protect you during the mission, but I can't shield you from the fallout."

"The fallout?" Tobey crossed his long arms.

"This is a smash-and-grab outside Commonwealth space. We'll be breaking numerous laws, and if things go sideways, the easiest thing to do is to burn us." Elise leveled her gaze at Tobey. "How did you know to request me? The sort of work I do is beyond your clearance. No, my name was placed in your path because I have a history of going off-book. My neck fits neatly into the guillotine of a rogue-behavior narrative. The fact that they let you come along means you either pissed someone off, or they simply don't mind throwing away the accountant with the bathwater."

Tobey frowned. "I admit, my superiors were highly skeptical of my conclusions. But the money trail is solid. They saw that. Otherwise, why authorize the mission at all?"

Elise wanted to say, *Because some among your superiors would really, really like to see me fail.* Instead, she shrugged. "If you're right, that's a big win. But I'm skeptical, too. How could an artificial intelligence be hiding out in a place where anything with a microchip is only good as a doorstop?"

"I don't know how the Lady is doing it, but she's running her terrorist cells across the Commonwealth from down there. I'm certain of that. I'd stake my life on it." Tobey looked Elise in the eye. "I *am* staking my life on it. You've led missions into interdicted zones before. That part was no fabrication. Right?"

Elise thought back to the times she'd led people into technological dead zones on alien worlds, of the good people she'd lost along the way. "Yes," she said. "That part is true."

"All right, then," said Tobey. "How do we ensure there's no fallout?"

"First, let me be perfectly clear. It's your operation, but down there, I'm in charge. You follow my lead," said Elise. "Second, you have to be *right*. It can't be some lieutenant down there. We have to capture the Lady and bring her hardware back to the commonwealth. Nothing short of total victory. The victor is not to be judged, that's the principle I live by."

Tobey nodded. "It was the Russian empress, Catherine II, who is said to have coined the phrase when she dismissed the charges at a court-martial of one of her commanders. The story may be apocryphal, but the underlying principle remains true today."

Against odds, Elise found herself impressed by the young accountant.

Tobey stared at the fake stars on display. "I don't know how the AI is operating in the interdicted zone, but the sort of money and materiel being moved on orders that I've tracked back to that hideout could only come from the Lady herself, and we're going to get her. I got where I am today following a very similar principle to yours." He refocused on Elise. "Winner takes all."

"Landfall in three minutes." Elise looked to each of her operatives, decked out in protective gear and armed with projectile weapons. They were packed tight into the small cabin on a nanofiber glider launched toward the rebel base from their descending shuttle. In addition to Elise and Tobey, there were four soldiers. Elise had hand-selected Mahmud, Peña, Kovalich, and Swenson for their experience operating in interdicted zones.

Such zones existed on over a dozen worlds in this part of the galaxy. An alien race had left satellites in orbits of those planets millennia ago, that projected a field disabling high technology—a sort of continuous EMP signal, only infinitely more sophisticated. Interdicted zones could be as large as a continent or as small as a valley. In a couple of cases, they seemed to encompass entire planets, forever trapping any ship that managed to land in one piece.

Their glider was designed to operate in such low-tech environments; it contained no microchips. Instead, it relied on wind and a carefully calculated flight plan to reach its target. The shuttle itself would land outside an interdicted zone and await their return.

"Remember, we want the hardware that houses the Lady AI above all else," said Elise. "It's a sphere the size of a grapefruit, which means the rebels can hide it or carry it away easily if we don't catch them by surprise. We need the sphere intact. You're authorized to use lethal force on any other rebels if they resist— and they will."

The Lady had been the leader of a secessionist movement for a better part of two decades, and her followers revered her with the blind faith of zealots. Tobey's data suggested minimal defenses and staff, but there was no doubt they'd put themselves in harm's way to protect their digital overlord.

Elise momentarily flashed back to missions past, when people she had led into other interdicted zones had had to fight with guns and swords and sometimes nothing but their fists against humans and aliens alike. There had been so much death; a fraction of what she'd done would horrify an average Commonwealth citizen. But it was people like her who kept them safe, kept them coddled enough so they could be horrified by such things. She had to believe that.

The glider made landfall in a field, fifty meters from a single-story house in the middle of nowhere.

"Go, go, go!" The soldiers unstrapped from their safety harnesses and ran toward the house. "Keep behind me," Elise told Tobey. By the time the two of them had exited the glider, the soldiers had covered the distance to the front door and were inside the house. The sounds of gunfire rocked the eerie quiet of the rural landscape.

Elise rushed across the field and toward the house. There were only two bursts of gunfire. It had ceased too soon, which felt wrong. Either her soldiers had somehow failed, or there were too few rebels in the house, which would mean their quarry was never there to begin with.

She burst into the house, Tobey a step behind her.

A burly man lay on the ground facedown in the hallway. He was bleeding from a headshot, his right hand still clasping a scythe. An unarmed alien sat on the ground a few steps from him, its clawed hands clutching a stomach wound. It moaned softly but made no attempt to move as the two humans rushed past it and through the interior door.

Inside, the four soldiers leveled their guns at the gaggle of humans and aliens cowering in the middle of the living room. None of them appeared to be armed.

"On the ground!" shouted Swenson. She pointed with the muzzle of her weapon. "Get down on the floor with your hands on top of your heads!"

The rebels obeyed. Three humans and two aliens of different species lowered themselves to the ground, until only an alien child remained standing.

The little girl was humanoid and appeared to be about ten years old. Wavy turquoise hair reached down to her shoulder blades. Strands of it curled around her cartoonishly large eyes. They were at least twice the size of a human's, oblong, and set parallel to her nose. She held a metal sphere in her slender four-fingered hands. Several cables connected the sphere to a coronet-like device she wore on her head.

"There's no need for violence. Please, do not shoot. My people will not resist."

For a moment, Elise thought it was the alien girl who spoke. But the child's lips hadn't moved. The smooth, calming voice of a grandmotherly news anchor was coming from the metal sphere.

"These people aren't armed. They pose no threat to you. Although their first instinct was to defend me, they are going to stand down now. They will not interfere, so long as you promise me you won't harm them."

"All right." Elise motioned to the soldiers, who in turn lowered their guns a fraction. "We only want you. If they keep out of our way, they get to live."

"You heard her, my friends. Please, respect my wishes."

After the AI spoke, the little girl gingerly stepped around the rebels prostrated on the floor and approached Elise in a languid, nonthreatening manner. The girl stood calmly in front of the armed woman, the sphere still clutched in her hands.

The sound of Tobey chuckling broke the silence. After the AI's witchy voice, his laughter sounded jarring.

"So that's how she did it!" Tobey leaned in, studying the girl as though she were a museum exhibit. "She's an Angotrean. Their planet is pretty far from its sun, not a lot of natural light. Look at those eyes."

"So?" Elise asked, without taking her eye off the AI and its subdued followers.

"Bioluminescence," said Tobey. "Her people generate a tiny amount of electrical current. Enough to power the hardware the Lady runs on, apparently."

"This doesn't explain how a computer can function in an interdicted zone," said Elise. "Care to explain, Lady?"

"I do not," said the Lady. Her mesmerizing voice made the curt answer seem reasonable; almost made it sound as though she regretted being unable to provide the information they sought. Elise made a conscious effort to shake off the effect—she wasn't about to get brainwashed by a sweet-talking tin can.

"Maybe she runs on biohardware," said Tobey. "Or some other alien tech sufficiently advanced to be indistinguishable from magic and to overcome the interdiction. Makes this thing that much more valuable."

Tobey stepped forward and grabbed the sphere from the girl's hands. He then took hold of the coronet device and pulled it off her head. He yanked on tiny wires hidden beneath it, severing the connection to a number of small sensors attached to her skin.

The child gasped once the device was removed. It was the first sound Elise heard her make. The sphere, on the other hand, had gone dead as soon as it became disconnected from the child. The intricate spell woven by its voice shattered at once.

Tobey held up the AI shell like it was a Faberge egg. "Winner takes all," he mouthed to Elise.

She nodded. "Peña, Mahmud, sweep the area. The rest of you, tie them up. That means you too, Choi. Put that thing away, and let's go."

Peña and Mahmud slid out the door to check around the house. Elise trained her weapon on the rebels as her soldiers expertly bound their hands. As long as the rebels couldn't get themselves free for a couple of hours, her team would have an insurmountable lead on any countermeasures the Lady's followers could possibly muster up within the interdicted zone.

A middle-aged man mumbled something as Tobey was restraining him.

"What's that?" Tobey pulled on the bindings, harder than Elise thought necessary.

"I forgive you," the man said, louder. He turned his head to the side as much as his position would allow. "You're an unwitting tool of a tyrannical, xenophobic regime. You know not what y—"

"Shut up before I have you gagged!" Elise had no patience for self-righteous speeches. She knew the Commonwealth wasn't perfect, but she'd seen firsthand what happened to an occasional human colony founded outside its bounds. Those people ended up eradicated, eaten, or enslaved. The universe was a cold, dark place, and fools like this rebel wouldn't live long enough to gripe about injustice if it weren't for the government and people like her keeping the worst of the horrors at bay.

The soldiers finished securing the rebels on the ground. Kovalich rummaged through his pack for another zip tie and made toward the girl.

"Not her," said Elise. She looked at the child who remained still, her large alien eyes glistening with what looked like very human tears. Elise put down her weapon and lowered herself onto one knee in front of the girl so they were face to face. "What's your name?"

"My human name is Savitri." The girl spoke softly but clearly. She met Elise's gaze straight on, without averting her eyes.

"Where are your parents, Savitri? Are they here or on Angot?"

This time the girl looked away, down toward the floor. "I have no parents." She pointed at the rebels. "Tessa and Karim take care of me."

Elise frowned. Her definition of care was very different. It certainly didn't involve using the child as some sort of an external battery. "Not anymore. You're coming with us."

The woman identified by Savitri as Tessa wailed at this. Kovalich leveled his weapon at her, and she stifled her protests.

"She'll slow us down," said Tobey.

"I'm not leaving a child with these people." Elise flashed back once again to missions past. The violence she'd seen, and the violence she'd been forced to inflict on others. This was a chance to counterbalance a tiny sliver of those wrongs; to give this girl a chance at a safe, boring life that Elise never had and never would have.

An explosion thundered outside, the blast wave rattling the wooden house.

Leaving Kovalich behind to cover the captive rebels, the rest of the team rushed outside to the soundtrack of machine-gun fire punctuated by occasional shots from another, unfamiliar projectile weapon.

The glider's light and malleable nanofiber had been annihilated by the explosion. Their supplies, including a set of all-terrain bikes they were going to use to leave the interdicted zone, were a total loss. Two dead rebels, including one with a rifle still in his hands, lay on the ground. Mahmud stood by the remains of the glider, his face covered in blood.

"They snuck up on the glider while we were sweeping the barn behind the house," he said, his breathing heavy. "Sorry, boss."

Elise nodded curtly. "Are you hurt?"

Mahmud wiped his eyes with his sleeve. "I'm fine, but they got Peña. This . . . She was standing right next to me."

Elise rushed forward. "Where is she?"

Mahmud pointed.

Peña's still body was obscured by the glider. A rebel's bullet had entered just under her left eye.

"Mahmud, Swenson, finish the sweep. Make sure we don't get ambushed again." Elise managed to issue the command without her voice cracking. She stared at Peña's lifeless body. Another soul gone under her command. Another nightmare to haunt her dreams.

With the other soldiers gone, Elise bent down to collect Peña's dog tag. She'd make certain it was returned to her family, if she managed to make it back herself.

"They didn't destroy the glider as a symbolic gesture," Tobey called out. He was looking at each cluster of vegetation, each hill with deep suspicion, expecting an attack. "They're trying to delay us. Can we make it to the ship on foot? How long would that take?"

"Ten, maybe twelve hours, depending on how often we rest." Elise closed Peña's remaining eye.

"We can't bring the girl," said Tobey. "She'll slow us down."

Elise ignored him.

Swenson returned after a few minutes. She led a wooly alien animal by the reins. It resembled a boar but was the size of a large horse. "All clear," she said. "That was all of them. Found this critter in the barn, though."

"How fast does this thing go?" asked Tobey. "One, maybe two of us could ride it out of the interdicted zone, get the AI back to the ship—"

"Let me guess," Elise interrupted him. "You're volunteering?" She turned to Swenson. "Get Kovalich and the girl, please."

When the soldier left, she sized Tobey up. "Remember our

deal. Keep your head down and follow my orders, and I'll get you back to the ship. Got me?"

His pale skin flushed, but Tobey nodded. Working with civilians in dangerous circumstances was often like this. She could deal with the likes of the accountant; she had babysat far worse through more dangerous missions.

When the soldiers returned, Kovalich's knuckles were bruised, and there were scrape marks on his cheek.

"That woman went nuts when we were leaving," he explained. "Had to fight her off."

"She was babbling something about half the zone rising up to hunt us down, and how we won't live to see the sunset," added Swenson.

"I told you!" said Tobey. "Maybe they have some local version of carrier pigeons, or maybe a few of the rebels ran to get help, but they'll try to wrestle their artificial leader back from us."

Elise addressed the girl. "Savitri, were there more people outside the house? Could help be coming?"

The girl glanced back at the house, then at the two dead rebels outside. When she spoke, it was softly but steadily again. "Two people are missing. There are several other farms and settlements. When they learn that the Lady is in trouble, they will come to save her."

"Right. Anyone know how to ride this beast of burden?" Elise asked her people.

When no one volunteered, she drew a handgun from her holster and put two bullets into the animal's head. The shots rang out across the plane, and the animal fell where it stood, its body threshing.

Savitri flinched and swallowed visibly, but said nothing.

"All right. Let's move out." Without waiting for a response, Elise took one last look at Peña and began walking east, toward the ship.

Tobey caught up to her and matched her pace. "You rescue the girl, leave the rebels alive, but kill the animal?"

"Someone there can ride it; let's not make it any easier on them once they manage to get themselves free." She glanced back to the house and the smoldering remnants of the glider. "Speaking of which, as soon as we clear the line of sight, we'll be heading northeast."

Tobey nodded. "I see. They may travel faster than us, so we don't want to take the most direct route out of the zone, right?"

"That, and there's another compound on the map, a few hours' walk that way," said Elise. "Perhaps we can get horses or bikes or some other assistance there."

"What if we run into more of the Lady's zealots instead?"

"Unlikely. That compound is on the official map. This place"— Elise pointed back—"isn't, and neither are any of the other farms the girl mentioned."

Tobey nodded. He rested his hand on the pocket where he carried the captive AI. "This can still be a major, major win for the both of us."

"Sure," Elise said. She squeezed Peña's dog tag tight in her pocket.

About an hour after they changed directions, Elise slowed her pace a little and let Mahmud take point. She walked alongside Savitri, who had managed to keep pace with the rest of the group so far and hadn't voiced any complaints. She had only asked for water once, since she didn't have a flask or a canteen of her own.

"How'd you come to be with the rebels, Savitri?" she asked.

"The Lady rescued me from a bad situation," said the girl. "I was too young to remember, and Tessa said she would tell me about it when I'm older."

"You don't remember your parents? Your home world?" Elise pressed.

"No." After a brief pause Savitri added, "My home's back there."

They walked past drooping vegetation that somewhat resembled weeping willows. The air smelled musty, and it was eerily quiet—if this place had some equivalent of birds or insects, they didn't advertise their presence.

"They were using you," said Elise. "They're bad people."

"I could say the same about you." Savitri looked at her, and her strangely shaped alien eyes seemed old. "The people who sent you, they're very afraid of the Lady because she wants to make changes that would make them less powerful. So they tell all kinds of lies and accuse her of all sorts of crimes, but the common folk hear her message and recognize the truth."

Elise wiped sweat from her forehead. "The truth is, the Lady is a terrorist. The way she goes about accomplishing her goals is not acceptable in modern society."

"The Lady once said that one man's rebel is another man's

freedom fighter, and that the people who write the history books centuries later will be the ones to decide which is which," said Savitri.

"Centuries from now, we'll both be dead. Each person has to decide what's moral and just in their own lifetime," said Elise.

"You've come to a free world outside of your Commonwealth to kidnap the Lady and abduct a kid," said Savitri. "Do you really believe what you're doing is moral and just?"

Elise had faced alien spies, warlords, and organized crime bosses in her time. She had never lacked courage to look any of them in the eye. But now, it took all of her willpower not to turn away, not to look down. Was it because the alien girl's accusation hit too close to home? Elise couldn't afford to dwell on that, at least, not until her people were safely off-world.

"You're too young to understand," said Elise. "But in time, you will."

"In time. When I'm older. That's what Tessa always says. Maybe the two of you aren't so different. You both seem to think you know what's best for me, but in reality you both need something from me. She needed me to help the Lady, and you need me to help you feel better about yourself."

This time, Elise couldn't maintain eye contact. She picked up her pace and resumed the lead position in their little expedition. She could swear she felt the girl's gaze boring into her back.

"This is a bad place," Savitri told Elise once the walls of the compound appeared in the distance. Two-meter-tall brick walls with barbed wire on top surrounded an area the size of a city block.

"Who's inside?" asked Elise.

"A man named Wasp grows the mala plant there," said Savitri. "They process it and make the drug."

Elise frowned. Mala was a highly addictive drug that ruined many lives in the Commonwealth.

"We shouldn't expect nice people to live in the interdicted zone," said Tobey. "If he can help us, great. We'll report the mala operation and let drug enforcement deal with this later."

"He uses slaves to grow and process the mala," said Savitri.

Elise gritted her teeth. Slavers were not entirely unheard of, but they were exceedingly rare on most worlds, in or out of Commonwealth space. In most cases, this was a matter of technological advancement rather than people's better angels; automation was cheaper and more effective. The labor-intensive process of making mala in an interdicted zone lent itself to this evil practice. She abhorred the idea of dealing with a slaver.

"We've got the firepower to rain fire and fury upon those scumbags," said Elise.

"Our mission comes first." There was a steel note in Tobey's voice. "It's safer to negotiate."

Elise knew to pick her battles, but she didn't have to like it. "I'll lead another team here personally if I have to."

Savitri made an exaggerated sigh and turned away from Elise.

"Don't adopt a holier-than-thou attitude with me, girl," said Elise. "The Lady has been aware of this thorn in her backyard for how long, and she's done nothing about it."

"I told you," Savitri replied. "The Lady is not violent."

"Bullshit," said Tobey. "Her followers are plenty violent across the Commonwealth. She probably didn't want to rock the boat. Didn't want to draw attention to this place, not from us or from the cartels or whoever this Wasp is selling to."

They walked toward the compound and approached the narrow gate. Inside, a large man armed with a spiked club sat on a wooden stool in the shade. Their approach roused the man, and he gripped his weapon tighter.

"I want to see Wasp," Elise said. "Take us to him."

The man sneered. "You don't get to tell me what to—"

Elise hefted her weapon. "This says I do. Open up. Now."

The man knew he was outmatched and didn't argue further. He unlocked the gate and led their group toward the large house at the center of the enclave.

All around them, there was cultivated land with green shoots of mala plants reaching upward from the dirt and toward the sky. At least a dozen people—most human—worked the fields under a watchful eye of another club-wielding guard. They were dirty and emaciated. A few stopped what they were doing and looked at the new arrivals with dull, hopeless eyes.

Rage boiled within Elise. This was the sort of thing she had signed up to prevent. What use were her successful missions if injustice like this was allowed to persist?

Inside, Wasp's four henchmen were armed with rifles and

handguns. Nothing as sophisticated as the submachine guns of her team, but it wasn't just clubs and knives. The slavers pointed their weapons at their unwelcome guests, and the soldiers took aim at the slavers. Elise supposed they kept projectile weapons inside for the same reasons prison guards do: so they wouldn't fall into the slaves' hands if there were ever an attempt at rebellion.

Wasp was a wiry man with dark eyes who bounced his foot compulsively, as though he'd been sampling his own product. "Who are you? What do you want?" he asked from his armchair throne at the center of the room.

"We need transportation out of the zone," said Tobey. Elise was annoyed at him taking the initiative again, but also somewhat glad. She wasn't sure she could control her temper in dealing with this man. "Something faster and more comfortable than walking."

"Do you, now?" Wasp's eyes darted between Tobey and the others, zeroing in on the weapons they hefted. "But you haven't answered my question. We don't get too many visitors here."

"Rest assured, we're here for reasons unrelated to your . . . operation," said Tobey. "It's in your best interest to have us leave expeditiously."

Wasp tilted his head. "Fine, don't tell me. I'm too polite a host to dwell on that. Suppose I can provide you with first-class transportation. What have you got to trade?"

"I can authorize a reasonable fee, transferred to a bank of your choice, once we're off planet," said Tobey. Elise wasn't entirely certain he was bluffing. The accountant wanted to leave with his prize badly enough.

"Try again. We deal in tangible goods around here," said Wasp.

"Sorry, I left my pouch full of diamonds in my other pants," said Tobey.

"We all make mistakes," said Wasp. "But that's all right. How about a pair of those fine guns? That'll leave you enough to tame the local fauna."

Tobey glanced at Elise. "You can have them once we board our shuttle," he replied.

"I don't operate on credit," said Wasp. "That's just bad business. How about a pair of strong hands instead? Leave me any one of those soldier boys or girls as collateral. They can help work the fields until we get our guns, and then hitch a ride into town, eh?"

"I could stay," said Savitri. She took a step forward and stared at both Tobey and the slaver defiantly. "You go to the ship, he gets his guns, and I go home to Tessa."

Fury roiled within Elise. She'd be damned if she left a soldier here, let alone a child. Elise wasn't sure what Tobey was going to say to this, but he paused a fraction of a second too long for her liking. In a fluid, practiced motion she raised her weapon higher and put two bullets into Wasp's heart.

Gunfire rang out across the hall. Her team was far better trained and had better reflexes than the slavers. They opened fire on the rifle-toting men, mowing them down before they could get off more than a single shot. Elise whirled toward the gate guard. The man was swinging his club, but he wasn't fast enough. A volley of shots to the chest sent him reeling back until he was on the ground and still.

When the gunfire ceased and the slavers were dead, Kovalich moaned and clutched at his side, where a bloodstain was growing on his pant leg like a blossoming flower.

"Mahmud, Swenson, sweep," Elise said as she leaned in to examine the wound. The soldiers rushed to check the rest of the house as well as outside. "No prisoners," Elise told them.

"What the hell?" Tobey was breathing heavily, trying to get his adrenaline under control. "That was an unnecessary risk. We would've fumigated this place later!"

"Looks like the bullet went clean through," Elise declared. She got out a foam tube and sprayed a gauzelike substance onto the wound. She addressed Tobey as she worked. "Would we, though? Would the Commonwealth even sign off on another trip to this zone, or would anything short of capturing a most wanted terrorist mean they'd have no stomach for another black ops mission outside their borders? This nest of vipers might've been left undisturbed, and you know it."

"You're far too reckless," said Tobey. "You risked all of our lives."

"No harm, no foul. Like I said before, the victor is not to be judged."

"No harm? He got shot!" Tobey pointed at Kovalich.

"I'll walk it off. Sir." Kovalich made the last word sound like an insult.

Savitri sat on the floor, massaging her leg.

"Are you injured, too?" Elise asked.

"I think I twisted my foot when I tried to duck out of the way," said the girl.

Elise did her best to ignore the look Tobey gave her.

"This is entirely unacceptable," Tobey declared as a string of wagons headed eastward. A beast similar to the one Elise put down at the rebels' hideout pulled each cart, containing four of the workers from the slaver compound.

"We killed the slavers, and we freed the slaves," said Elise. "Something tangible and positive was actually accomplished on this mission." It was more than she could claim for many of her previous operations, Elise thought.

"They could have made their own way back," said Tobey. "We lost hours preparing this wagon train, and these animals barely move faster than our walking speed. Plenty of time for the rebels to find us."

"I'm sorry the slavers didn't have an air balloon or a horse," said Elise. "As is, we're moving at the same speed no matter how many wagons we've got, and this is safer for the people we've rescued. Just get some rest while you can. You have to get used to the fact that things happen a lot more slowly in the interdicted zones."

Tobey squashed a bug that was crawling on his neck. Apparently, the insects showed up after sunset. "I don't understand how people live in these low-tech hellholes."

Mahmud, who—like the rest of Elise's team—grew up in an interdicted zone, gave Tobey an evil look, but restrained himself from interjecting.

"The nights are short on this world," said Elise. "Sleep. We'll reach the shuttle by midmorning."

They were so close—less than an hour's travel away from the edge of the interdicted zone and their shuttle—when the rebels caught up with them.

They were on a plain, where one could see for kilometers, with nowhere to run or hide. Through their field binoculars, they could see twenty or so armed rebels approaching on horseback. They were riding real Earth horses and moved far faster than the caravan.

"Take Mahmud and Swenson and run," she told Tobey. "Get the AI to the shuttle. Kovalich and I will cover you." She knew she'd get no argument from the accountant. The fear on his face, combined with the desire to return victorious—bringing the AI and possible new tech to the Commonwealth—meant he'd abandon anyone else to their fates. She was more concerned about her team's response, so she added. "That's an order."

Her soldiers weren't happy about it, but they knew their duty. So did Kovalich, who couldn't run with his wound. He'd give up his life to protect the team and so would she.

Elise hoped it wouldn't come to that. Once Tobey reached the shuttle, then she and Kovalich would no longer be a top priority for the rebels, and they should have no disagreement with the freed slaves. If only she could lay suppressive fire, to slow them down long enough for Tobey to escape, then maybe they'd allow her to retreat rather than risk their lives only for the sake of revenge.

As she watched Tobey and the two soldiers dash away, she ordered the freed slaves to abandon the wagons, to get as far from them as they could in order to stay out of the line of fire.

Savitri awkwardly tried to climb out of the wagon.

Elise faced an impossible choice: she could either send the girl out to where she'd be certainly taken back to the rebel camp, or she could hang on to her and still try to save her, but at the risk of placing her in the cross fire for the second time in less than twenty-four hours. She knew what the girl would choose—the child was still brainwashed by the rebels, after all. Instead, she wondered what she'd want, were this her young self.

Elise stopped Savitri by placing a hand on her shoulder. "No. You stay with me."

They watched the rebels get closer and closer from the back of the wagon. When the riders got close enough, Elise fired a volley, aiming for their horses. They were still too far, but it produced the desired effect of slowing the riders down.

The rebels spread into a wide semicircle, the riders on the far edges of their group seeking to put enough distance between them and the wagons where they could pass by outside bullet range.

Elise regretted not having a sniper rifle. For this mission, they favored small and portable submachine guns. She could still see her three comrades running in the distance. It would be a close thing. Very soon now they'd be within firing range of the shuttle's weapons. Although it couldn't traverse the interdicted zone, it could fire projectiles into it, just like it could release the glider. But would it be soon enough?

The riders must've thought so, because they encircled Elise's wagon. The beast, which kept slowly moving eastward even without a driver, stopped once the rebels blocked its path. The riders began cautiously approaching the wagon from all sides. Elise and her companions cowered at the bottom of the wagon, its short sides a scant protection against the riders' rifles.

"Surrender, and we'll let you live!" shouted one of the riders.

Elise knew the man had no incentive to live up to his words. Once he discovered that she didn't have the AI...but then, wouldn't they assume it was the people running away at full speed that had what they wanted?

Elise rubbed at her temples as an idea began forming in her mind. The more the notion coalesced, the more it made sense. Then she let the submachine gun hang loose on its sling around her neck, drew her pistol instead and touched the muzzle to Savitri's temple. She rose slowly to full height, dragging the alien up with her.

"Stand down!" she shouted to the rebels. "Stand down, or I will shoot her!"

Kovalich stared at her, mouth agape. Savitri's look of shock slowly morphed into the look of fear, and she began to cry. The rebels halted, several of them huddling atop their horses.

"Cut the waterworks," Elise told Savitri. "I know you're the Lady."

Savitri quit crying mid-wail, and her facial expression changed to tranquil so quickly, it was unsettling. "How did you know?" she asked, in the familiar voice but an entirely different tone; a tone of a person both certain of themselves and used to issuing orders.

"I didn't, until moments ago," Elise admitted. "It was the actions of your people that convinced me. They chose to zero in on this wagon instead of pursuing Tobey and the prop he's carrying, even though they still had the chance to catch him."

The Lady nodded, very slightly and carefully with the gun still at her temple. "In their zeal to protect me, my people aren't as disciplined as I would like them to be."

"I should have figured it out sooner," said Elise. "It makes a hell of a lot more sense than an AI functioning in the interdicted zone. That was one hell of an effective subterfuge. And back at the slaver compound—provoking me to act, to free those people, all so you could slow us down a bit, give your followers a better chance to catch up. You only pretended to hurt your ankle, didn't you?"

"I shouldn't have pushed so hard. You're cleverer than a typical operative. You're the first to see through my ruse. People's belief that I'm an AI, added to the fact that adults of my species look like human children, has previously been sufficient to shroud me from all suspicion. I could use a person like you—"

"That's a nonstarter," said Elise. "Don't praise my intelligence and then insult it with such an offer in the same breath."

"What now?" asked the Lady. "If you shoot me, you will die, too."

"You know I'm not afraid to die for the right reasons," said Elise. "You saw this at the slaver compound. I believe you will get your people to stand down and let us ride our wagon out of here."

"Perhaps I'm willing to die for the right reasons, too," said the Lady. "After all, being captured by the Commonwealth is hardly better for me than death."

"That's not how your mind operates, I gather," said Elise. "While you live there's always a chance you can trick someone, manipulate someone in order to get free. Those fools may believe you to be their Jesus, but I don't think resurrection is one of your powers." She nodded to Kovalich, who grabbed the reins and nudged the beast forward. "I'm willing to play Russian roulette with you. Winner takes all."

The rebels clutched their guns tighter, but the Lady raised her hand palm forward to make them halt. "You seem invested in this zero-sum-game idea, but there's no reason both of us can't win," she said. "You're willing to break Commonwealth law, so long as you're doing the right thing. I operate in the same manner, in my own way. I can give you money, resources, leads. The slaver you took down yesterday? There are so many more like that man on the edges of the human space. You don't have to work for me, but you could do far more good under my patronage than you ever could while constricted by the Commonwealth bureaucracy."

"No," Elise said firmly. "I believe in the Commonwealth, warts and all. I will do what I must to protect it."

The Lady sighed. "Your identity and self-worth are so invested in this role of savior of humanity that you choose to play, that I don't believe I can make you see reason. Please listen to me. I'm not a terrorist. I merely want a better system, a system where different species can co-exist, in place of an entrenched government that values human interests above all else. I want you to know this, to consider this later, even though you have no reason to believe me now. But you will in a few minutes."

"What does that mean?"

Elise searched for some kind of a trick, a last-minute gambit the Lady or her supporters might pull. But the wagon was moving ever closer to the shuttle, and the riders remained crestfallen where they stood, until they were far enough to be out of range.

The Lady didn't say a word that whole time. It was only when they were outside of the interdicted zone and within the shadow of the shuttle that she spoke again.

"The reason I didn't do this earlier is because I didn't want you to die," she said. "You are misguided, but you're a good person. So I waited until we reached your ship."

"Do what?" Elise asked.

"I can't risk being captured alive," said the Lady. "The information your people might extract from me will put too many of my followers in grave danger. Remember what I told you."

Before Elise could respond, the Lady twisted with the speed of a coiled snake. She grabbed for the submachine gun hanging in front of Elise's chest, aimed it at Kovalich, and fired a burst of bullets.

Of all the horrors she'd lived through, this was the moment Elise would relive in her nightmares. She was certain she could have pulled the trigger on her pistol quickly enough to stop the Lady. She was absolutely certain of it, but she'd hesitated. She never expected the Lady to shoot Kovalich. She had been willing to risk her own life to bring the Lady in alive, but not the life of her soldiers.

Elise pulled the trigger a moment too late.

She sat in the wagon, her face in her arms, with the bodies of both the Lady and Kovalich, while Tobey and the others raced from the shuttle toward them. Why would the Lady do this? Why commit suicide rather than be captured? Why spare the life of her executioner when she could have had her post-mortem revenge by pulling the exact same stunt while still surrounded by her people? Why do any of it, if the things she said weren't true?

"What happened?!" Tobey was next to her, and then Mahmud and Swenson, too.

Her soldiers grieved over Kovalich's body. She had lost half her team on this mission, and all she had to show for it was a prop.

It took an inhuman amount of effort to stand up, look Tobey in the eye, and speak without her voice breaking.

"I bluffed our way out, but then the crazy girl went for my gun. I guess she was more loyal to the Lady than I had realized. This is what I get for trying to save her."

Tobey rested his hand on her shoulder. "This doesn't feel like a victory now, but it still is. We did it. We got the Lady, even if we paid a high price for it. Winner takes all. Right?"

Elise nodded. She didn't trust herself to speak.

"Take the bodies to the shuttle," Tobey told the soldiers as he gently tried to nudge Elise toward the ship.

"No," she said. "Leave the girl." She straightened up, removed Tobey's hand from her shoulder, and walked toward the shuttle. "That Tessa woman loved her like a daughter. It's how I managed to escape," she lied. "We have what we wanted. Let Tessa have the body."

Elise wasn't entirely sure why she decided to leave the Lady's body behind. She was, however, certain of how things would turn out in the following few days.

Tobey would file a report claiming the lion's share of the credit for capturing the AI. It was clearly in his nature not to share too generously. Once it was discovered the gadget he brought back was nothing but a paperweight, the report would sink him. Not her, however. She had succeeded in her part of the mission: getting the accountant there, retrieving the object, and getting him out again. The death of two soldiers was unfortunate, but the powers that be would see that only as the cost of doing business.

She would go on more missions, and she would use those missions to balance the karmic scales. To make up for the lives lost, for Peña and Kovalich and countless others before them. Was leaving the Lady's body a tiny act of compassion toward her followers and a first small step in that direction, or merely an instinctive move to obfuscate Elise's own failures? She didn't trust herself to decide, just then.

One thing she was certain of was that she wanted to investigate more of what the rebel leader was talking about: to root out slavers and warlords festering on the edges of human space. In the game of winner takes all, the Lady had somehow managed to turn defeat into a gambit that resulted in a non-zero-sum-game solution.

The shuttle roared as it took Elise back toward the stars.

The End

LAST STAND AT EUROPA STATION A

David Boop

Welcome, Settlers, to Europa Station A—brought to you by the Coca-Cola Corporation—the first nonterrestrial, human-occupied, underwater colony.

When the cost of producing drinkable water on Earth exceeded Coke's profitability model, our multitrillion-dollar company sponsored exploration into the far reaches of the solar system to find more. You might not think water a necessity for soda, but if you'd pull up the ingredients, you'd see it right there... toward the bottom. Plus, even our executives still needed to drink something other than our product, so off to space we sent dozens of red-and-white-striped probes.

Europa's water had previously been examined by Earth, Luna, and Mars, each hoping to claim the moon for their own, but before anyone could develop the colonization technology to make it feasible, we had planted our flag. Being an interplanetary company serving the entire Sol System, we claimed Europa as a neutral zone. Other parties would be allowed to build refineries on the moon, as long as they understood that Coke would take a percentage of all water harvested as our fee. No one complained as they considered the royalty share preferable to going to war with our beloved brand. The now defunct Pepsi, Coors, and McDonald's corporations all learned that lesson.

Virgin Galactic's magnetically shielded, toroidal-shaped transports—dubbed "wagon trains" by those who named

*things—shipped colonists to Jupiter, once the shortest route
was negotiated through the Microsoft Asteroid Belt™. Before
then, it took nearly three years to get from Earth to Jupiter
via Ceres, but now your trip will only take you about a year.*

*The first habitat, bored into the ice nearest the North
Pole, was assembled by robots before any humans could even
attempt a landing, due to Jupiter's radiation upon the surface, which made placing a frog in a microwave seem kind
in comparison. Once the HAB had been sealed up, drained,
and dried, wagons dropped down through thirty-two miles of
ice into the docking bay.*

*Those initial plucky colonists had to figure out how to
turn Europa's salty ocean into safe, drinkable water. The station's original Radio-Thermoelectric Generator, or RTG, was
enough to get the colonists started; however, it didn't have
the raw output to power the filtration system of the refinery
needed to quench our solar system's thirst. Thus the latest
fission reactor was printed out and brought online, doubling
the refinery's capacity.*

*But with Europa Stations B and C having been authorized,
harvesting and refining had to be done smart—sustainably,
as you will, so we wouldn't cause the moon's very delicate
environment to collapse in upon itself.*

We at Coca-Cola have learned our lessons from the past.
—From the *Coca-Cola Corporation's*
Europa Station A Newcomer's
Orientation Training Manual

Aldo "Brake" Bargman walked down the ramp from his wagon
and breathed in deeply the manufactured air of Europa Station,
noticing how much better it tasted than the manufactured air
of his wagon or the manufactured air of Mars Station, or Lunar
Station. And it certainly was cleaner than what passed for air
back on Earth.

A drone delivered his personal bags to him and gave him a
receipt for the containers of lab equipment it would take directly
to his new medical examiner's office.

In a dozen years, the only deaths on Europa had been clearly
accidental, or so the reports had said, but as more colonists
arrived and water refinement picked up, certainly the confined

space would eventually lead to someone killing someone else. Thus, the local security force requested a medical examiner be assigned to the twelve-hundred-person colony.

Brake had no family to leave behind on Earth. No obligations, no outstanding warrants, and despite years exposed to Earth's toxic air and water, his health was surprisingly within tolerances, making his application and approval process with the Coke Corporation go smoothly. He grabbed the last train out for Europa that week and, *boom!*, one year later, he stepped onto the alien moon. Well, onto polycarbonate plating in a HAB under the moon's surface, but close enough.

During his layovers on Luna and Mars, he hadn't gone "outside" either, so it had been no great disappointment. However, the wagon train's pilot had brought them in on the night side of Europa, giving them full view of the moon's legendary North Pole. The icy surface glowed soft blue with rust-colored linnea woven into it like yarn in a scarf. Jupiter's intense radiation passed through the dayside ice shell to produce the most magnificent effect on the opposite side. It reminded him of those old cyberpunk movies where people ended up inside a computer.

Unfortunately, that effect also drove Europa Station down farther undersea, as it messed with their instruments. He couldn't see anything but water from any of the portholes.

"Mr. Bargman?"

The question came from a woman wearing the red-and-white fatigues of a C.C. Ranger. The Rangers were the law on Europa, with their understood priorities being to protect the corporate assets first, then the people. Occasionally, the company realized its people were also assets, which was why they'd hired him.

"Yes, I'm Brake."

The Ranger extended a hand. "I'm Lieutenant Thana Suvari, and I'll be your guide as you acclimate to Europa Station and your responsibilities."

"My shadow, you mean."

She nodded. "Exactly, though I'll be on your ass tighter than Peter Pan's shadow was."

Brake laughed. He liked her straightforward attitude immediately.

"Excellent!" He bent forward and spoke loudly to her ranking badge, as to if indicate he were talking into a hidden microphone.

"I want to make sure my employers don't ever doubt that sage decision to hire me. It's a long way home."

He leaned back, smiling at his joke, but then Thana pointed up to her beret, to the Rangers insignia. "It's up here," she said, a sly smirk gracing her full lips.

Thana had a touch of Middle Easterner to her skin tone, but these days, most people had some pigmentation that made anything but genetic identification impossible to tell what their true racial origins were. Only health care providers and MEs like himself cared, as sometimes genetic traits could lead to a cause of death. His own DNA contained a mix of the combined UK gene, along with some Ashkenazi and Dutch with just a touch South African. Once humans left Earth, it didn't matter much where you started from, you became a citizen of Luna, or Mars, or now Europa. There wasn't room for racial prejudices when you needed to count on everyone to have your back.

Brake straightened his shoulders and saluted Thana's hat. "Lead on, MacDuff."

The ME's office had previously been occupied by a massage therapist. Brake deduced this by the stuff left behind: an eerie salt lamp, aromatherapy gel packs, and a display rack filled with flimbrochs on chakras, mindfulness, and getting enough sleep. Over the adjustable massage table hung a jerry-rigged step-therapy frame that might have once belonged in a medieval torture chamber. Stepping inside the room, he banged his head on the hatch's lower clearance. Rubbing his forehead, he knew it wouldn't be the last time he did that.

"Where is the Inquisitor now?"

"He was so popular the station commander approved a new space, complete with waiting room. He decided you probably wouldn't have repeat business."

"Unless I'm bad at my job."

She raised an eyebrow. "Sorry?"

Brake began to unpack his supplies. "There's an old joke among examiners. How can you tell a bad coroner from a good one?"

Thana, deciding to help out, picked up the salt lamp and unplugged it from the wall. "How?"

"A bad one is in the bar, drinking heavily, and complaining he 'gained' one on the table that day."

It took her a moment, but then Thana chortled so suddenly, she nearly dropped the lamp.

As they emptied a container, they refilled it with the therapist's leftover accoutrements.

"Why 'Brake'?" Thana pulled down and rolled up a reflexology chart.

The new ME chuckled. "Well, my parents were on the way to the hospital for my impending arrival but got caught up in traffic. Dad had taken the car off self-drive, hoping to jump ahead into any openings he saw, but then he kept being distracted by my mother's screams, as one would expect. He'd just turned back around in time to slam on the brakes before hitting a truck in front of them, and I sort of... popped out."

Thana raised an eyebrow. "You what?"

Brake blushed. "I just slid right out, right there in the back seat. Landed on the floorboards and everything."

"That's..." Thana paused, gauging her words. "That's quite a story."

"Anyway, Dad often told his friends that I was his big Brake from that point forward, and it stuck."

Once Brake had satisfactorily claimed the lab as his own, he yawned.

Thana tagged each container of the former occupant's items for the drones to pick up and deliver to their new home. "Let's get you to your apartment. While you got the short end of the stick here, you've been assigned private quarters, seeing that the nature of your work requires you *not* be mixed with any of the general worker bees."

"Yeah, would suck to find out your bunkmate is a murderer."

"Indeed."

His place wasn't far from his office, which was nice. He expected he'd often be working late. Any crime solving on Europa had to be done expeditiously to alleviate uncertainty in a small, confined space. Confining crew to quarters while an investigation was ongoing was a bad thing.

Along the way, they made a plan to tour the station, then meet the actual medical team and Thana's superiors.

Thana showed him how to key his finger in the hatch's lock, which would scrape a micro-particle of skin before opening.

Brake thanked her.

She nodded, which he realized was her answer to most things. "Will you be needing a massage or blow job before bed?"

His jaw hung loose. "Um, what? I mean, is that part of what—"

Thana cut him off, her expression indicating she knew where his mind had gone. "In your dreams. I'm not that type of escort," she stated matter-of-factly. "In addition to the aforementioned therapist, we have licensed sexualists on staff—male, female, and nonbin. It cuts down on the awkward nature of unwanted advances on coworkers, and keeps the staff focused on the task at hand. I thought maybe after such a long journ—"

Embarrassed, it was Brake's turn to cut her off. "I'm fine. For now, at least. I'd be too tired to enjoy it, anyway. Plus, I tend to, y'know, like to get to know someone beforehand."

Thana titled her head slightly. "I hope I didn't offend you. Corporate-sponsored sex services are pretty common on new colonies."

Brake knew that. He wasn't prudish or opposed to it, she'd had just caught him off guard. "No offense was taken. Now, if you'll please. The sun will be up in twenty hours, if I understand that correctly, and I'll need my shadow rested and ready, as well."

Giving him one last nod in acknowledgment of her dismissal, Thana left.

He turned and, still distracted by their last conversation, smacked his forehead hard on the hatch.

After unpacking, having dinner delivered, watching some of the orientation streams on Europa again—this time with more context—showering, and then crawling into bed, he realized he still had fifteen hours before the new day started. Europa had an eighty-five-hour day, which meant that concept of day and night were set by the lighting in the station. But as he lay there in his new bed for hours, trying to sleep, he debated if he shouldn't have gotten the nobber after all.

Over the next month, Brake wondered if the company had made a bad call. He'd only had one autopsy, which COD turned out to be from a previously unknown allergy to a sealant used specifically on Europa. The doctors on staff had already determined that, but he backed their findings. They, too, didn't understand why he was there, as modern medical scanning technology took most of the guesswork out of cause of death. The team didn't socialize with him, or invite him to gatherings, nor visit his office. Brake thought they were all pretentious dicks, anyway.

However, as simple as the worker's death had been, he'd learned about "the Locker" because of it.

Thana piloted a submersible through the dark waters, the only lights at their depth coming from the Über-Manta submersible.

"Who came up with the idea of calling it Davy Jones' Locker?"

"Leo Edwardson, the refinery's super. He was the first to lose a worker under him. Pipe burst and the poor lady burned instantly."

The temperature of the seawater was well below freezing, due to its chemical nature. Any exposure to the skin was like dipping toes into liquid nitrogen.

"So, since there's no morgue, and no place to bury them, you just sink bodies to the ocean floor." Brake wondered what the next of kin thought of this arrangement. He didn't remember reading any clause of that sort in his contract.

"Until we come up with something better. Maybe cremation, but right now, the station can't support any sort of open flame."

Brake shrugged. He couldn't think of anything better. He was sure there was an ethical reason not to turn them into mulch for the farm. He looked behind the Manta to where the bagged corpse trailed behind them. Sealed in a fiberweb coffin, a blinking locator tag had been attached should the body need to be recovered by drone. It reminded him of a trolling lure.

Thana slowed. "This is as deep as we go. The ocean floor isn't as deep at the poles as it is closer to the equator. Normally, we'd just send an Alvin to do this, but I thought you might like to go walkabout."

Brake agreed it was nice to get out of the station, and just as nice to be in the cramped submersible with Thana—who he'd grown fond of. He thought the feeling was mutual, but neither acted on it out of professionalism. Besides, as the Corp clearly sanctioned, why risk rejection when sex was not only available but paid for and covered under his insurance benefits?

"What now?" Brake asked.

"Funeral services were done back at the station. Now, we just cut her loose."

When they stopped, the weights attached to the victim's coffin pulled her down below the Manta. Thana hit the release button, and the victim began her descent.

"And the biology teams haven't found life down here yet? Nothing that might nibble on the corpses?"

Thana nodded. "Yeah, disappointed a lot of scientists. Everything you'd need for spontaneous evolution is below the surface, save for carbon. Sure, you've got some meteor debris on the surface, but nothing can survive up there. Sadly, no carbon. No life."

As they swung the Manta around, Brake followed the blinking locator tag on the coffin as the body sunk slowly into the darkness.

Then, out of the corner of his eye, Brake thought...

"Wait," he said, and Thana put the submersible in hover.

"What?"

No, but that must be just a trick of the light. She just said, no life down here.

"Nothing. Let's head back."

By the time he was home, Brake had already forgotten about it.

Besides that one autopsy, Brake mostly toured Europa Station with Thana, whom he'd taken to calling "Shadow," and learned everything he could about the inner workings of the colony.

All the better, he considered, *to determine what might be used to kill someone someday.*

Like him, security had little to do until something went horribly wrong. His shadow was the second-highest-ranking officer on the station with six guards under her command. She delegated much of her daily tasks to her subordinates, allowing her the freedom to teach Brake the ins and outs of the station. She told him she was "investing" in his future success. Brake worried that eventually those subordinates might grow resentful of doing all her mundane jobs.

The HAB itself consisted of the living quarters and social area, the farm, the power plant, and the water refinery. The first three were conjoined closely together like Cerberus, while the refinery hung farther back, like its spiked tail.

The plant brought in ocean water through feeder tubes and filtered out any contaminants, such as sulfates, nitrates, and sodium, some of which would be added back in for taste in drinking water. He heard that the lines often got clogged with the silicate sand that made up Europa's mantle.

The more he learned about Thana, the more he grew to admire

her. She'd served during the resource riots on Earth, protecting the corporation's food and soda distribution centers as they handed out rations. Next, Thana pulled dozens of people from a Coke Café on Luna when the ALON window cracked due to a manufacturing flaw. The Corp awarded her with a promotion for reducing the number of survivor benefits they would've had to pay out.

"My ticket to Europa came," she told him while playing *Catan: Mars Uprising* in his office, "was when I arrested a group of water pirates who'd attacked a supply ship. The execs said they needed someone like me on Europa. I came in with the fourth wave a year ago."

The first colonists settled thirteen years ago. Now a new wagon arrived every other year or so. The Earth-Luna Conglomerate, backed with Microsoft money, landed their colony three years earlier, and Mars had just bored in less than a year ago.

"Have you been to B or C?"

She shook her head. "No, the 'Es on B,' as we call them, are very much Earth first and get angry at the Corp for not choosing to send water there exclusively. The Martians at station C are all right, but they also have this 'we were the first off-world colony' thing going on. Elitist dicks, if you ask me."

Since Brake had encountered much the same thing on station A, he didn't say anything, but thought it fascinating that each group felt they were owed something over the other.

And so his days went, with him researching the various aspects of underwater life, never seeing the sun save through vidscreens. It took him quite by surprise when Thana said she was coming in hot with a frozen corpse.

"What's going on?" he asked.

"Refinery worker found a guy, frozen solid, in one of their feeder pipes. No one knows how he got in there, but it clearly doesn't add up. I'm bringing the witness and Leo Edwardson, the refinery boss, with me."

Brake prepped his autopsy table for frozen matter. "Do I need to drop the temperature in the lab and put on my PPE-0s?" The gear would allow him to handle a body exposed to subzero conditions.

"Doesn't matter," Leo said, cutting in. He snorted in a way both disgusting and dismissive. "He's not melting anytime soon."

Leo was right.

Even after the stretcher bots hoisted the body onto his table, and Brake turned on the warming lamps normally used for frost-bite victims, the structure of the deceased didn't change in the slightest. It defied everything he knew about cryo-death.

Brake bent over him. "What was his name?"

"Omar Chapman," the coworker witness, Sophia, answered. She was an older woman of Hispanic decent. "He'd only arrived about a month ago."

That put the man on the same train as he'd arrived on, Brake realized. He didn't look familiar. Maybe their cars were at opposite ends? Most likely.

Omar was unlike any hypothermia victim he'd ever read about. He'd studied prehistoric bodies recovered after the glaciers receded. He'd reviewed the data that came out of the cryo-revivalist movement of the 2080s when cancer had been cured and a bunch of bodies from the 1980s had been thawed so they could be "revived." None of them had been successfully, but the research went a long way toward understanding the long-term effects of cryostasis. Brake had viewed every type of aquatic death in full 3-D holo recreation, and nothing matched what lay before him.

The refinery worker had become solid ice down to the cellular level according to the lab's scanner. He'd literally become an iceman.

Brake ran his reader glove over Omar's body. "Tell me what happened."

Sophia recited what seemed to be a preestablished accounting. Her voice didn't carry with it the raw, unsure emotions that came with finding someone you knew dead. Brake wondered how long it'd been before the C.C. Rangers were notified of the discovery. "Omar and I were following up on a slowdown in the Number Three and Number Four feeder tubes. I took Three and he took Four. By the time I ran a diagnostic, my tube was running back up to normal, but Omar's had plugged up completely. I called him on the comm, but he didn't answer."

Sophia looked up at Leo, who nodded. He was an intimidating, barrel-chested man of Scandinavian decent, and Sophia had waited for his confirmation to keep going. "When I got over to where Omar should have been, I found nothing but a patch of ice on the floor. I thought maybe he went to get some tools or something to unplug the line, but that's what we have the crunchers for."

"Crunchers?" Brake asked distractedly. His reader glove, which allowed for very specific subatomic scans, had picked up something he couldn't rationalize. He reached over for a micro-laser to carve off a piece of Omar to place in his analyzer. It barely made a divot.

Thana answered. "Spinning blades that travel the feeder lines to break up ice. ALON-diamond composite, able to cut through anything, supposedly."

ALON, or aluminium oxynitride, dubbed "transparent aluminum" after some old movie, was the hardest polycrystalline ceramic science had invented so far. It was the final piece for building colonies on other worlds. If they'd found a way to make it harder, that was news to Brake.

"There's never a reason to open a live tube," Leo added. "It would have to be shut down to the outside, boiling decontaminate run through it to clean off any residue, then drained and dried before anyone set even a finger inside."

Thana nodded. "Opening a live tube would risk pumping thousands of gallons of cryoprotectant-level water into the plant."

"And killing scores of people before it could be turned off," Brake agreed.

Brake finally managed to cut a sliver of Omar away, and he dropped it into the subatomic analyzer unit.

"So, how'd you find out he was in the tube?"

Sophia looked down, embarrassed. "I turned on the cruncher... and it broke."

"Broke?" Brake asked.

"Broke," Leo echoed.

"Like broke broke?"

Thana nodded. "Stopped dead, teeth shattered."

Brake whistled. He found several small nicks in Omar's body, down near his legs, where the cruncher must've bit in.

Leo made his scoffing snort again. "There is no ice in the known galaxy a cruncher can't chew through. Rock or metal, either. It's what they're designed to do. Well, when Sophia called me down, I authorized a drone sent into the line, and that's when we found"—he indicated the corpse—"him."

Thana, a slight tone of irritation in her voice, said, "They'd already drained the line and went through the procedure Mr. Edwardson described before calling the Rangers."

Leo didn't react to the admonishment. "We had to see for ourselves. I mean, it couldn't be him, right? Thought it was sabotage by the Es on B, or a prank."

The analyzer beeped and Brake checked the readout on his glove.

"Well, I know why the cruncher broke, now. That's not ice he's encased in. It's a complex silicate composite that just looks and acts like ice. It's part ocean water, part Omar, which is why the scanners didn't see it at first. But the silicate material has bonded at the subatomic level. He's... well, he's no longer a carbon-based being." Brake looked back and forth from Leo to Sophia. "Ever see anything like this on Europa before?"

Leo looked unsurprised at the news, though he tried to act like it. Sophia stared at the floor, uncomfortably, and the ME could tell she had more to tell him.

Brake subtly got his shadow's attention, and then Thana got Leo's.

"Mr. Edwardson, I'd like to review the security footage from the last forty-eight hours around feeder number four."

"Can't you access that remotely?" Leo didn't want to move.

But the Ranger was equally undaunted. "For a potential murder investigation, I'll need your authorization."

The plant manager grew instantly agitated. "Murder? Who said anything about murder?"

"There's no way he got in that tube by himself, not with it open. Someone had to have shut down the line, thrown him in there, and reopened it in just the short time Sophia was gone."

Leo waved his hand dismissively. "Not possible. And there's no data to support that."

Brake chimed in. "But wasn't that what Sophia and Omar were checking out? A slowdown or blockage?"

"Well, yes, but..."

Thana took Leo's elbow. "Which is why I want to review the footage to see if that could've been done."

Though he initially resisted, Leo gave in and let her lead him to the security office.

Once he was out of earshot, Brake asked Sophia, "So, what haven't you told me—or more precisely, what doesn't Leo want me to know?"

Sophia blushed. "Nothing, sir. I've told everything I know."

Brake shook his head. "I don't think so, and as you're now the prime suspect in Omar's murder..."

"I'm what?"

Shrugging, Brake told her, "According to your account, there was only the two of you. And if he didn't drag himself into the tube..."

Sophia found her voice. "Oh, hell no! No way I'm going down for that idiot."

And then she told Brake everything.

Thana piloted the Manta toward the Locker as fast as she could, following the locator tags of the nearly twenty souls that had been sent to Davy Jones' Locker in the last thirteen years. The Manta creaked as the pressure and cold increased on its outer walls.

"How could this even be possible?" Thana asked.

Brake reviewed the data again. "It isn't, not if we keep thinking of life as being carbon-based exclusively."

"And we aren't."

"Not anymore. Whatever this is, it's silicon-based, and when it bonds to carbon, it creates a new thing, like when heat and sand make glass."

Thana shook her head. "And Leo knew about this for nearly three years?"

"According to Sophia, the first silicon symbiote—or silibiote—showed up about a year before I was hired."

"And right before I was transferred, so the timing is suspect. I can't believe he kept it a secret."

"Apparently, the station's dead would swim home and get stuck in the feeder tubes, their only way in. Leo would rebag them, and sent them back to the Locker with more weight and stronger coffins." Brake checked the schematics. "No matter what sort of vent they put over the tubes, somehow the silibiotes found a way in."

"And he never figured out how?" Thana shook her head, disgusted.

"Or why? What are they after?"

Thana shuddered at what they'd found on the raw security footage, the feed that Leo hadn't scrubbed before he'd initially called in the Rangers. Luckily, the Corp had a secondary feed of all surveillance footage sent to the security office without the rest of the station knowing, just for that very reason.

Omar was at his station when the silicate life-form had leaked out of the feeder tube, masking itself as condensation frost. When Omar returned to the pipe, it leapt and encased him in a matter of seconds. It stopped the water in the line, climbed in, sealed the hatch behind it, and tried to swim back down the tube. Only, it found it could not fit anymore.

The silibiote Omar was now sealed behind an energy wall with several armed Rangers guarding it, in case he suddenly came back to life. It hadn't reanimated since its discovery, and Brake wasn't sure why. Leo Edwardson sat in the next cell over.

"Leo used threats of termination or bribes to keep the whole thing quiet." Thana cursed that such a huge secret was kept right under her nose.

Behind them, the lights of two more Mantas blinked into view.

"Um, Shadow? Did you call for any of your Lost Boys to follow us?"

Thana swore. "I have a feeling that's Hook and his pirates. Edwardson must have someone on retainer in the Rangers."

"Safe bet. He couldn't have kept this quiet for so long without one."

"Can you pilot a Manta?"

"I can try."

"Then take the wheel."

They switched places, and Brake couldn't help but notice the way she crossed over him: very, very close, her butt grazing his crotch ever so slightly. She made no outward indication that she did this intentionally, but he'd also known people to be turned on by danger in the past. Maybe it was a hint that she wanted him to risk rejection. Unfortunately, he couldn't explore those thoughts at the moment.

Brake's dad had taught him how to drive a car on manual, especially after the circumstances of his birth. Overall, the Manta didn't handle much differently, save for the pressure of water forcing him to give it more power than the old beater back home he'd inherited.

Thana crawled to the back of the submersible and pulled down a targeting display.

"Um," Brake said, looking over his shoulder, "I've never seen that as an option on any Übër vehicle I bought."

"The C.C. Rangers get a fleet discount, and we have special upgrades available to us. Circle the Locker, but don't go down yet."

Brake said he would.

Thana fired her first torpedo.

On the dash monitor, Brake watched the missile intentionally streak past the Mantas without hitting either of them, after which, Thana contacted Leo. "This won't look good on my report if you come any closer."

The refinery boss replied, "The only report you'll be making is to Davy Jones. I'm sending you and this anomaly back to—"

Brake shouted into the comm, "You freed him from the containment unit? Don't you understand yet?"

"Understand what? That Europa's water somehow bonds with a dead body's cells and reanimates them like a chicken with its head cut off?"

"Sophia was right. You *are* an idiot. Omar wasn't dead, and that wasn't water!"

But before Brake could explain further, a scream rattled the communicators. The second of the two pursuing Mantas veered sharply down. Then, the cabin suddenly compressed and it imploded. The duo had no doubt as to which Manta had been carrying Omar's body.

"What the f—"

Brake interrupted. "The silibiote. It's not just some chemical component bringing the dead back to life. It has a conscience and a goal."

Leo stumbled over his words after that until Thana turned his feed off. This was bigger than the refinery boss could contain anymore. Thana would make sure of it.

Feeling that they were no longer in immediate danger, Brake took the Manta down into the Locker. The pressure outside increased, but they made it without imploding. Leo arrived right after them, and the twin Mantas' searchlights illuminated an eerie scene.

All the coffins, including the one that Brake and Thana had just delivered weeks earlier, were empty, the shredded remains of the fiberweb wafting in the current like reeds in the wind.

☆   ☆   ☆

As they raced back to the station, Leo frantically called to his people, but no one answered.

Thana also tried to reach the C.C. Rangers, connecting once and hearing only the sound of energy weapons before the comm disconnected.

"Those energy rifles won't get through the silicate. My concentrated laser had a hard enough time."

"What are we dealing with?" Thana asked. "Really."

Brake shrugged. "I'm not a xenobiologist, just familiar enough with what happens to dead bodies after they die, but I'm guessing they're parasitic microorganisms that have been waiting for carbon hosts to bond with for God knows how long."

Thana tilted her head to stare at him. "You said 'waiting.' Like, they didn't evolve here?"

Again, he couldn't answer her. "I can't say for sure, but a parasite needs something to attach to, right? Otherwise, how could it ever form in the first place?"

"Sure."

Brake waved his hand around. "You said it yourself. Do you see anything for them to bond to here?"

"Well, we did miss these things."

"No, I don't think we did. I think whatever they are, they don't activate until they have a suitable host, so we wouldn't register them as life. Probably just looked like sand."

Thana ground her teeth. "What activated them, then? Carbon?"

"They've been dropping bodies down in the Locker for years. The question is . . . why now? Why in just the last couple of years has this started happening?" He brought up a holo of the solar system. "I think it's because Jupiter entered its 'summer.' For about four Earth years, Jupiter is the closest it gets to the sun. Add Sol's radiation to its own, and the silicate heats up and searches for a life-form to possess."

"Possess?"

"Yes."

"Like a ghost."

He nodded. "Yes."

"Why?"

"It's just a theory, but until we get back to the station, I can't know for sure."

Thana went white. "The other refineries. Are they in danger?"

"C is still using water that's already been filtered by us, and they're on the other side of the planet. B? I don't know. This might be localized."

"Regardless, I'll send a message they should shut down their plants temporarily due to a recently discovered contaminant."

It took all her security clearances to get through to the heads of each refinery, even conferencing Leo in before they all agreed to shut down. By that time, they were in the approach vector to Europa Station.

As they passed by the ALON windows of the refinery, they could all see hazard lights spinning and bodies strewn about.

"Ghosts?" Leo echoed, as he exhaled a cloud of cold air. The silibiotes had flooded the refinery HAB up to about an inch of the Europan ocean water they lived in. The refinery was as cold as fuck.

"Yes," Brake said, exasperated. "But I need to talk to one to be sure."

"Talk to one? Are you serious? Those things kill anything they touch!"

Once they got into the station, Thana brought up the Rangers' security feed.

As water cascaded over the workers' feet, silicate would rise up and form a cocoon, bonding solid for several minutes until the "ice" cracked and the newly formed silibiote walked free.

The C.C. Rangers fired on these walking dead with zero results. Then, one creative solider came out of the residuals room with three modified energy rifles slung over his back, and one in his hands. When he fired, it shattered the silibiote's leg. It stumbled and fell to the floor, causing the silicate creature to slough off the body. The once-human corpse instantly freeze-dried and crumbled in the water. The parasites apparently had no use for a defective host.

"There goes your glass theory, Doc," Thana had said.

That Ranger tossed the other rifles to his team, and together they were able to pull several survivors out of the area. They all backed out of the refinery, and sealed off the central hub behind an energy barrier.

Thana found the improvisational Ranger from the vidstream, and Brake asked him what he'd done to modify the rifles.

"I remembered that one of the residuals we pulled from the water was neodymium. My dad is a jeweler on Mars, and he uses a neodymium YAG laser to cut diamonds. I figured, what the hell? I swapped corundum for the neodymium and boo-yah!"

"Good work," the ME said, "but let's not kill any more of them than we have to."

"Why in the eighty-three fucking moons of Jupiter not?" Leo said.

Brake held up his hands in mock protection. "I know. I know. But I think they might be sentient, so let's not shoot them unless our lives are in danger."

"What do you mean 'unless'?" Leo scoffed. He grabbed one of the rifles from the Ranger. Thana held the young man back from retrieving it, with a hand across his chest. "You saw the feed. They killed a lot of my people."

"What I saw a species doing what it was designed to do. I'm just not sure what that is."

Leo stayed true. "You're an Earth-pounding coroner, not some first-contact expert. What are you trying to do?"

Brake spun on him, ignoring the man's size and armament. "First off, I'm a medical examiner, not a coroner. I went to school for this, you canned air–sucking moron, and I've dealt with the dead every day since. Every body I examine tells a story. That story then helps save other lives."

Thana added, "There're nearly a thousand people on Europa Station, plus the other stations, and we don't have time to evacuate everyone off-world if this plant falls and they decide to attack. Don't you think reasoning with them is better?"

Leo seemed unconvinced, but he didn't object further.

Thana authorized letting Brake, Leo, and herself back into the refinery HAB. She and the boss each had a rifle, but Brake chose not to carry. "I'm about saving lives, not taking them."

The trio moved cautiously along the strobe-lit passageway. The klaxons finally turned off. They stuck to the sides, avoiding the frigid water that ran down the center as much as possible.

Once they reached the central hub, they took a set of steps just on the other side of the entrance up to a mezzanine. Below, in addition to the twenty-plus reanimated corpses, fifty or so new silibiotes wandered around aimlessly.

Brake thought they looked . . . confused.

Ironically enough, Sophia, the woman who'd found Omar's body, was the first silibiote that noticed them standing there. She stared up at them with a mix of distant recollection and concern on her frozen face.

Brake's voice cracked, knowing that just hours ago she had helped him. Now, she was dead, or something akin to dead. "H-hello, Sophia. Remember me?"

The Sophia silibiote opened and closed its mouth, seemingly to mimic speech, but unable to create words. She looked behind Brake to Thana and Leo and took a step back cautiously.

Brake motioned the others to get farther behind him.

"I don't know if you can understand me, but your vocal cords are frozen solid. Along with your lungs. I don't know how much control you have over your host, but you'll have to unthaw them or release them to speak to us."

The silibiote seemed to understand his words, but just kept opening and closing her mouth.

Brake then placed his hands on his chest and mimed lungs expanding and contracting.

The Sophibiote, as Brake started to think of her, morphed. The area around its chest softened, but it still struggled to speak.

Next, the ME ran his hand up and down his throat to indicate that air came in and out of it.

When Sophibiote softened that part of its body, a low moan came from its lips that grew louder and louder as it drew in more air.

More moans came from elsewhere and fed Sophibiote's.

"They're a hive mind!" Brake shouted, covering his ears.

"Fuck this!" Leo said and aimed the energy gun at the silibiote, but before he could pull the trigger, Thana plowed into him, knocking his aim off. The blast hit the wall and traced up the ceiling, scorching a huge path.

"Asshole!" Thana said. "You'll punch a hole through the HAB, and then we're *all* fucked!"

Sophibiote and the other silibiotes moved to the opposite side of the HAB and huddled together scared.

"Dammit!" Brake moved behind Leo and pulled the leads from the pack. "She was just learning to how speak."

Leo grabbed the smaller man by his envirosuit and slammed him against the wall. "It was calling for reinforcements! I'm not the asshole. You are!"

Thana grabbed Leo's arm and twisted it behind his back. She let it go, though, when they spun around together to the sound of rushing water.

The water came from down the feeder access shafts and started to fill up the HAB.

Leo ran down the steps. "I'm out of here!"

Brake shouted for him to stop, moving to intercept him, But Thana held him fast. Maybe the refinery boss thought he could outrun the rising water and make it through the energy barrier in time.

The wave caught Leo's heels as soon as he hit the floor, and he spilled forward. The silibiote-controlled tide washed over his immense body like the oceans of Earth once washed over a sand castle. Apparently, none of the silicates inside wanted him, and his body blackened in the frigid waters before crumpling away.

The silibiotes approached the mezzanine overhang and looked very angry, as a whole. Sophibiote moaned, but at a lower volume than before. "Mmmm. Mmmm. Nnnnah. Nnnnah."

Thana, who had the energy weapon poised and ready to shoot, looked out of the corner of her eye at Brake.

He motioned for her to lower it. When she did, Brake noticed the "temperature" in the room dropped.

"Naaah. Naaaht. Mmmd. Naaaah mmdr."

"What?" Brake asked.

"Naaht muddrar. Naht muddarar."

Brake dropped to his haunches, staring down at Sophibiote through the guardrail. "Not murder?"

Sophibiote nodded. "Naht mmeen to muddar."

"What was that, then?" Thana pointed at the rapidly dissolving body of Leo.

"Iddddeeaatt."

Brake looked at Thana. "She's not wrong."

"Waaytt ffer ttyymm."

Thana asked, "Wait for what time?"

Sophibiote addressed her. "Ttym auf ttelleeng."

"Time of telling? Telling what?"

The water stopped rising, and one by one, the other silibiotes stepped up beside Sophibiote; each speaking in turn.

"Telleeng arrr ttayl."

"Telliing oor tayl."

"Telling our tayle."

Sophibiote said, in nearly clear English, "T-telling our tale. H-how we lived. How w-we died. Are...Our m-memories. W-we were never m-meant to bond with y-your species, b-but our own." She bowed her head. "Your re-refin-ary. Eras-sing our history."

And over the next several hours, and for years to come, the silibiote ghosts told humanity the tale of how they were not alone in the universe.

One Year Later

Thana slid up along Brake's body until her head poked out from the sheets.

"Okay, so that was *still* not part of the services the C.C. Rangers provide," she said with a grin. "But, consider it a special bonus for saving Europa Station A."

Brake pulled her into his arms, kissing her forehead. "As a bonus, I'll need to report this on my taxes." When Thana scowled at him, he scrambled, "Wait, let me rephrase—"

"Too late," she said, making to get out of bed. "That was disresp—"

He pulled her back to him, both of them giggling. "I'll choose my words more carefully in the future."

Thana snuggled in. "Well, you do have a way with words."

"And with dead people, apparently."

She nodded. "It's disappointing that they can only merge with living humans. I'm sure there are some families who would take even a bonded loved one, even if they have to share memories."

"Yeah, I couldn't get the reanimated dead to do more than moan. After conferring with some actual xenobiologists, who were overly excited to have actual data—and not just theoretical data to work from after all these centuries—they suggested that the Zicrei need living cells to bond with to access both genetic memories."

"Which is what their species does."

"Well, when they merge with their own kind, it's a nonlethal process. Like accessing stored data, the Zicrei can link with their dead, ask questions of the possessed, and then disconnect like a vidstream. With us, it's permanent." He shrugged. "A shame really. Maybe we can someday leave genetic recordings of our lives the way the Zicrei can."

"It's baffled me how many people are willing to sign up for your bonding project." Thana wiggled in a way that let Brake know it was his turn now.

Brake began kissing her neck while talking. "Elderly, mostly." Kiss. "And some terminal patients who figure, 'why not?'" Kiss.

She purred. "You never did tell me how you figured out the silicates were actually cells of an alien race."

"Well..." Brake stopped for the moment to answer. He smirked, thinking himself quite clever. "They often say that a medical examiner is a speaker for the dead. That we tell the last story of a person's life."

"Yes?" Thana looked over to him impatiently, wanting him to continue where he left off, but then sighed resignedly because *she* had asked the question.

"Well, something didn't make sense. If Leo hadn't reported the Locker's secret to headquarters, how had they known I was needed here?"

Thana got up to an elbow. "What do you mean? They hired you because of the increase in colonists coming to the station."

He shook his head. "I don't think so. The timing is suspect. Leo discovers reanimated corpses, and then I'm hired almost immediately after? And you, their best and brightest, getting transferred here? That's too much of a coincidence. I think something greater is at play."

"I like the 'best and brightest' part." She poked his chest. "But, pray, continue."

"Well, we know now that Europa's north pole is near the aliens' burial ground, or more accurately, their memory repository."

The Zicrei dead existed nowhere else on the planet, which is why the Corp was able to plan on moving Station A and resuming production. The area around the Locker would be left as a protected habitat.

"Okay?" Thana still wasn't following him yet, he could tell.

"Why did they pick the North Pole and not the south? Why bring in an ME when the onsite medical staff could essentially do the same thing? Why bring in a known loyalist instead of just letting the compromised Rangers continue covering up for Leo?

And why time it so that all these things would happen during Jupiter's summer?

"And the biggest question of all: Where are the rest of the Zicrei? Who abandons such a repository of knowledge?"

"They could have died out?" Thana suggested.

But Brake shook his head. "I think they're closer than we suspect."

Thana furrowed her brow. "You're not suggesting..."

Brake looked over to where Thana's pile of clothing lay.

"Is your beret turned off?"

She giggled and nodded.

Brake shrugged. "I'm not saying that the Coca-Cola Corporation is run by aliens, and they knew that Europa was a graveyard *and* wanted to see what would happen if alien DNA merged with our own to form a new species. I'm not saying that. I'm just saying that it's just a theory."

When Thana snuggled back in, she said, "Well, your theories do tend to pan out."

"What can I say? Sometimes you catch a lucky Brake."

And that's when she punched him.

The End

RIDERS OF THE ENDLESS VOID

Cat Rambo & J.R. Martin

Usami sucked sweetened red wheat paste from the tube as she watched newcomers stream through the *Capitola*'s arrival lanes. She kept her distance. Weeks cramped on board a passenger ship, where water had to be saved for drinking, gave travelers what the locals called the "new settler" smell. Best to let them air out a bit.

The new settlers would focus on arranging quarters and making sure their funds transferred to the accounts here aboard the ancient generation ship the original settlers had cannibalized to create a makeshift home.

Usami glanced at the datapad containing the job request. She could do the job herself, but Uncle Leone shot that idea down as soon as he'd heard it. Get an experienced pilot, not a child, he'd said scornfully. But how long could they wait? As she slurped down the last bit of red paste, she studied the faces streaming past. None of them looked like pilots.

The lanes cleared. Usami hopped on her leviboard and slipped through the remaining people. Kids gasped as she eased by, and she heard one begging their parents for a board. She laughed, circled a trash can to toss her paste tube, then glided toward the recruitment office.

The lines here remained empty. People had given up on posting new jobs months ago, when the accidents began. Uncle Leone had told Usami and her mother that people stopped applying for work as the accidents grew worse, and leaving jobs posted on the board cost too much when the wait stretched into weeks.

121

Usami hopped off the board, kicked down, and flipped it into a waiting hand. The normally cramped office felt uninviting without the noise and warmth the job seekers had once brought to it. She stepped to the clerk and dropped her datapad down.

"How's it going, Emee?"

Emee clicked her tongue. When she exhaled, Usami smelled cotton candy and mint.

"It's going fine, Usami. Obviously." She motioned to the empty room.

"I know, I know. Have y'all come down on those fees yet? My uncle thinks it'll help get business going again."

Emee rolled her eyes. "I'm already going to the poor house 'cause of the accidents. Your uncle wants me to get there faster."

Usami sighed. "Anyone looking for work?"

Emee clicked her tongue again. "Do you even have to ask?"

"Well, we need a pilot." Usami held up the datapad.

"Good luck finding one."

A chime sounded as the door to the office slid open.

The man who entered wore a standard travel-issue jumpsuit, but something about the way he held himself made Usami pause. Pilots walked with that kind of swagger.

He was also augmented, his sleeve rolled up to reveal a forearm inset with controls and a datascreen, while the silver beads of input jacks gleamed on his temples. As he crossed the room, Usami could see the spacer's roll to his steps, the easy movements of someone used to coping with a wide range of gravities.

His voice was low, edged with sleepless gravel. "Sorry to interrupt. I was told I might have some luck finding work here. Wanted to come before the rush."

"You a pilot?" Usami asked.

The man glanced between the two. "I am."

"How can I—" Emee began.

Usami interrupted. "Emee, those fees come down yet? Didn't think so." Usami handed her datapad to the man. "I got a job if you're interested. What's your name?"

"Gem." He took the pad, but studied Usami's face rather than the data. "Aren't you a little young to need a pilot?"

"I'm fourteen. Can you fly the ship on the pad?"

He didn't bother to look. "If it has thrusters, I can make it move."

"You're hired. Emee, lower those fees. Follow me, Mr. Gem."

Gem nodded. "Just Gem is fine."

Emee clicked her tongue twice. "You tell your uncle, since your daddy is gone, someone's gonna have to get things under control soon. Or ain't no reason any of us came here, trying to make new lives."

"I'll let him know."

Usami let Gem keep the datapad as she walked toward the exit. As they stepped out of the office, leaving Emee's scowl behind, she realized he didn't have that new settler smell. The man's scent seemed more like new circuits and chemicals. Not pleasant, but aggressively neutral as scents went.

"Long flight, stranger?" Usami asked.

"Yeah, but my ship handled it while I slept in stasis," Gem said.

Usami raised an eyebrow. "Your ship handled it?"

Gem nodded.

Usami waited, but he remained silent.

"How can a ship navigate star systems while the pilot is in stasis?" Usami asked. "That goes against protocols."

"Ini is an advanced AI. He..." Gem frowned and looked at his arm. "He told me to shut up."

Usami's eyes went wide. "Your ship talks to you?"

Gem pointed at the pad. "Yeah."

He went silent and refused to speak again.

Around them, people swarmed the ship's barracks section, searching for their new residences. During the initial exploration of the *Capitola*, Usami's father and uncle had discovered over ten decks filled with crew quarters forward and aft on the capital ship. Thousands came to the *Capitola* each year and, in the five years since the original settlers had arrived, they'd only managed to fill three decks.

Every section had its own flavor, a mélange of colors and smells and sounds created by the mingled remnants of humanity, the refugees and veterans of the Void Wars or others from planets devasted by the ravages of the corporations that had plundered their resources. This section, established by Usami's father almost six years ago, had corridor walls painted with the saying of Khons, handprints along the edges of each mural showing where those praying had touched the border in tribute.

"Do you have quarters yet?" Usami asked.

"Nah, I went straight to the job office as soon as I got in."

Usami took the datapad from Gem and pulled up the job. "It's your lucky day. Previous pilot's quarters are available."

"That's appreciated. Are they far from a hangar?" Gem asked.

"They're only for work ships, normally. I'll check with my uncle about giving your ship access. But, yes, your quarters will be near the hangars."

Gem nodded. "Thanks for that."

They arrived at the old pilot's quarters. Usami keyed in a code on the datapad and waved it over the door's keypad. It slid open, and they stepped inside.

The previous occupant's belongings still littered the apartment. Clothes lay on the couch midway through folding. A cup with the dregs of sour blue liquid sat on the table. Each breath filled Usami's lungs with stale and scentless air.

"No one's been here for a while. Whose place is this?" Gem asked.

"Guy whose job you're taking. He took off in a hurry. It's why I could get you accommodations so quickly."

"Why'd he leave without packing?"

Usami sucked her teeth. "You gonna run if I tell you?"

Gem shook his head.

"Cetus and his attack drone, Carina, ran him off."

Gem raised an eyebrow.

"Cetus thinks he should run this place. My uncle Leone and father thought different. Especially after Cetus tried to claim *Capitola* and the debris field for himself. My father caught him and made sure he could never sit on the council."

"Interesting. But why run off the pilot?" Gem pressed.

"Good pilots help us salvage the ships in the graveyard. Without the pilots for the cutters, we can't get in. Most pilots are having trouble staying spaceworthy. The guy here seemed to have a sixth sense to avoid the accidents."

"You don't think they're accidents?"

"Everyone knows they aren't. My uncle thinks it's Cetus. The accidents started after he hired Carina."

"Why Cetus?"

"Because he's got the cash and backers now to pay for our claim, if we can't pay our taxes. No cutters, no taxes."

Gem nodded.

Usami rolled her eyes at his lack of verbal communication. "Consider this place a bonus for hazard pay."

Gem nodded again. Usami couldn't read the man. He continued to study the apartment.

"Please don't run." Usami covered her mouth, shocked she'd spoken out loud.

Gem stole a glance at Usami. "Never that."

They shared a smile.

"We're down the corridor a ways. Come by for dinner. My uncle will be there, and you can talk to him. The black door."

"Still mourning?"

"Nah, mourning time is over. We just haven't had time to strip the black off."

Gem nodded. "It's nice to see you folks keep the old customs here. See you there."

"Don't forget to enter your new key code."

Usami headed home to let her mother know there'd be one more for dinner.

"Time is relative. The hours, days, and years we measured our lives against were in reverence of Sol. Now, time is malleable as millennia separate us. Khons forever guides our journeys as Sol shall forever be our origin. If they know Khons, and are of Sol, then they shall forever be our family. Blessed be they. Amen."

"Amen," Usami and Leone said in unison, unfolding their hands.

"Beautiful prayer, Lyra," Leone said.

"Thanks, Leone. I wish we'd waited for the new pilot."

"I figured he'd have been here by now. It's hard to miss the door," Usami said.

She reached for a roll as Leone took thin protein strips from another plate. A yeasty aroma burst from the roll as she split it open, and her mouth watered in anticipation. Usami grabbed some strips to stuff in the roll, splashing it with spice oil before taking a bite.

Someone scratched at the front door. Usami stared at Leone, who eyed the door with a raised eyebrow. Lyra glanced between the two as the scratching intensified. Some new scheme of Cetus's to intimidate them? Her stomach twisted with tension, and she was unable to swallow.

Leone stood, pulling his plasma blade from its sheath. Usami and Lyra followed.

When Leone flipped the outside view screen on, Usami saw Gem scraping at the door and frame, methodically removing the mourning coat applied there.

"Uncle Leone, it's okay. That's the new pilot, Gem."

Lyra stared at the man stripping the coating's layers from the door. "He's handsome, isn't he?"

Leone cut his eyes at Lyra.

Lyra stared him down. "I said what I said."

He slid the cutter back into its sheath and opened the door.

Curls of black paint furred the flooring near the door. Gem's face was moist with sweat as he mopped at it and gave Usami a quick smile where she stood with the first bite still in her mouth.

"Hey, Gem, I'm Leone. Nice to meet you." Leone extended a hand to Gem.

He shook it once, then got back to scraping.

"What are you doing?" Leone asked.

"Usami said that the mourning had passed. The final journey can't be made if the traveler thinks his family still misses him. I want to help your brother along his way."

Leone's mouth opened, then closed. Lyra and Usami nodded their approval.

"I guess I've been slacking on my brotherly duties over the past year." Leone chuckled. He grabbed a grinder and started removing the coating from around the door as Gem continued scraping the entryway.

Usami waved the door closed and took a seat on the corridor bench outside it with her mother as the two men worked. The nausea she'd felt earlier disappeared, and she continued eating her sandwich.

Leone's shirt became soaked with sweat, and he took it off. Lyra slapped her daughter's leg as Gem did the same. The mechanisms set into his arm gleamed metallically, but the rest of him was quite human. Usami rolled her eyes at her mother, but noticed the chiseled body and wondered why a pilot needed to be so fit.

After an hour the two men had finished stripping the mourning coat from the entrance. Usami stood and rubbed her fingers along the door and walls surrounding her home. She buried her face in her mother's chest. Lyra pulled Usami closer, stroking her head as heavy sobs shook the young woman's body.

"It's fine, Usami. Khons is flying with your father on the final journey."

Leone slapped Gem on the back. "Thanks for reminding me of my duties. My brother can fly free now."

"No worries," Gem said.

Leone stared at the man, waiting for more, then laughed when nothing came. "Usami wasn't lying when she said you were a man of few words."

Usami listened to Lyra sing her father to rest, the sweet voice rising up in the final act of mourning. Usami knew Lyra missed her husband as much as Usami did. So far she'd politely refused any of those who'd thought they might replace him, holding her grief close. Her eyes were closed now as she sang.

> *Riders of the endless void,*
> *Khons has led us home.*
> *Our journey through the timeless night,*
> *No more shall we roam.*
> *But you are called to move along,*
> *And we speed you on your way,*
> *You follow Khons and wander on,*
> *We'll follow you one day.*

The gathered crowd clapped and cheered.

"Thank you all for bearing witness. We are honored you were here with us as the mourning ended," Leone said.

The cheers grew louder.

Another hour passed before the crowd began to shrink. Usami hugged the neighbors and thanked them for being there as Lyra and Leone walked around shaking hands and sharing stories. Gem stood off to the side watching the people and studying his forearm datapad. Usami walked over to him, distancing herself from the emotions she felt near the crowd.

"Thanks for doing that, Gem," Usami said.

"No worries. Ini thought it would be a good idea."

"Your ship?" Usami raised an eyebrow.

"Yeah, he's always listening. Aren't you, Ini?" He spoke to the datapad.

"Of course. What else is there for a lowly, sophisticated AI such as myself to do? I can't very well come inside, now can I? I live vicariously through you. Which is difficult with your personality—or lack thereof," a voice replied from it.

Gem frowned, and Usami snorted with laughter.

"See, Gem? I've made the girl laugh in less than a minute. You spent an hour thinking about jokes to break the ice."

Gem's eyes went wide with shock. "You promised."

Usami roared with laughter at Gem's embarrassment. She laughed so hard she had to sit down on the bench. Her legs kicked out as she rocked back.

"Ini, I'm going to dismantle you and sell you like cheap scrap," Gem said.

Usami wiped the tears from her eyes. "Thanks, you two. I needed that."

A silvery face took shape on the datapad. "Any time, dear. I know your father's loss is deeply painful. We're both glad we could help your family in some small way. Thanks for giving my partner here a job."

Gem's head dipped down. "He's right."

Usami and Gem bumped fists.

"I do all the work, and this lout gets all the love," Ini lamented.

"I'd hug you if I could, Ini."

The face on the datapad smiled.

Lyra strolled over. "Thank you again, Gem. Looks like you two are having fun. I hope we can all get to know each other better."

"Yes, ma'am. Let me get washed up. Is dinner still available?"

"It is. You can clean up in our place. We have some towels you can use. Why don't you head on in with Leone?" Lyra said.

"Yes, ma'am." Gem followed Leone, who'd just stepped inside.

"*Mama*," Usami pleaded.

"It's been over a year, and a lady has eyes. Now get inside, and let's finish dinner with our guest."

Usami laughed and followed her mother.

From afar, the debris field marking the ship graveyard looked like a murky cloud. Over the past two months Gem had approached the cloud from different routes every few days. As Ini neared, the ship's lights reached out, glittering swathes made from metal bits and glass tilting to catch the light and return it. Usami released the breath she hadn't realized she'd been holding.

Gem glanced back at her, half-smiling. "Still don't trust my flying?"

She shook her head.

Leone frowned. "Stay focused," he said softly.

They approached the ship that was their target. An old Cooper-Stevens XR, its heavy armor plating would be good salvage, relatively easy to cut loose from the wreck.

"I'll strip the pilot chamber electronics," Usami said.

Leone nodded. While she did that, he and Gem would start tethering pieces and using the plasma cutter to sever the plating connectors.

The ship's system pinged. "Incoming ship."

"What?" Leone said, startled. "I've filed the paperwork on this section. No one else should be here."

"The signal is from the *Raptor*."

Carina's ship. Of course.

Usami took a deep breath. The air inside Ini smelled like Gem, the same neutral smell of circuits and chemicals, rather than rank human sweat.

"Open up a channel," Gem said.

Carina didn't even bother with pleasantries. Said, "Left you a present, Leone." Her voice was low and mean, even over the comm channel. "Call it a goodbye gift. Because you and yours need to say goodbye and move along."

"Not going to happen!" Usami yelled before Leone could reply.

"In that case..." There was a click as Carina cut comms.

"They're powering up!" Leone said, staring at the screen.

Gem slid into the pilot's chair faster than Usami had ever seen anyone move. "Turn that plasma cutter on," he snapped.

"What? You can't use that as a weapon..." Leone began, but Usami was already swinging into place at the cutter's controls.

"Can't use it as a weapon," Gem said, fingers flying over the controls, "but I can use it to turn something else into a weapon. That drone started the fight cold, and it's going to take a good three minutes to get its systems ready."

He was feeding numbers to Usami as quickly as she could enter them, so fast she could barely keep up.

Leone was watching the monitor. "Carina's at half power now," he said.

"Execute!" Gem said.

Usami slammed her finger down on the execute button, and the cutter began firing according to the calculations, each time hitting one of the wrecks around them, stirring them into motion. It was impossible to have calculated that on the fly, Usami thought. How had he accomplished it?

"Three-quarters power," Leone said.

Gem's voice was as calm as though Leone had said it was time for dinner. "One more wave of shots, Usami."

Just as she hit the last one, and the plasma cutter's blue bolt flashed out one final time, Leone said, "She's firing!"

Red light struck out from Carina's ship. Every time it fired, somehow, impossibly, one of the revolving bits of debris was in front of it, reflecting it, and then a bolt even doubled back to strike the attacker.

Usami wanted to shout victory, but she saw Leone staring at Gem, wide-eyed. "How did you do that?"

Gem pushed himself up from the chair.

"Just lucky, I guess." His eyes met Leone's in challenge. Something hovered in the air, unspoken. Leone was the first to look away.

"If you did that, could have hit her directly," Leone muttered. "Instead you just tapped her enough to drive her away."

"And that was enough," Gem said.

All the way home, Leone was silent.

There, Usami told Lyra in great detail what had happened, trying to convey the sheer wonder of the precision of those shots. Leone stayed silent, and Gem was modest, shaking his head and changing the subject when Lyra tried to thank him. In the end, she simply leaned down to kiss him, saying once more, "Thank you," and getting a mumbled, "Wasn't an issue" in reply.

But late that night, Usami got up to get a glass of water and heard Leone and Gem talking.

"I know you're a man of war," Leone said. "Here. We're celebrating." From where she stood in the hallway, holding her breath and listening, Usami heard the gurgle as Leone poured something. There was a clink as the two men touched cups.

"Celebrating?" Gem said, letting the word trail off in question. "Celebrating what?"

Leone cleared his throat. "You stood up to them. Reminded us that it's . . . well, that it's possible to stand up. I've been talking to the other salvagers. We're going to stand together. Won't be run off."

There was the soft slap of him clapping Gem on the shoulder. "Night."

Usami shrank back into the shadows as Leone exited. She was about to turn to go, when she heard Gem murmur something. Was he talking to her? She paused.

"I don't know, Ini," he said.

She breathed out silent relief. Talking to his ship. She did turn to go but couldn't avoid hearing his last words, "I thought we'd left all that behind. I said I wouldn't kill again."

Usami stared across the launchway as Ini sat in a refitting bay. Over the past three weeks, crews had removed the plasma cutter and reinstalled Ini's original weapons. Everything about the custom ship screamed murder as Usami watched the refitting team make their final checks.

It wasn't what Gem would have chosen, she knew. Her eyes were hot with unshed tears as she saw him moving toward Ini, his steps slow and reluctant.

"Where's that pilot of yours, little girl?" Usami turned as Carina spoke.

"Doesn't matter, does it? And you better not touch me, there are witnesses here."

Carina grabbed Usami by the shoulder. "Little girl, let me be clear. If your uncle doesn't give Cetus the rights to this capital ship, and all the salvage rights, then I can't be responsible for what happens next. But I guarantee you'll have nothing."

Carina's increasingly painful grip brought the tears to the girl's eyes till they spilled out. She tried to pull away, but the woman's grip held her like a vise.

"Now where's your pilot and that fancy ship of his?" Carina dug her fingers into Usami's shoulder.

Usami slapped Carina across the face. The woman let go in shock.

"You think your hard attitude is gonna help you? You're just Cetus's lapdog, and you're only good for fetching, so go fetch somewhere else."

Carina's face turned red with rage. "Little girl, I don't care who's watching. You're about to feel more pain than you can imagine before they pull me off you."

Carina stepped toward Usami, fist raised. Before she could strike, she tumbled backward.

Lyra stared down at the other woman lying on the ground before her.

"Carina, if you ever in your life think about putting your hands on my daughter again, you won't have much life left to live."

A crowd gathered around the women as Carina stood.

"I'm telling Cetus to quit playing nice with any of you. You're all gonna be dead."

Carina pushed through the crowd and stomped away.

Usami wrapped her arms around her mother. "Mom, that was awesome."

"I can bluff with the best of them, love."

A chuckle ran through the crowd as everyone separated.

"Where are you headed, Usami?"

"I was going to talk to Ini, Gem's ship. It looks like it's being refitted for something dangerous."

"Gem's ship can talk?"

"Yes, ma'am, I'll introduce you."

Usami took Lyra's hand and led the way to Ini. Crews made final checks on the remounted hard points before moving on to the next ship.

"Where's Gem?" Usami asked the passing workers.

"Not sure, but the ship's still open."

Usami and Lyra boarded the ship and walked to the cockpit. Lyra studied the ship as they went.

"This isn't a regular ship. Where was this made?"

"I was made a long time ago, Ms...."

Lyra jumped as the voice spoke from everywhere.

Usami laughed. "Ini, this is my mom, Lyra."

A chime rang throughout the ship as if Ini were laughing.

"*The* Lyra. I've heard good things about you. I see why Gem has been smitten."

Lyra blushed. "Oh really? What did he say?"

"I'm not at liberty to repeat those words, but I will say all of them were good."

Usami snorted. "Ini, don't tease her."

"I'm not teasing."

Usami rolled her eyes at the smile on Lyra's face. "Ini, what's going on? Why'd they mount your original weapons?"

A sound similar to a human sigh passed though the ship. "I'd prefer not to say, Usami."

"Ini, please."

The mechanical sigh passed through the ship again. "This Carina woman, she's dangerous. We've seen her type before. She won't stop until she's stopped."

"Stopped how?" Lyra asked.

A voice spoke up from behind them. "With the only thing our type really understands: force."

The two spun around to find Gem standing in the doorway to the cockpit.

"Here's the deal: I've asked around to where the ships are Cetus uses. After working a few guys over in the bar I found out where they're keeping them. Luckily, it's not too far. It's where Cetus is holed up."

"What are you doing?" Lyra pressed.

"They'll ride with Khons on the endless void. They can figure out the toll once they arrive."

Lyra reached for Gem's hand, then stopped. He stepped up and grabbed her hand, interlocking their fingers together. Lyra blushed and turned away.

Gem gently turned her face back to him. "Look after Usami. Let Leone know so he can be prepared if this goes nova."

"Of course."

Gem leaned in and kissed Lyra.

"Usami, watch your mother. Keep her safe."

"Yes, sir."

"Ready, Ini?"

"I'm never really ready for this, Gem."

"Ladies." Gem pointed to the exit.

Lyra squeezed Gem's hand before exiting the ship. Usami followed.

Ships leaving for the day lined the launchway, and the two had to walk all the way around to leave the area safely. Usami sucked her teeth.

"Mom, I forgot to give Gem a hug. Can I go back and do that?"

"Sure, he could use our support. I'll meet you back at home."

Usami kissed Lyra on the cheek, then ran back to Ini. She peered through the door. Gem studied star charts while talking with Ini. As they spoke, Usami slipped through the door and back into a storage closet, where she sat on the floor and waited for takeoff.

"Ini, keep the throttle down and drop a mag-mine array."

"Gem, I'm noticing odd signals..."

"Ini, shut up and do your job." Gem's voice was harsh. How much did he hate this? Usami wondered. How much had it cost him to go back to being a soldier?

"Gem, I must report—"

Gem cut the ship off again. "I. Don't. Care. Let's get this job done."

Usami crept out of the closet and made her way toward the cockpit in silence.

Gem punched in calculations at a terminal as the ship charged toward Carina's base. Usami wanted to know about the mag mines, but decided against revealing herself. Red dots blipped onto a screen behind Gem, then faded away. In their place, yellow lights began flashing.

Usami studied the dark mass through a porthole as they circled it. No light reflected from its surface, and she only knew it was there because it blocked the stars on the other side. As she watched she saw a flash from the inky blackness surrounding the station. It burst out two more times, changing direction with each movement and lighting the side of the station briefly. Usami's eyes went wide when she realized what the lights were.

"Gem, a ship just fired maneuvering thrusters to get behind Ini!" Usami ran to the cockpit as she yelled.

Gem whirled in shock. "Usami, what the heck are you doing...?"

"Gem, you may plan on suicide, but we're not letting her die. There's a target lock on us. Taking evasive actions," Ini snapped.

The g-forces threw Usami against the opposite wall as Ini made a hard turn at full throttle. Gem unstrapped himself and ran to Usami to help her up as Ini straightened the ship. He dragged her to a seat and strapped the young girl in. Usami's head rolled as she tried to regain focus.

"Ship. Behind us," she stuttered.

"I know. We'll talk about why you're on board *this* ship once we get home."

"Indeed, young lady. A firefight is no place for a civilian."

Usami gave a shaky double thumbs-up as Ini made another sharp turn. The ship's hull rattled as explosions detonated nearby. Ini made two more sharp turns as Gem's hands flew over the console.

"That ship is dark to radar, but I see others exiting the base."

Usami stared at Gem, who hadn't strapped himself back into the seat but easily handled every maneuver Ini made. The man stood as Ini made another sharp turn and went over to the comms panel and pressed a few buttons.

"You have two minutes to stand down. If you don't, you'll all be next week's salvage," he said into the comm.

Silence filled the cabin.

"Crap, I hoped she'd be piloting the dark ship. Ini, you've led them long enough. Let's make this three dimensional."

A rumbling tone sounded over the internal speakers.

"Is Ini laughing?" Usami asked as her head cleared.

Gem stared at the girl as if surprised to see her. "You could say that. Usami, you knew what I was coming out here to do. Why'd you hop on board?"

"I felt like if I didn't, something bad would happen."

He stared at her. She stared back. Then he nodded, almost imperceptibly. "It might have," he said. "I guess it was good you were here."

Usami's stomach lurched as the bottom seemed to drop from under her. She and Gem floated as Ini changed direction. She felt the ship twist as it began a flip end over end. Gem punched a console, and the screen blew up into a holographic display.

"Light it up."

Ini's hard points moved to fire as the ship continued to shift. The sharp staccatos from the turret's barrage echoed throughout the ship, deafening Usami and reverberating through her bones.

Explosions from the initial volley flashed with each hit on the opposing craft. The dark ship disengaged and pulled away.

"You're losing your touch, Ini. I thought you'd take her out for sure."

"That ship has moves. It'll be a shame to scuttle it."

"Shouldn't it have picked up the target lock like we did?" Usami asked.

"Remember the calculations I made before? Ini and I can do

that in our heads. We don't normally turn the targeting laser on. It's there if needed."

The flashing yellow lights began turning green as the ships leaving the base passed through them.

Gem waved a hand, and the green lights replaced the previous view.

"The mag mines have cameras. Can we use those to find some way to see that ship?" Gem asked.

Usami shrugged right before Ini spoke. "I don't think so. We need her to respond to your comms call so I can get a lock through that channel."

"Fine, then. Detonate and let's see what happens." Gem flipped the comms panel button again to broadcast his next words. "You were warned."

One by one the green lights erupted, sending flashes like a distant nova burst popping all over the screen. The ships collided together as they scrambled to figure out what was happening.

Usami stared at the views, eyes wide.

"Mag mines only turn on once they make contact with a ship's hull. We remote detonated them instead of setting the timer."

Usami nodded at the explanation.

"I saw the dark ship flash into view a few times, but it's dark again. Calculating all intercept vectors based on last known positions."

"I'll take over the piloting while you do."

Gem sat down as three remaining ships flew toward them to attack. Gem's fingers ran across the console and Ini's movements became more erratic. Usami heard a ringing sound as munitions fired from the other ships hit and bounced off the hull.

"Really, Carina must have kept the good rounds for herself."

A target lock indicator came on, and Gem cursed.

"Ini, looks like she beat you. Brace for impact."

Usami's straining stomach emptied itself as Ini lurched end over end after the impact. When the spinning stopped, Gem lay on the floorboards. Usami unbuckled herself as alarms sounded. She found blood on the console Gem had sat at before she noticed the gash on his head. He pushed himself up slowly, and Usami moved to help him.

"Looks like those other three ships are coming back, Gem," Ini said.

Gem accepted Usami's help with a nod as he sat back in the chair. "I got them, find Carina. She's smarter than I thought she'd be."

Gem's fingers flew across the console.

Ini made a sharp turn and flipped to face the three ships coming toward them. Gem fired thrusters and flew at the lead ship. Usami stared as the two ships came within two hundred meters of crashing.

The lead ship veered off, and Gem's fingers danced across the console, causing Ini to strafe the lead ship. The turrets let loose on the other ship's broadside.

The target lock indicator flashed again.

"Not this time." Gem engaged full burn toward one of the two remaining ships while deploying countermeasures. As the ship veered, Usami saw it heading into the remaining flashing yellow lights. Two turned green as the ship made contact.

"It's only a hundred meters out, Gem!" Usami screamed.

"Stay calm, Usami," Gem said.

Gem passed Ini below the other ship, narrowly avoiding a collision. He did a hard burn on the other side, putting distance between the two ships as fast as possible. The screen showed the missile beginning to pass under the ship. Gem detonated the mines.

The screen turned into a bright white light as the mines detonated the missile.

"Only one scrub and Carina left," Gem said.

Usami pointed at the screen. "Looks like the scrub is taking off."

Gem followed her finger with his eyes. Where she pointed the remaining ship had begun turning toward the capital ship.

"When he gets to the *Capitola*, he'll have a lot of explaining..."

Before Usami finished the sentence, the ship burst apart as another missile cracked it like an egg.

"We've got to find her," Gem growled, "Any luck, Ini?"

"None. I didn't think she'd shoot down her own men." Ini's voice sounded flat to Usami's ears.

"I have an idea. Can I use your comms?" Usami asked.

"Sure," Gem said.

Usami flipped the comm switch and licked her lips. "Hey, lapdog, looks like we took out all your buddies. How about you run back to your daddy Cetus with your tail between your legs? How do you think a stray like you will be punished?"

Gem's mouth hung open as Usami turned to him smiling.

A crackle came across the comms, followed by an enraged voice screaming at Usami. "Little girl, you're about to get what's coming to you! How dare you slap me? This is going to be so sweet when I tell your brave mommy that her daughter was killed on that ship. I can't wait to see her tears. Your uncle will—"

The comms went down.

"Ini, did you tag it?" Gem asked.

"You know it. Let's go hunting." Usami thought she heard a smile in the ship's voice.

A crackle came across the comms again. This time it was a man's voice. "Usami, this is Cetus. I'm going to call your uncle and mother now. I wonder if they'll sign over the deeds knowing I have you here."

Usami glanced at Gem. He switched the view, and she saw Carina's ship creeping up behind them. Gem smiled.

"Cetus, you *sound* as greasy as I remember you *looking*. Just remember, your mourning coat will remain forever, and you'll never make the final journey."

"Why, you rude little—"

Ini cut comms and pulled Gem's strafing maneuver. Without acquiring a target lock, the turrets and missiles launched toward Carina's ship. The screen went white one last time as the dark ship became star stuff.

Usami rushed toward Gem and wrapped her arms around the man, nearly knocking him over.

Gem laughed and squeezing her gently. "He's right, you were being rude."

Usami pulled away, grinning. "Maybe somebody can teach me better?"

Gem sucked his teeth. "Maybe someone could stick around and do that."

Usami nodded. "You shoulda seen Mom earlier when she stared Carina down. I guess I've still got some things to learn from her."

Gem tousled Usami's hair. "Guess I'll stick around to see that, too."

The End

SEEDS

Patrick Swenson

In the year 2049, Rosenquist left Earth with his girlfriend, Maggie, and cast through *the flicker* to the Skystone system. It meant giving up almost everything, but he knew they could survive, just like his ancestors did in the 1800s. When Rosenquist's grandparents bequeathed the family farm in Iowa to his dad, they had learned everything on the fly.

Skystone wasn't well known. It had been given a name, because scientists and astronomers gave names to only the brightest stars, like Sirius and Rigel and Vega. This system was so far out that few knew about it, but the flicker decided to cough up some of the first settlers that way through the wormhole, and that's how Skystone came to be, star and planet.

He was nineteen the day he left Earth, a year into college. He came to the door of Maggie's house at three in the morning and knocked softly, his nerves all jangled. They'd decided on this course without their parents knowing.

She showed up at her bedroom window. "That you, Bud?"

"You expecting someone else?"

"Just a minute."

He waited for her while she came down with her bag.

"What if there's no preacher on Skystone?" Maggie asked.

"There will be. Don't you worry."

"We should've done it here."

"No time, Maggie."

They drove to the flicker and showed their authorizations, and the clerks wondered why they were so early.

139

"Just in a hurry to get out of here, is all," Rosenquist said.

For a half hour they walked through the complex hand in hand, passing checkpoints and signing forms. He carried her bag, and she his, because hers was twice as heavy. Those bags contained everything they had—or at least everything they were allowed to *take* to Skystone. They would live off the land, barter for supplies and medicines—whatever they could find—and live a simpler life. His father had seeded farming into his family's blood; Rosenquist vowed to work as hard as possible to find it, even on an alien world.

Fifty-six years later, sickness took Maggie. Late fall of '04, she fell ill. She seemed to recover a few weeks after, but no: she could never quite shake it, and she struggled all winter. A week into March of '05, not willing to let her help with the planting, he returned in the evening from the field and found her wrapped in the ratty quilt she'd brought with her from Earth, her head slumped on her chest, feet still tucked underneath the bottom chair rung.

He didn't remember crying then.

Planting season would be an agonizing effort for just one old man. He'd probably die out here on his own. Other colonists were spread far and wide, and town was a day's ride on the mule—or what passed for a mule on Skystone. But he didn't like socializing, and he limited his contact with the other folks in town. He kept Maggie in his heart, though, and that was enough.

It was spring 2109 now, and Rosenquist stood in the rough patch of cleared land closest to his cabin, early morning, the sun still low in the sky. In the distance, he heard something rattling down the rutted road, but he didn't pay much attention to it.

He always put the garden in early so he'd have a food source he could count on—adding to the last of his winter stores—before tackling the larger fields to cultivate crops such as wheat, corn, and potatoes to stretch the cold months. There were the crops native to Skystone, too, such as aradip and flasp. Flasp was a fairly bland tuber that grew fast and had plenty of vitamins. And damn if his first crop of carrots didn't come out purple. It took some getting used to. All the seeds they planted, even those that originated on Earth, yielded abundant crops, but they all tasted quite bland.

He expended a great deal of his own energy to work the fields. Even this little garden would be an effort, and he sweated just thinking about it. The area had been short of rain the last few weeks; there was just this humid air sitting heavy over his land, and it reminded him of the day Maggie died.

It wasn't at all fair that a simple bend of elbow, knee, or back should create such torment. Tightening his jaw, Rosenquist willed himself to get through this year's planting, no matter how many times he had to stop and rest. When a man couldn't plant his own *garden*, he might as well lay down and die.

Four years earlier, Rosenquist made a makeshift grave for Maggie next to the woods bordering the west end of the fields. He figured no one else would lie in this patch, not even him, unless some passerby found him dead in the cabin, or the field, or halfway to town. Someone, perhaps, might chance upon the other grave on the property and put two and two together. He didn't *expect* to be buried next to his wife. Maybe he should leave a note—his last will and testament. Legal enough around here.

The day Maggie died, Rosenquist did nothing but his chores. He let her sit there in that chair, the quilt still draped over her, but maybe a little more snug because he'd fussed with it some. The next day, she was too much a reminder of his solitude, and an odor had started. It had been humid the last few days and that didn't help matters much.

Under a tree that was a pine, but not quite a pine, he buried her in the shade, amid the pinecones that were not quite pinecones. After, drenched in sweat, holding his hat, he stared at the unmarked mound of dirt, and at this woman who'd been his wife for nearly sixty years. He stood over her, crumpling his sweat-stained hat in his fists, and he whispered "Maggie" once, then again, and said rest in peace and goodbye and turned away. He put on his misshapen hat and faced the cabin in the distance, his face slick with tears, and he was overcome and couldn't move. He waited several minutes before finally leaving the grave behind. He thought: *I've planted you and made you full of growing.* He wasn't sure where that came from, but he thought it might be some Shakespeare he read when in school on Earth.

☆   ☆   ☆

He listened to the rattle coming down the road from town and heard clanking and a horse's whinny and knew a horse-drawn wagon was headed toward the cabin. No one had come down his way for a long time, and he only ventured into town once a month himself, if necessary. He didn't like other people.

He was ready to shoo this nuisance away.

The wagon appeared, and Rosenquist knew right away the man driving it was a salesman. He shook his head at the ill-made wagon. The salesman had probably constructed it with Skystone materials if he'd flickered here from off planet. Funny to think a traveling salesman so far from Earth could have anything Rosenquist needed. He turned over a patch of Skystone's ultra-black soil with his shovel, then thrust the blade into the ground and waited.

The salesman wore a tailored suit and there wasn't a wrinkle in it. He was lean and had a sculpted look to him—very precise—and his thick hair, heavy brows, and sunken face suggested he might not be from Earth. Certainly not from Skystone. He said, "Whoa" to the horse pulling the run-down wagon, took hold of a briefcase by his feet, and stepped down even as Rosenquist waved him away.

"You should get on out of here," he said as he bent over and picked up his hoe that lay nearby. He needed to make progress on his garden, and he didn't want to talk to this guy.

The salesman didn't stop.

"My wife," Rosenquist said. "She's . . . well, she's quite sick, and I doubt you want to be here. Contagion being what it is."

The salesman didn't need to know she'd been dead four years. The thought of disease usually stopped most people inching too close. The man didn't stop, though. He looked up, smiled, and walked past the small shed into the tilled soil of the garden. He tried to walk lightly, deliberate in his movements, as if the soil were covered with manure, which it wasn't, but soon would be.

"Sorry to hear that," the salesman said. "Is it plague?"

He meant a nasty Skystone virus that laid people low for weeks and forced a monthlong recovery—if they didn't die first from extended bouts of fever. "No, not plague."

"Flicker sickness, then. It happens, poor souls."

He was a young man looked fresh from schooling, dressed in his suit, those heavy eyebrows nearly obscuring brown laughing

eyes. He looked far too put together for this line of work, put-
tering about in his dilapidated wagon.

Rosenquist wiped sweat from his forehead. "It isn't those
things," he said. "Something else took hold of her and won't let
up. You should go. Best not to tarry."

The man held out his hand when he was close enough. He
smiled wide. "Name's Medak. Ted Medak, and I represent Agri-
Corp."

Rosenquist ignored Medak's hand. "Yeah? And what's that?"

Medak shrugged and dropped his hand. "AgriCorp? The
company that sends me to pique the interest of settlers out here
past the flicker. You know. To guarantee you a more comfortable
life. I've flickered in from Palacade, our biggest colony—have you
heard of it?—where the company is based. We've got all the classic tools, of course, right on up to modern luxuries."

"Isn't that illegal? We all leave Earth with what we have and
what we're allowed to leave with and nothing else. How can you
come and offer more?"

"I've a special travel permit granted by Palacade Provincial,
so my trips through the flicker are backed by law."

Rosenquist would have to disappoint him. "I don't have the
capital for anything other than what I've a need for," he said.

"Didn't catch your name?"

"No, you didn't."

"I like to help folks like you out," Medak said. "Perhaps you'll
let me have my say and maybe we can come to an arrangement."

"You're not worried about the sickness?"

"Now, now," Medak said, amused. "You know there's no sickness. Why, a reputable salesman such as myself might get the
idea you were trying to get rid of me. I've got the permit, but
the trips to and from Palacade eat into my profits, and I like to
see things through when I reach a colony. Perhaps I could talk
to your wife in there."

"She's dead. And it *was* illness."

"Ahh." He bowed his head. "Well, again, sorry to hear that.
My condolences."

"Thanks. Now, whatever it is you're selling, I don't want it.
You can just scat."

The salesman looked up and smiled at Rosenquist. "You know,
I had a hard time figuring out who's who in this settlement. No

phones, no directories, no *maps*. And by gods, *you're* a good distance away, aren't you?"

"A bit far, the way I like it."

"Lucky for me someone knew where you were and pointed me in the right direction. To be honest, I wasn't sure where I was going the entire trip out."

Rosenquist sighed, leaned, and put his weight on the hoe handle. He scooted his boot up on the nearby shovel blade planted in the ground. "My name's Rosenquist. Bud Rosenquist."

"Bud. Okay, Bud."

"Well? Give your spiel."

"Mighty kind of you."

"Just be quick about it."

Medak grinned. "Bud, that wagon has a lot of goodies you'd find helpful. Look right over here."

Rosenquist stared at the wagon. "In there?"

"Yes. In the wagon."

"No, I don't think so. If you have something specific, maybe I'll listen."

"Well then, here." Medak dug into his jacket's inside pocket and brought out a brochure. "You an educated man? How long you been here?"

"Long enough, and I can read and I can write from long before Skystone. What is it?"

Medak held out the brochure.

Rosenquist didn't look at it. "Actually, I need to get back to work."

"Just give it a look."

"Perhaps you just explain it."

"All right."

Medak pulled the brochure and slipped it back into the suit pocket. He smiled and said, "I'm here for just the rest of the day, Bud. You're my last run, so give me a listen, and then I'll get out of your hair and on my way back to the flicker."

"With your special permit. Fine. Go on already."

"I mentioned AgriCorp, the company that sponsors my livelihood? Well, they've developed an exciting piece of technology I think you'll be very interested in. Palacade has created a rigorous technology—in accordance with the new statutes, of course—and we're second only to Earth in technological prowess. AgriCorp is *so* confident you'll like their new planting device, they're offering a once-in-a-lifetime challenge."

"Did you say planting device?"

"We'll plant half your garden with our new product, and if you like the results, you can contract with us to buy one."

"I'm not signing any contract."

Medak waved away Rosenquist's distrust. "No, no, you're right. It's an option. Of course. Just an option. You can buy it outright, but the guarantees only come with the contract."

"Yeah, of course they do. Did you say *planting* device?"

Medak smiled. "I *did*."

Rosenquist let go of his hoe, and it thumped into the dirt. He passed his sleeve across his forehead and hitched his coveralls higher on his shoulders. He couldn't imagine anything better than the old-fashioned way and told him so.

"But you haven't even seen it."

"Well then, let me see it."

Medak crouched, placing his briefcase on the ground. He opened it and fished around inside while he spoke. "This beauty is so special it gets top billing in my inventory. A ride in *here*, always close by me. It's basically an automated planting system."

"What do I need that for?"

Medak stood and showed him what looked like a large silver bullet. "We call it a seed." He returned his hand to his inside jacket pocket.

"A seed?" Rosenquist asked. It wasn't like any seed *he'd* ever seen.

Medak had the brochure out again, and he flipped it over to a page that sported a logo and large block letters.

Rosenquist read it out loud, using his finger like a pointer. *SeEDS*, it spelled. "What is that supposed to mean?"

"Self-efficient Embryo Dirt Sower. *Seeds*. Sounds plural when you say it, but the acronym represents a single device."

Rosenquist looked at the card without emotion and took a long look at the silver bullet before shrugging. "So?"

"The future, Bud. You're looking at the *future*."

Rosenquist said nothing, thinking about his future, thinking about Maggie's lost future, and not really caring about Medak's future, which, he reckoned, was Earth's *past*. Probably a cast-off, this contraption: old technology that no one on Skystone had ever seen, no matter how much Medak tried to wow him about Palacade tech. It would likely malfunction the moment Medak flickered back home.

"Maybe you could say something," Medak said.

"I'm not interested."

"That's not what I hoped you'd say. Look, this baby does everything. You program in the dimensions of the garden—"

"How about a field like over in my west forty?"

"—or, yes, the biggest field you've got. Program, start, and away it goes. It burrows to the proper depth and sows the seeds in a perfect line, correctly spaced. Measures soil density, acidity, water content—well, yes, including a unique planet's specifications, such as you have here on Skystone. It even tags the end of the row with a designation of what's been planted. We also have specialized SeEDS available, but those *are* a bit on the costly side. One of them will help you maintain your garden as it grows. No weeding, no fertilizing. Just add water."

Medak laughed at his joke, but Rosenquist bent down to his hoe and retrieved it from the dirt. "I'm still not interested."

The smile on Medak's face lost its good-natured outlook. "Now, now, I understand it's difficult to change, but I assure you—"

"I can plant it myself. This garden. My fields."

"But surely, now, with your missus gone, and you alone out here? You could use the help."

Rosenquist nodded at the wisdom behind this, but he'd already made up his mind he'd finish out his time on Skystone on his own; he owed it to Maggie to see it through. "I've been doing fine."

"At least consider the benefits. Face it, Bud, you're not getting any younger."

"Everyone dies when it's time," Rosenquist said. "Time for everything, season for everything, right? There's a verse about that in the Good Book."

"I'll make a believer out of you, then. Let me show you what SeEDS can do."

"No."

"If you're not interested after my free demonstration, you owe me nothing. You can plant the rest of your garden today by yourself, and you can plant all your fields after that if you're still standing." He winked.

There he is, Rosenquist thought. Standing in the garden with his pressed suit and polished shoes, his SeEDS in one hand, the brochure in the other, looking as if he knows everything there is to know about planting. Pretending he knows what makes things grow on an alien planet other than his own. Rosenquist squinted into Medak's brown eyes, looking for wisdom and finding nothing there, and he was a mite sad that the young man was spending his future this way, wasting his life flickering from one shithole outpost to the next.

"Okay," Rosenquist said.

"Okay?"

"*I* have a challenge."

Medak frowned. "Pardon?"

"We'll divide my garden in half. You plant one side with your silver bullet, and I'll plant the other my way. We'll see which of us makes a garden first."

Medak considered it silently, probably searching for a reason not to accept, thinking there might be a scenario in which he might not win.

"If you win," Rosenquist continued, "I'll pay the price for the thing. No goddamn contract, though. If I win, you just head home and leave me alone."

Medak took more time, and Rosenquist was fine giving it to him. He watched the sky. The sun was higher, but there were clouds now, and in the muggy air everything seemed to curl. There was rain coming. Across the garden, toward the west field, was the tree Maggie was buried under. He could spot that tree from anywhere on his property.

"It's absurd," Medak said. "You wouldn't have a chance. Do you know how fast SeEDS works? Do you have any idea what you're saying? This is modern tech, Bud." He held the silver bullet higher. "This would have my half of the garden planted in under—"

"I want three rows of carrots—*our* purple carrots—two of peas, and one of flasp on your half. Can your gadget do that?"

"Certainly, but—"

"Fine. And by the way—since this is my property, a tie is a win for me. Are we agreed?"

Medak hesitated, as if still struggling to figure him out.

Rosenquist looked at the wash of sky again, the hint of rain out on the horizon. "Tell me, Medak, do you know the story of John Henry?"

Medak straightened and squinted, trying to remember. "Now that's an old one. I think so. Didn't he go against some modern machine that lay railroad tracks?"

"I'm impressed you know that, Medak. The machine could supposedly lay track faster than any ten men."

"No chance for him to win, then."

"He won."

"Got his reward, did he?"

"He died afterward, so I'm not sure I'd call that a reward."

"Oh."

"Died of a broken heart," Rosenquist added, and he thought again of Maggie.

"It's a myth, Bud. A tall tale. It doesn't compare with what you're proposing. Technology is our future, not some old story."

"Not out here past the flicker. Not on Skystone."

His father, back in the days when they lived in Iowa, on the old family farm, taught him that *people* took control, not technology. You couldn't count on anything or anyone but yourself, and maybe your loved ones. When Rosenquist was a kid, if his father was tired, he'd order his son to do those chores, but the things he *really* wanted done he did on his own. *If you want something done right...*

His old man didn't start life as a farmer, but he caught on quick, and one could see knowledge pooled in his eyes when he mended a fence, milked a cow, or planted a field.

"Carrots, peas, and flasp," Rosenquist said. "Six rows. Three, two, and one. I'll plant four rows of green beans, two of lettuce."

Medak nodded, having finally calculated the fine details of the challenge, thinking, no doubt, he had nothing to worry about.

Rosenquist raised an eyebrow. "Deal?"

"Very well. Frankly, Bud, if you win, you can *have* the bullet. It can't lose, so let's do it. Now, how do you want to—"

Rosenquist turned away, and with his hoe, started a furrow to mark the midpoint of the tilled soil. The heat beat down on him as he trailed the hoe behind him; the humidity had soaked his shirt through. He felt his bones creak even with this simple task.

Medak was probably right. Technology took over Earth, apparently had taken hold on Palacade, and maybe it would out here too someday, even though the powers that be had insisted colonists tackle the frontier with very little—unless you had a special travel permit. Maybe modern conveniences were a good thing for most people—maybe it helped more than it harmed—but there were some things technology had no business intruding upon, no matter how wonderful or efficient.

He knew he couldn't beat the SeEDS, not in any way he could think of right now, but he'd give it his all, even if it killed him. He started humming "John Henry" to himself.

I'm a seed-planting man.

When he got to the end of the garden, Rosenquist turned and raised his chin at Medak. "Ready?"

Medak blinked, confused.

"Set, go," Rosenquist said, and started his first row.

"Shit," Medak mumbled, and while Rosenquist hoed, the salesman fumbled in his briefcase, his dress shoes sliding in the dirt.

With a mixture of amusement and curiosity, Rosenquist watched the salesman work, looking up from his hoeing every few minutes. By the time Medak had taken the measurements of his half of the garden, Rosenquist had finished hoeing his first two rows. By the time Medak had programmed his SeEDS, Rosenquist finished his third row, but his back hurt like a son of a bitch. He tried not to let his discomfort show. During the fourth row, Medak put the actual seeds inside the silver bullet and did some more programming.

Rosenquist started his fifth row. Maybe he had a chance after all. That is, if he didn't keel over before then. His heart thudded, his head throbbed. One more row to hoe, plant the seeds, and he was done. What was that saying? Slow and steady wins the race. The Good Book said the race was not to the swift, no favor to men of skill, that time and chance happened to everyone. Something like that.

Rosenquist's fifth row was nearly done, and he panted like a dog in need of water. God almighty, he thought, pressing his free hand to his chest. Just keep going. Keep *going*.

A high-pitched whine made him wince. He clapped one hand to an ear and grimaced, looking up at Medak.

Medak waved the silver SeEDS tauntingly at him, holding the casing between thumb and forefinger. Rosenquist squinted. Medak looked all smug and sure of himself as he placed the

SeEDS on the ground, dug his hand in another suit pocket, and withdrew a device.

"You lost," Medak said, and he punched the device.

The silver bullet screamed. It dove into the soil and disappeared, its high-pitched whine suddenly muffled. Rosenquist followed its progress by the tiny mound of dirt it left behind like a high-speed gopher. He watched, fascinated, as a small plastic tag sprouted at the far end of the row. Then, one row over, another tag, a new trail, and soon after that, a tag at the end of that row, and so on, and so on.

Rosenquist hobbled over and inspected the first white tag.

CARROTS, it read. The carrots pictured on the tag were purple. And in smaller print: AGRICORP SEEDS.

Well, *that* was impressive.

The whine stopped.

When Rosenquist looked back, Medak was holding the silver bullet. *Jesus.* Six rows done, just like that, bordered by twelve tags marking the ends of the rows.

"You haven't even finished hoeing, Bud," Medak said. "Where are your seeds? Why, they're still in their containers over there! You see what I was saying?"

Rosenquist felt his face redden. "You enjoy that, Medak?"

Medak nodded.

"Your hands aren't even dirty. You're not even sweating."

"So?"

"There's nothing to it. Your SeEDS are a toy. A gimmick. It's not natural."

"It's not a toy, and it's *not* a gimmick."

Rosenquist gripped his hoe tighter, and he felt as though he might be having a goddamn heart attack. But he knew what he knew. The joy came from planting the seeds himself, doing it while he was still able. His body ached with the thought of the hard work ahead of him. Someday, he would become ill, and like Maggie, he would die.

"There's no joy in it," Rosenquist said.

"Still," Medak said, "you lost."

"No. I didn't."

Medak stuttered, looked uncomfortable. "But—what do you—of *course* you lost."

Rosenquist shrugged. "I don't think so."

"You *what*?"

"Let me tell you something, Medak."

Rosenquist explained how his father had to quit the farm in Iowa when, sure enough, technology caught up to him, as did his age, and he was asked by folks to move into town and let someone else take care of it. A big company gave him a good price, and as much as his father missed the farm, Bud was happy to spend more time with Maggie, whom he'd started dating his senior year.

His old man did some real estate, and, without fanfare, the town dwindled down to near nothing. The earth swallowed everything up. New life sprouted, but the people flickered away. Rosenquist held on as long as he could with Maggie while attending the state college.

He never forgot that last night on Earth, picking her up at her house, and the two of them taking the endless walk to the complex, ready to leave for good. It didn't matter what happened on Earth anymore. It only mattered that Maggie left it with him and they spend the rest of their lives doing what they wanted amidst the flicker of new beginnings.

"It doesn't matter what you think, Medak," Rosenquist said. "I won, because soil gives and soil takes, and it gives back again, no matter the planet. You can do all the fancy divinations and complicated science you want, but you don't rush life or death. We do things right in Skystone."

"That doesn't explain shit."

"The challenge was, we'd plant our halves and see which one made a garden first."

"My memory's fine, Bud."

Rosenquist turned and motioned toward Medak's side. "I see a bunch of white plastic markers. I don't see carrots, peas, or flasp."

"Well of course not," Medak said, "they have to grow—"

"And they'll grow at the same rate as my green beans and lettuce. I'll finish planting my side here in a little bit—hopefully before this rain starts—then both sides of the garden will grow together."

"That means nothing. That's not a win."

"You're right, it's not. But it's not a win for you, either. We have to call this a draw. A tie. Which means I win, you lose."

Medak's mouth dropped. He stepped toward Rosenquist and

raised a finger to object, but slipped in the loose dirt and landed on his ass on one of the rows of planted seeds.

"Goodbye, Medak."

"Son of a bitch," Medak mumbled as he picked himself off the ground and dusted his hind end.

"Thanks for the demonstration."

"That's not fair. Not fair at all."

Rosenquist returned to his side of the garden and began hoeing again. "Oh, it's fair and square. That's the bet we made, and I think you should hold to it, don't you?"

"I was just trying to bring you some ease," Medak said.

"I'm good. I've got to get back to the garden here."

Medak stood still, the SeEDS in his hand, his face showing some anger. Or disappointment. Rosenquist wasn't sure what that look was.

He focused on his row, letting the hoe divide the soil carefully and at its own speed. He hoped Medak would go away, that he wouldn't try to stick him with a bill for the SeEDS.

After a while, Rosenquist looked up and saw Medak had retreated to his wagon. The salesman hoisted himself up and, with a last look at Rosenquist, clucked the horse and maneuvered his way back to the rutted road. The wagon screeched and clattered and set off toward town.

Rosenquist stopped, leaned on his hoe, and watched until the salesman disappeared over a small hill. He looked toward the horizon and saw the rain sheeted over there and knew he better hurry with the rest of the garden. It was all he'd get done today, what with the storm coming.

He looked over at the other half of the garden. A black bird—a crow that wasn't quite a crow—was hopping aimlessly along the first row, searching for seeds.

"Bird, shoo now," he said, walking as fast as he could toward it. It squawked and flew away.

Shining in the dirt where the bird had been was the silver bullet. Rosenquist had forgotten that part of the bet. Medak had left it, as promised. He wondered how the salesman would explain *that* to his AgriCorp people.

Rosenquist picked it up. The weight of its casing felt unnatural. The future, he thought, rubbing his lower back with his free hand. Every year life started again, with the seeds. They sprouted and produced. By winter, crops died. In the spring, he buried seeds and started over.

Where they see SeEDS, we see seeds. See?

A cool wind picked up off the plain, smelling like wet dog. Maggie's tree swayed, but the pinecones from last season had dropped in the late fall. They were still there on the ground—they took a long time to break down, and they did some good fighting soil erosion. They even provided a habitat for spiders.

Rosenquist turned his attention to the other half of the garden and noticed right away something wasn't right. The seeds planted by Medak's device had already sprouted, breaking the surface of the dirt.

What? He shivered at the strange sight of life visibly creeping from the dirt. The yellow sprouting leaves of the flasp. The dark green leaves of the purple carrots. How could that be? If Medak had known this would happen, he would have waited. He would have seen that his SeEDS had *won*.

Medak had used the wrong one. One of those "specialized" SeEDS he talked about. That had to be it. Rosenquist saw the plants inch up, growing, taking shape. At this rate, he'd have fresh vegetables for dinner. By morning, after a good dousing from the approaching rainstorm, he'd have enough vegetables to sell to the farmer's market in town and make some extra money, if he felt strong enough to make the trip.

Were the seeds that Medak put in the silver bullet unique? Or was it the contraption itself?

He twisted the bullet back and forth, holding it up to the sky where columns of clouds were forming, and he tried to get a better sense of its nearly featureless surface.

There's no joy in it.

He lowered his arm, and in an instant his back seized up. He swore and reached around with his other hand, searching for the source of the ache and pain. He massaged the bottom of the spine.

Of *course* he would keep the bullet. After seeing what it could do? He wasn't stupid.

Medak hadn't left the brochure, so Rosenquist would have to figure it out, but he was decent at tinkering with things, like his old man had been before him. He knew someone in town might be able to help if he couldn't puzzle it out for himself. If things worked out, he might even loan the bullet to other farms for some extra cash.

Tomorrow, if he worked out the secret of the thing, he'd try the bullet out on the west field closest to Maggie. He couldn't help but wonder if...no. That would be ridiculous.

In the meantime, the impending rain wasn't going away.

Just add water.

He figured he'd better get right to it, so habit took over; he wanted to finish the garden the way he started. He put the silver bullet into his coverall pocket and picked up his hoe. He had another row to finish, and there were seeds to plant.

The End

RIDING THE STORM OUT

Martin L. Shoemaker

I looked between my feet and down into the crawler below, where Erica Vile stared up into the pilot pod.

"I'm ready to drive if you need, Chief," she said.

I checked the navigation display. "Wow . . . Four hours of driving already." I had not noticed the time, as I had been too busy dictating reports. I did not want to feel the trip was a *complete* waste.

We had accomplished our goal: we had picked up Brad Andreesen from the Gander Settlement and were bringing him back to Maxwell City to face charges.

But that was no job for the chief *and* the deputy chief. Sending us both out here would put us far behind on paperwork and processing. So I was trying to keep up as best I could.

I nodded. "That sounds good, Vile," I said. I slid back the throttle, and the crawler came to a halt. We were in the middle of Mars's Meridiani Planum, and in other circumstances I might have liked to stop and look around. But orbital weather control said there could be storms coming through, and I wanted Andreesen safely locked up before those hit.

"Deputy Chief Vile," I said, "you have the wheel." I clambered lightly down into the interior of the overland crawler.

As I stepped aside, Vile climbed up. "Chief Morais, I relieve you." As she nudged the crawler up to speed, I went back to look at Andreesen and check his restraints. He was asleep, so at least I didn't have to put up with his mouth.

Andreesen wasn't to blame for my bad temper, not really. He was just an excuse. I was annoyed that Maxwell City had been taken over by a xenobiology conference, with Initiative security commandeering my troops. *But it makes sense, Rosalia,* Mayor Grace had said. *The scientists are traveling from all across the Solar System. They want to know that interplanetary authorities are managing security, not locals.*

That is foolishness, I had said. *My officers know the city better than they do.*

Chief Hogan knows that, Grace had answered. *That's why he's deputizing your force. But he has to be in charge, not . . .*

Not the police chief who let Andreesen get away, I had finished.

No one blames you for that. He eluded the Initiative, too. Andreesen has plenty of connections and money. It's not your fault.

That is what she had said. That is what my husband, Nick, had said, and Vile, and even Chief Hogan from Initiative security. But space it! I did not believe it. We had been *so* close to making the case on Andreesen, and he had gotten away. On my watch. I took that personally.

I resisted the urge to kick Andreesen as he slept, instead sitting in the other couch where I could keep an eye on him. We had been shutting down Andreesen's operations and his resources. We had cut off every contact and every stash of credits we could find. He could not get off Mars, and authorities in every settlement were looking for him. And sure enough, in the middle of the xenobiology conference, Gander Settlement had reported his capture. Since all of my team had been working for Hogan, Vile and I had taken the extradition assignment ourselves.

A gruff voice came from across the crawler. "Hey! I need a drink."

I looked over at Andreesen as he lay on the bunk. He was tall and thin. His dark brown hair was tousled, and he bore a stubble beard, brown mixed with white. Not exactly the picture of the polished crime lord from his dossier. He had been living rough for weeks now. "You have a bulb," I answered.

"It's dry!" he said. "I think it has a leak. This cheap suit . . ."

I smiled at that. "Not up to your standards?" I stood carefully. Riding in a crawler on Mars is tricky. They are not fast, less than twenty kilometers per hour, so on Earth you would feel safe walking around in one. But on Mars you only have forty percent as much weight holding you down. It is easy to get tossed around if the crawler hits a bump. So I stood in a low crouch, and I gripped the safety rails as I made my way to the environment station and pulled out another water bulb.

I carried the bulb back to Andreesen. "Sit up," I said. Andreesen made a show of it, groaning and straining as he tried to sit up with his hands cuffed. "Cut the act," I continued. "You are not that injured."

"I am!" he said. "Those goons you sent beat me. I'm going to sue!"

"I sent no goons," I answered. "We just announced a bounty for your capture." And it had worked. If Andreesen had had access to his funds, he might have bribed his way free. Instead the bounty hunters would get paid with some of Andreesen's own money. "I cannot help that you resisted arrest."

"An unlawful arrest, Chief. I'm going to sue you, and Mayor Grace, and the whole city. I'm going to *own* Maxwell City."

I scoffed at that. He had nerve: on the run with all his funds cut off, beaten, captured, and he still acted like he was in charge. "You remember I said you do not have to speak without an attorney?" I asked. "This is a really good time for not speaking." I snapped the bulb hookup closed, and stepped back.

Andreesen grinned, and I could still see the oily charm with which he had insinuated himself into the confidence of the gullible. "Are we a bit sensitive, Chief?"

"No, just bored with your noise. You should save your breath for when you see the magistrate."

"I won't ever come before the magistrate. Not as a defendant. My lawyer will do all the talking when I sue. By the time he's through with you, you'll be done in Maxwell City, done on Mars. Your reputation will be fouled from here to Earth. I'll bring you down."

I laughed at that. Andreesen thought he was a big man, but admirals and billionaires had tried to crush Nick Aames and me in the past. Compared to them, he was an amateur.

Andreesen's eyes grew wide. "You think I'm funny?"

I shook my head. "You are pathetic. Funny will be when I see you locked in the stockade for twenty to life." I sat back in my couch, picked up my paperwork, and did my best to ignore Andreesen's taunts. He was powerless, but persistent.

Eventually Andreesen lay back on his couch and closed his eyes. Vile's voice called from over my head. "How's our prisoner, Chief?"

"Quiet now. He tried to bait me for a while, but I ignored him."

"Smart move," she answered. "He's manipulative."

"Oh?"

"He made a pretty good push on me," Vile explained. "He hinted at money, connections, and power. He even suggested I could have your job if I helped him."

"Do you want it?"

"Hell, no! I work hard enough as it is. But it was fun playing along as if I was interested. When the player finally figured out he was being played, he got royally pissed. He dropped the façade, and he hit me with a string of invective that would make any drill sergeant proud. He's used to being able to turn people, and he doesn't know how to handle it when he's out of power. I think he's on edge. We have to be careful, he might blow."

I nodded. "Speaking of blowing, what's the word on that storm?"

I looked up just in time to catch the hint of a scowl. "I'm glad you asked, Chief. It's not looking good. Orbital weather says it's building up speed, and picking up a lot of dust. It's ahead of their earlier track, and accelerating. I see haze on the horizon."

I tapped my console to pull up a weather report as well. "What is the long term on that?" But I found the answer before she could respond. "Seven hours?"

"At least," Vile answered. "It'll get heavy pretty soon. What do you think we should do?"

I shook my head. "Vile, you are a better crawler pilot than me." I had seen her records. Earthborn do not really grasp Martian storms. They underestimate or they overestimate. Some of them expect horrendous windstorms, like a tornado or a sirocco, at a hundred kilometers an hour or more; but they do not understand the low density of the Martian atmosphere, only 0.6 percent of Earth normal. The winds move fast but are so thin as to exert no pressure at all. They are barely strong enough to lift a piece of paper.

But can they lift dust! Martian dust is fine and powdery, and can be lifted high into the atmosphere. So much dust moving at that speed can blind you and interfere with instrumentation. It cuts off radio traffic for common communications frequencies, and it shuts down solar power.

So a traveler facing a dust storm has a choice. You can drive through it, dead reckoning and blind, and hope you run into no obstacles. That might work on a well-mapped path, since new obstacles were uncommon on Mars. Or you can hunker in place and ride the storm out. Assuming you packed reserve air and water and food, the crawler will be a safe place to spend to sit through an average Martian storm—if a bit cramped. The risk is that sometimes the storms run longer, even for weeks or months. Plus a storm can leave you buried so deeply that it takes you additional hours to dig out. The dust is fine, but it is heavy if it piles up deeply enough.

Still, hunker in place was the safer choice. Unless...

"Chief, there's a settlement only twenty minutes off our path."

"There is?" I checked my map. "I do not see it."

"It's new, and pretty small," Vile answered. She pushed the data to my console. "There. It's a scientific outpost. Everett Base. Founded less than a year ago, a corporate-university partnership."

"Let me see." I patched into the Initiative data network—noting that the performance was already sluggish from the storm—and pulled up survey information on Everett Base. Founded by a team of xenobiologists looking for historical signs of Martian life, led by Dr. William Everett, as well as a geological survey team and corporate laboratories. It had been under construction for a couple of Martian years with full operations starting ten months back. "It is small," I said, "but they do have crawler garages. Give them a call, Vile, and ask if they have room to shelter us through the storm." I looked back toward Andreesen's couch. "And ask them if they have a lockup."

Visibility was down almost eighty percent by the time we approached the crawler garage, the northernmost in a hexagon of domes connected to the Everett Base main dome by surface tubes. Satellite connections to the Initiative were completely down, and local comms were patchy. The air was filled with hazy streamers of dust, thick enough to sound like very soft static is it struck the side of the crawler. The stuff was fine, but it was fast, and $\frac{1}{2}mv^2$ said it carried a lot of energy.

The garage door cycled open, and we rolled inside. Once we cleared the door it closed, and the purge cycle began. The air in the garage was Martian thin, having been evacuated to let us in. Now the locals were pumping the air up to half pressure, while running giant fans to keep the dust circulating. Electrostatic filters along the wall and ceiling trapped the dust, cleaning the air for several minutes. Then the fans stopped and more air pumped in. Soon our external pressure light showed green, and two figures in suits without helmets approached the crawler.

I started cycling both doors on our airlock as Vile climbed down from the pilot pod. When the door slid open, I stepped out to meet the pair: a young, redheaded man and a tall, graying Asian woman. "Greetings," I said, "I am Police Chief Rosalia Morais of Maxwell City. Thank you for offering us shelter."

The woman reached out to shake my hand. "Welcome," she said. "We're glad we could help. I'm Dr. Iwa Sakura, and this is Dr. Jacob Fletcher." She pointed to the man, and we shook hands as well.

I looked back as Vile stepped out of the lock. "This is Deputy Chief Erica Vile. Vile, Dr. Sakura and Dr. Fletcher."

More handshakes all around, and then Sakura said, "Your message mentioned a prisoner?"

"Yes," I said, nodding. "Extradition from Gander Settlement. I can push you the authorization and the case files, just so we are clear."

Sakura shook her head. "We're just a small scientific base, Chief," she said. "Just a tiny, tight-knit community of academics—plus a few corporate researchers. We don't have law enforcement here, and I wouldn't even know how to read your paperwork. But your credentials check out, so we're good."

Vile's eyebrows rose. "No law enforcement? How does that work?"

Fletcher chuckled. "We're scientists," he said. "If there any serious disputes, there's an Initiative judicial team that runs a circuit through the frontier bases. But really, we don't need it. The only disputes we have here are academic, and those get settled in the journals."

"And in the conferences," Sakura added. "I'm sure Dr. Everett would be happy to welcome you here, but he's actually at the xenobiology conference in Maxwell City."

"Presenting two papers," Fletcher added, a broad grin on his face.

"Yes," Sakura continued, "so we're holding down the fort while he's out. Experiments don't stop just because the prime researcher is away." She lowered her voice and leaned closer. "We do all the day-to-day work, anyway."

I checked some readings on my comm. "We are definitely grateful you could take us in. If we could purchase some air and water to replenish, that would be good. We can bunk in the crawler. No need to put anyone out."

"Nonsense!" Sakura said. "Have you checked the storm track? It moved into the major storm category before we lost satellite contact. The current estimate is it'll last thirty hours, and there's another front behind that. If those merge, you're looking at fifty, even sixty hours. Why would you want to spend that in the crawler?"

"Well . . . There *is* the matter of our prisoner."

"We thought of that," Fletcher answered. "We have an outside equipment shed, left over from the construction of the base. If you take him out there and don't leave him a suit, he can't go anywhere, right?"

I paused. "What do you think, Vile?"

Vile shrugged. "You're the chief," she said.

At last I said, "Let's take a look at it, check the security. It may work."

Fletcher grinned. "I'm sure you'll find it suitable," he said. "And we have some visiting scholar quarters for the two of you, just inside the tube to the main dome. They're much more comfortable than being cooped up in that crawler."

Vile and I had inspected the locks on the utility shed. Neither of us was as good with data security as Officer Moore, but we were not inexperienced, either. We confirmed that the lock could not be operated from the inside—and there was nothing inside that Andreesen might use as a weapon or tool—and we uploaded our own security algorithms into the door lock. We agreed that this was a safe, secure place for Andreesen to ride out the storm. We might have to blow a path out to him after it passed, but he would have food and water and air, and he would be able to flex his limbs a bit. I did not like the man, but there were still

standards of prisoner treatment that had to be maintained. So we
suited him up, led him in, checked the supplies that Dr. Fletcher
provided, took his suit, and left him there.

Then we went back to the garage to fetch our bags. I peered
through the dust, trying to see the layout of the facility. Besides
the main dome and the six big peripheral domes, I could see
three smaller domes. I could only guess how many others might
be around the far side. A network of wide tubes connected the
domes.

Fletcher led us to the visiting scholars' wing near the garage.
Our lugbots followed closely with our bags. He showed us two
compartments in a row of doors on the west side of the tube,
gave us security keys, and let us settle in. "But Dr. Sakura would
like to throw a dinner party in your honor. We don't see a lot
of new faces around here."

"It *has* been a long day," I answered.

"Count me in," Vile said. "And Chief, you haven't had a day
off in a month. You really could use it."

"Maybe," I said as I closed the door to my quarters. I took
advantage of the shower, glad to get out of my suit and freshen up.

But Vile's words stuck with me. I looked through my duffel,
trying to decide which of my clothes were most festive.

Vile had already left for the party by the time I headed south
through the tube to the main dome. While the doors along the
east wall had no markings, the west doors were labeled for different corporations. The last door in the line, heavier than the
rest, was marked simply MAINTENANCE.

As I entered the main dome, I heard laughter, conversation,
and clinking utensils. The dome had a high ceiling, nearly four
meters, and the space was divided into rooms by partitions only
two meters high. No one but a tall loonie was likely to see over
those, but sound could travel. A blank partition faced me as I
entered the dome, forcing me to choose left or right.

Instead I raised my voice and called, "Dr. Sakura?"

"In a minute, Chief," she called back. It took her far less than
that to appear from the right and lead me through the maze of
rooms and corridors. The compartments were all empty. Everyone
must be at the party.

Finally Sakura brought me into the assembly hall in the

center of the dome, where a few dozen people were engaged in laughter and conversations. I saw one cluster around Vile, and people laughed at some story she told.

Sakura raised her voice above the din. "Everyone!" The voices quieted. "I know you're all having a wonderful party, but I wanted to introduce you to Police Chief Rosalia Morais from Maxwell City. The putative reason for this party."

"I thought *I* was the reason," Vile said, and people laughed more.

"You both are," Sakura answered. "And now this party can really get started. Clear away from the tables so we can bring the food in. There's plenty for everyone. I contacted Dr. Everett, and he authorized open rations for tonight." At that, there was a scattering of excited conversation, and a few broke out into applause. "Enjoy it, because it's back to work in the morning."

With that, conversation resumed, and I was distracted as staff introduced themselves and asked about Maxwell City. After several minutes, Sakura pulled me away and led me to the food tables.

The fare was plentiful, if simple. Frontier research bases like this operated on carefully rationed food and air and water. There were a few well-funded research bases, but not many on Mars. The focus on academics over exploitation meant that a place like Everett Base operated primarily on grants and fundraising efforts—and dedication and faith. They might celebrate today, but they'd be back to the budget tomorrow.

And the alcohol . . . that I found myself sampling, encouraged by a medium-built, jovial man who introduced himself as Dr. Burke. "A *real* doctor," he said as he handed me a tall glass.

I took a sip. "Pretty good gin," I answered. "It must cost a lot to import."

Burke smiled and shook his head. "No, I distill it myself. Strictly for medicinal purposes, you know."

I nodded. "So you're the doctor for the doctors?"

He smiled at my small joke. "I lead the clinic staff. There are four of us here. For anything major, we summon a hopper from Maxwell City. But we're good with lesser injuries, allergies, and the occasional infection that slips through quarantine. Oh, and bad lifestyle decisions."

I sipped some more gin, and then gently inclined the glass toward him. "Such as hangovers?"

He laughed. "Too many of those. There's not a lot of recreation out here in the frontier. A lot of it comes down to what you can put in your body or do to your body. Or do to somebody else's body. That has consequences, too."

I chuckled. "It has been known to."

"Good and bad." He smiled. "We've had a few fights, usually friction between the university people and the corporate folks." He finished his drink and poured another. "We've also had three pregnancies since we arrived. Two mothers transferred to Maxwell City for better obstetrics facilities. The third is still making up her mind. So I might get to deliver a baby in five months."

I smiled. "I hope you do."

"We'll see," he answered. "Dr. Everett would really prefer we stay child-free."

"Oh? He doesn't like kids?"

Burke shook his head and lowered his voice until I almost couldn't hear him over the din of the party. "I didn't say that, I just... Budgets and rations are tight. He won't make parents leave, but it's easier if they do."

Again I contemplated the tight margins on the frontier; but before I could ask more questions, I was cut off by the sound of musical instruments tuning up. I looked across the hall, and a small band had set up.

"This should be good," Burke said. "No one hires researchers for their musical skill, so we take what we can get; but these four have some talent."

The musicians started playing, and it took only a few bars for me to hear what Burke meant. When the second song started, partiers pulled aside tables and chairs to make a dance floor in the middle of the hall. Dr. Burke stood up. "Chief, may I have this dance?"

"Certainly, Doctor." I never passed up a chance to dance, one of Nick and my favorite pastimes. Dr. Burke wasn't nearly as good as Nick, but he was enthusiastic. We started with a fast, improvised routine as we got to know each other's steps. Next was a slow number in three-four, and we settled into an easy waltz. The band picked up the tempo after that.

It felt good to relax and unwind for once. I looked around for Vile so I could admit she had been right.

I could not see her. Vile is a taller woman than me, and

she often stands out in a crowd in Maxwell City; but a lot of the researchers at Everett Base were tall, probably loonies, and I couldn't see her.

I scanned the crowd. "What's the matter?" Dr. Burke asked.

"I was just looking for Vile. I do not see her anywhere."

Burke looked around as well. "Maybe she left the party."

I shook my head. "It is not like Vile to leave a party in full swing. She works hard, but she knows how to unwind."

Burke's mouth turned up in a slight grin. "Maybe she didn't leave it...alone?"

I mentally kicked myself for overlooking the obvious. I was Vile's boss, not her big sister. If she wanted a little privacy with a scientist, that was her decision. Let her enjoy herself.

I turned my attention back to the dance, with Dr. Burke and with other willing partners through the night. And I had more fun than I had had in months.

When the band finally packed up, I said my goodnight to Dr. Burke and navigated my way back to my room and into my bunk.

I was just settling into a light dreaming state when the voice of Dr. Burke intruded over the comm. "Chief Morais, come to the infirmary. Immediately, please."

I stared through the plexi wall and into Vile's isolation chamber. "She's all right," Dr. Burke said. "For now."

Vile's face had a blue tinge to it. "You're sure?"

Burke shook his head. "I won't be sure for a while. This isn't Maxwell City General. We've got some damn good bio labs, but they're not set up for medical work. I've got teams reconfiguring them to test her blood for what did this."

"So you don't know?"

"I know her oxygen uptake is deficient. She's young and healthy, that shouldn't be an issue. Maybe if I had her medical records..."

"Can't you get them from Maxwell City?"

"Still can't cut through the storm," Burke answered.

"What about her suit comp? Her medical records should all be encoded there."

Again, Burke shook his head. "That's the other bad news. Her suit comp was missing when we found her."

"What do you mean, missing?"

"She was in a conference room not far from the party, just lying in the dark in a corner. A maintenance drone stumbled upon her about twenty minutes ago, recognized a possible medical emergency, and summoned help. I checked her vitals, got her on oxygen, and hauled her in here. But there was no comp on her."

"So this is not an illness."

Burke's tone was bitter as he nodded. "What are the odds she caught a mysterious illness at the same time her comp mysteriously disappeared? It's a toxin, I just don't know what yet. With all these labs around here..."

I was only listening with half my brain. Vile's suit comp had the encryption keys for the cyberlock on Andreesen's storage shed.

Space it! I needed to be in three places at once. I needed to check on Andreesen, I needed to find out who the hell had poisoned Vile, and I needed...

No, I did not need to keep an eye on Vile. There was nothing I could do there that Dr. Burke couldn't do better. He was a stranger, a dance partner for a few brief hours. I did not really know him at all. But I had to trust somebody in Everett Base; and if I could not trust him, then Vile was dead anyway. So it would have to be Burke.

"Doctor," I said, "find out what did this to her, and who had access to it or could make it. I am counting on you."

"That's what I'm doing," Burke said. "I am *not* going to lose her." Then more softly he added, "But you take care of yourself, Chief."

"What?"

"I can see what you're thinking," he explained. "This is Andreesen's doing. Somehow he got to somebody. He's probably already escaped."

"I know, that is—"

"But whoever did this won't just be after Vile," he interrupted. "If they expect to get away with it, they're gonna have to get rid of you, too."

"I do not—"

"With you gone, their odds of getting away with it go up. They'll have an easier time covering their tracks then."

"They will have to get rid of all the evidence. The samples... Vile...*and* you, as you know too much."

Burke gave a thin smile. "They can try." With a fast, subtle motion, he had an automatic pistol in his hand. "I've worked frontier bases my whole career, Chief. Sometimes you're too far from any protection but your own."

Again, I had no choice but to trust Burke. If he could not protect himself, I certainly could not protect him *and* secure Andreesen. So I wished him well, and I headed back to my quarters to suit up.

But when I made my way to the crawler garage, the inner door would not open. I tapped my comm. "This is Chief Morais of Maxwell City. My access code is not working for the garage."

A female voice answered. "This is access control, Chief. I see your guest credentials are valid." She paused. "Oh, here it is. The garage is under Mars pressure. We don't know why, but the outer lock is open. The inner door won't open until the garage is at normal pressure."

I cursed inwardly. "It is vital that I get to my crawler right now. Is there a lock to let me cycle into the garage under Mars pressure?"

"There is, Chief, let me see if I can authorize you. It will take a second."

As I waited, I wondered if I had made a mistake. I could have gone through a surface lock and gone straight to check on Andreesen. But my instincts told me that he was gone already. This scheme made no sense unless he fled quickly, dust storm be damned. I needed the crawler and its drones so I could find where Andreesen had gone.

The woman's voice returned. "Chief, security has a lockout because cameras are out in the garage, but I got my manager to authorize an override. You should see a blinking light over the maintenance door in your tube." I looked back just as the light started blinking. "It will lead behind the corporate quarters and to a small personal lock. From there, you can cycle through into the garage."

"Thank you!" As soon as I reached the maintenance door, it opened. Beyond was a tight corridor filled with mechanical and electrical access panels. I reached a simple air-lock door at the end, and I checked my suit seals and cycled into the garage.

Once inside, I saw the problem. "Everett access control, can you still hear me?"

"I can," the woman answered.

"I cannot explain the cameras, but I can explain your door. There is a personal crawler parked in the doorway. The outer lock cannot close."

"That sounds like this was deliberate."

"I think it was." But I said no more. She had been helpful; but there were only two people I trusted in the base, and one of them was unconscious.

I ignored the personal crawler. It suited me just fine to have the door propped open so I could launch scan drones. I hurried to our crawler.

I cycled inside and went straight up to the pilot pod. The scan drones were operated from there, giving the pilot extra eyes and sensors for Martian surface conditions. I sped through the checklist and launched all six drones. They floated out through the open door, and I followed behind at crawler speed.

One drone reached the storage shed in under a minute, while the others spread out, searching for heat trails and other signs of escape. That would be difficult, with high velocity dust obscuring the readings, but it was all I could do.

The first drone did a sweep around the shack, and I was not surprised when I saw through the swirling sands that the panel was unlocked. But I could not assume anything. Andreesen was crafty. He might still be hidden inside. So I parked the crawler by the shack and got out to check. I had my automatic at the ready.

Before I operated the external lock of the shed, I summoned two more drones to join me inside the airlock. When they were ready, I closed the outer door and started the pressure cycle. Then I stepped to the side of the door, reached over, and slapped the button to open the inner hatch. As soon as it was open far enough, the drones zoomed in and gave their reports. I followed through their video feeds.

The scene inside was grim, but probably safe. All that blood on the floor was still warm, so Fletcher probably was not faking as he lay in the middle of the pool, a big gash in his head.

The rest of the shack was empty, so I came in and inspected. Vile's comp lay next to Fletcher's body. There were boot tracks in the blood. Fletcher's helmet sat on a rack by the door. If the fool had had enough sense to keep the helmet on, Andreesen would not have been able to whack him with Vile's comp.

Or maybe it would not have mattered. Fletcher did not look

like much of a fighter. Andreesen was not, either, relying on others to do his violence. But he might have found another way to overpower him.

Somehow Andreesen had got to Fletcher and offered him a bribe big enough to tempt him. Fletcher had poisoned Vile, grabbed her comp, and taken a suit out to Andreesen. And now Andreesen was gone...

But where?

The next step in my investigation was back in the garage. I left my overland crawler parked outside, and I walked up to the personal crawler. The haze had thickened again. Though I could barely see, the crawler hatch hung open. Vehicles that small did not have airlocks. You depressurize the entire crawler, and then you enter or exit. I climbed into the personal crawler and backed it out of the doorway. As soon as I did, the outer hatch started sliding shut.

From old habit, I was disinclined to leave the personal crawler in the middle of the garage. I saw where more crawlers were parked against the southeast wall, so I steered in that direction. I approached marked parking lanes for the six personal crawlers that were already there and spaces for two more. I also saw a much larger parking slot for an overland crawler like my own. The overland was gone, no doubt to take Everett and his team to their conference. But after I parked the crawler, that left one unfilled slot. The odds were good that Andreesen was driving that crawler right now.

There had been too many security breaches. It did not add up. I wanted to talk to Dr. Burke, but I did not want to distract him from Vile's treatment. Plus I was not sure if that channel was secure. So instead I went back to my crawler, clambered in, and went up to the pilot pod to check communications.

Space it! Still too much particulate interference. I had no channel to Maxwell City nor to orbit. No one I could turn to.

So I pulled up an onboard database of settlements and locations. It included brief reports of all staff nearby, because you never knew when you might need a hydrologist or a chemist in an emergency. It was not as good as full personnel records, but I would take it.

I checked Fletcher's record. The man had been a skilled geologist with no indication of any aptitude for chemistry or biology. Nor for computer security, for that matter. I could not see a timeline where he could have done everything necessary for Andreesen's escape. He was a scientist (and an administrator, according to the file), but not the right kind of scientist.

So I ran a search for someone with advanced biological skills and also computer security skills; but no records matched. Fletcher would need at least two accomplices, maybe more, to have freed Andreesen.

But then I thought again. If Fletcher was an administrator, he would not need to break security. He could just turn it off and wipe the records.

That was harder to search. It took me over twenty precious minutes to write the query. Finally I got a list and cross-referenced it with biology skills. Again, Fletcher was not in the intersection. In fact, the set was practically empty. It had only one name, the second in command of the base: *Iwa Sakura*.

I connected to local comms and entered my chief credentials. Soon I had a secure channel. A young male voice answered, "Infirmary."

"This is Chief Morais," I said. "I need to talk to Dr. Burke."

There was a pause, then Burke came on the line. "What's up, Chief?"

"How is Vile?"

"She's . . . her body is fighting, but she's losing. I can give her six hours, and hope the tests come back in that time."

"But if you knew what it was . . . ?"

"That would be a whole different story. She'd have a great shot."

"Then let's give her that shot. You should know what it was in a few minutes."

"What? How?"

"A few minutes, Doctor." I ran through the comm directory until I found Assistant Director Sakura. I opened the channel, and when she answered, I wasted no time. "What did he pay you, Sakura?"

Sakura's face showed puzzlement. "I don't understand, Chief."

"Space it! Sakura, Vile's dying, and Fletcher's dead!"

Her mask dropped. "Fletcher—"

"You idiots trusted Andreesen. For that, Fletcher deserved what he got." Maybe not, but I wanted to hammer her hard. "So that is one death on your conscience already. When Vile goes, that will be two."

"No!" she said. "I was going to let the lab 'discover' the answer in a couple of hours. I didn't want anyone to die. I just—"

"You just what? What did you want, Sakura? Money?"

A tear ran down her left cheek. "Not money, *independence*. He offered so much...we could've held off the corporate teams for five years, maybe longer. We would've been able to do pure science."

"And all it cost you was your soul."

"Damn it, Chief, I didn't know he was a killer!"

"He was a desperate, wanted man, and you knew that. Tell Dr. Burke, *now*, what the toxin was."

"I'm...sending the message now. Chief, you have to believe me..."

"You had better hope that Vile makes it through, or I will personally see you up on murder charges."

"You can't—"

"I damn well can. You are already an accessory to murder for Fletcher."

"No..."

"It's going to get worse, Doctor," I said. "Think what this will do to the reputation of Everett Base."

"No, please..."

"All of your research will be tainted."

"No..."

"The base will *fail*, Doctor. The only way it will survive at all is if corporate interests come in and take over."

"You can't do this to us! The others...they had nothing to do with it!"

"None of them?"

"Just me and Fletcher. He kept up with the news. He'd read the reports about Andreesen and thought we could make a deal."

"He paid for his stupidity, and now you will pay for yours."

"But not the others! You have to do something."

"Doctor, I will tell the authorities that you have been cooperative if you'll do two things. First, you will turn control of the base over to Dr. Burke and turn yourself in to him."

She swallowed. "And?"

"I need to know—and do not lie to me—is Andreesen in your base, or is he out on Mars? I do not have time to search both."

"He's gone. There have been no unauthorized entrances back into the base."

"Not even using Fletcher's credentials?"

She paused. "No, security reports him still... Why would he kill Fletcher? We were *helping* him!"

Why *would* Andreesen kill the young geologist? And where would he go? In the middle of the storm, he was as blind as me and as cut off from communications. And he certainly had less range. Overland crawlers were built for journeys of thousands of miles, personal crawlers for journeys measured in hours. So Andreesen could not plan to meet a confederate, even if he somehow had a chance to contact one.

I turned my attention back to Sakura. "You arranged a crawler for him. How much oxygen did you give him?"

"Eight bottles. That might be good for sixteen hours."

And the storm might last double that. I tried to remember how much surface experience Andreesen had. An experienced explorer knew to keep plenty of margin on air, but would he?

But then my thoughts turned back to Fletcher. The geologist. "Doctor, where did Fletcher do his work?"

I checked the dead reckoning against the few landmarks that I could see through the storm, matching them to my map. It was hard to tell when one rock pile could look like another, but my calculations said that DR was not off by more than two meters. I assumed four meters just to be safe.

So I stopped five meters short of the edge of the chasma, the deep Martian canyon indicated on the map. This was where Andreesen had an advantage with his smaller crawler. The overlander massed more than ten times his. There was a switchback trail down into the chasma, but it was unsafe above a certain mass. My crawler was four times that limit. If I got closer, I would go in for sure.

Somewhere in that chasma was Fletcher's geology station. My guess was that Fletcher had offered it as a hideout, and then Andreesen had killed him so that no one would know where he was. The station would have food, water, and air for a single person for weeks, maybe a month.

I sent the scout drones ahead as I packed up the lugbot. They could give me the lay of the land.

I pondered what to expect. Killing was new for Andreesen. Fletcher might have been his first. He had always been a manipulator behind the scenes, one who ordered killing, not one who did it. The man was desperate, and I had to keep that in mind.

I loaded the lugbot with extra first-aid supplies, air bottles, and ammo. Then I called one scan drone back from the chasma to check out the area around the crawler. There was no sense being ambushed before I even got down there. When I saw that the way was clear, the bot and I cycled through the airlock and onto the surface. I started toward the switchback trail. The lugbot followed on its treads.

Tracking on Mars is difficult. Vid dramas make it look easy, with long red Martian dunes and one set of wheel tracks crossing them. But the Martian surface is never the same place twice. Storms will wipe out any track as they pass. And right now, with the dust in the air, I had nothing but intuition to tell me I was on the right track.

If Andreesen was not at the geology station, I could not see where else he could be. So I navigated the switchback on foot; and as I did, I grew more confident. Dust blows away, but rock remains. The wall of the chasma was layers of shale-like rock—solid *unless* you stressed it. As I hiked down the slope, I saw distinct tracks of cracked stone all around me. Some of the broken rock looked fresh. It still had sharp edges since it had not been eroded by high velocity dust.

I needed to look ahead and see what the drones saw. I pulled up their feeds just in time to catch a bright flash of green on drone four's feed. Then the image developed a series of dark spots. I quickly pulled the drones back.

I ran diagnostics. Drone four's forward camera was practically useless. The most likely explanation would be a high-powered laser. Those were often used in geological excavations, because they were faster than a trencher.

So Andreesen was armed.

But he had made a mistake in his choice of weapon, one common to people who did not understand armaments. Despite years of science fiction vid shows, lasers had never displaced traditional firearms for personal defense. Lasers had their advantages, but their energy consumption was prohibitive. You could not pack enough power in a handheld pack for more than a shot or two.

What Andreesen had must be a scientific tool, not handheld, probably mounted on a power cart. That gave him limited mobility, and I assumed he was not familiar with the weapon. Plus a laser was a poor choice in the middle of a massive dust storm. A geological laser should have burned drone four out of the sky; but the beam was scattered so much by the dust in the air that the power had been cut to a fraction. Enough to blind the sensor, but not to get through the drone's armor.

But *my* armor wasn't as thick as the drone's. I might survive a hit from the attenuated beam, but it was a risk I was unwilling to take.

I ducked behind some rock fall, just to be safe. I fed the drone stream to a modeling analyzer to build a 3D model of the chasma floor. Once I saw where Andreesen was now, I knew where the geology outpost was. I could even see the crawler parked at the outpost lock. Andreesen could not move far from that location, given the storm. He could, however, cover the switchback and the chasma wall, if anyone climbed down that way. Assuming he could see them, of course.

The next move was mine. And I had only one choice.

I watched Lieutenant Kilgore of Initiative Rapid Response as he marched Andreesen up the switchback. For the next hour or two, the air would be almost free of dust.

I called Kilgore on my comm. "What's he saying, Lieutenant?"

Kilgore chuckled. "Let me patch him in, Chief."

There followed much sputtering and profanity. I let it go for over a minute before I said, "Problem, Andreesen?"

"Fuck you!" Then he paused for breath before continuing, "I *had* you. There was no way you could get me. I could blast your drones out of the sky."

"No, you could not," I replied.

Ignoring me, Andreesen continued, "I had the laser. Better range, deadlier. No matter how you came at me, I had you!"

"Andreesen, you are an idiot. You do not understand violence and risk. This is not stock fraud, it's life and death. Did you expect me to just come at you?"

"I—"

"You did! You thought this was a vid, some showdown in the canyon."

"You—"

"I was angry. I might have killed you if I could, but I did not need to. I had more range, more supplies, better intel, and better weapons for the conditions. All I had to do was wait out the storm and call for assistance when it broke."

Andreesen had called for assistance, too. Two hoppers had launched from Gander Settlement not long after comms cleared. But by that time, *three* Rapid Response hoppers had been in flight. Whoever had been piloting his hoppers, they had changed course immediately. Nobody smart messes with Rapid Response Teams.

Andreesen's people had been smarter than him when it came to violence. He had planted crude booby-traps, geological charges on tripwires. Amateur stuff that had not even slowed down the RRT. He did not know how to do his own dirty work.

I cut off Andreesen's channel. "Thank you, Lieutenant," I said. "I shall tell Chief Hogan that your team did an excellent job."

"Wasn't nothin', Chief," Kilgore answered, and he cut off.

I switched back to my other channel. Right after reaching the Initiative, I had contacted Dr. Burke, and he had set up a comm channel inside the isolation unit. I smiled at the new color in Vile's face.

I said to her, "Got him!"

The End

INCIDENT AT RAVEN'S RIFT

(A Short Story of T-Space)

Alastair Mayer

"So, Dr. Carson, tell me about Jackie," Satoshi said as the two of them rode through the arid, winding canyons gouged out of the floor of the great valley known as The Rift. "If she's coming out to Montresor to see you, it must be more serious than your usual shipboard romance."

Hannibal Carson grinned back at his grad student. "What do you mean, 'usual'? Are you implying something?" Carson didn't dispute the claim. Three weeks aboard a starship did sometimes lead to temporary involvement with other passengers. But this last trip out had been different.

"Anyway," he continued, "Jackie Roberts, *Commander* Jackie Roberts, is crew, not a passenger. She's smart . . . and attractive." His voice trailed off, thinking about her.

They'd met aboard ship, en route from Alpha Centauri to the Beta Hydri system, halfway across the bubble of settled stars known as T-Space. She'd caught Carson's eye as she entered the passenger lounge. She was crew, and her uniform had enough gold braid to mark her as an officer. She looked far too young to be the captain, but with anti-aging drugs, looks could be deceiving. The green hair, though, wouldn't be the affectation of a captain. First officer, perhaps?

She chatted with a couple at the table nearest the lounge entrance, glancing up and around while talking in a casual appraisal of her surroundings. She caught him eying her, and smiled at him. Carson's first impulse was to look away, pretending he hadn't been staring, but she'd caught him. He smiled back.

She finished talking to the couple and made her way toward him. "Welcome aboard the *Arabella*. I'm First Officer Jacqueline Roberts, Mister...ah...?"

"Carson. Dr. Hannibal Carson, but call me Carson. Everyone else does."

"And I'm Jackie. So what are you a doctor of, Carson?"

In his experience, most people assumed that "doctor" meant a medical doctor, unless they'd worked with or grown up around academics.

"Xenoarcheology, or exoarcheology if you go by the department name. I'm a professor at Drake University. I take it you know a few PhDs? And please," he said, gesturing to an empty chair, "have a seat."

"You could say that," she said, remaining standing. "Both my parents, for starters. And thank you, but I'm on duty. Just greeting the passengers. So why is an archeologist going to Raven? Going to visit the ruins at The Rift? I thought they'd been completely excavated."

"They mostly have, although that doesn't mean there isn't more they could tell us. But no, there's a new site."

"Really? That sounds exciting. Where?"

Carson hesitated. "Sorry, I'd rather not say just yet. With a new find there's always a risk of tomb raiders. Not," he hastened to add, "that I think you'd be connected with such."

"You mean grave robbers."

"Artifact smugglers. There's a demand for alien artifacts on Earth, and illicit dealers like to raid archeological sites, going after the pretty baubles without caring what that does to the site's integrity. Even if the artifacts are later recovered, they've lost their historical context." Carson's temper was rising, and he forced himself to relax. "Anyway, that's one reason any archeologist is reticent to reveal a new site until it's been thoroughly documented."

"That's all right, Dr. Mysterious. I understand."

Carson started to protest the title, but she smiled to show she was joking, her green eyes twinkling. He couldn't help but smile with her.

"What about you?" he asked. "I don't mean to offend, but aren't you rather young for a first officer? You must have started early."

"No offense taken. I did. My mother's an astrophysicist, and I grew up on a starship. Don't worry; the ship, and you, are in good hands."

"That's not what I meant ...." His protest trailed off at her teasing grin.

She clapped him on the shoulder. "I know. I do need to get back to my duties, though." Her hand lingered a moment. "If you like, you're welcome to join my table at dinner."

"Thank you, yes. I'd like that."

That dinner had turned into others, and more.

"Carson?" Sato's voice.

"Sorry. My mind wandered. Anyway, Jackie might not be the only one we're meeting. If my messages caught up with him, my old friend Marten will be arriving with her. Her ship was headed to Zeta Tucanae and back. Last I heard, he was at a dig there."

Messages between stars could travel no faster than a starship could carry them, so coordinating meetings was an iffy prospect.

"Is Marten his first or last name?" Sato wondered.

"Neither. It's a nickname; he's a timoan. His first name is *Mcchartengha*"—Carson sounded like a Scotsman trying to speak Swahili—"and timoan clan names are complicated."

As they rode, a shadow swooped overhead, spooking their *ghorsels*.

"Easy boy," Carson said, and they urged their mounts closer to the cliff face so the overhang helped conceal them. He glanced up as the *roc*, far bigger than an Earthly condor, glided above the canyon walls. Carson loosened the pistol in his holster, just in case. The 12mm slug wouldn't do much damage to the huge bird, but the flash and bang might scare it off.

As they rode, keeping close to the overhanging cliff, the roc continued to soar overhead, banking this way and that, then circling back to keep pace. Ahead, the slope of the cliff face lessened. They would soon be out of cover. The ghorsels knew it too, growing increasingly skittish.

"Screw this," Carson said, drawing his pistol.

"You'd be better off with a *giranno* gun," Sato said dismissively. "That's not going to do anything."

"A roc's big, but it's still a bird. It's nowhere near as massive or thick-skinned as a giranno. Anyway, I don't want to bring it down, just give it second thoughts." That said, Carson had to agree. He'd rather have a weapon more suited to the giraffe-rhinos of Sato's homeworld. He drew a bead on the roc, willing it to keep to its glide, wings outstretched.

BANG! Feathers burst from the roc's wingtip, and the great bird squawked and banked away, flapping for altitude and then gliding off in search of easier prey.

"You almost missed," Sato said.

"No, I didn't want to wound it." A feather fluttered down near them and Carson snatched it out of the air. It was more than half a meter long. He handed it to Sato. "Here, a souvenir. Come on, let's ride before that roc changes its mind." With that, he urged his mount to a gallop, with Satoshi following.

The birds were one reason the men rode ghorsels—horselike animals with some characteristics of mountain goats and camels, suiting them to the hot, dry, chaotic terrain in the canyons of Raven's Rift. Rocs had been known to attack the lightweight, open-frame aircars used elsewhere.

The danger now passed, Sato picked up their conversation again. "So why is she coming all the way here from Ravensport? You must have made quite an impression; Montresor isn't exactly a tourist town."

It wasn't. It was a small town of one main street and perhaps a score of buildings, a trading hub for the surrounding community of small farms and wildcat miners and prospectors. The old riverbeds at the bottom of the canyon held occasional troves of placer gold deposits, and the sandstone walls were laced through with deposits of an exotic opal. The gems, called firestones, outdid the finest Australian fire opals, iridescing in multiple deep reds and oranges with flashes of green and blue. The best of them glowed with their own inner light, thanks to radioluminescent inclusions.

Above the canyon, but still on the floor of the greater rift valley, small farms tapped into the aquifer to grow crops that thrived in the heat and daily sunshine. It wasn't an easy life, but frontier planets attracted people looking more for liberty than luxury. As Satoshi had said, it wasn't a tourist town.

Carson had also wondered why when Jackie had suggested she visit him in Montresor. "I'd like to see your dig site, if that's allowed.

I showed you my starship." Indeed, she had shown him a few places that were normally off-limits to passengers. And they'd done things together that went beyond normal crew-passenger relationships, Carson remembered, smiling to himself. "Anyway," she had added, "if nothing else, maybe I can get a good deal on some firestones." He'd agreed, and noted that the occasional green flash would complement the color of her hair and eyes. She'd smiled at that.

She had a wonderful smile.

"To be honest," Carson said with a pang of doubt, "there's no guarantee she'll be there. She said she would be, but that was two weeks ago."

"You haven't called her? Her ship would have landed yesterday, wouldn't it?"

"It would, but no, not until we get to Montresor. Radio silence, remember?"

"I thought rank had its privileges. I assumed you didn't want any of us blabbing about where we were," Sato said. "Are you that worried about tomb raiders triangulating the site?"

"After what we found three days ago?" It had been a large firestone, elaborately carved, the work of the ancient Raven aboriginals... and priceless. "Damn right I am. But even without that, I've seen too many archeological digs picked over by treasure hunters not to worry about it. Even when they don't take everything, they make enough of a mess of the context to ruin its scientific value."

They came to a spot where the canyon narrowed and forked. The town lay in the direction of the right fork, but Carson took the left, signaling Sato to follow, the clop-clop of their ghorsels' hooves echoing off the narrower canyon walls.

"Are you sure this is the right way?"

"I've made that mistake before," Carson said. "About three kilometers in, that other fork peters out, with no way to climb out. No, we go this way."

Two hours later, they climbed a zigzag trail up the sloping canyon wall to come out on the floor of the rift valley proper south of Montresor, an easy twenty minutes farther.

They tied up their ghorsels at the livery stable, then crossed the street toward the hotel. A man Carson hadn't seen before angled to intercept them. "Dr. Carson, a word with you, please," he said, gesturing him aside.

Carson turned to his student. "Go on ahead, I'll be right there," then turned back to the man. "What can I do for you?"

The man paused, waiting as Satoshi entered the hotel, then spoke in a low voice. "My name's Herbert. I wonder, have you turned up any aboriginal firestone carvings? I have clients who would pay a lot for that kind of thing. If you're not interested in the money for yourself, think of the archeological digs you could finance."

Carson frowned. He'd heard this pitch before. He turned to the man, keeping his voice low but firm. "No, and they wouldn't be for sale if I had. For one, they wouldn't be mine to sell, and for another, that kind of thing belongs in a museum, not locked up in some private collection."

"You're sure?"

Carson's glare was all the answer Herbert was getting, and he backed off. "All right. Just making the offer."

Carson watched him walk away. Something about the man's tone bothered him. He shook it off. There was no way anyone here could know what they'd recently found.

Carson found Jackie Roberts waiting for him at Montresor's only hotel—such as it was—as he entered.

She was in the hotel's saloon. A cluster of prospectors and ranch hands had gathered around the table where Jackie sat. Sato hung back, unsure of himself. The locals were all polite enough, and Jackie didn't seem fazed by the attention she was getting.

"I see you found something to amuse yourself with," Carson said as he approached.

"Hannibal!" she said, her face brightening as she jumped up from the table to greet him with a hug.

There was good-natured grumbling from the other men. "Shoulda known Doc Carson would show up when a pretty woman did," muttered one of them.

Jackie heard him and raised an eyebrow. "Really? Is there something I should know about, Hannibal?"

"Vicious rumors, don't believe any of it," he said, then as an aside, "Thanks for nothing, Zeke."

"The boys here," Jackie began, although Carson knew at least three of them had to be more than twice Jackie's age, "were telling me about mining for firestones."

"Then definitely don't believe any of it," Carson said, grinning. "These guys exaggerate more than fishermen."

"Hey now, Doc, that ain't fair. We might embellish a little, but we don't brag about the one that got away."

"No? What about that stone that Old Pete supposedly pulled out of his claim, only to have it break into pieces just as he got it loose?"

Zeke grinned. "Oh, well, yeah, but that's Old Pete. Nobody pays him no mind."

"Old Pete?" Jackie asked.

"He was one of the first settlers in these parts," Zeke said. "Still works a claim twenty klicks north of town. I swear, if he wrote his stories down and sold them he could make more than he gets from firestones."

"You might be right," Carson said. "Jackie, maybe you'll meet him when we get back. He's in town every couple of weeks."

"Get back?" Zeke said. "Are you taking this lovely young woman somewhere?"

"I promised to show her some of the aboriginal ruins. Nothing you'd find exciting."

"Hey, Jackie, we can show you ruins too."

"I'm sure you can, but Hannibal here is the archeologist."

"How about firestone mines? Want a tour?"

She shook her head. To Carson, it seemed almost a shudder. "I'll pass. I'm not a fan of tunnels or being underground; I'm a spacer," she said. "Anyway, Hannibal owes me. I showed him my starship."

She grinned, and her wink was answered with chuckles and a whistle.

"All right, guys, settle down. Jackie, we should hit the trail soon."

"Roger that. Let me go up and get my things. I'll be right back."

As she went upstairs, Carson looked around at the others. "Sorry to break up the party, gentlemen. Can I buy you a round before we go?"

"Hell, Carson, you don't *have* to do that," Zeke said, "but since you're offering...."

Carson signaled the waitress. "A round for the house," he said, feeling generous, and sat down to join them.

☆　　☆　　☆

Marten—*Mcchartengha*—was at a nearby table, sitting backward on his chair and surveying the crowd around Jackie with amusement. One curious local had been talking with him, but most of them had been more focused on the new woman in their midst rather than the timoan. Carson called him over.

"Mcchartengha, come meet my current grad student, Satoshi Rodriguez."

"Please, just Martenga. Human throats can't handle my timoan name."

The crowd around the table shuffled to make room for him, some ignoring him, a couple of others looking him up and down appraisingly. They were all used to seeing nonhumans, of course, since a few of the indigenous natives still lived in and around the canyon, but they were tall and gangly, with a tawny skin that blended with the ochres of the surrounding sandstone.

Martenga, from Taprobane in the Epsilon Indi system, was shorter than most adult humans, with a fine, blue-gray pelt. Unlike the Raven natives, who descended from a distant primate-like ancestor, timoans had evolved from something like a terrestrial meerkat. More distantly still, the ancestors of both had come from Earth, brought by the mysterious Terraformers some sixty-five million years ago.

"Should have known the alien was Carson's too," Zeke said, *sotto voce.*

"That's funny," the timoan said, "I thought Carson was *my* alien." He grinned. "No offense meant nor taken," he added.

"Ha! You're all right, Martenga," Zeke said, careful to keep both his hands in view.

Carson's eye shifted warily as he watched the exchange. He knew most of the men here, and they were generally a good bunch, but he had seen arguments lead to drawn pistols. Not that he was worried about Martenga, specifically. Timoans had lightning-fast reflexes, and Zeke apparently knew it.

The waitress came back and distributed her trayful of drinks.

"Cheers, folks," Carson said, hoisting a mug of the weak brew that passed for beer here. This early in the day, they were drinking more for the water and electrolytes than the alcohol. At least, that was the excuse.

The group chatted for a while, but with the timoan now the center of attention rather than Jackie, several of the men left to attend to whatever daily chores they had. It gradually dawned on Carson that Jackie had not returned.

"She's taking her time," he said.

"Women," said Zeke dismissively. "She'll be along."

"No, she's a starship officer. It's not like her." He stood up. "I'll just go check at the desk."

He came back a few moments later, signaling to Sato and Martenga. "They haven't seen her, and there's no answer from her room." He pulled out his omniphone and tapped the screen.

The timoan looked at Sato, who shrugged and shook his head.

"No answer," Carson said, slapping the omni against his wrist so that it curled around and held. He looked at Martenga. "Did she say anything to you? Maybe she went shopping?" His tone said he didn't believe it.

"No. She was out at the exchange this morning, looking at souvenirs and firestones, such as they were. But I don't know her that well. We only met on the way here."

Zeke got up from the table and came over to them. "I don't mean to butt in, but you look worried. Somethin' wrong?"

"Probably not," Carson said. "I'll just check at the desk again."

"Never mind that." Zeke beckoned the waitress over. "Millie, get the key to Ms. Roberts's room, would you? Likely nothin', but Doc Carson here is getting anxious. You know these city fellers." He said the last with a wink at Carson.

"What? Oh, sure, boss. Be right back, gents."

"Come on, Carson," Zeke said. "Sit back down and relax. Have another beer."

"But you just sent the waitress away," Carson said, grinning and allowing himself to be led back to the table.

"I guess I did, didn't I? That was dumb."

A few moments later they heard the sound of hurried footsteps on the stairs, and Millie came in looking flustered. "Sir," she said, agitated, "you'd better come up and see this."

Carson was halfway up the stairs before the last word was out of her mouth.

The door to Jackie's room was ajar, as Millie had left it in her hurry. Carson pushed it open, half dreading that he would find Jackie's body within. The room was empty. He took a step inside, puzzled, glancing around. Jackie's gun belt hung on a peg near the door, and on the bed was a bag, still open. But aside from her absence, he didn't immediately see anything wrong.

Just then Martenga, Sato, Millie, and Zeke arrived at the doorway behind him.

He turned to Millie. "What...?"

She pointed to the bed. "There, on the pillow."

There was a note. Carson grabbed it up and read it out loud, "Carson. You have the artifact we want. We have something you want. Trade? Stay put. We'll be in touch."

Carson felt a knot in his stomach, then a slow, simmering rage. It was all he could do not to crumple the note into a tiny ball, but instead, stiffly, he passed it to Martenga. "Fucking tomb raiders," he snarled, in a tone that would blister paint.

Back in the saloon, the four of them—Carson, Zeke, Martenga, and Sato—sat in a quiet corner discussing the situation.

"It was that bastard, Herbert," Carson growled. "Somehow he knew about the artifact we found."

"He said that?" Sato wondered.

"Not in so many words, but I got that impression. The timing."

"Who's Herbert?" Zeke asked.

"No idea. Guy came up to me on the street soon after we got to town. You don't know the name?"

"Nobody local." He turned to Martenga. "Anyone else come in yesterday with you and the lady?"

"Not that I noticed, and I think I would have."

"Huh," Zeke snorted, and thought for a moment. "We did have a few folks come in last week, didn't stay at the hotel. I figured they were new hands for one of the ranches."

"But how could they have known about the artifact?" Satoshi asked.

"There must be a leak in the camp," Carson said, "maybe unintentional. It wouldn't be the first time."

"What's this artifact you're talking about?" Martenga asked. "It must be something special for all this trouble."

"What do you know about the natives here on Raven?" Carson asked him.

"The basics. They flourished here in The Rift circa ten thousand years ago, neolithic civilization, not quite bronze age, but they had agriculture and worked gold and silver, and softer gems like firestones. Moved north as the climate warmed and the valley dried out. Still around, but more nomadic now. What am I missing, Carson?"

"What about their legends of sky people?"

Martenga made the timoan equivalent of a shrug. "Lots of cultures have legends of sky people. Heck, so do we, and ours are justified." He grinned. The timoan people had been in their iron age when discovered by human spacefarers.

At Carson's scowl, he added, "But that's not what you meant. Okay, legends of gods from the skies, taking on aspects of local animals, as well as the timoanoid or humanoid natives. Some cave art and carvings, a mix of figures and symbols like stars and triangles." He looked around the table. Carson was nodding slightly, but Zeke was shaking his head. "Something else?" Martenga asked him.

"You ain't wrong," Zeke said, "but the legends here are much richer. The sky gods were powerful, with flying chariots that even the rocs avoided. Flying mountains, even. Stories of heroes and monsters. Great battles!"

"Oral history," Carson said, breaking in on Zeke's enthusiasm. "Some of the natives tell stories. With no written records, it's hard to tell how much was passed down over time, and how much is recent embellishment. Some of it correlates with tales from other planets, but it could be contamination."

"So this artifact you found," Martenga said, "it somehow relates to these legends?"

"It doesn't prove anything itself, but—"

They were interrupted by a boy of about twelve who came in, breathless, carrying a small package. "Which one of you is Dr. Carson?"

"That's me."

"A man told me to give you this."

"What man, where?" Carson demanded.

"Easy," Zeke said. "This is Arne Jackson's boy, he's a good kid. Answer his questions, son."

"I never seen him before. At the edge of town. He said to deliver this to you here, and then he rode off."

"Okay," Zeke said. "You did good. Go tell Millie at the bar I said you could have a soda or ice or whatever. Off you go." He waved to her to give the okay.

"Thanks, Mr. Zeke." The boy scurried off.

Carson opened the package. Inside, in a plastic bag, was a cheap-model omniphone and a lock of green hair. Jackie's. Carson's grip threatened to crush the phone.

"Now what?" Satoshi said.

"We wait."

Satoshi seemed flustered. "But shouldn't we call the police or something?"

Zeke snorted. "Nearest law enforcement's in Ravensport," he said. "Wouldn't get here before tomorrow, day after, even if they deigned to scramble out here for something as minor as a missin' person."

"But—"

"We'll handle it," Carson said.

Some minutes later, the omniphone rang, with the caller identified as "Herbert."

Carson stabbed at the screen to answer, and without giving Herbert a chance to talk, snarled, "You want the artifact? Then we deal on my terms. I want Roberts and ten thousand credits for the trouble."

The others at the table stared at him, horrified. He motioned them to silence, but beckoned Martenga to listen closer. He continued, "You were willing to pay cash for the artifact before, so you've got the money. I'll tell you when and where we make the exchange."

"*You're crazy, Carson. The deal is Roberts only, and—*"

"She's a spacer, she takes risks all the time. But if anything happens to her, the price will be half a million credits. If you know what the artifact is, you know it's worth it. You'll also have the UDT after you for murder."

"*Roberts only, and we don't cut her fingers off. Otherwise, we start sending them to you one at a time until you deal.*"

Shit, Carson thought. This was going in a direction he didn't like. "How do I know she's still alive? Or that you even have her at all?"

"*She's right here. She's been listening, and she ain't happy. I'll put her on.*"

A female voice came on. Carson recognized it as Jackie, but not the edge of panic in her voice.

"*Hannibal, what the fuck are you doing? These guys are serious, let them have the damned artifact!*"

"Not before I get you back safe, Jackie. It's the only leverage I have. And I *will* get you back safe!"

"Just get me—" Her voice cut off as if someone had muffled her.

The man came back on. *"Of course you'll get her back safe, Carson. Just bring us the artifact."*

The defiance left Carson's voice. "All right. Let's do a trade. When and where?"

Herbert gave map coordinates and a time late in the day.

"That won't work. I need time to go back to the camp to get it."

"Tomorrow noon, then. Same place."

"Okay. Call me at ten, and we'll work the details. You're not getting anything until I see Jackie safe."

"And you're not getting her until I see the artifact. We'll talk. Now you'd better get moving." The connection clicked off.

Martenga leaned away from the omniphone and stared at him. "What are you doing, Carson? Trying to get Jackie killed?"

"No, just the opposite. But I wanted to get a feel for the opposition. There has to be at least two of them, one to deliver the omni, one with Jackie. More likely at least three. Did you hear anything in the background?" Timoan hearing was more acute than a human's.

"Not really. There was a slight reverberation, like they were in an empty room, or underground in a tunnel with hard walls, not dirt."

"A mine tunnel, perhaps? The rock around here is sandstone."

"Maybe. I can't tell *that* much from the sound."

Carson turned to Zeke. "You know the area as well as anyone, right?"

"Yep, better'n most."

"Okay," he said, unfurling his own omni screen to full size and laying it out on the table. He brought up a map of the area around Montresor, showing the valley floor and part of the canyon. He pointed at a spot. "They suggested doing the trade here." It was an area where the floor sloped downward, scabland terrain that merged into the main canyon. The rendezvous was where two smaller coulees crisscrossed in an X.

Zeke looked at it and nodded. "I see what they're doing. Plenty of cover, several ways in and out. And if they've got the people, they can see who's coming and going."

"They don't even need the people if they put a couple of cameras up there," Martenga said.

"Good point, but the people have to come from somewhere," Carson said. "Zeke, do you know of any old mines, ones that aren't being worked by folks you trust, that would be an easy ride from there? Assume they'd be bringing a prisoner with them, and also that they'd have to make a getaway after."

Zeke examined the map, panning and zooming it a bit. He tapped several locations, marking them with a symbol. "There are mines here, here, and here that, far as I know, have been worked out. There are a couple of smaller pits there and there," he added, tapping the map again, "but they never amounted to much and don't go back far. This one"—he pointed to one the mines he'd marked earlier—"is near the Johnson claim here." He added another symbol. "That's still being worked, so if they're trying to hide, they wouldn't be near it."

Zeke studied the map a moment longer. "For what it's worth, there's an old aboriginal site in the cliffs just over the canyon rim here." He pointed. "The place goes pretty far back in. They were mining too, but it was pretty much looted clean twenty years back. There's nothing much there now."

Carson and Martenga examined the map, comparing the marked mine sites with the terrain.

"These two mines are pretty close together," Martenga noted.

"They are, aren't they? Zeke, were these part of the same claim?"

"Might have been, I'd have to check. Why?"

"They're on opposite sides of the same ridge. I wonder if they tunneled straight through."

"Let me check." Zeke pulled out his own omni and began tapping through to access the claims database.

"What are you thinking, Carson?" Martenga asked him.

"I'm thinking that either of those make a convenient spot to get to the rendezvous from, and that if I were holed up after doing something illegal, it'd be nice to have a back door."

"Okay, but there could be side tunnels all through that ridge. And even if that is where they've got Jackie, what do you hope to do about it? We can't move on it without risking her."

"Perhaps. I need to check something myself." He opened another window on the screen showing the map and started tapping away.

Zeke closed his omni and said, "Yep, those two are the old McPherson claim. He had most of that ridge staked. Closed up seven or eight years back. I remember now, he'd had a problem with cave-ins, and it was pretty much dry by then anyway."

"Bingo," Carson muttered, and then looked up. "Cave-ins, you said?"

"As I recall, yes. Didn't pay much attention at the time. Why?"

Carson pointed to the window he'd opened on the map. "That native site may have been looted, but it was still part of an archeological survey done back around '07. I've got the map from that here. Give me a sec." Carson fiddled with the display for a few moments, rotating and zooming the inset, then dragging it to the edge of the canyon on the larger map.

"There," he said, and sat back. The archeological survey showed the outline of ancient tunnels underlying part of the ridge the McPherson claim spanned.

Zeke let out a low whistle. "Well, hell, no wonder he had cave-ins."

Martenga looked thoughtful. "That's quite a coincidence, don't you think?"

"Maybe," Carson said. "But think about it. The natives were mining firestones. So was McPherson. Firestones form when water seeps through the rock and leaves dissolved silica behind. Water follows paths of least resistance. McPherson and the natives were probably both mining the same vein from different ends."

"Okay," the timoan said, "but we still don't know if that's where they're keeping Jackie. Or if it is, how well guarded it is. Or if we can even get into it from the cliffside."

"True. But that last bit, my tunneling timoan friend, is where you come in."

"Me? I may be descended from cousins to your meerkats, but that doesn't mean I can dig. Not through sandstone, not without a boring machine."

"I'm hoping you won't have to do any actual digging, just follow existing tunnels. Maybe move a few loose stones."

"How am I supposed to do that without a map?"

"I'm going to trust your judgment and knowledge. You *do* know how to use a ground-penetrating radar, don't you?"

"Wait, you have a GPR? Handheld?"

"Yes, back at the camp."

Zeke had been listening to the exchange between the two archeologists, not entirely following, but he got the gist. "So I take it you boys have some kind of plan?"

Carson looked at him. "Well, it still has some holes in it, but it's starting to come together."

☆   ☆   ☆

Carson's return to camp alone raised questions among the crew there. But he was the boss; he brushed them off.

"Where's Satoshi? And I thought you were bringing someone else back?"

"Change of plans. I'll explain later," Carson said, scrambling to pull together the artifact, in its lockbox, and the portable GPR. "I have to get back."

"Now? You're going to ride at night?"

"Pallas is almost full. There's plenty of light. No worries. Back in a couple of days."

On his way back, he paused outside of town to swap a rock for the artifact, and hide the latter.

Carson rode to the rendezvous, expecting trouble. Herbert waited for him, holding a gun on Jackie who sat, blindfolded, on another ghorsel, her hands tied to the saddle.

"No sudden moves, Carson. You're covered. Now, dismount and set the artifact on the ground."

Carson did so, placing the lockbox on the ground a couple of meters away. "Now, let Jackie go."

"Not yet. Bart! Check the box."

Crap, this isn't going to work, thought Carson, hearing footsteps behind him.

"It's not in the box," Carson said.

"What do you mean?" Herbert raised his gun to Jackie.

"Lower your weapon. Do you want the artifact, or do you want a world of hurt? You're not the only one with backup."

"*Hannibal?*" Jackie shouted. "What are you doing?"

"Yeah, what are you trying to pull?"

"I expected a double-cross. I had to see Roberts alive. Let her go, then I'll tell you where I hid the artifact."

"No. Bring us the artifact, and we'll trade. You've got three hours. No tricks this time. Boys, keep him covered until we're gone." With that, Herbert turned to ride off with Jackie's ghorsel in tow.

As they disappeared up the canyon, he heard Jackie yell back. "*Carson, you bastard!*"

Shit, he thought. *That didn't go as planned.* He mounted up and turned to ride south.

☆   ☆   ☆

Martenga and Sato wriggled over the rubble pile that, according to the GPR, separated the old aboriginal tunnel from the McPherson mine. It had taken most of Carson's allotted three hours to get this far, once they'd confirmed where Herbert had taken Jackie.

It was a tight squeeze, and they'd already crawled more than ten meters with no signs of the passage widening.

"Are you sure this is right?" Satoshi gasped as he squirmed through yet another tight gap between two boulders. Martenga, ahead of him, wasn't having it much easier. Although smaller than Sato, he was burdened with the GPR.

"Ask me again in ten minutes," Martenga muttered.

"At least Jackie's skinnier than I am. Getting back should be easier."

The plan was for the timoan to bring Jackie back the way they had come, with Sato and Carson creating a distraction. Carson would be outside the main mine entrance, while Satoshi escaped out the back. Carson hadn't wanted to put his student at risk like that, but the young man had insisted.

They pushed on, and soon the heap of rock debris they'd been climbing over sloped down to the floor of a larger passage. They were in the McPherson mine.

"Now what?" Sato whispered.

Martenga put up a hand for silence, listening. There weren't any choices here. The tunnel went straight ahead, then bent to the right. "Turn your light off," Martenga said quietly. His own light was much dimmer than Sato's; his dark vision was better. He turned it off anyway.

A scattering of glowing flecks shone from the walls, tiny fragments of low-grade firestone not worth digging out. Farther on, a more general lessening of the darkness indicated a lit tunnel ahead.

"Okay," Martenga said, keeping his voice low. "Keep the lights out. Quietly now, let's move."

They crept on, rounding the curve. Soon they came to a wider cross tunnel, dimly illuminated by lights strung along the ceiling. The timoan called a halt a couple of meters short.

He held the ground-penetrating radar against the wall of the tunnel, checking its display, then did the same on the other side. "Stay here, keep quiet. I'm going to figure out which way." He moved forward silently into the cross tunnel. He paused, turning to listen intently one way, and then the other. He did it again, this time tapping his omni each time. Finally, he nodded and beckoned to Sato.

"What's with the omni?" Sato whispered.

"Sonic pulse. I can hear higher frequencies than humans." He pointed down one branch of the tunnel. "I don't hear anyone that way, and it sounds like it opens up. That's the back entrance. This way"—he pointed down the other branch—"sounds like where Jackie is." He checked the pistol at his side, and Sato did likewise. "Okay," Martenga said, "we go this way."

Carson halted his ghorsel at the rendezvous point, a kilometer from the old McPherson mine. He was deliberately early, but he knew that the kidnappers would be watching for him. He dismounted, unfastened the lockbox from where he'd secured it to his saddle, and walked a few paces away from his mount. His gaze swept the surrounding ridgetops.

"All right," he shouted, his voice echoing off the surrounding walls. "I've brought what you wanted." He raised the box, then put it down on the ground. "Where's Jackie?"

There was no answer, only the whisper of the wind over the rocks. Carson turned and paced around, not wanting to stand in one spot for too long.

"Hello?" he shouted again.

This time he was answered, an amplified voice shouting back at him, the weird acoustics of the crossed canyons making the direction impossible to determine. "Okay, Carson. Open the box and walk away."

"Not until I see Jackie. Bring her out where I can see her!"

"That's not how it works this time."

What's keeping Marten? Carson thought furiously. *He was supposed to signal when he had Jackie. What if the omni signal was too weak to penetrate the rock over the tunnels?* He had to stall longer.

"Then I guess you don't really want this," he shouted back, walking over to pick up the box and moving to put it back on his ghorsel's saddle.

"Enough!" A shot rang out, spalling chips off a boulder a few meters from where Carson stood. He spotted the flash; it came from a point on the lip of the coulee to the northeast. *That's one,* he thought. He stepped away from his mount and put the box on the ground again, then took a casual step toward the boulder the shot had hit. It was potential cover.

"That was a warning," the voice came. "Next one is either in you or in Roberts."

"I hear you!" Carson called back. "Just relax, and we can still both get what we want." *Come on, Marten! What's keeping you?* "Just show me Jackie!"

"Okay, here she is. Look to your one o'clock!"

Carson looked. Across the canyon from where he'd seen the muzzle flash, silhouetted against the sky, a figure stood and waved at him. It was too far away to tell who it was, something the kidnappers were probably counting on. *If that's Jackie,* Carson thought, *then I'm a timoan. But that's two.*

"Now show us the artifact!" The figure atop the ridge disappeared.

Carson swore to himself. He was out of time. "All right," he shouted back, raising his hands in appeasement.

Martenga and Sato found Jackie bound and gagged in a side tunnel off the passage they'd been following. Her guard was fifty meters farther on, near the main entrance to the mine, his back to them. Good, that would ruin his night vision. "Stay here," Martenga told Sato, and then slipped in to release her.

The side tunnel was dark, but there was enough light for Jackie to recognize the timoan as he sneaked up and motioned her to silence. Since she was gagged, the gesture was redundant, and she rolled her eyes. He unfastened the gag and began working on her bindings.

"I hate this place!" she hissed. "What's happening? Where's Hannibal?"

"He's providing a distraction. I'm going to sneak you out a secret tunnel."

"Secret tunnel? What are you talking about?" By now Martenga had her hands free, and they both began working on untying her legs.

"There's a partly collapsed passage that connects to an old aboriginal mine. It's a squeeze, but that's how we got in here."

Her eyes widened as if in terror. "No fucking way! Sorry, I'm not going out that way."

"What's the problem?"

"I-I'm claustrophobic. There must be another way. Give me a gun, I'll shoot my way out. How many guards are there?"

"Don't you know? Never mind. I've got another idea. This way." They caught up with Sato, still watching the guard at the entrance.

"Anything?" Martenga asked him.

"There might be someone else out there, and I thought I heard a shot in the distance. Why aren't you taking Jackie back?"

"Change of plan. You take her out the back entrance, not the side tunnel. I'll distract the guards." To Jackie he said, "Stick with Sato. It's a tunnel, but a big one, and it should be lit all the way. You'll be fine."

"Are you sure?"

"Promise. Go! And quietly!"

As Sato and Jackie darted off down the tunnel, Martenga keyed his omni to send Carson the signal. Then he drew his pistol. Getting around the guard at the main entrance shouldn't be a problem, he had the advantages of surprise and speed. If it came to a shootout, though, well... The timoan knew he was a quick draw, but he also knew he couldn't hit the broad side of a barn.

Carson had started to step back toward the box when the omni on his wrist beeped. *Finally!* He leaned down as if to reach for the box, then converted the motion into a roll behind the boulder, drawing his pistol as he went, and snapping off a shot toward the gunman on the north ridge.

Answering fire came back from both sides of the canyon, and Carson alternated shots between the two. Bullets ricocheted off the rocks around him, scattered enough that he wasn't worried about their marksmanship, but the sheer volume meant they'd get lucky sooner or later. He picked his own shots more carefully, aiming for the flashes. Zeke was supposed to be giving him backup; where the hell was he?

Then he heard shots coming from the ridge behind him, and the fusillade around him lessened. Zeke must have arrived, at last, to help take the pressure off. But Carson was pinned down, and Herbert and his men could retreat under cover. If Marten and Sato hadn't gotten Jackie clear, things could end badly. He had to pursue.

He fired again, then, with Zeke laying covering fire, he dashed across the open toward the cross canyon. From there he could climb up and flank the gunman on the north ridge. Herbert, if Carson was lucky.

Martenga rode to the sound of the guns. He'd easily evaded the guard at the mine, firing enough shots to panic him into fleeing, then stealing his ghorsel. But gunshots ahead told him Carson needed help, and he had to distract the gang from following Satoshi and Jackie.

A shot came from behind him, probably the guard. Martenga fired back over his shoulder. Then for the hell of it, fired a few rounds toward the gunfire ahead. That should keep them off balance.

Carson was down; he'd been hit crossing the clearing, but he'd made it to cover, and the wound didn't seem bad. Above him, the firing continued sporadically. Someone else had joined the fight. Satoshi, maybe?

His omni sounded again. It was a message. JACKIE IS SAFE. ON OUR WAY BACK TO TOWN.—Sato. Then who was shooting?

Marten!

After that, things got kind of blurry.

Later, back at the saloon in Montresor, Carson, Sato, Zeke, and Martenga sat around a table drinking beers. Carson's left arm was in a sling. He'd taken a hit in his upper arm, but the town's autodoc had patched it up. He was pretty sure they had taken out at least one of the kidnappers, but there'd been no sign of them, save for some bloodstains, when law officers from Ravensport had finally shown up.

Sadly, Carson had missed Jackie when she left with them. He'd still been in the traumapod, and she hadn't wanted to stick around. Partly, Sato had said, because she was worried about getting back to the *Arabella*, her ship, before it departed.

But Carson suspected it was because she blamed him for everything.

"So, what was all this fuss about an artifact anyway?" Zeke asked while Millie brought another round of beer. "Most of what I've ever seen has been arrowheads and potsherds, with a few bits of carved firestone. Nothing worth that much trouble over."

"That's partly because a lot of it was cleaned out by tomb

raiders a long time ago," Carson said. "But remember the legends of the sky people we talked about before?"

"Yeah, so? I've seen a few petroglyphs and scratchings on cave walls. Triangles and alien-looking creatures." He glanced at Martenga. "No offense."

The timoan grinned back. "I don't have feathers or scales," he said.

"Exactly," Carson said. He looked at Martenga and Satoshi, then back at Zeke. "These guys know what I'm talking about, but have you ever heard of Quetzalcoatl or Kukulkan? Aztec and Mayan names of a certain god, from back on Earth?"

"Can't say that I have. What's the significance?"

"Maybe none at all, it might just be coincidence. But a number of ancient cultures, on different planets, have legends of sky gods. I find it interesting. What I also find interesting is that Quetzalcoatl, etcetera, are Earth legends of a feathered serpent." He lifted the lockbox from under his chair, set it on the table, and unlatched it. "This," he said, raising the lid, "is what all the fuss was about."

Even in the subdued lighting of the saloon, the fist-sized carved firestone gleamed and iridesced brilliantly, glowing with deep reds and flashes of green. There were gasps from around the table. Carson smiled and lifted it out of the box. It was an exquisitely carved head, something like a snake's or a lizard's, with a crest of feathers running from the brow up over the head and down to the neck.

"I'm just sorry Jackie didn't get a chance to see it," Carson said.

"You'll see her again," Sato said. "Isn't her spaceline based out of Sawyers World?"

"It is," Carson said, "but the university's talking about leasing its own ship. I'm not sure we'd cross paths."

"You could, you know, call her," Martenga said. "I think she likes you."

"I thought so too, until I botched the swap," Carson said wistfully. The last thing he remembered was her shouting at him, *Carson, you bastard!* Would they ever be on the same planet, at the same time, long enough for him to explain himself to her? He could hope.

T-Space wasn't *that* big, was it?

The End

CLAIM JUMPED

Jane Lindskold

"Phoenix, I didn't murder Gus," Jun pleaded, squeezing her hands tightly between his. "Whatever else I did, I didn't murder him. You do believe me, don't you?"

As Phoenix leaned forward to softly kiss her husband on one cheek, she wondered if she did believe him, but she said what he needed to hear. "I believe you, Jun."

The jury was out, but neither of them had any doubt what the verdict would be. In a few short hours, Jun wouldn't be able to remember anything. No matter what he'd done, Phoenix could give him this small comfort... even though she wondered if he deserved it.

The case had started out bad, gotten worse. The facts were plain and simple: Jun East and his partner, Gus Ganon, were working their isolated claim: the asteroid listed in the catalog as NG721, but which they called Nugget. It was a sizeable bit of rock, particularly notable for a vein of silver, along with a second vein of high-grade iron.

On the fatal day, the partners had gotten into an argument. The vid feed from the camera monitoring the ore processing and smelting machinery showed what had happened in vivid—if silent—detail. The silence was because the crushing stage was deafening, so the boys had long-ago disabled the audio. Like everyone in the courtroom, Phoenix had watched the unfolding scene with fixed attention.

Jun stood in the processing room. He was a handsome man in his mid-thirties, broad-shouldered and muscular, because not all his work could be done wearing an exoskeleton, like the one he was wearing today to help him shift the bricks of processed metal from the conveyer. He wasn't unduly tall, but then height wasn't an advantage for a miner or really for anyone who lived in a contained environment, as most spacers did.

Because he was wearing ear protectors, Jun didn't hear when Gus entered the room, though calling it a "room" was a stretch. Like most of the chambers on Nugget, it was a repurposed area, in this case, one of the early excavation areas, so the walls were rough rock and its shape irregular.

Gus strode over to Jun, every line in his lean, wiry body showing his tension. He moved to where Jun could see his face, then tapped one ear as a signal that he wanted to talk. Jun nodded, touched buttons on the wrist-mounted remote he wore to shut down the ore crusher. Then he removed his protective earmuffs, slinging them around his neck as he prepared to listen to what he partner had to say.

Gus, in turn, had slid open the cover on his data tablet, called up a file, and then angled the tablet so Jun could see what was displayed. It didn't look like much, several columns of numbers, but Jun's reaction made clear that whatever these numbers were, he was horrified to discover that Gus had seen them.

Gus said something to Jun. Jun replied angrily. Gus snapped the tablet cover closed and began to stalk from the room. When his back was turned, Jun struck, grasping Gus with the grippers on the exoskeleton, grippers meant to handle heavy blocks of refined metal and buckets of unprocessed ore. What would have been a solid grasp from a man's hands smashed Gus's collarbone. Blood spurted forth, flesh and fragments of bone oozing up through the metal claws.

Gus opened his mouth in a soundless scream. Jun panicked. Raising his partner's writhing, screaming body in the exoskeleton's claws, he held it in midair, staring in shock. Then, almost certainly realizing that Gus was doomed, he slid his ear protectors on before turning back on the power to the crusher. A machine built to pulverize ore makes short work of a human body. Temperatures needed to separate ore from waste rock render a person into nothing in no time at all. Jun might have gotten away with it, might have cleaned up after himself, made some excuse for

Gus vanishing, but the bad luck that had plagued him from the moment Gus confronted him continued.

The door opened, admitting a stocky woman clad in an EVA suit with the hood off and the gloves dangling loose at her wrists. Her name was Tisi Tone, and she was the owner of a shipping company. On the fatal day, she was due to deliver supplies to Nugget, and take away a load of silver bricks. When she hadn't raised either Gus or Jun, she'd docked, let herself in, and gone to the processing room, thinking that the partners were getting together the cargo.

She arrived in time to witness Jun sliding Gus's mangled body into the hopper. Without a pause, she pulled her sidearm from its holster. Within moments, Jun was in custody.

The video image ended there, and Napier Oakes, the prosecutor who was trying the case on behalf of the Rolling Rock Asteroid Belt Conglomerate Government, took up the account.

"Although the tablet itself was destroyed along with Gus Ganon's body, forensic techs were able to retrieve the data from the database on NG721. What Gus confronted his partner with was evidence that Jun East, far from being a simple miner, was actually involved in hacking and fraud on a grand scale. In an attempt to cover up his criminal actions, Jun murdered his partner."

Over and over, Jun denied having killed anyone. Chanel Sulwyn, his defense counsel, did her best, but with that recording, with the blood and tissue samples the forensics team collected and analyzed, there was little she could do but attempt to get the sentence changed from murder to manslaughter.

Sulwyn emphasized that Jun's crimes had been of the Robin Hood sort. Not all miners owned their own claims, as Gus and Jun did. Many worked for large companies. These companies paid in scrip that could only be redeemed at company stores. Jun's crime had been altering the electronic scrip records so that, as he himself put it when questioned, "The miners would be paid enough to balance the horribly inflated prices charged by the mining companies."

That Jun himself took nothing was a point in his favor, but one that, in the end, was not enough to save him.

By the time the jury went out, Phoenix felt as if she, as well as Jun, had been on trial.

When presenting his case, Oakes hadn't been willing to stop at the obvious scenario: that Jun had been involved in fraud and theft; that Gus had apparently caught Jun, confronted him, then paid with his life. His voice silky and insinuating, he'd made much of the fact that Phoenix had been romantically involved with Gus, that she'd met Jun through Gus, then, after a whirlwind courtship, had married him.

The way Oakes had presented events, Phoenix had been transformed into a succubus who had seduced Jun away from his "partner." On Oakes's lips, the word that simply defined a business relationship became a synonym for "spouse." Phoenix was the homewrecker, the destroyer, the one who had driven her man to murder.

It helped Oakes's case that Phoenix was gorgeous. Pixy small, with a figure her close-fitting EVA suit showed off to full advantage, she had adorned her depilated head—for like most who spent a lot of time in space, she viewed hair merely as an inconvenience that clogged filters—by having an elaborate coif tattooed onto her scalp. This depicted her namesake bird resting its head atop her own, its feathers trailing down and to the sides of her head before vanishing beneath her collar, inviting speculation as to whether the bird's embrace continued beneath.

Nor did it help that Phoenix herself was a skilled miner, although she favored prospecting over actual mining. That preference had been turned against her. She'd been presented as a wanderer, a flitter, more at home in *Mustang*'s pilot chair than at her spouse's side. It had even been implied that if anyone bothered to search, they'd probably find she had an undeclared lover or three dotted around the Belt.

All untrue. The deceiver had been Jun. Faithful to the terms of their wedding vows, Phoenix didn't doubt, but not honest, or at least not honest in the way the law designated honesty. She wished Jun had confided in her, but out of a misguided belief that he was keeping her "safe," he hadn't.

"We find Jun East guilty of the murder of Augustus 'Gus' Ganon," Judge Quenby boomed, obviously enjoying the sound of her own voice, "and sentence him to serve a term equivalent to the lifespan during which his late partner could have been expected to benefit the community."

Phoenix had been expecting this. Hard labor had long been the "humane" penalty, one made easier to accept once some genius with more talent than common sense had invented the device commonly called a "slave driver," which enabled the will to be overridden, while the skills remained intact.

Phoenix had been expecting this sentence. What she hadn't expected was for it to hurt so much. As she rose from her seat, she resolved that she was going to clear Jun, and—she had to be honest—herself, as well. And if she couldn't clear him, somehow she'd set him free.

Goodbyes were brief, since statutes against cruel and unusual punishment had been interpreted to mean that a sentence should be carried out as quickly as possible. Why not? If there was a successful appeal, the unjustly condemned could be released, compensated for his time at guild rates minus a set amount for his room and board, then sent on his way. Meanwhile, why let him feel anguish? Why let the community go uncompensated for one minute less than necessary?

The rationale made perfect sense until you were the one watching your husband being led out the door, knowing that if you chanced to encounter him again, he'd have no idea who you were. Phoenix didn't want to take that chance. As soon as she and Jun had shared a final kiss and the prison guards had led him away, she all but ran out of the courthouse, down the steps, to where *Mustang* waited in the slips reserved for those called in as witnesses.

She glimpsed Tisi, whose testimony had been so damning, a few slips down, apparently reveling in being interviewed by the numerous newsbots that floated around her like planets around their primary star. When they saw Phoenix, several newsbots unceremoniously abandoned Tisi and sped toward her. Phoenix flung herself into *Mustang*'s cabin. The ship's AI didn't wait for her to give the command. As soon as the restraint harness had dropped over her shoulders, *Mustang* bolted.

Phoenix let the ship have his head, and leaned back in the seat that was the key element of her home: pilot's chair, office, entertainment center, gym, bedroom, and lab—bathroom and shower, too. The ship had cost—if not the Moon, as the old saying went—then a very nice asteroid that, a decade later, still produced pay dirt for one of the companies, ironically, Jun had been defrauding.

And worth every cred, Phoenix thought, and affectionately patted the seat.

Mustang—the AI—got them out of the vicinity of Rolling Rock City in record time, without violating any of the many safety regulations, then spoke. Sometimes Mustang affected a deep, nasal voice that was his idea of how a stallion would sound if it could talk, complete with a variety of snorts, whinnies, nickers, and even hoofbeats. The fact that he chose to address her in a neutral, vaguely masculine voice told Phoenix how deeply concerned the AI was.

"Did it bug you as much as it did me?"

"What? Jun getting life?"

"Not that. That was a given if he was convicted. No. The way Oakes went after you."

Phoenix forced a laugh, which came out more like a groan. "Well, I can't say that was exactly fun, but compared to what Jun came in for, I guess lascivious slander isn't much."

"But why did Oakes bother? I checked your background files and cross-referenced them with Oakes's résumé. He's only been out in Rolling Rock for two years. Unless you're hiding something from me, it's highly unlikely that you encountered each other in the years before I met you."

"You're right, I never laid eyes on him until court," Phoenix replied. Unasked, Mustang had sent her a cup of black coffee and a thick slice of pound cake. She sipped the one as she reviewed her recent excursions. "Last two years, I've either been out trying to strike pay dirt, or visiting Jun . . . and Gus. Heck, the boys even did most of the shopping. You haven't needed an overhaul. I've met with some company types, but pretty much been riding the range."

"Yet, given a perfectly good case," Mustang persisted, "based around the undeniable evidence that Jun was involved in some petty theft, and Gus caught him at it, Oakes decided to spend most of his designated time building a case around jealousy, hinting at you playing the two men off each other."

"Which I didn't," Phoenix said. "Heck, Gus and I were cooling even when he introduced me to Jun. I'd wondered if he'd introduced us because he thought we might clinch, and Gus liked the idea of keeping me—I am a damn fine prospector, thank you very much—in the family, so to speak. I said as much when was on the stand."

Mustang spoke in an eerily accurate echo of Oakes's rolling oratory. "How many a man has, once he has given something away, realized that he has lost a treasure? Perhaps Gus hinted at his lingering affection? Perhaps he suggested a triad? We will never know what he felt, but looking at the witness, we cannot imagine his heart did not carry a flame for the lovely Phoenix."

"Horse-hockey!" Phoenix let herself show the anger she'd hidden in court. "When Oakes went on like that, I wanted to shake him, but the judge had already made clear that 'irregularities' would not be tolerated. I didn't see how getting cited for contempt would do Jun—or me—any good."

"Unfortunately, your restraint could have been taken," Mustang interjected, "as an admission that the prosecution was onto something. And there's another thing that's bothering me: the judge's behavior."

"What did Judge Quenby do?"

"While we've been chatting, I've analyzed the courtroom proceedings. Chanel Sulwyn was repeatedly told not to speculate, but Oakes was permitted to heap up sufficient lascivious innuendo to make his subtext clear to the dullest juror before being told to get back on track. I'll shoot you the details when I have them charted, but I think the judge was bought."

"Judge and prosecutor both?"

"And maybe part of the jury."

"But who's going to gain from getting a miner brain-slaved? Sure, Jun had some excellent skills, but he wasn't unique."

Except to me. Except as a person. Except as the hardworking idealistic idiot I loved enough to marry, in the "till death do us part" romantic way. I'm realizing more and more, now that he's been taken from me, that I meant it then and I still mean it. Jun's alive, and I'm gonna get him back. While I'm at it, I'll find who killed Gus, because he was our friend, as well as Jun's partner.

"Are you sure Jun wasn't specifically targeted?" Mustang persisted. "Maybe someone needs a bunch of miners for some secret project?"

Phoenix shook her head. "All of this is just to recruit Jun? Easier to pay him. Sure, he and Gus owned Nugget free and clear, but that didn't make them rich."

"I remember you telling me that Gus had suggested they issue shares so they'd have the ready cash to hire help, but Jun wasn't interested."

"Part of Jun's fear of big business," Phoenix explained with a sad smile, rolling her empty coffee cup between her palms before stuffing it into the recycler. "Jun was certain that as soon as he gave anything away, it would be used as a hook to yank away the rest."

I wonder if that fear was why Jun proposed a life-contract marriage. I wonder if, rather than loving me, he was afraid of losing me. But, no. Stop being stupid. Don't let your hurt get in the way of your head.

Mustang said, "Another argument against my proposed Recruitment Motive is why kill Gus? Better to get him as an accessory to Jun's crimes. That wouldn't get Gus brain-slaved, but he'd probably have been sentenced to a year or so of remunerative labor. All right, if we discard pushing Jun into involuntary servitude, what's left?"

"Let's see . . ." Phoenix stuffed the uneaten pound cake after her coffee cup. "We can rule out someone having a grudge against Gus, killing him, then framing Jun. Oakes went out of his way to establish that no one had anything against Gus. Neither of them owned much—except for Nugget, of course, but there're a lot of asteroids out there. Why commit murder to get this one?"

"Hang on, don't toss that so fast." Mustang nearly whinnied in excitement. "Getting ownership of Nugget would explain the attack on you, as well."

"Why?"

"With Jun out of the way, you own his share of Nugget. Do you know who Gus's heir would be?"

"I'm pretty sure Gus mentioned a brother, but that brother wouldn't get Nugget. Jun's paranoia again. When the boys bought Nugget, Jun insisted that they will each other their share. When Jun and I got married, they amended the agreement so that I would inherit his share. Gus wasn't thrilled until we added a clause that he would get first right to buy me out."

"Work with me on this," Mustang said, adding the sound effect of racing hoofbeats beneath his words. "There's one circumstance where the provision to inherit wouldn't hold true: if *you* were complicit in Gus's death. A murderer cannot benefit from her crime. So if later evidence showed up that you goaded Jun into killing Gus, neither of you would inherit Jun's share. Then Nugget would go to whoever is Gus's heir."

Phoenix didn't need to look at the med readout at the corner of her panel to know her heartrate had just jumped to a dangerous level. She gripped the arms of her pilot seat.

"Could there be something on Nugget? Something someone else wants, someone who wants it enough to kill Gus, frame Jun, frame me? Damn! If that's true, we've got to get there and find out before they take it, or before charges can be brought against me."

"Shifting to gallop," Mustang said with a wild whinny. "You get some sleep. I'll wake you when we're there."

Mustang woke Phoenix well before they arrived. "Long-range scans showed anomalies," he announced as she was scrubbing grit out of her eyes. "Thought you'd better see. Putting on your screen. Coffee's almost ready. Rye or wheat toast?"

"Rye," Phoenix replied absently, her gaze skimming the sensor report. "Thanks."

The singleship *Mustang* had been designed as Phoenix's ideal of what a prospector's ship should be. She'd insisted on the best scanners that could be fit in the ship's relatively small profile, and hadn't even winced too much when her mech-tech offered her some scavenged from a military "scout"—which she had taken to mean "spy"—craft. She'd never regretted it, because those sensors had kept her from wasting time and fuel investigating a promising asteroid whose promise proved superficial.

This time, I think those sensors may have saved my life. There's a ship inside the hangar bay, and that bay should be empty.

"No one should have been able to get in there," she said to Mustang. "After the on-site murder investigation, I wiped the codes and sealed Nugget. Didn't want gawkers or reporters in there."

"How good are the protocols?" Mustang asked. "Nugget's not my department."

"Good," Phoenix said. "Better than good. Only three people knew the cycle: me, Jun, and Gus."

"Could Jun have given away something when he was interrogated?"

"No. I thought of that. I supervised the investigation, then changed the codes after. I didn't tell even Jun that I'd done it."

"Well, no one should be in there," Mustang said. He paused, and Phoenix knew he was going to try a joke. "I guess you locked the barn door after the horse got out."

"Ha-ha...Or someone set a Trojan horse to let them get in no matter what I did. It wouldn't have been easy, but neither would framing Jun. Damn! I should have wiped the whole system and reloaded from scratch."

"Give yourself a break. Your husband had been arrested for murdering his partner, who was both of your close friend—and, as Oakes wouldn't let you forget, your own former lover."

"Is there a reason for bringing that up?"

"You know there is. We talked about how there might be an attempt to frame you, too. What if this is part of it? Who would guess that you'd turn around and come back so soon after the trial had ended. Many humans would avoid a place with such painful associations for a long while after."

"Or go get drunk or whatever." Phoenix's breakfast had appeared, and she made a sandwich from rye bread, fried eggs, and slices of sharp Swiss cheese, and then ate half while she thought about how best to explain. "They probably didn't consider that my reaction to getting publicly shamed would be to run to my ship."

"Or on your ship being so insightful," Mustang added, very pleased with himself. "So, let's assume they don't expect you here. Still, I don't think going in the front door is a great idea."

"Me either. But I don't want to delay. Plot us a course that will use the local rocks as cover, then bring us in." She finished the other half of her sandwich. "Pull up the specs for Nugget."

"Done, and doing." The AI's voice sounded flatter than usual.

"And thank you very much. I'm sorry I've forgotten my manners, O best and brightest of companions."

"I like that. You can heap on praise anytime."

"Sure, O Faithful Steed. Now, some peace and quiet, so my slow human brain can process. I'm going to trust you to handle everything else—including getting me another breakfast and more coffee."

"Do I get an extra nosebag of oats?"

"You do, but you get something even better."

"What?"

"You avoid the likelihood that if I fail, you'll get mind-wiped like poor Jun. You don't think that whoever is after me is going to leave you around as a witness, do you?"

There was a long pause, especially for the AI. "Would you believe I'd overlooked that?"

"Yeah, I would." Phoenix patted her armrest, like she might have the neck of a real horse. "You've been so busy looking out for me that you didn't realize that, in doing so, you're also looking out for yourself."

"Consider me reprimanded, and my enlightened self-interest activated. Let's find out who drygulched Gus, framed Jun, shamed you, and had the gall to decide I could be sent to the knackers!"

The design specs proved extremely useful. Like many asteroids, over its many repeated journeys around the Rolling Rock belt, Nugget had been repeatedly holed, dinged, and dented. Like any sensible, economy-minded asteroid miners, Gus and Jun had repurposed various of these dings and dents. The largest had become the hangar bay, which had been fitted with doors, so that it could also serve as a secure storage area for the processed ore. Others had been used to hold for various other necessities.

"Fuel conduit," she said aloud. "That's my best way in."

Mustang's reply came after a pause, so the AI's attention had been elsewhere.

"Yes. That should work. It's a tight fit, but you're small. Then what?"

"Then I find out who's there, what they're doing. If it's at all iffy—which we're both assuming it is—I make a record of it. Then I sneak back to you. We clear out and let the law take over."

"If we can trust the law." Clearly the prospect of being sent to the knackers had Mustang spooked.

"I think we can. Not Judge Quenby, certainly, but if the whole legal system is corrupt, then this setup wouldn't have been necessary. One of the things you can do while I'm creeping around is some research into just who we might be able to trust. I was planning on starting with Chanel Sulwyn, but we'd better check in case she might have been bought, too."

"I can do that." Mustang sounded moderately more confident. "I downloaded a lot of material about the legal system when Jun was arrested. I thought we might be able to advise Sulwyn, but when that video was revealed, well, I guess I gave up."

"You and me and him and her, all," Phoenix said. "Don't blame yourself. Now, let me get suited up."

After the singleship *Mustang*, Phoenix's most expensive business investment had been a very good EVA suit. Although spectrographic analysis and densitometer maps were useful, actual physical specimens were required to register a claim.

Phoenix's suit had several useful bells and whistles, including a chameleon coat, because she preferred to see rather than be seen. She'd opted out of built-in jets, because they were killer expensive to repair and meant the whole suit would be in the shop if one went out. Temporary jets were cheaper, and a lot easier to replace, even if they didn't look as good. Even better, especially for today's job, Phoenix could unstrap the units after she'd landed, slimming her frame down, the better to get into tight places.

Never been in a tighter place than I am today, Phoenix thought as she drifted to a soft landing only a few meters from her target crater. *I hope you appreciate this, Jun. Heck, Gus, I hope you do, too, because this'll hopefully get the real murderer.*

"Mustang," she tight-beamed over her comm-link, "I'm going in. Eavesdrop as you can."

Both she and the AI knew that it was possible they could be cut off from each other once she was inside and thick layers of dense ore-laden rock got between them.

I always meant to get a drone for Mustang so he could come along if he wanted. Definitely move that up on the shopping list.

Smelting ore required a lot more fuel than could be supplied by solar collectors. Jun and Gus had invested in a small reactor that, being sensible, they'd mounted in a hollow on Nugget's exterior, where meters of solid rock provided shielding in case of a malfunction. As with the hangar, they'd built bay doors to protect the reactor from rocks and dust—as well as their more opportunistic neighbors. Phoenix had an access card, so she slipped in without triggering any alarms.

The power conduit had been laid in a tunnel wide enough to permit maintenance and upgrades. While not within anyone's definition of "roomy," there was space enough for Phoenix to pull herself along. When she came to the conduit's end, she eased open the access panel enough to listen. Once she was sure she was alone, she dropped through and pushed down until her lightly magnetized boots caught hold of the metal flooring. She'd long been proficient in the art of glide-walking, and moved soundlessly to the door between the fuel room and the rest of the interior complex.

Once again, she eased open the door, listened, and reassured herself that she wasn't about to bump into anyone before going out. Initially, Gus and Jun had camped in their ship, which was quite a bit larger than *Mustang*, but (or so Phoenix thought) not nearly as comfortable. They must have thought so, too, because as soon as they had raised enough credits, they'd created a small, sealed habitat. Then, over the years, in the way of burrowing animals of all sorts, they'd expanded their warren. Air and pressure had been the first big luxury, enabling them to work without risking the integrity of their EVA suits. Metal walkways connecting frequently used areas had been another quality-of-life investment. They hadn't bothered with lighting throughout, though, settling for luminescent striping, color-coded by level.

Phoenix guided herself by these strips now. They were arrayed in a classic rainbow pattern: ROYGBIV. The first, central level was green, and as the dig had expanded, the spectrum provided a directional guide—a useful thing where "up" and "down" were optional concepts. She had emerged from the conduit on Green Level, which had largely been mined out and now contained living quarters, storage, and processing facilities—but no intruders.

The hangar bay held a sleek passenger craft. Phoenix made a note of the registration number before continuing her inspection of Green Level and confirming that it was empty.

She drifted over to the nearest cross-shaft and listened. Nothing. Not giving herself time to get nervous, she dropped toward Blue, choosing that direction because that was where the most recent work had been done. If there was a new find, it was likely that way. She paused at Blue and Indigo, inspecting for light or sound, but only oppressive darkness and silence met her. Then she dropped toward the newly opened Violet Level.

Phoenix hadn't been down here since joining the boys for a ceremonial drink and coin toss when they'd opened the cross-shaft. They'd always done that, with whoever won the toss getting to choose which direction they would excavate—the new tunnels were too narrow to admit more than one person at a time. If one or the other hit something good, then they'd concentrate their attention that way.

Silly, I suppose, but that friendly competition kept them fresh. I remember that day. Jun won the toss and chose to go deeper into the interior. Gus tried to make out he was perfectly happy with the other way, but since the densitometer readings showed he was likely to hit a pocket pretty soon, he wasn't thrilled. Still, they both knew it didn't matter. They'd share equally in any profit.

To Phoenix's astonishment, when she did hear voices, they were coming from Gus's tunnel. Subconsciously, she'd expected the intruders to be inspecting Jun's, since Jun had struck silver, the same he'd been smelting on the fatal day, and that'd been where new work was being done.

But could one of Gus's pockets have held something of interest?

Gus's tunnel expressed his personality. It was carefully cut, with shoring at appropriate points, as any experienced miner would do, but the shoring was almost always at maximum recommended distances, expressing his impatience with "fuss." The tunnel was cut tall enough for him to stand with room to spare. Gus claimed this was because an old slag burn on one leg made it awkward for him to crouch, but Phoenix had always thought it was because Gus hated being uncomfortable. He'd been the one who insisted they keep modifying Nugget to make it more livable.

Jun would probably still be living in the ship and breathing bottled air, spending his money on tools like the exoskeleton—and probably giving away too much to whoever showed up with a hard-luck story. They were good for each other, balancing priorities.

Whatever the reason, today Phoenix was grateful for Gus's indulgences. She took advantage of the minimal gravity and went high, pulling herself along the ceiling. No matter that humans now inhabited interstellar space, humanity hadn't changed in that "up" was usually the last place anyone looked.

The voices grew clearer as Phoenix moved closer but were far from distinct. Instead of trying to understand what was being said, she activated her recorder. She might not be able to understand the words, but the audio pickups were a lot better than human ears. Looking for the first indication of ambient light, she moved closer.

Three voices. Higher-pitched. Lower-pitched. And...vaguely familiar? Trying to place that last voice distracted Phoenix so much that she reached, gripped nothing, and only then realized that there was no more tunnel roof.

Pocket. Jun told me Gus had encountered a large cavern a couple of shifts before Jun confirmed he had hit that rich silver vein, so they shifted operations over there. This must be it. This is a heck of a cavern. No wonder the voices were distorted. I bet Gus would have wanted to make it into a recreation area or something.

Smiling sadly at the memory of her murdered friend, Phoenix eased forward. A faint glow told her that artificial light was in use. Trusting her EVA camo, she gripped the uneven surface of the "roof" and crept to where she could get a look at the three figures clustered close together, apparently inspecting something.

Score one for Mustang. There's definitely something here other than silver and iron. But what? And why didn't Jun tell me about it? Was he going to surprise me? Or—the thought was unsettling— maybe he didn't know? Did Gus discover something and held out on Jun? Possible, I guess.

The unsettled feeling that had been surging in Phoenix's gut since she first heard the "familiar" voice grew. She felt suddenly desperate to get a better look at these three intruders. Staying "up," she angled until she could see faces, then activated the distance vision on her EVA optics. All wore EVA suits, open, with the helmet back, collar loose, taking advantage of the interior atmosphere.

Higher-pitched was speaking, so she oriented on him first. Ground-pounder built, a grizzle-jawed male. Maybe retired? Likely military. There was something in his posture, even though his EVA suit was generic "rack." Maybe *too* generic, like it was a disguise.

"The images you sent were promising," Military was saying, "but this is even better than I dared hope. I suspect this is a cache from the last Incursion."

"Incursion" was the polite way of referring to periodic attempts by various company interests within the Rolling Rock Conglomerate to take over a competitor by extralegal means. Every mining camp and rock habitat told tall tales of caches containing everything from combat drugs to weapons to extraordinary devices, even to singleships that would make *Mustang* seem a spavined hack ready for the scrapyard.

Deeper Voice—rich baritone to Higher Voice's tenor—was elegantly androgynous after the current fashion for corporate types, which called for a lack of individuality that proclaimed loyalty to the company, rather than to the self. Corp was clad in a very fine EVA rig, the sort used by those who didn't expect to work or fight, who wanted to forget that they were surrounded by vacuum.

"I concur, except that I'd hazard a few Incursions further back, based on some of the tech specs, but that hardly matters. This is excellent material, and so varied! Pity we can't just take it now, but some of the best is too bulky. We're going to need to bring in a cargo hauler, and that can hardly be expected to go unnoticed."

"We've already discussed that," said Familiar Voice, his tones tough and uncompromising. "If this stuff could be easily crated and taken, we wouldn't have needed to get Jun out of the way."

His EVA suit was miner-styled, belt loops almost empty except for orientation jets and a few other tools. Phoenix angled to get a better look at his face, suddenly placing the voice.

Is that Gus?

No, there was a physical similarity, sure, but so many differences, as well. This man was fleshier, softer, more stooped. Where Gus had shaved his head, this man had short, neat brown hair. His skin tone was darker, too. His brown eyes seemed smaller, surrounded by pouchy skin.

Familiar Voice went on. "Now that the trial is over, we can move ahead. Gus's twin brother will show up to claim his inheritance. He'll offer to buy out Jun's widow at a fair rate. Phoenix Diaz will sell. She's more interested in finding treasure than doing the hard work of extracting it."

Twin brother?

She hadn't realized she'd spoken aloud, but Mustang's voice replied, holding that weird muffled sharpness that meant he was using a tight beam.

"I can't tell. Appearance is one of those things that means little to me. If this is an identical twin, then DNA would match. But that this *is* Gus seems a possibility worth considering."

"But we saw Gus killed on that video!" she subvocalized back, even as her mind was spinning through possibilities.

"We saw someone killed," Mustang replied sternly. "Jun denied over and over that anyone had been killed. No one believed him since there was ample evidence to the contrary."

Phoenix forced herself to take several deep breaths. "All right. Recorded images can be faked. Tisi could have been bought. But what about the blood and gore, the flesh dangling from the exoskeleton's claws?"

"Use that brain humans are so proud of," Mustang prompted with an equine snort of disgust.

"Cloned," Phoenix replied. "If Gus was in on this, he could have supplied material for culturing."

"That's better," Mustang replied. "Now you're thinking, rather than feeling."

"So, if we allow that's Gus," Phoenix went on, her gaze locked on the trio below, "here's my guess as to what happened. After Gus's tunnel intersected this cavern, he found whatever they're all gloating over. Either he didn't want to share, or it's something he didn't think Jun would agree to sell. So he sniffs around and finds a buyer."

Mustang interjected. "I've moved to the outer side of Nugget, approximately where you are. There are several hollows that could conceal an entry. Whoever put the cache there probably used a densitometer to locate a hollow near the surface, drilled through, put the cache in, then sealed the opening. For whatever reason, they never retrieved the stuff."

"I think you're right," Phoenix agreed. "So, after Gus finds whatever it is, he frames Jun for his murder, and . . . now that I think about it, I never heard Gus mention a brother until over my last couple of visits. I always had the impression he was an only child, though I couldn't swear to it. Gus must've been planning this for a while, but to prove it, I'm going to have to take him alive."

The cavern was too large a space for Phoenix to control, so she opted to wait in the one area that Gus and his companions must pass through to return to their ship: the entry foyer between Nugget's interior complex and the hangar bay. This had begun as a tunnel, then been expanded into the boys' first camp. Later, when they carved out residential areas from played-out tunnels, it had become the entryway into Nugget's interior, complete with a double airlock to protect their investment in air.

Although she'd delayed making her ascent until the intruders were departing the cavern, Phoenix waited longer than she'd expected, which gave time for doubt to creep in. What if Gus did have a twin? What if she was about to confront a grieving brother?

When the inner airlock began to cycle, with a weird sense of relief that it was time to act, she eased back next to a locker that provided ample concealment. Military and Corp were carrying battered suitcases. Gus—it must be Gus—was wheeling a dolly on which crates were stacked.

Phoenix waited until they'd all come in and the airlock into Nugget was sealed. Then, sidearm in hand, Phoenix stepped forth.

"Drop and reach!" she ordered.

Their reactions were interesting. Corp responded with the automatic response of someone accustomed to obey. Military paused, saw that Phoenix held a no-recoil beam cutter that would make short work of solid rock, much less his EVA suit, and dropped the suitcase. His hands went up so fast that they were above his head before the magnets on the suitcase's base snapped onto the floor plates. Only Gus—it had to be Gus, right?—kept his hands where they rested on the dolly's handles.

"You," he said, looking at her as if trying to place her, then brightening, "I know who you are! You're Phoenix Diaz, wife of the man who murdered my brother. I assure you, we're not doing anything wrong. I have as much right to be here as you do."

"Cut the patter, Gus," Phoenix said. "I've figured out that you framed Jun. Save the song and dance for the courts."

"I assure you," the man continued, looking hurt and, for the first time, a bit frightened, "I'm not Gus. I'm his twin brother, Julius. I came out from Sirene—I'm an accountant—as soon as I was notified of my brother's death. I was too late for the trial, so I came out here to retrieve some of my brother's personal items. I was going to contact you to see about buying out your part of the claim. These two people"—he indicated Military and Corp with a wave of one finger—"are interested in buying Nugget."

"Don't move another finger, Gus," Phoenix said. "After what you've done to Jun, I wouldn't hesitate to hurt you, but I'd prefer to let the law do its job."

"I suppose you could take me in," said the man Phoenix was pretty sure was Gus, "but it's going to be your word against mine. I assure you, I can support who I say I am. Can you support your accusation?"

Phoenix laughed, which sounded pretty crazed, but she was at her limit.

"I'm sure you can support your claim. You would have made sure of that before starting this scheme, but I think I can jump it, just like you tried to jump Jun's."

Without taking her eyes off Gus, Phoenix addressed the other two.

"General," she said, probably promoting Military, "I'm sure you're an honest man." (She wasn't, but what she *was* sure of was that he was solidly scared, not of her, but of what was going to happen if his part in this scheme came out.) "Peel off Gus's suit. He's got a nasty scar on the inside of his right thigh where he got hit with some hot slag, as well as pockmarks on his butt from an unfortunate encounter with a sander. Somehow I doubt that Julius 'the Accountant From Sirene' could claim the same."

Military didn't have a chance to obey before Gus—now definitely Gus—shoved the dolly at him and bolted. He slapped the access panel open, then dove into Nugget's interior.

Phoenix cursed. If Gus got into the maze of tunnels, he just might make his escape.

Kicking off the wall, she dove after him. The interior was pitch dark, except for the glowing strips, but she could hear Gus breathing hard, his exhalations becoming fainter as he put distance between them.

Damn! If he gets into the lower levels, he can lose me, then get out via one of the service tunnels. Later, he can signal his pals to pick him up. I can't let that happen.

She oriented on the closest cross-shaft, so certain that she had guessed what Gus would do—because it was what *she* would have done—that she forgot that this Gus wasn't the man she thought she knew, but someone far nastier.

As Phoenix was rounding a bend, a whipcord-strong arm snaked out and wrapped around her, pinning her weapon arm to her side. Gus's free hand wrenched her cutter from her hand, then pressed the tip to the side of her head.

"Gotcha!" he crooned triumphantly. "Now, what to do with you? Should the grief-stricken widow simply vanish? Naw. That'd delay probate. Maybe if you'd sign over your share of the mine to me, I'd let you go."

Phoenix didn't believe him, not for a moment. Gus'd get rid

of her, far more irreversibly than he had Jun. So easy to make it look as if someone had broken into the mine, killed her, stolen some things, then fled.

"Why do you keep acting as if I'm here alone?" Phoenix asked, forcing herself to sound far calmer than she felt. "That no one would miss me?"

"You're alone," Gus said confidently. "You're always alone. Even when you came to visit Jun, part of your heart was out there, yearning after the next find."

"I'm never alone," Phoenix said, hoping her bluff wasn't going to be called. "Right, Mustang?"

The ship's AI spoke through her suit. "Right, Phoenix. I'm here, and I've been recording this recent exchange. Even if he kills you, Gus is sunk. I can't testify, but I can get the recording to those who can. Chanel Sulwyn is going to be really pissed when she finds out how she was played. I bet she'd even take the case *pro bono*."

"Hear that, Gus?" Phoenix asked. Raising her voice, she called to the pair she felt certain were listening from a safe distance. "Hear that, you two? I'm sure you had no idea what a ratfink you were dealing with, did you? Mustang's got video of you, as well as your ship's ID. If Gus takes me out, you'll go down with him."

Self-interest won, bringing Military and Corp out of the shadows, along with the powerful lighting unit that they'd had down in the cavern on Violet. Military had a sidearm out, and looked very menacing.

Phoenix could hear Gus's breath coming fast. *Will Gus kill me anyhow? He's got nothing to lose.*

Unlike the others, she hadn't opened her EVA suit. The hard coat wasn't military grade, and certainly wouldn't stop a beam cutter, but...

She didn't let herself think, but went limp, dropping her head a few inches so that the cutter tip was no longer at her temple. Given the choice of keeping his hold on a potential hostage or re-orienting the weapon, Gus froze for a single crucial instant.

Phoenix flexed her knees so she could drop below the level of his chin then came up hard, smashing her EVA suit's armored helmet into the underside of his jaw. She heard the click as his teeth connected, followed by the crack as his jawbone broke.

Even before Military stepped forward to help, Phoenix had

flipped open the med panel on Gus's EVA suit. With her left hand, she hit the tab that would dump an emergency-level dose of soporific pain meds into Gus's system, while her right reclaimed her beam cutter.

Military took an involuntary step back but Corp, either cooler or simply dumber, smiled ingratiatingly.

"I believe you and your soon-to-be released husband will now be the sole owners of this claim. Perhaps we can do business."

As a gesture of goodwill, Corp and Military helped transport Gus to Rolling Rock City, and freely added their testimony to Phoenix's. As soon as Gus was identified, Jun was released. The compensation for Jun's uncompensated service turned out to neatly balance the fines leveled for his hacking into store credit accounts.

So bribed, they left, Jun promising to mend his ways.

Several days later, Phoenix and Jun stood, arms around each other's waists, examining the cache that had made Gus turn murderer. It included some nasty weapons they both agreed were better slagged, but there was also plenty that Corp would be happy to buy.

By mutual agreement, Phoenix and Jun kept back a very high-end drone. This, after being gussied up with a retractable ornament of a buckskin stallion, was presented to Mustang.

"For my faithful steed, without whom I never could have come to the rescue," Phoenix said, kissing the drone on its nose.

Mustang, for once at a loss for words, proclaimed his delight with a very authentic whinny.

The End

DOC HOLLIDAY 2.0

Wil McCarthy

John Henry Holliday walks up to the guards as bold as you please, smoking his favorite cigarillo and tipping his hat against the cold glare of the sun. He takes the cigarillo out of his mouth and, with a twinge of regret, drops it into the dirt, not bothering to grind it out with his boot, because there's not enough damned oxygen here to keep it burning unattended.

"Afternoon, gentlemen."

"What's this? What are you doing?" one of the guards asks him. It's a man—a beefy one—dressed in the kind of brightly spangled coverall some people wear here on Mars. He doesn't look worried or even particularly suspicious. He looks like a man who feels he's got everything under control, and doesn't need to do much to keep it that way.

"Yeah," says the other guard. "Whadya want?" He's smaller, and wearing a similar but blander coverall that, although it's all one piece, somehow suggests a puffy white shirt atop puffy black trousers. He's like an actor in some hastily thrown-together play, wearing a third-rate pirate costume.

"The conversation will be brief," he tells them both. "I'm about to draw my weapon and fire, so I advise you both to kill me before you're hit."

"Excuse me?" the larger man says, not afraid but simply confused.

"Who the hell are you?" asks the other.

Patiently, Holliday pulls his coat aside to reveal his iron. "I

221

prefer not to gun a man down in cold blood, but I warn you I'm not above it. Defend yourselves or not, as you please."

One of the guards needs no further urging. He's cradling a rifle of some sort, and he swings it around and raises it just in time to receive a round through the center of his heart from Holliday's pistol, which is not difficult to draw and cock and fire in time. The man pauses for a moment, a look of confusion spreading across his face, and then drops into the dust.

The other guard looks suddenly afraid, as well he ought to, and asks, "What . . . what do you want?"

It's a natural enough question, particularly as Holliday has already holstered his pistol out of sheer polite sportsmanship.

"What do I *want*?" Holliday muses. "Sorry, I don't *want* anything, or not from you at any rate. Your people have made my people very angry, and I'm the consequence. You might say I exist because of you, though I'm unlikely to appear grateful about it."

An explosion sounds somewhere nearby.

"Why, there's my friend Wyatt, right on time with some dynamite. Are you cut from marble, sir? Perhaps you're a good man who deserves better than your friend here, but it hardly matters. I'll have satisfaction. Now raise your weapon."

The man does so, far too slowly, and Holliday answers: drawing and firing and re-holstering. It's an ugly business, but it's over in just a moment, and Holliday is moving past the two twitching corpses, into the warehouse they were supposedly guarding. Inside are "trucks"—vehicles like coaches or small locomotives—and stacks of crates, and smaller stacks of metal ingots. And three men caught in the act of loading a crate into the back of a truck. The look on their faces is a mix of confusion and alarm, but the box is heavy, and they cannot simply drop it.

Holliday surprises himself by simply gunning all three of them down. Not very sporting, but these men are thieves and killers, and there are limits to even a gentleman's patience. They fall with the box on top of them, and it isn't a proud moment, but Holliday is moving past them toward a glassed-in office at the rear. Two more men inside, fumbling for weapons as Holliday approaches. If there'd been a door they would have locked it, but there wasn't, and although these men were willing enough to cut down miners and truck drivers to steal their hard-won metal, they seem rather less eager to take on an armed opponent.

"I aim to tangle with you boys!" Holliday calls out as he moves around to where he can shoot through the doorway. They're already firing by the time he gets there; quiet sounds, more like the bark of a hare than the report of a firearm, and Holliday feels a disturbance in the air as the shots move past him. A bit too close, actually, so he dispenses with manners once again and simply shoots them both as soon as he has the angle, grateful that they are in fact mere criminals and not true gunfighters. One he shoots through the heart and, for good measure, through the head as well. For the other, he aims more carefully and blasts the rifle out of his hands. It's a tricky shot, but he's done it a time or two when there was no need for a duel to turn fatal. The man screams and flails his arms, fountaining blood from one of his hands, and then drops to his bottom, howling and moaning and clutching his wounded appendage.

And then, just like that, the confrontation is over.

Holliday takes a moment to collect himself, finds a match and a cigarillo in his breast pocket, lights up, and vomits on the concrete floor of the warehouse.

"Doc?" a voice calls out to him. "Are you all right?"

Holliday takes a quick puff on the cigarillo before answering, "Over here, Wyatt. In one piece and, I believe, free of holes. And how are you?"

"The same," Wyatt says. "They never knew what hit 'em."

"This one might," Holliday says, inclining his head toward the wounded man as Wyatt approaches.

"You left one alive?"

"I did. I thought perhaps he could carry a warning to others who may be running this operation from afar."

"Ah. Good thinking."

And it *is* good thinking, because men like these will not complain to the authorities, and yet, if they wonder, without knowing, what happened to their warehouse, they might get uppity ideas of trying to steal from Wyatt's employers once again. The Dawes Crater Mining Company is a no-nonsense operation, and Wyatt is, for the most part, a no-nonsense kind of man.

"Get up," Wyatt says to the injured man. "Come on, I said get up. You've riled the wrong dogs, but we're done here. For now."

"Let me see your hand," Holliday says to the man. "Come on, I'll not harm you."

Nearly weeping now, the man gets unsteadily to his feet and walks toward Holliday, his wounded hand outstretched.

Holliday draws a cotton handkerchief out of his pocket and gently binds the wound. He might be a dentist by trade, but that was always just a matter of family honor. With licensing requirements in Georgia so lax, any quack could claim to be a medical doctor, whereas only a schooled and certified man could be a dentist. And yet, Holliday had come from a long line of surgeons, and knew his business well enough.

"You'll have it seen to proper," Wyatt says. "Keep it balled in a fist until then, and you'll be all right."

"Who's the doctor here?" Holliday chides.

"Not you," Wyatt says. "He's bleedin' fine there. Make a fist, I tell you."

"Who are you?" the man wants to know.

"We're retribution," Holliday tells him, with a sudden stab of anger. "Or I am, at any rate—created for that one purpose. Wyatt here was created to make peace among brawlers, but I've no such talent. Now come with me. Come with us." He leads the man past his murdered comrades and out into the daylight. "You're going to have a long walk. Wyatt here has dismantled your fax machine—that was the boom you heard—and it means your friends here aren't getting refreshed from any local backups. By the time they're dusted out of archive and back on their feet again, they won't know what happened here, or why they died. But *you* will. The nearest settlement is Silver Canal, ten klicks that-a-way, and I suggest you get about it before you bleed to death."

"Or die of thirst," Wyatt offers. And it's no empty threat, for the noontime sun of Mars, while no match for that of Earth, can dry a man out in a day and a half if he's not careful.

"Please," the man says, like he's been ordered up a gallows, and it occurs to Holliday that this fellow may never have walked ten kilometers in his life. He seems fit enough, but of course he's printed that way. Printed fresh every time he steps through a fax from one place to another, and why walk when you can do that instead? Why bother getting any exercise at all?

"If you don't like the walk, you should contemplate the alternative," Holliday tells him, and gives him a shove. "Things could have gone worse for you, make no mistake. Perhaps some day you'll appreciate what a fine shot it was that saved your life today."

"Next time will be worse," Wyatt says darkly. "You tell your people to stay the hell away from Dawes Crater, and the Dawes Crater Mining Company, and from the two of us."

"Who are you?" he asks.

"I'm Wyatt Berry Stapp Earp 2.0 Faxborn. That right there is Doc Holliday. Look it up before you even *think* about crossing our paths again. I've got an eye for faces; I surely won't forget yours."

Once the shooting stops, the place is overrun by Wyatt's ragtag posse of blacks and Chinamen and whatever else he'd found here on Mars. And Holliday is of two minds about that, because the faxborn part of him knows a man's skin means less than nothing. In this day and age, anyone can be black or white or red or yellow any time they feel like it. Or polka-dot blue! And it says nothing about the person inside, all right. But Holliday came up in Georgia during Reconstruction, and that left little burrs in his heart. Burrs that don't seem to mind he isn't real, and never lived in Georgia at all, and never drew a breath until a week ago Sunday when Wyatt Earp printed him out of a fax machine. He has no reason to feel any way about anything, but he does. Yep, he does.

The trucks are loaded up with stolen metal—all the wealth hijacked away from Dawes—and soon the trucks are on their way back there to repatriate the loot. Holliday doesn't quite understand why these ingots have to travel overland—can't they just be shoved through a fax machine like everything else? But apparently not, so away they roll, bouncing over the ruts and rocks of a landscape very much like Utah. Holliday and Wyatt are alone in a truck of their own, with Wyatt driving and Holliday riding beside him with a shotgun across his knees.

Holliday's been born with a detailed knowledge of Martian geography ("areography," they call it), and this road goes only back to Dawes. So he knows well enough where he is in the world. But what a world! The sky is purple-gray, like a hemisphere of slate, the light of the sun punching through. An alien sun; it seems bright enough but too small by half, and too cold, and somehow too blue. The same sun that shines down on Earth, he supposes, though it doesn't look it. Thin clouds streak the sky here and there, moving faster than it seems they ought to, and on the other side of this celestial dome, opposite the sun, hangs the pearly orb of Phobos, the nearer moon.

The most unsettling thing about all this is how normal it feels. How proper, as though John Henry Holliday were born in this place, born *for* this place, and all his other memories no more than daydreams. Which is exactly true.

"That was awful," he tells Wyatt.

"It's always awful."

"Indeed, yes, but this time feels different. A greater sin than I've previously committed. Which can't be right, can it?"

"No," Wyatt tells him. "I've seen you do worse."

And that's true. The two of them had been mixed up in some bad business in their day. Some of that had been Wyatt's fault, or at least Wyatt was the reason Holliday became involved. But not too much. Wyatt was a lawman, and a law-abiding one, for the most part. If anything, he'd been a brake on the worst impulses of the man he called "Doc" Holliday. Things could, perhaps, have gone worse if the two had not become friends—the lawman and the gambler.

"Is it always this way?" Holliday wonders aloud. "Sickening? Churning in the belly like a bad meal? I wouldn't know. This was only my second gunfight, wasn't it? My second."

Wyatt only grunts to that, and so the two ride in silence for a while, with only the whistle of the wind and the squeaking of the truck to acknowledge their existence.

But there are thoughts in John Holliday's head that want to get out, that want to be spoken aloud and acknowledged by his fellow man. In a very real sense, he has never unburdened himself, never had a real conversation at all. A construct, like Wyatt, printed by machines for a world that had no real men of its own, no one capable of chasing down and murdering a few miscreants. Because that was illegal, yes, but also because it was *difficult*, because it required a hard and violent heart that even the roughest miners and teamsters of this age seemed to lack.

"I never asked to be a gunfighter, you know."

"None of us did," says Wyatt.

"Oh, I beg to differ, Wyatt. You pinned any number of badges on your chest, carried all manner of firearms all your life. What did you think would happen when you moved to Kansas, eh? You'd be arranging flowers? Take up blacksmithing? No, you were born to this life of turmoil in a way I never was. I was a good dentist, Wyatt, I really was. I won awards for my dentures and bridgework, and I'd've been quite content to live out my days that way, with a wife at my side and children underfoot. It was all I wanted, all I needed out of life. It was just bad luck I caught my mother's illness."

John Holliday had moved west for the clean, dry air, but found it difficult to practice his trade. People in Texas had better uses for their money than to give it to a dentist who coughed, so he'd fallen back to his other great skill: reading a deck of cards. And, when necessary, manipulating one.

Wyatt just snorts at that. "Way I hear it, Doc, you had your share of scrapes back in Georgia, as well. You're as fine a gentleman as I've met, but you're a born fighter, and there's no shame in it. Where would the world be without gentlemen who know how and when and why to be angry?"

"I believe we're in that world now, Wyatt." He thinks about that for a moment and then laughs. "Some god of war Mars turned out to be. When men finally reached up to settle this world, I guess the fight had gone right out of them."

"Exactly. There's men here know how to steal, men who know how to throw a punch, maybe. Nobody who can take a real beating and keep coming. But you, you're a mean cuss when crossed, Doc. It's what I always liked about you."

There is some truth to that, but Wyatt had never known the younger Holliday. Gambling was a respectable enough profession for a gentleman—it brought no shame to him or to his fine Georgian family—but it surely did rub him up against some unsavory characters, often drunk and even more often angry about losing. He didn't *seek out* conflict, he truly didn't. But it seemed to dog him wherever he went, and he just seemed better at it than most. He didn't want to cough himself to death from tuberculosis, so there were definitely days he'd've been just as happy to lose a duel as win one. But no, he was too fast. He was the fastest man he'd ever met, and the corpses piled up until it was his very reputation for violence that seemed, at times, the only thing that earned him any peace.

Holliday thought again for another while, and finally said, "If you and I are reborn, Wyatt—reborn into a more peaceful world—then perhaps it's a greater sin to continue in our old ways. To look a man in the eye and pull a trigger on him when he has no quarrel with you. Shouldn't that sicken us? Is that any way for the resurrected to behave?"

"If that's *why* they were resurrected," Wyatt says. But he doesn't sound convinced.

"Most men aren't six days old, Wyatt. Most men aren't created for a purpose. Have I just fulfilled mine? Should I now vanish?"

"Aw, hell, Doc, you haven't even been paid yet. And no, you haven't outlived your usefulness. Not by a long shot. There's a whole world here, and nothing eating you from inside. Resurrected, like you said. You can be anything. I mean, to the extent that people can."

"Well. Well. That begs the question, then, doesn't it? What's a man to do with his second life?"

After a pregnant pause, Wyatt admits, "I'm still figuring that out myself."

"I see."

They finish the rest of their long drive in silence.

In the dormitory room assigned to him by the mining company, Holliday sleeps roughly that night, haunted by dreams of violence. How many men has he sent to Valhalla? A dozen and a half, all told? Do past sins still burden his reborn soul? Has he been snatched from divine retribution, and if so, do the cheated gods await his second death? They might have a long wait, for all persons are "immorbid" in the Queendom of Sol, where a freshly printed body awaits anyone careless enough to momentarily expire.

It's only strong drink that allows him any rest, and when he awakes it's only strong drink that controls his hangover. Like a man still consumed from within, Holliday lies abed until his pocketwatch calls it well past noon. Then, like a half-animated corpse, he finds his way to the mining company's cafeteria, where he fills his belly with starchy biscuits drowned in a kind of sawmill gravy, and chases them with iced tea and then, again in his room, another nip from the whiskey bottle Wyatt bought for him as a resurrection gift.

"Wouldn't be right, you starting altogether fresh," Wyatt had told him. "I've also put a thousand dollars to your credit account, which is all I can free up from my own this morning. Be warned, it's not as much as it sounds like."

"You always were cash poor," Holliday had said back. "Paid in promises on a good day, and daydreams on all the rest."

These were very nearly their first words to each other here on Mars, which John Henry "Doc" Holliday 2.0 Faxborn later came to realize were part of the first conversation he'd ever had.

Afternoon finds him walking down Main Street, between the rows of brightly colored buildings. He turns on Third Avenue (aware somehow that these street names were chosen ironically and anachronistically by the town's founders), and realizes then that what seemed an aimless stroll was in fact a beeline for The Metal Bar. In his week among the living, he's found this ironically named drinking establishment suits him better than either of the town's other two choices.

Soon enough, he's sat down, shuffling a deck of cards and offering to teach a table of strangers the basics of Five-Card Draw. The cards are a thing Holliday had to order by providing a detailed description to the fax machine, for while a few card games are known in the Queendom, they're played on touchscreens or else entirely in the mind. A physical deck of celluloid-coated paper, inked in bright colors and static as a painting, is something else entirely.

"It's like something out of a storybook," says a miner named Glenn Abbott. He doesn't say it kindly, nor does he look that way on Holliday's person.

"Well, then, perhaps Go Fish will be more your speed," Holliday tells him.

"You weren't invited to sit down," Abbot says, in what he seems to imagine is a warning tone. Then he adds, in a tone of clear insult, "Faxborn. Take it somewheres else, or find out why."

Holliday laughs at that, in genuine amusement. Out of respect for Wyatt's town, he carries no gun or knife, nor even a nonlethal "tazzer," but there's loose cutlery on the table, along with drink glasses and a China plate Holliday could use to bash in a man's nose or skull without breaking a sweat.

"I came to play," Holliday tells him, "and there's no other occupied table."

"Come on, Glenn," says another man, who introduced himself simply as "Fuzzy" before Holliday sat down beside him. "Hain't you seen trouble enough this month?"

"Not looking for trouble," Abbott replies. "He's the one who sat down here."

"Just looking for a friendly wager," Holliday says, not moving.

"I'll play you," says a thick-boned woman, whose name Holliday doesn't know, but whose face he remembers from his last time in here.

"Hell you will," says Glenn Abbott, getting up from his chair. "He looks like a cheater to me. Why's the deck physical like that, if he doesn't mean to use it crooked?"

For a moment, no one says anything.

"Hain't that my business if I want to play?" the woman finally asks.

"It's mine," Holliday tells them all, "if my honor is so impugned."

And he's ready, quite ready, to take the matter as far as it will go, but then he reminds himself that he's not in fact dying of tuberculosis. He doesn't need to get himself killed over a petty insult. Also, nobody here knows anything about him. He might *be* a cheat for all they know, and he has, in fact, from time to time, cheated at cards. He remains seated.

To Abbott, he says, "What do you have against the faxborn, exactly? Has one of them hurt you? Has Wyatt? He's a hard man, I know, and harder when crossed."

"What business is it of yours?"

"None, sir, and I apologize if I've aggrieved you in some way. I'm just here to play cards." Holliday says this as soothingly as his nature allows, which isn't very. In truth, even his kindest words have a way of coming out as though spoken to an inferior, and for a moment he's afraid he's going to have to fight it out after all. But Abbott sits back down, grumbling vaguely.

A few pleasantries are exchanged, and drinks are ordered, and his charm seems to have done the trick, because in another minute he's dealing out four hands, as if among friends.

Although civility got the card game started, in the end, he needn't have bothered with it, for Glenn Abbott accuses him thrice more of cheating. He surely isn't, but he does have the advantage, teaching them a game he knows well.

"Come now," Holliday says, that first time. He's just won his third pot, and while there are no bills or chips or coins on the table to mark the transfer, a thing called a "living contract" has allegedly transferred the funds into his account. "You earn that much in an hour, I expect. You think I'd risk hellfire over such a small sum?"

The second time is worse. Abbott says, "No one's that lucky, faxborn."

And Holliday warns him, "Sir, I've told you I turn these cards honestly. Poker's a game of skill, as well as luck. If you call me a liar, as well as a cheat, then I hope your hands are quick."

"Steady, boys," says Fuzzy.

That cools Abbott off for no more than a minute before he's on his feet again, saying to Holliday, "A goddamn thief is what you are."

And with that, Holliday's had enough of this man. He was a fool to ever sit down with him, but a gambler can't always be a chooser, and anyhow he held a hope that this new world was somehow better than the old one. Alas, no, so he stands up, grabbing the China plate as he rises and cracking it on the edge of the table to get a point on the end of it. And he's ready, quite ready, to drive that point into Glenn Abbott's heart and send him back to his maker. But no, that's not right. Killing Abbott would merely get the man refreshed from backups, missing at most a few weeks of memory. Solving nothing.

Holliday pauses for a moment, knowing even while he does it that hesitation is death in a confrontation like this one. But Abbott is wide-eyed with surprise at finding a weapon by his belly, so much so that Holliday thinks he was perhaps not expecting a fight at all. Simply expecting Holliday to back down to his repeated insults? The thought is so strange, he hardly knows what to make of it.

"Drop the plate, Doc," says a familiar voice behind him.

Without turning, Holliday says, "Hello, Wyatt. Have you come to play cards with us? We're having a wonderful time."

"So I hear."

Holliday keeps his eyes on Abbott's hands, not trusting to luck or to Wyatt's intervention. But he sets down the broken China and waits.

"Gambling is legal here," he says mildly.

To which Wyatt replies, "Not in public, it isn't. In a bar, you can play for points, but not cash. That leads to fighting, which leads to broader trouble."

"Does it?"

Holliday is simply being difficult; his whole life has been about that broader trouble, and he knows it very well indeed. He isn't surprised that Wyatt, late in life, has decided it's too much to put up with on his watch.

"Everyone, look at me," Wyatt says in measured tones, then repeats it less evenly when Abbott and Holliday fail to comply. "Look. At. Me. Doc!"

Holliday finally turns to face his friend.

"This game is over. You boys and girls stay here and talk about your feelings. Doc, you're with me."

"Have I caused you some embarrassment?" Holliday asks, when the two of them are out on the street together.

Instead of answering directly, Wyatt asks him, "Do you remember what Charlie Bassett said to Katie that night in Dodge? About drinking when you gamble, and gambling when you drink?"

"Who's Katie?" Holliday asks.

"Very funny," says Wyatt.

"I'm serious, Wyatt. I don't recollect anyone by that name."

"She was your wife, Doc."

"Are you referencing Big Nose Kate? She and I were never married, as you know, and she'd've shot any man with the temerity to call her Katie."

"I used to call her that all the time," Wyatt says.

"You did not. Your memory betrays you. And if you're speaking of that conversation in the Long Branch Saloon, it was Bat Masterson who thought to school me on temperance. Charlie Bassett and I were *drinking companions*, before you ever set foot in Dodge."

Wyatt, who's been walking down the edge of the street, where the wellstone-paved road seemed to kick most of its dust, now stops. "That's not how I remember it. Are you sure, Doc? You're not just gabbing?"

"I'm not," Holliday assures him.

"Well, damn. Damn it all. The surgeon who helped birth you said our memories would be synchronized."

"Eh?"

"It's all bullshit, you know. All the memories, all the moments of your life, just made up. How could anyone know all the actual moments of Doc Holliday's life? But damn it, yours were supposed to crystallize from mine. That quack."

"Wyatt, what are you talking about? I know you and I are

not authentically resurrected, but are you saying we're not even authentic simulacra?"

"No. I mean, we're well crafted."

"We're what?"

Wyatt harrumphs at that. "Study of history is serious business here, and it doesn't miss much. The accents, the sceneries, the turns of phrase we grew up with...those are all real. And everything you ever said or did that got written down and remembered. Or photographed. They can reconstruct an awful lot from one photograph, Doc. It's the little details that'll trip you."

"Like the name of the woman who loved me best?"

"Yeah," Wyatt says, with a tinge of sadness in his voice. "Like that. Now I've got boxing practice in half an hour, which you're welcome to attend. Or not, but I'll ask you to stay out of trouble, please. You're my responsibility, and I'd rather this time we not drag each other into something we'll have to run away from."

"You appear to be the one getting me into it, Wyatt. I didn't ask for this. Am I half imaginary, now, and half ghost? I certainly didn't ask for that. Maybe I *will* run away."

Wyatt seems to think on that a moment, before saying, "You're a free man, Doc. Free as anyone. But take warning: it's hard to run in the Queendom of Sol, and near impossible to hide."

"It was just a card game, you know."

"It wasn't. It never is."

"Well, then, I believe I'll take a walk. Assuming my legs are real enough to carry me around."

"Cute. It does get easier, you know. Being alive again."

"Does it? Well, then. Good day, sir."

"Thank you for coming, John," says Jonathan Adisa, the "site manager" of Dawes Crater. Rising partway from his chair, he reaches out to shake Holliday's hand.

"A gentleman," Holliday says, mildly surprised. He accepts the handshake—the first he's been offered here on Mars—by anyone other than Wyatt, that is.

"I'm old," Adisa says, with a slightly fake-looking smile. "And my parents were strict."

"As were mine," Holliday allows.

Adisa seems to be waiting for something, then finally says, "Ah. You're waiting for an invitation! Please, sit."

"Thank you."

Holliday sinks into one of the two chairs positioned in front of Adisa's desk. The chair looks like wood, but yields under his weight like a feather mattress, conforming to his shape while still managing somehow to feel both rigid and light. It's a sort of magic Holliday is slowly becoming used to, here in the world of six hundred years in his future.

"Your friend Wyatt wanted to be here with you," Adisa says, "but I thought for our first meeting it might be more productive if we spoke alone."

"Wyatt does drive a hard bargain," Holliday says, with unfeigned sympathy. "To his detriment at times. I suspect his preference would be to negotiate this matter with me out of the room entirely."

"Oh, he has. He did. The price for your services was set before you were born."

"Oh? I see. Come to think on it, I'd expect no less from him. What, then, is the purpose of our meeting?"

"To discuss your future."

"Ah."

Holliday understands immediately. Though Adisa has the powers of a mayor, the "site manager" is a company man, not an elected official. This puts Dawes Crater City in a category of company towns with which Holliday had some familiarity. In his old life, he'd tended not to spend too much time in places like this, because mining companies discouraged gambling. It was anyhow practiced mainly by the lowest-paid workers, so the big-money games from which Holliday made his living were rare. Complaints of cheating were taken seriously, too, which made it hard sometimes to hang onto a worthy score.

Even worse were the towns where there'd been some sort of a scrape—someone shot, someone stabbed, something burned down to create a diversion. Regardless of the underlying events and reasons, Holliday was generally put to blame, and had more than once fled with nothing but the coat on his back and the contents of his pockets. If the life of a gambler was hard, the life of a gunfighter was harder still. Even if that man had a sense of honor that his opponents lacked.

And here he is, post-scrape in another goddamned mining town.

"At the age of one week," he muses, "I'm already being asked to move on." By a black man, no less. The burrs in Holliday's heart snag on that fact, though the faxborn part of him knows they shouldn't. "Racism" is a word people never used in Holliday's time, as it was so prevalent as to be unremarkable, and people do not use it in the Queendom, either, because no one living has ever seen it practiced. But Holliday is aware of it as part of an ugly history, in which he himself played some part. He's not so much resentful of Adisa's dark skin as he is surprised, but he knows that's also a thing he shouldn't feel. So perhaps he's simply confused, and uncomfortable at his confusion. He's used to moving on, though; that much doesn't surprise him.

"I'm not necessarily asking you to leave," Adisa tells him.

"Oh, come now. There's work to be done here, by serious men. And serious women, too, and not by persons such as myself. If Wyatt does his job correctly, there'll never be another gunfight in Dawes."

"I certainly hope that's true. But I'm told you have other skills."

"Cardplaying and dentistry. One of which is not wanted here, and the other not needed. Every man, woman, child, and dog here has the most perfect teeth I've ever seen."

Adisa sighs. "Look, the hijackers could come back at any time. I'd like you to stay on here for at least another few months, as a deterrent. You don't have to *do* anything. During that time, I can offer you training toward new employment."

Holliday pauses, taking that in. He has come to learn that as a faxborn construct, he is basically the stories and reflexes of a long-deceased gunfighter, grafted onto a generic fax template of a male human being from the Queendom of Sol. That template is equipped with a sort of generic recognition of things and a generic knowledge of how things work, and this part of him recognizes Adisa's offer as a serious and valuable one. Most men of the Queendom are idle in the lowest sense of the word, without any sort of meaningful work to do. This is true even here in Dawes Crater, where a small but growing share of the population simply eat and drink and take up space, perhaps dedicating themselves to art appreciation clubs, which seem quite a popular affair. In Holliday's week among them, he's been tempted to lead them all into mischief. Tempted, hell—he's gone and done it, or tried at any rate.

"What sort of employment? A formal joinder to the Security force?"

"Better," Adisa says. "I've heard the Provincial Authority might be interested in a man of your background. And, uh, manners."

Holliday snorts. "They haven't met me. Those manners, alas, lie thin upon the surface."

He almost adds, "Scratch 'em, and you may find nothing but rage underneath." But why talk himself out of an opportunity? A man needs something that needs him back. And anyhow, that rage came partly from the hand he'd been dealt back on Earth: the consumption, and the ghastly death it promised if no one came along and shot him first. But he met that ghastly death honorably enough, and is now every bit as resurrected and immortal as his mama could have hoped. Perhaps the time for rage has passed.

Holliday's never met an officer of the Provincial Authority, or anyone else from outside Dawes Crater, except of course the hijackers he was brought here to kill. But he knows them by reputation. They're the despised "whitecaps," who come to town only to haul people out of it, for trial in distant lands. No one but Wyatt seems to think kindly of them, and it's telling that Holliday knows this after only a week in town.

"This is Mars," Adisa tells him, after musing a long time. "A lot of us would welcome any manners at all. Especially from a man as . . . dangerous as yourself."

In moments of doubt, it's Holliday's practice to say nothing, so another long pause stretches out before Adisa speaks again: "The training I'm talking about would be partly neural stim and partly memory surgery. Quite expensive, but the company's willing to pick up the cost."

"And why is that?"

Adisa spreads his hands. "Are three reasons enough? As your creators, we're legally responsible for your introduction into society. Some . . . mistakes were made with your friend Wyatt, and I'd rather not see those repeated. That's the first thing. Second, you're correct that we don't really want you staying here indefinitely, in anything like your original capacity. It doesn't send the right message."

"Towns like yours welcome a gunfighter," Holliday agrees darkly, "until they don't."

"It's a big world," Adisa counters. "Full of better places than this. You could always return, once you've acclimated and things have settled down, but I doubt you'll want to."

Annoyed now, Holliday asks, "What's the third reason?"

At this, Adisa looks slightly embarrassed. "We'd, uh, like some friendly faces in the Provincial Authority. You were born here, and you're familiar with our problems."

"I'm only a week old, sir."

"Still."

Holliday says nothing, until Adisa finally fills the silence again. "Look, you're *our* creation. A history program told us what kind of champion we needed, and we made it happen. You're Wyatt's creation, really, and he's Tom Clady's. Both of you, made right here. That means something."

"I see. And in my filial gratitude for the privilege of existing, I'll gallantly keep the feds off your back?"

Adisa sighs unhappily. "That's not how I'd put it. But yes, basically."

He doesn't say anything else. Eventually, Holliday realizes it's his own turn to fill the silence. "I hope you'll forgive my cynical nature. What child was ever grateful for the hand his parents dealt him? Satan himself was a child of God, which I suppose makes him a brother of Jesus. Now *there's* a sibling rivalry for you. All right, then, Wyatt gets Dawes Crater, and like any second son I get to move along, free of inheritance. Your offer is a fair one, and I shall think on it some, ere I give you my answer."

The walls of the buildings on Mars can both display text and speak in human voices, and by a sort of wireless telegraph system, invisible messages can be sent through the air. Holliday for some reason finds none of this remarkable, so he is not particularly surprised when, while he's sulking in his room, "avoiding trouble," such a message announces itself with a little chirp. A string of glowing letters announces AN INVITATION FROM ELIZABETH M. GONZALES, EPAULET CAPTAIN OF THE MARTIAN PROVINCIAL AUTHORITY, LANDOWNER, REGISTERED PRE-PARENT, AND BACHELORETTE OF SCIENCE IN CRIMINAL INVESTIGATIONS AND ENFORCEMENTS.

"Receive and display," he tells the wall, as though he's been doing such things all his life.

"Mr. Holliday," the message says, both in printed text and in the pleasant speaking voice of a human female, "it pleases me to extend an invitation to speak on a matter of possible mutual interest. If interested, please make my acquaintanceship at the Provincial Emulative Firing Range, today at one P.M. your time. If not interested, please accept my heartfelt apology for any intrusion. RSVP requested. Thank you."

There's something oddly stilted about the words, as though their speaker is reading from a carefully prepared script in a not-quite-native dialect.

"Reply yes," Holliday says. Then, thinking better of it, he adds, "Reply yes, thank you. Any meeting outside this damned crater would delight me, Madam."

It's already past noon, so he climbs up off his bed, combs his hair and moustache with a quite magical little styling comb, and puts on a tie and hat. Wyatt seems to have gone native in the clothing department, or at least to have met the natives halfway, but Holliday finds the local fashions clownish, and will not stoop to them. He looks much as he did toward the end of his life, when he lived in Leadville, high in the mountains of Colorado, and was never warm even in July. Shirt and trousers, vest, cravat, jacket, riding boots with woolen socks underneath, and over it all a broad-brimmed hat, to keep the bright sun from burning his skin. Leadville hadn't been good to him, but by the time he realized it was worse for his lungs, rather than better, the damage was done. After that, there was nothing for it but to ride the stage down to Glenwood and hope its vaporous, sulfur-dripping caves and pools might heal him. They didn't, and so he died, but he was *well dressed* until he actually took to bed for that final time.

Of course, his present outfit must seem quite outlandish by the standards of Mars and the Queendom of Sol, so he supposes he'll have to adapt at some point. But damn it, he's a week-old faxborn historical construct, and anyone who doesn't like that can bugger right off.

He's never traveled by fax before, but he understands the process, so he slips downstairs to use the dormitory's own fax gate. It's a metallic-looking slab mounted up against a wall of the building's atrium, and apparently surrounded by a whisker-thin layer of unmoving fog or smoke or fine gauze. It's the same machine from which he obtained his deck of cards.

"Outbound travel, Provincial Firing Range," he says to it.

"Deconflict," it says back to him in a gentle, sexless voice that might almost belong to a child. "Provincial Live Firing Range, or Provincial Emulative Firing Range?"

"Emulative, I think. Which one was I just invited to?"

"Emulative," says the fax. "Destination established."

Holliday simply assumed the thing knew his business, and indeed it does, and the Queendom part of him thinks, well, why wouldn't it? The Old American part of him finds this all a bit unsettling, but he goes ahead and steps through the plate, spreading his hands before him as though he's walking through a curtain.

On the other side, he's outdoors. It's dawn or dusk or something, and a chilly wind carries fine, stinging, alkaline grit. Grateful for his coat and boots, he unties the cravat from his neck and wraps it over his nose and mouth, tightening the bead of his hat's chin strap underneath it to keep it from slipping. He wishes, suddenly, that he had a pair of those damnfool Martian goggles.

"*Malo e lelei,*" says a woman's voice. "Thank you for coming."

He turns, and sees a woman wearing exactly the aforementioned goggles, above a sky-blue uniform and below a distinctive white cap, which Holliday recognizes at once as the finery of the Martian Provincial Authority. Her mouth and nose are fully exposed to the grit, although a white mask dangles around her neck, unused.

"Captain Gonzales?" he asks. He's never met a female with any sort of rank at all, much less a captain. She's brown-haired, of medium build, and looks like she means business.

"The same. Doctor Holliday?"

"You know I am." That seems a bit terse, so he follows it with, "Thank you for your kind invitation."

Her smile and nod are professional, as well as warm, and Holliday can see she's sizing him up, as if for a fight. "I'm sorry for the short notice. It's time for my monthly shooting drills," she says, "and my scheduled partner had a last-minute conflict. It occurred to me this might be an opportunity for us to meet."

"I see."

Holliday doesn't know what "emulative" shooting is, or why it needs to be out in conditions such as these, but he's bored and (he realizes suddenly) lonely, so he's going along with it.

"Do you consent to being shot at?" she asks, with the seriousness of a Texas Ranger.

"Do I what?" The question rocks him back. He realizes he's both immorbid and archived. In fact, the fax machine he's just stepped through retains a seconds-old image of him that would be automatically reinstantiated if this current body were, for some reason, to stop functioning. But it's a strange question, isn't it? Like asking a man if he'd like to be beaten unconscious with sticks. Flummoxed, he says, "I think you'd better unpack that question a bit."

"Ah. Yes. Sorry," she says. "It's actually easier if I show you."

She walks away from him, and although there's nothing lurid about her uniform, he'd be a fool not to notice she's got a fine derriere. Everyone seems to, here in the Queendom.

He follows her to a broad wellwood table. They're in the middle of what looks like a stage set of some kind of ancient Greek village. The walls and columns are thin and fake-looking, and not attached to anything, and it's open on every side to what looks like many kilometers of hardpan desert, broken here and there by low hills covered in scrub oak.

The table is covered in neatly arranged weapons: pistols and rifles, tazzers and wireguns, and even the sort of long knives David Bowie made famous in the Republic of Texas. Every weapon matched with a single duplicate. It is a table full of weapons in pairs.

"Are we dueling?" he asks.

"We are," she confirms. "These are nonlethal dummy armaments. They'll sting, but won't leave a mark. Do you consent?"

Holliday studies the weapons, then Gonzales's face. It's not that female leaders were completely unknown in his time. Why, Queen Victoria of England had ruled over hundreds of millions of people, and he did not doubt she'd been loved and respected by a great many of them. But a police captain was another matter. He supposed she was something between a federal marshal and an army captain, and her bearing is consistent with this. Authoritative, but not overbearing.

Her face, though, seems both serious and friendly, a bit like other people he's met who are aware of him by reputation. She seems to think she knows something about him, and perhaps she does. If she's thinking about offering him a job, she will certainly have done some research, and found something agreeable about him.

"I've never worn a badge," he cautions her. "I've been sworn into a posse here and there, on a mostly informal basis, and that's the sum of my experience. And I've more than once killed men dead who were not directly about to kill me. I'd be a strange choice for any agency of the law."

"Maybe," she says, picking up a gun belt and buckling it around her waist. "You want to fight about it?" She seems genuinely eager to try her luck against him, and this too is something familiar. Back in Kansas and Texas and Colorado, and especially in Arizona, men would hear about him, how fast he was, how deadly, and would take it as a personal challenge, though he'd never met them. Many bad men, and a few good ones, had gone to their graves that way.

"Madam," he says, then falters. He doesn't know what to say to her. It would be ungentlemanly in the extreme to duel a woman. And yet, if these things are no more lethal than a hot cup of tea, and the duel no more meaningful than a game of hearts in a hotel parlor, then refusing it would also be rude. "You have me at a disadvantage."

"I'm sorry," she says sincerely. "Have I presumed too much?"

"Or I too little," he says, flummoxed. But he *is* bored and lonely. And he's deadly fast with a weapon, and he's in a new country where the customs are different. This isn't an invitation he ought to refuse. "When in Rome, I suppose, one must do as the Romans, or be marked forever a barbarian."

Now her voice is playful: "Would it help if I insulted your honor?"

"It would not," he tells her, strapping on a gun belt. And then says, with a tentative humor of his own, "For then I should have to kill you in earnest."

She laughs at that, then marches ten paces away and turns to face him. "Try it."

She seems to know the forms, better than most men in the West ever did. Very well, then. He paces off ten yards of his own, then turns to face her, his arms and hands relaxed at his sides.

"Draw," he says mildly. Then waits for her hand to move toward the hilt of her pistol. When it does, he waits some more, and finally, lackadaisically draws his weapon and shoots her once in the forehead. BANG! Calmly, patiently, he fans the hammer back with his other hand, and puts two more rounds into the middle of her chest. BANG! BANG!

She falls backward, a familiar look of surprise and pain and fear on her face. Her hand never did touch that gun, and he fears for a moment that he's actually killed her. But she steps back and catches herself before actually toppling over. Then she drops her iron and leans forward, grabbing at her face with one hand and her chest with the other. She cries out in pain, then melts into laughter and shoots upright again, a broad smile splitting her face.

"I knew it!" she barks. "Oh, I knew it! Look at you! Fastest gun in the Old America. My God."

"Are you all right?" he asks, with both friendly and gentlemanly concern. He thinks to lower his weapon.

"I'm excellent," she chortles. "My God. I'm excellent. When you crank the reflexes that high, you normally get tic disorders and a bad case of Tourette's Syndrome. But if you interconnect the cerebellum directly with the motor cortex, bypassing the sensory cortex entirely... The surgeon who created you wasn't sure it would work, but I knew it had to. It *had* to, because you were a real person. Oh, my God, it's such a pleasure to meet you, Doctor."

Holliday, who understands about half of what she just said, puts his pistol back in the holster. "So you've spoken with my surgeon. You knew me even before I was born? Faxborn?"

"I did," she says, retrieving her weapon from the dirt where she's dropped it, brushing it off and then gently holstering it. "I'm sorry if that feels like an invasion of privacy, but Dr. M'chunu consulted with me before performing the birth, as he was concerned you might be used for... extralegal purposes."

"He was right about that. I've killed six men since I've been here."

She looks hard at him now, then raises her goggles up to her forehead and looks at him some more. Her irises are difficult to discern at this distance, particularly since she's squinting against the blowing dust, but he thinks they might be the color of worn-out pennies.

"No one has complained," she says, finally.

He snorts at that. "No witness, no crime?"

She nods slowly, the tip of her tongue peeking out at an angle at one corner of her mouth. "And an inadmissible confession, yes. But I don't want to hear anything about it. I don't want to *know* anything about it."

That seems rather a lax attitude for a police captain to take, and, for a moment, he's not sure what to say or do. Walking back to the table, he unbuckles the gun belt and lays it back down where he got it.

"I've never worn a badge," he tells her again. "I don't understand why someone like you would want anything at all from someone like me."

"A fair question," she says, walking up a laying her own gun belt down. She lowers her goggles back down over those worn-penny eyes. "Shall we get out of this wind?"

"And go where?"

"For a drink? I'm off duty for another twelve hours."

"I think you shall tire of my company long before that," he says, then wonders if he's joking or serious, and whether it even matters. Since his birth, he's had zero romantic interest in any goggled Martian lady, and her own interest in him seems more scientific than personal. This is an audition, and he seems to be doing his best to fail it.

"Clear the range!" she calls out in a strong voice. Whereupon a trio of mirror-bright, willow-thin mechanical men come whirling out of the fax machine, clearing the table with astonishing speed and efficiency, then picking up the table itself. In another moment, they're gone, vanished back into that vertical slab.

"Come on," she says, neither commanding nor wheedling, but just simply issuing the invitation.

"I have nothing else on my calendar," he confesses.

She takes him not to Dawes Crater, but to a nearby city called Sabeeta, which Holliday knows is a regional capital of the Sinus Sabaeus Quadrangle. The drinking establishment is no saloon or music hall, but something more like a vision of heaven. They're outdoors, but sheltered from the wind and dust by a mazey arrangement towering triangular sails, white against the toffee-colored sky. It's early afternoon here, and the sails are brightly lit by the sun's warm rays, but he imagines they would look even grander and more imaginary if they were lit up at night. He resolves to find that out sometime.

The liquor is something called "hard tea," which is served in a clear mug and is roughly the same color as the sky. It isn't strong or sweet or bitter or sour, but it has a mild, cool bite to it, like mint.

"...the Provincial Authority has developed a rather prissy

reputation," Gonzales is saying. "We're better educated than the people we police, and that doesn't go over well."

She's packed away her goggles and mask in a sort of belt pouch, and she looks at him now over the tea mugs they're both holding.

Holliday's hat and jacket hang over the back of the chair he's sitting in. His cravat is draped loosely around his neck, and the top button of his shirt is undone. It's finally warm here on Mars, and he welcomes it.

"I'm an educated man myself," he tells her.

She waves that off. "Not the same thing. You were a dentist, which is a hands-on profession. And you were mostly a gunfighter."

"I was *mostly* a cardplayer," he says, feeling a need to be understood more precisely. "Though I'd've remained a dentist had the opportunity remained open. Tuberculosis had other ideas. As did certain rough characters, without whom I would never have fired a weapon in anger. You seem to have some odd ideas about me."

She sips from her mug and says, "I know you fought beside law enforcement several times in your life. You may not have worn a badge, but you had the respect and gratitude of men who did."

He snorts. "A badge did not guarantee a man was on the side of the angels. I gather it does now, which makes your interest all the stranger."

"You're not making this easy," she says. "Look, when we arrest a suspect, we show up in overwhelming numbers to forestall resistance, but this winds up making us look weak. I've seen how your friend Wyatt handles things, and I think that's exactly what we're missing. He makes people afraid of crossing him, without actually doing all that much. It's quite something to see."

"He's a *man*, yes, in a world of sheep. Pardon me if it's rude to say so. I wonder, then, why don't you extend this invitation to him?"

"And poach him away from the mining company? I'd never hear the end of it. Interfering with commerce is the *last* thing we want to be known for."

"He is a shareholder," Holliday admits, "of a profitable enter-prise. That's something he never quite managed back on Earth, so if I think a moment, I don't suppose you *could* pry him away. But Miss Gonzales, surely you know I'm nothing like him. Except insofar as neither one of us has ever worn a uniform, or ever would."

She frowns. "So it's 'no,' then? You haven't even heard the offer."

"Haven't I? All right, then, out with it."

He sounds ruder and less patient than he would like. Gonzales seems like a perfectly fine peace officer and human being, and Holliday is at loose ends. But he fears she's barking down the wrong hole, here, and doesn't like the idea he would let her believe otherwise.

She sips from her mug again, then sets it down and wipes her mouth with a knuckle. "Doctor, I know it's hard for faxborn people. You were literally created for one purpose, and when you're new there's nothing else about you. Nothing that's your own. But it doesn't have to stay that way. You're not limited by your memories, or how things were done in the Old America."

"No? Captain, we're all limited by who we are. By who we've been, and what we remember doing and feeling. You don't just brush that off like dust. Now, do you have an offer for me or not?"

"The rank of sergeant," she says, and from her tone he can tell she no longer thinks this will impress him. "In charge of a special liaison unit, five men."

"Men? Not 'men and women'?"

"Not for this."

He presses: "Not ternary? Not transdeterminate or agendered or celibound?" These are just words to him. He's aware there's nothing wrong with any of them, but he's never met such a person, so the concepts are quite alien. He presses further: "No *robots*? I've seen your robots; they're faster than I am. And slower to anger, I would think. Better at following orders."

"Our problems are mostly with men," she says. "Rough men, with no use for people like me. That's where we need the most outreach. Not enforcement; we need *persuasion*. A touch of fear, or at least respect. You think the people of Dawes Crater don't respect you? I know about that little hijacking problem, and I know it ended the day you were born. What do you think would happen if we put you on the road, town to town?"

"I think I would get in a lot of fights," he says. "Truly."

"And you'd have your men behind you to break it up. That could be their main job. Look, I'll even make it a plainclothes unit, so you don't have to wear the blue. You like your hat? We can make that the uniform. Not whitecaps at all; The Holliday Black Hats, if that's what you want. And if things go well, there'd be a path upward, to detective sergeant or even detective inspector. You could hunt for fugitives, like an old-time Texas Ranger."

He blinks three times, slowly, before he speaks again, because in his old life he'd done exactly this a time or two, hunting fugitives with his friend Wyatt Earp. It wasn't comfortable work, but he was suited to it. And having a posse of hard men at his back, keeping his trouble from getting out of hand, or standing with him when it did... Why, that was exactly why he'd had Wyatt for a companion all those years. He did not want to be a peace officer, and he did not want to be an instrument of unchecked violence, and the world had never really wanted him to be a dentist or any sort of quiet citizen. But Captain Gonzales seemed to be offering a fourth option: to be an agent of mild intimidation. Why, that was practically his natural state.

"Perhaps you know me better than I'd surmised," he says. Slowly and thoughtfully, he tells her, "I know there are places in the Queendom—even right here on Mars—where people live in the traditional manner, without fax machines. Living and dying and suffering ailments of the body. I'd had some thought of settling in one of these colonies, and resuming the dental trade."

"Sadly," she says, "they'd have the right to refuse you. As a faxborn person, I mean. Some of them might not mind, but some of them very definitely would."

"Convenient," he says, "that my hopes should be unattainable."

"I can help you find out," she says.

"Really? Can't I just ask any wall?"

"Not necessarily. I mean, you can try it, but walls don't know everything. Particularly about what happens in the unlivened regions, right?" An unhappy expression passes over her features, as though she's just realized she might be on the wrong side of this issue. "Look, I'm sorry. I'm not here to squash your dreams. It's just that your actual needs may be aligned with those of the Provincial Authority. And the mining company, who've agreed to pick up the cost of your training." She pauses, then adds, "You don't have to answer right away, but you should know, the pay is also generous."

She names a figure, and he recognizes it to be more than he could plausibly need to make a life for himself here. More than a dentist made in the Old America, and steadier than what a card player could bring in.

It's quite an offer, really. Quite a surprisingly attractive offer.

"Would I be free to quit if it doesn't suit me?" he asks.

"You would," she agrees. "And I'll personally help you craft a backup plan, which you can revert to anytime you like."

"Well," he says.

There's silence, which she declines to fill.

"Well," he says again.

"Take your time," she tells him.

"No," he says. With one long swallow he drains his mug, then sets it upside down on the table's wellcloth covering. "No, I think I've taken enough time already. The answer, Madam, is yes."

And that, quite frankly, is how the Martian Civility Wars began.

The End

ABOUT THE CONTRIBUTORS

David Boop is a Denver-based speculative fiction author & editor. He's also an award-winning essayist, and screenwriter. Before turning to fiction, David worked as a DJ, film critic, journalist, and actor. As Editor-in-Chief at *IntraDenver.net*, David's team was on the ground at Columbine making them the only *internet newspaper* to cover the tragedy. That year, they won an award for excellence from the Colorado Press Association for their design and coverage.

David's debut novel is the sci-fi/noir *She Murdered Me with Science* from WordFire Press. A second novel, *The Soul Changers*, is a serialized Victorian Horror novel set in Pinnacle Entertainment's world of Rippers Resurrected. David was editor on the bestselling and award-nominated weird western anthology series *Straight Outta Tombstone, Straight Outta Deadwood,* and *Straight Outta Dodge City* for Baen.

David is prolific in short fiction with many short stories and two short films to his credit. He's published across several genres including media tie-ins for *Predator* (nominated for the 2018 Scribe Award), *The Green Hornet, The Black Bat,* and *Veronica Mars.*

David works in game design, as well. He's written for the Savage Worlds RPG for their Flash Gordon (nominated for an Origins Award) and Deadlands: Noir titles. He owns Longshot Productions, a multimedia company that, among other things, produces a line of *Author Centric* T-shirts, and a comic strip about the adventures of a new author called "Sign Here, Please."

He's a summa cum laude graduate from UC Denver in the Creative Writing program. He temps, collects Funko Pops, and is a believer. His hobbies include film noir, anime, the blues, and history. You can find out more at Davidboop.com, longshot-productions.net, Facebook.com/dboop.updates or Twitter @david_boop.

David would like to give a special thanks to Hugh S. Gregory III, Daniel D. Dubrick, and C. Stuart Hardwick for their insights on Jupiter and Europa. You made the station a reality.

Elizabeth Moon grew up on the Texas-Mexico border, and started writing as soon as she could hold a pencil. She has degrees in history (Rice University) and biology (University of Texas) with graduate work in biology at U.T. San Antonio. Besides twenty-eight novels and over fifty short fiction works, she has written poetry, essays, and one-act plays for school and community production. Her first published book, *Sheepfarmer's Daughter*, won the Compton Crook award in 1989; *Remnant Population* was a Hugo nominee in 1997, and *The Speed of Dark* won the Nebula in 2004. Her most recent book, *Into the Fire*, came out in spring 2018. Then she got bucked off a new horse and acquired a fourth concussion...do not try this at home; it's not fun. On the other hand, it's an excuse for confusion other than simple aging.

In addition to writing, Moon's interests include nature photography, prairie restoration and wildlife management, horses, music, and just about anything but housework. She lives in central Texas with her husband, enjoys making epic soups and "fusion" burritos, and is busy with a new book in the Vatta universe.

Michael F. Haspil is a geeky engineer and nerdy artist. A veteran of the U.S. Air Force, he had the opportunities to serve as an ICBM crew commander and as a launch director at Cape Canaveral. The art of storytelling called to him from a young age, and he has plied his craft over many years and through diverse media. He has authored original stories for as long as he can remember and has dabbled in many genres. However, science fiction, fantasy, and horror have whispered directly to his soul. He hosts the *Quantum Froth Dispatches* podcast, which examines storytelling through pop-culture classics and shares author interviews.

When he isn't writing, you can find him sharing stories with his role-playing group, cosplaying, computer gaming, or collecting and creating replica movie props. He devotes the bulk of his hobby time to assembling and painting miniatures for his tabletop wargaming addiction. Michael is a regular contributor to *The Long War*, a premiere podcast and webcast dedicated to tabletop gaming, but especially to Games Workshop's Warhammer 40,000. He has also collected and made replica movie props for over twenty years and enjoys the way a particular collectible lets an individual connect with a meaningful story.

His novel from Tor Books, *Graveyard Shift*, an urban fantasy story about an immortal pharaoh out to stop an ancient vampire conspiracy in modern-day Miami, was well-received by critics and readers alike and was a finalist for the Colorado Book Award. Michael is currently working on other stories within the same world, known as "Umbra Case Files," as well as other novels. He is represented by Sara Megibow of the KT Literary Agency.

Gini Koch writes the fast, fresh, and funny Alien/Katherine "Kitty" Katt series for DAW Books, the Necropolis Enforcement Files series, the Martian Alliance Chronicles series, and, as G.J. Koch, the Alexander Outland series. Gini's made the most of multiple personality disorder by writing under a variety of other pen names as well, including Anita Ensal, Jemma Chase, A.E. Stanton, and J.C. Koch. She has stories featured in a variety of excellent anthologies, available now and upcoming. Writing as A.E. Stanton, she has an audio release, *Natural Born Outlaws: The Legend of Belladonna Part 1*, from Graphic Audio.

Gini is an in-demand speaker who panels regularly at conventions and conferences such as San Diego Comic-Con, Phoenix Comicon, the Tucson Festival of Books, Multiverse, and LibertyCon. She's also been part of the faculty for the San Diego State University Writers Conference, Jambalaya Con, the Desert Dreams Writers Conference, the James River Writers Conference, and High Desert Book Fair, among others.

As Anita Ensal she writes in all areas of speculative fiction and has stories in many fine anthologies (such as this one) including *Love and Rockets* and *Boondocks Fantasy* from DAW Books, *Guilds & Glaives*, *Portals*, and *Derelict* from Zombies Need Brains, *The Book of Exodi* from Eposic, *A Dying Planet* from Flame Tree Press, and the upcoming *The Reinvented Heart* from CAEZIK SF & Fantasy. She also has the novella *A Cup of Joe* and will be re-releasing her The Neighborhood series sometime in 2022.

Born in New York City in 1946, **Alan Dean Foster** was raised in Los Angeles. After receiving a Bachelor's Degree in Political Science and a Master of Fine Arts in Cinema from UCLA (1968, 1969) he spent two years as a copywriter for a small Studio City, California, advertising and public relations firm.

His writing career began when August Derleth bought a long Lovecraftian letter of Foster's in 1968 and, much to Foster's surprise, published it as a short story in Derleth's biannual magazine, *The Arkham Collector*. Sales of short fiction to other magazines followed. His first attempt at a novel, *The Tar-Aiym Krang*, was bought by Betty Ballantine and published by Ballantine Books in 1972. It incorporates a number of suggestions from famed SF editor John W. Campbell.

Since then, Foster's sometimes humorous, occasionally poignant, but always entertaining short fiction has appeared in all the major SF magazines as well as in original anthologies and several "Best of the Year" compendiums. His published oeuvre includes more than 120 books.

Foster's work to date includes excursions into hard science fiction, fantasy, horror, detective, western, historical, and contemporary fiction. He has also written numerous nonfiction articles on film, science, and scuba diving, as well as having produced the novel versions of many films, including such well-known productions as *Star Wars*, the first three Alien films, *Alien Nation*, *The Chronicles of Riddick*, *Star Trek*, *Terminator: Salvation*, and two Transformers films. Other works include scripts for talking records, radio, computer games, op-eds for the *New York Times*, and the story for the first Star Trek movie. His novel *Shadowkeep* was the first-ever book adaptation of an original computer game. In addition to publication in English, his work has been translated into more than fifty languages and has won awards in Spain and Russia. His novel *Cyber Way* won the Southwest Book Award for Fiction in 1990, the first work of science fiction ever to do so. He is the recipient of the Faust, the IAMTW Lifetime achievement award.

Though restricted (for now) to the exploration of one world, Foster's love of the faraway and exotic has led him to travel extensively. After graduating from college he lived for a summer with the family of a Tahitian policeman and camped out in French Polynesia. He and his wife, JoAnn Oxley, of Moran,

Texas, have traveled to Europe and throughout Asia and the Pacific in addition to exploring the back roads of Tanzania and Kenya. Foster has camped out in the "Green Hell" region of the Southeastern Peruvian jungle, photographing army ants and pan-frying piranha (lots of small bones; tastes a lot like trout); has ridden forty-foot whale sharks in the remote waters off Western Australia, and was one of three people on the first commercial air flight into Northern Australia's Bungle Bungle National Park. He has rappelled into New Mexico's fabled Lechugilla Cave, white-water rafted the length of the Zambezi's Batoka Gorge, driven solo the length and breadth of Namibia, crossed the Andes by car, sifted the sands of unexplored archeological sites in Peru, gone swimming with giant otters in Brazil, surveyed remote Papua New Guinea and West Papua both above and below the water, and dived unexplored reefs throughout the South Pacific and Indian Ocean. His filmed footage of great white sharks feeding off South Australia has appeared on both American television and the BBC.

Besides traveling he enjoys listening to both classical music and heavy metal. In April of 2020, he began writing orchestral music and to date has written a number of short pieces in addition to two symphonies. Other pastimes include hiking, body surfing, and scuba diving. In his age and weight class he is a current world and Eurasian champion in powerlifting (bench press). He studied karate with Aaron and Chuck Norris before Norris decided to give up teaching for acting. He has taught screenwriting, literature, and film history at UCLA and Los Angeles City College as well as having lectured at universities and conferences around the world. A life member of the Science Fiction and Fantasy Writers of America, he also spent two years serving on the Planning and Zoning Commission of his hometown of Prescott, Arizona. Foster's correspondence and manuscripts are in the Special Collection of the Hayden Library of Arizona State University, Tempe, Arizona.

The Fosters reside in Prescott in a house built of brick salvaged from a turn-of-the-century miners' hotel/brothel, along with assorted dogs, cats, fish, several hundred houseplants, visiting javelina, roadrunners, eagles, red-tailed hawks, skunks, coyotes, bobcats, and the ensorceled chair of the nefarious Dr. John Dee. He is presently at work on several new novels and media projects.

Alex Shvartsman is a writer, translator, game designer, and anthologist from Brooklyn, NY. His adventures so far have included traveling to over thirty countries, playing a card game for a living, and building a successful business. Alex resides in Brooklyn, NY, with his wife and son.

Over 120 of his short stories have appeared in *Analog, Nature, Strange Horizons, Fireside, Weird Tales, Galaxy's Edge*, and many other venues. He won the WSFA Small Press Award for Short Fiction in 2014 and was a two-time finalist (2015 and 2017) for the Canopus Award for Excellence in Interstellar Fiction. His political fantasy novel *Eridani's Crown* was published in 2019.

Alex's translations from Russian have appeared in *The Magazine of Fantasy & Science Fiction, Apex, Samovar, Amazing Stories*, and other venues.

He's the editor of the Unidentified Funny Objects series of humorous SF/F, as well as a variety of other anthologies, including *The Cackle of Cthulhu* (Baen), *Humanity 2.0* (Arc Manor), and *Funny Science Fiction* (UFO). He's the editor and publisher of *Future Science Fiction Digest*, a magazine that focuses on international fiction.

His website is www.alexshvartsman.com and his Twitter handle is @AShvartsman.

Cat Rambo lives, writes, and teaches somewhere in the Pacific Northwest. Their 200+ fiction publications include stories in *Asimov's, Clarkesworld Magazine*, and *The Magazine of Fantasy and Science Fiction*. Their most recent work is space opera *You Sexy Thing*, the first in a series from Tor Macmillan. Upcoming in 2022 is the sequel, along with the final book of the Tabat Quartet, *Gods of Tabat*, and anthology *The Reinvented Heart*, co-edited with Jennifer Brozek. A former two-term president of the Science Fiction and Fantasy Writers of America, Rambo continues to volunteer with the organization's Grievance Committee and other projects. Rambo also runs The Rambo Academy for Wayward Writers, an online school featuring some of the best genre writing instructors in the field. Their website is www.catrambo.com and their Twitter handle is @Cat Rambo.

J.R. Martin was born in Fort Hood, Texas. He started writing to bring worlds to life that reflected his background and experience. Recently, J. R. finished a steampunk novel and is working on a new short project. When he's not writing he's spending time with his two boys and dog in Dallas, Texas.

Patrick Swenson runs Fairwood Press, a book line, which began in 2000. A graduate of Clarion West, his first novel, *The Ultra Thin Man,* appeared from Tor; the sequel is *The Ultra Big Sleep.* His new novel is *Rain Music,* a ghost story with music and magic. He has sold stories to the anthology *Unfettered III, Seasons Between Us, Like Water for Quarks,* and a handful of magazines. He runs the Rainforest Writers Village retreat every spring at Lake Quinault, Washington. He's been a high school teacher for thirty-five years. He lives in Bonney Lake, Washington.

Martin L. Shoemaker is a programmer who writes on the side... or maybe it's the other way around. Programming pays the bills, but a second-place story in the Jim Baen Memorial Writing Contest earned him lunch with Buzz Aldrin. Programming never did that! His work has appeared in *Analog Science Fiction & Fact, Galaxy's Edge, Digital Science Fiction, Forever Magazine, Writers of the Future,* and numerous anthologies including *Year's Best Military and Adventure SF 4, Man-Kzin Wars XV, The Jim Baen Memorial Award: The First Decade, Little Green Men— Attack!, More Human Than Human: Stories of Androids, Robots, and Manufactured Humanity, Avatar Dreams,* and *Weird World War III.* His Clarkesworld story "Today I Am Paul" appeared in four different year's best anthologies and eight international editions. His follow-up novel, *Today I Am Carey,* was published by Baen Books in March 2019. His novel *The Last Dance* was published by 47North in November 2019, and was the number one science fiction eBook on Amazon during October's prerelease. The sequel, *The Last Campaign,* was published in October 2020.

Born in London, England, and raised in Canada, **Alastair Mayer** apparently inherited the gene for science fiction from his father, who published Arthur C. Clarke's first stories. He's always had a sense of adventure, and served in the armed forces, scuba dived, parachuted, became a pilot, an astronaut candidate, and space activist, as well as more mundane things like farmhand, mapmaker, and software developer. In 1989, he moved to Colorado, ultimately working for a satellite network company.

He began writing as a contributing editor to *Byte Magazine*, breaking into fiction with five stories in *Analog Science Fiction* magazine, plus stories in several anthologies, including *Footprints* and *Space Horrors*.

As of this writing, Alastair has published nine novels set in his T-Space (terraformed space) universe, including the five-volume (and counting) Carson & Roberts series, beginning with *The Chara Talisman*. His story in this collection, "Incident at Raven's Rift," is a prequel to that novel.

Larry Niven's *Tales of Known Space* convinced **Jane Lindskold** that being a prospector and miner out among the asteroids would be the coolest job ever. The *New York Times* bestselling author of over twenty-five novels and seventy-some short stories, her novels include the Firekeeper Saga, the Breaking the Wall series, the Artemis Awakening series, the Athanor novels, and a number of standalone works. She's also written in collaboration with David Weber, Roger Zelazny, and Fred Saberhagen. Jane lives in New Mexico, and when she's not writing, she rides herd on a passel of cats and guinea pigs.

You can find out more about her and her publications at www.janelindskold.com.

Engineer/Novelist/Journalist/Entrepreneur **Wil McCarthy** is a former contributing editor for *WIRED* magazine and science columnist for the SyFy channel (previously SciFi channel), where his popular "Lab Notes" column ran from 1999 through 2009. A lifetime member of the Science Fiction and Fantasy Writers of America, he is a two-time winner of the AnLab award, has been nominated for the Nebula, Locus, Seiun, Colorado Book, Theodore Sturgeon and Philip K. Dick awards, and contributed to projects that won a Webbie, an Eppie, a Game Developers' Choice Award, and a General Excellence National Magazine Award. In addition, his imaginary world of "P2/Sorrow" was rated one of the ten best science fiction planets of all time by *Discover* magazine. His short fiction has graced the pages of magazines like *Analog*, *Asimov's*, *WIRED*, and *SF Age*, and his twelve published novels include the *New York Times* Notable *Bloom*, Amazon.com "Best of Y2K" *The Collapsium* (an international bestseller), and, most recently, *Antediluvian* and *Rich Man's Sky*. He has also written for TV and video games, appeared on The History Channel and The Science Channel, and published nonfiction in half a dozen magazines, including *WIRED*, *Discover*, *GQ*, *Popular Mechanics*, *IEEE Spectrum*, and the *Journal of Applied Polymer Science*.

Previously a flight controller for Lockheed Martin Space Launch Systems and later an engineering manager for Omnitech Robotics and founder/president/CTO of RavenBrick LLC, McCarthy now writes patents for a top law firm in Denver. He holds patents of his own in seven countries, including thirty-one issued U.S. patents in the field of nanostructured optical materials.